Raves for *Master of None* by Sonya Bateman

"Sonya Bateman's prose will keep you captivated from page one."
—Jennifer Armintrout, *USA Today* bestselling author
of the Blood Ties series

"If *Reservoir Dogs* and *Aladdin* had a baby with *Alice in Wonderland,* it would look something like *Master of None.* . . ."
—Bitten by Books

"First in an exciting new series, this book brings a refreshingly different twist to urban fantasy. . . . Plenty of action and memorable characters add up to an entertaining read that's tough to put down."
—Romantic Times (4 1/2 stars)

"The hostile Ian, his beloved wife, Akila, and their djinn friends and foes provide a refreshing change from [urban fantasy's] habitual hordes of vampires, werewolves, and fairies."
—*Fantasy* Magazine

"A book that will take you on a surprising journey. You will laugh, cheer, and root along with these vibrant characters."
—Smexy Books

"Fun, touching, and exciting. . . . I couldn't put [it] down."
—Debuts & Reviews

"Tongue in cheek . . . loaded with action . . . a likeable antihero."
—Genre Go Round Reviews

Also by Sonya Bateman

Master of None

SONYA BATEMAN

MASTER AND APPRENTICE

Pocket Books

New York   London   Toronto   Sydney

Pocket Books
A Division of Simon & Schuster, Inc.
1230 Avenue of the Americas
New York, NY 10020

This book is a work of fiction. Names, characters, places, and incidents either are products of the author's imagination or are used fictitiously. Any resemblance to actual events or locales or persons, living or dead, is entirely coincidental.

First Pocket Books paperback edition April 2011

POCKET and colophon are registered trademarks of Simon & Schuster, Inc.

For information about special discounts for bulk purchases, please contact Simon & Schuster Special Sales at 1-866-506-1949 or business@simonandschuster.com.

The Simon & Schuster Speakers Bureau can bring authors to your live event. For more information or to book an event contact the Simon & Schuster Speakers Bureau at 1-866-248-3049 or visit our website at www.simonspeakers.com.

Interior designed by Jacquelynne Hudson.
Cover design by Lisa Litwack.
Illustration by Craig White.

Manufactured in the United States of America

10 9 8 7 6 5 4 3 2 1

ISBN 978-1-4391-6085-5
ISBN 978-1-4391-1207-3 (ebook)

To my core unit at home, with much love.

ACKNOWLEDGMENTS

There are so many people that I'm grateful for when it comes to my writing, I hardly know where to start—or when to stop. But here I go, trying to thank you all.

My love and eternal gratitude to my family, every last one of them, including Lori and Eileen, whose names I left out last time (I'm sorry!), and all my lost friends from high school who resurfaced on Facebook. My family is huge, crazy, and the best on Earth.

My agent, Cameron McClure, and my editor, Jennifer Heddle: thank you for saving me from lame jokes, underdeveloped scenes, and plot holes the size of Texas. And for all the other awesome stuff you do. I'd be lost without you.

My writer friends, who keep me sane: Aaron, Kim, Marta, Val, Nichola, everybody at the League of Reluctant Adults. Bronwyn, Mia, Brynn, Kris, Jen, Selena, Diana, Kathy, Connie, Stella, Jim, Froggy, and everyone I met at Authors After Dark. And more I'm probably forgetting. Please don't kill me in your next book.

My coworkers and friends at Bradley Communications and the National Publicity Summit. I hug you. I hug you long time.

All the reviewers and bloggers who were so enthusiastic about *Master of None:* Jackie Uhrmacher at Bitten By Books, Stella at Ex Libris, Tia Nevitt at Debuts & Reviews, Tori and Mandi at Smexy Books, Vicki Browning, whose blog name escapes me, Derek Tatum at Mondo Vampire, Natasha at Wicked Lil Pixie, and the anonymous ten-year-old reviewer at Flamingnet Book Reviews. You guys rule!

Also, everyone who took the time to read the book and write a review, even a bad one—thank you so much.

And, of course, all the readers. Everyone who's written me a note, or talked about my books to friends, or read *Master of None* and remembered me long enough to pick up this book, or who's never heard of me and my djinn, but is reading this right now . . . thank you, from the bottom of my heart.

CHAPTER 1

They tell me flying is safer than driving. Every day, millions of people take to the skies and fail to crash and die.

Maybe that's true when flying involves spending hours being delayed in an airport, eating bad airline food, and hoping the person who bought the seat next to yours has showered sometime in the past week. Maybe it's safer being surrounded by an experienced, professional pilot and crew, a bunch of life-saving devices, and decades of engineering precision.

But when flying means riding piggyback on an airborne djinn who isn't very good at it, and who might be cranky enough not to notice—or care—if you fall off and drop a thousand feet to your death, it's safer to swim in a pool full of hungry sharks. When I fly, nobody offers me peanuts or a watered-down drink. I don't even get a lousy seat belt.

Lucky me.

"Ian, we've been up here an hour," I shouted. "Where's this damned cave?"

"Close."

"You said that the last three times I asked."

"Then stop asking, thief."

"You're lost, aren't you?"

I felt him tense beneath me. "I am not lost."

"Bullshit." We were definitely lost. And even if we weren't both guys, we couldn't exactly ask for directions. There wasn't anyone else flying around the open skies above the Appalachians in Virginia right now. I didn't bother opening my eyes to see if I could help. Every damned mountain looked the same to me. "You sure this is the right area?"

"Yes. Now be silent. I am attempting to scry."

"Great," I muttered. Scrying was basically remote viewing, a mental camera that could travel anywhere and focus on anything magical. A nice trick to know—and yet another type of magic Ian wasn't good at, and I couldn't do at all. Ian's wife, Akila, usually did the scrying for us to find our targets, since it was one of her clan's strengths. We were never going to find the thing on our own. "Maybe we should land before you try that."

"Donatti."

"Fine. Shutting up." I'd give it a few more minutes before I complained again. My arms ached from the awkward grip across Ian's chest, and my cramped body begged for a stretch. At least we hadn't flown all the way here from upstate New York. We had a hotel room in some little village farther down the mountain, and when we finished this, we'd use the mirror there to get home the same way we'd come down.

If we finished this at all.

My gut clenched, and not from airsickness this time. We'd dragged ourselves here to kill another Morai. For the past year, I'd been helping Ian hunt down and destroy the snake clan, the djinn responsible for wiping out the Dehbei, his clan. Well, our clan, I guess, since technically he was my great-great-great-you-get-the-idea-grandfather. But I was mostly human, and there were at least ten generations between Ian and me.

I didn't like killing. I assumed the Morai didn't like being killed. But they were vicious bastards, and Ian's revenge became mine when their clan leader, Lenka, had tried to take out him, Akila, me, and my woman and son. We'd destroyed Lenka, and had been tracking the rest ever since.

Ian assured me that after this one, we had only seventy-eight or so more left. At the rate we were going, I figured I'd probably be ancient and drooling in my oatmeal when we caught the last one. If I lived that long.

"There you are, snake." Ian spoke softly, but I heard him just fine. The venom in his voice would've transcended a tornado. Louder, he said, "We are landing now. Hold tight."

"Like I'm not doing that already." Still, I shifted and locked my hands together. I felt him slowing, losing height, and finally we landed with a dull thud. I opened my eyes to make sure there was ground beneath us, then let go and stumbled back a few steps while my legs remembered how to stand. "There's gotta be a better way to travel," I said. "Any suggestions?"

He ignored me. I would've been insulted, but I was used to that from him.

I let out a sigh and scanned the area. This was just about the summit of the mountain. In front of us, a jagged opening in the rock face revealed a deep cavern, dappled with sunlight that streamed through what I assumed were holes in the ceiling, and fading to black beyond. Cool, dank air wafted from the mouth of the cave like an ancient breath. Anything could be hiding in that patchwork of light and shadow.

With my luck, it'd be something with teeth.

It actually took me a few seconds to find Ian again. Nature wasn't my element, but he blended right in. As always, his clothing was earth toned, dirt brown everything—boots, pants, vest, no shirt. He hated shirts. The leather duster he always wore, no matter the temperature, had rumpled a bit during the flight. Standing perfectly still, staring into the cave with coiled bloodlust in his eyes, he looked every inch the predator he was. A wolf ready to strike.

I cleared my throat. "Maybe we should wait awhile before we go in there."

Ian's black-ringed eyes narrowed, and his lean features drew into a scowl. "Are you afraid, thief?"

"Ex-thief," I said automatically. "I'm retired, remember? And no, I'm not scared. Unless there's bears. But my point is, you've been flying forever, and you scryed too. You can't have much juice left." Djinn magic drained when they used it in the human realm, and it took time to recharge. "I won't be able to save us if things go wrong."

Ian snorted. "This one is still sealed inside his tether. Nothing will go wrong."

"Those sound suspiciously like famous last words to me."

"What?"

"Never mind." I shook my head. Once he decided on something, that was what'd better happen. We were going in. The great Ian had spoken. I frowned and said, "Look, when we're through here, do you think you could show me a couple of useful spells? I can do the invisible thing, and turn knives into different knives. I've got mirror bridges and tether destruction down. But that's it. I can't defend myself against these guys, and I'm human. Unlike you, I'll die."

Something that resembled surprise eased over his face during my rant. "I have told you, he is sealed. And djinn cannot kill humans."

"No, but they can cause death to happen. And they aren't all going to be sealed."

Ian frowned. "We will discuss this later."

"Yeah. Sure we will." I knew a dismissal when I heard it. With a scowl of my own, I crossed my arms and nodded toward the cave. "Confident assholes first."

He looked like he'd say something else. Instead, he shrugged carefully and walked inside.

I gave it a few seconds and followed. Wasn't quite as pissed as I made out, but I was getting a little tired of feeling like a fourth-rate lackey. We'd gone into some nasty fights with the Morai over the past year, and my little handful of pathetic tricks never prevented me from coming out banged up and bloody. Ian or Akila always healed me afterward, but there had to be a way to avoid the pain in the first place.

A quick glance around revealed rocks and more rocks. "Remind me what we're looking for again," I said.

"It is a bracelet." Ian stirred a pile of stones with a foot and avoided looking at me. "Thick, tapered. Likely gold."

"Got it." I moved toward the left-hand wall, where the most light came in. Ian had the senses of a wolf, and could see in the dark. I couldn't. The thought strengthened my resolve to push the issue of learning more magic after we killed this guy.

Snake, I told myself. Not guy. I had to think of them as snakes pretending to be humanish—it was the only way I could go through with destroying them. I didn't believe in murder. At least if Ian was right, this time would be a little easier. I'd only see the tether.

Tethers were important to the djinn. They were personal objects, usually small and made of metal, that bound them to the human realm when they crossed over. And since the djinn were basically immortal, the only way to kill them was to destroy their tethers with a blood spell.

Ian never brought his tether along on our hunts. For obvious reasons.

I reached the wall without seeing anything shiny. From here, I could see about four feet in any direction before darkness bled into the light. Looked like a standard cave to me—not that I'd been in many caves.

Only there was something on the wall that wasn't standard. Marks not made by weather and water and time. Curves, squiggles, dots, and hash marks arranged in slanting rows, drawn with something dark and maroon tinged that was probably blood. I couldn't make sense of it, but Ian could.

It was djinn writing.

"Ian, get over here." I spoke low, knowing he'd hear me and hoping there wasn't anyone else around to listen. A tingling sensation prickled the back of my neck, and I backed away from the wall. The marks weren't recent—but they shouldn't have been there at all.

I blinked, and he was next to me. He noticed before I had to tell him. Cursing in djinn, he reached out and brushed fingertips across the nearest line. "Ward spells," he said. "They are no longer active. And here . . ." His hand trailed down a few lines. "A warning."

"About what?"

"It says, 'Beware the deceiver.' I cannot make out the rest."

"Terrific. Who wrote it?"

Ian gave me a dry look. "How should I know?"

"Make a guess, then." The tingling on my neck crawled down my spine, and a breeze whispered over me. A warm breeze. From the back of the cave. I turned and squinted into the blackness, saw shadows painted on shadows.

One of them moved. Something flashed briefly, a yellow glint in the dark.

Likely gold.

"Oh, shit," I breathed. "Ian. I found it."

A figure oozed silently from the shadows. The bracelet wasn't lying around the cave—it was on the wrist of the Morai who owned it.

Like all the other Morai I'd seen, this one was bald, with pale white, almost scaly skin. His eyes were yellow, reptilian, with slitted pupils. But there, the resemblance ended. At least the rest had looked half alive.

Filthy rags hung loosely around a gaunt, wasted body only a few steps up from skeletal. He was barefoot, the nails on his toes and fingers way too long and gnarled into thick, yellowed curls. His lips and the sunken pockets under his eyes were an ugly bluish-purple, and the eyes themselves bulged from his head, glittering madly.

He grinned around blackened, pointed teeth and rasped, "Gahiji-an."

When a djinn knew Ian's real name, it was never good news.

His burning gaze shifted to me. *"Lo an riisal,"* he said.

Panic flooded me while I tried to figure out what spell he'd just cast, and how much it'd hurt. I couldn't speak djinn too well, but I was starting to understand it better—through instinct, not because Ian had taught me any of it. Except the spells I needed to help him out. Finally, my mind plucked out a rough translation: *and the apprentice.* I stared back.

The Morai hadn't moved. He was still grinning.

If he knew who Ian was, why the hell hadn't he attacked? They all did, usually right before we found them. But this one had apparently been standing there watching us, and then revealed himself completely without so much as a threat. Maybe he was insane. I'd seen the same wild-eyed stare from people who lived in alleys and talked to shopping carts.

The Morai shifted his gaze back to Ian. *"Rayan. Ken-an ni—"*

Ian snarled something, too fast for me to understand, and definitely a spell. A tremor passed through the cave, and the Morai's feet sank into the ground. The rocky surface closed around his ankles. He blinked, glanced down, looked at Ian. The grin slid away.

My brain worked out what the Morai had started to say. *Prince, do you not know* . . . Not know what?

I had actually started to ask when Ian interrupted. "Donatti. Kill him."

"Christ, Ian. He didn't do anything."

"He is Morai!"

Before I could respond, a harsh cry tore from the trapped djinn. Eyes narrowed, teeth bared, he cast a hand out toward Ian and shouted something that was unpleasantly familiar. Ian dropped with a scream and writhed on the ground. I understood what had happened seconds before the Morai sent the same spell at me.

Crud. Why did all the evil djinn have to use flame curses?

I had no way to stop it. The magic hit, and burning pain surged through me and drove me to my knees. I dragged myself back across the floor of the cave, inch by painful inch, hoping this one wouldn't last long. My flesh had so far failed to erupt in fire, but it sure as hell felt like I'd drunk kerosene and swallowed a match. I could practically smell charbroiled Donatti.

As I attempted to crawl into a shadow, hoping snakes didn't have night vision, the Morai yanked free of the cave floor. He steadied himself, cried, *"Ela na'ar!"* and gestured in Ian's direction. I couldn't see Ian, but I heard him shout in pain.

My own situation forced my focus back to the sensations consuming me. I blinked against imaginary smoke and tried to forget that flame curses could actually kill if you believed in them enough. Screaming nerves, boiling blood, the faint crackle of fire . . . it was all in my head.

Yeah, right.

I heard one of them mutter something in the djinn tongue and really hoped it was Ian. An instant later, the false fire consuming me vanished. I gasped in relief and twisted semiupright to see the Morai doubled over and coughing up viscous black fluid. Ian had cast a soul drain on him. I'd seen him do it once—but unfortunately, it hadn't taken the djinn he'd thrown it at long to shake loose.

Speaking of Ian, where the hell was he? I glanced around, saw nothing in the light, then a flickering glow from a corner caught my attention. It came from Ian, who was executing a strange little dance while he smacked at the flames spreading across his torso.

Shit. I'd never seen one of them actually set someone on fire before. This was bad.

I heaved myself up from the floor just as the Morai got himself under control and stopped leaking soul gunk. He glared at Ian, pointed up, and snapped, *"Yiiksar-en."* An alarming crack echoed through the cave.

Ian threw a hand out and shouted something. The Morai went rigid and immobile. Ian must've locked him down to keep him from casting more spells. I knew how that one worked—temporary whole-body paralysis. He'd done it on me before. But only to shut my big mouth long enough to prevent us both from getting killed.

More cracks sounded, and a grinding groan announced hunks of rock breaking away from the edges of the roof vent. They fell straight for Ian.

A soccer-ball-size chunk struck his back and knocked him flat. Another big piece landed on his arm, and I heard a bone snap. Smaller stones pelted his legs. Jagged shards rained on his head and sliced his face. He groaned, tried to drag himself away from the rubble.

"Jesus Christ!" I stumbled toward him with no idea what I intended to do. Before I reached him, he glanced up at me and shook his head.

"Get the tether," he said through his teeth.

Crud. I really didn't want to do that.

I shifted direction and lurched toward the stiff, furious figure. So much for him not doing anything. I guess Ian was right about them all being evil.

I grabbed for his wrist. The Morai blinked. A hiss rose from his throat, like air escaping from a punctured tire. Hoping there were no spell incantations that went "ssssss," I wrapped a hand around the bracelet and pulled.

It didn't budge.

Ian coughed. It was a wet, ominous sound. "Quickly, thief."

"What do you want me to do, cut his hand off? It's stuck."

"Whatever it takes."

My gut clenched and rolled. I didn't think I could bring myself to hack somebody up like that—even if it was an evil djinn. I yanked on the bracelet again. It moved down about a quarter inch and stuck at the base of his thumb.

The Morai's hissing grew louder. This time, I heard a few vowels in there.

"Blast you, Donatti, kill him!"

Ian had pulled himself up on one knee. The broken arm dangled limp and twisted at his side. Sweat drenched his ashen face and mingled with blood from a deep gash on his forehead.

If he wasn't out of magic before, he had to be now, and there was no way I could fight this guy on my own.

I grabbed for my switchblade, flicked it open . . . and realized that even if I could pony up the guts to lop his hand off, it'd take too long to saw through with a lousy three-inch blade. Time to improvise.

A hasty mental inventory revealed I'd brought nothing useful. Cell phone, flashlight, a bag of trail mix. That'd help. I could temporarily blind him, force-feed him, and hope he had a peanut allergy.

With my limited magic options, that pretty much left tether destruction—if I could get the damned thing away from him. I might've been able to destroy it while it was still on him, but djinn tended to explode when their tethers went, and if I didn't move quickly enough I'd finish myself along with him.

There had to be another way. I scanned the cave floor, and my gaze lit on a crumbled spray of loose rock. Perfect. I dropped the Morai's wrist, grabbed a fist-size stone from the pile, and smashed it against his temple. He shuddered and collapsed.

Magic didn't solve everything.

A sharp gasp from Ian drew my attention. I dropped the rock beside the unconscious Morai and rushed over to him. He'd staggered back against the wall, collapsed, and slumped forward, barely conscious. Bright blood dripped from his mouth.

"Ian." I shook his shoulder. He stirred, groaned. "C'mon, man. You in there?"

He raised his head and looked at me with piercing eyes. "Idiot. Destroy him."

"He's out of it—"

"*Now.*"

"Fine." I turned, palmed my blade, and crossed over to the Morai. His closed eyelids twitched in erratic rhythm, and his open mouth had frozen in a sneer around his ruined fangs. The Morai could look more human if they wanted to—Ian didn't resemble a wolf much, except for his eyes. Their appearance was a testament to their hatred. If they were smart, they could make it a lot harder for us to recognize them.

The arm bearing the bracelet lay flung out from his side. I crouched as far away from him as I could and still be within reach of the tether, sucked in a breath, and sliced my finger open. Blood was an unfortunate necessity for most of the few spells I knew. At least this one didn't require drawing a symbol, like the mirror bridge. My hands shook enough to ensure a lack of precision.

I smeared a thick band of blood on gleaming gold and tried to concentrate. There were words I had to speak. I always had trouble with those.

Before I could spit out the incantation, the Morai's eyes fluttered open and found me. A cold smile wrenched his lips. He struggled to breathe and spoke in a guttural whisper. *"Riisal'a gekki. Ken'an ni shea-wa. Fik lo jyhaad insinia de sechet."*

A translation ripped through my head, and dull weight settled in my gut—then fingers seized my wrist. The Morai's lips attempted to form words. More weird warnings . . . or a spell?

"Ana lo 'ahmar nar, fik lo imshi, aakhir kalaam."

My relief that the words had come from me didn't last long. The tether glowed white-hot, and the Morai erupted in flame. I wrenched my hand free, but not before the fire singed my flesh. Real burns this time, turning my skin a ghastly, blistered white. I scrambled toward Ian, half blind, the Morai's dying scream chasing me like a wounded banshee.

His explosive end shook the world and knocked me prone

on the cave floor at Ian's feet. I curled around my throbbing hand and waited for things to settle down. No need to witness the Morai's destruction. I'd already seen plenty of them die.

A gray haze settled over me, and I drifted on the edge of senselessness. Eventually Ian nudged me and said something. It took a minute for his words to impress on my brain.

"Donatti. Your hand."

I tried to move. Pain sliced a ribbon up my arm. "Still there," I gasped. "How 'bout a nap? Wake me up next week."

"We must get out of this place."

"Why? It's a nice cave. We should camp here." Though I intended sarcasm, I came across like a doomed Boy Scout in a horror movie. Using major magic always took a toll, and exhaustion weighed me down to the point of idiocy. I barely made sense to myself.

I clenched my jaw and maneuvered onto my back for a look at the injury. It was a lot worse now. My hand formed a frozen claw, the flesh a deep and angry red where it wasn't sickly white and threatening to burst. The sight of it threw my gut into full boil. I swallowed bile and turned away fast, before I could heave all over myself.

"Close your eyes, thief," Ian said gently. "I will attempt to heal you."

"Ex . . . forget it." I took his suggestion. "What about you? You're a wreck."

"That will have to wait. I do not have enough power left to transform."

"Oh. Right." Djinn could only heal themselves in our realm by taking their animal forms. Ian happened to be an oversize wolf, when he wasn't an angry, vicious, almost-seven-foot-tall human-looking bastard. This little bonus excluded me, since I wasn't exactly a djinn.

I sensed him move, knew he held a palm just above my throat like he always did when he healed me. The searing pain in my hand diminished to a deep, slow throb. Ian hissed through his teeth. "Not enough," he whispered. "I am too drained."

I risked a glance and gave my fingers a tentative wiggle. They moved, so at least my hand wasn't mummified anymore, but the skin remained red and blistered and streaked with white blotches. The missing top third of my index finger wasn't a result of the fire, though. I'd lost that a year ago against Lenka—and djinn magic didn't cover regeneration, so I'd never get it back.

"It's fine." I eased into a seated position, exhaled slowly. "I guess this is our cue to walk," I said. "Want a hand up?"

Ian nodded reluctantly. I knew he hated asking for help, no matter how much he needed it. He was a warrior, or at least he had been four hundred years ago, before he got banished to the human realm. And no self-respecting warrior would let a little thing like crippling injury stand in his way.

His banishment was another reason we hunted the Morai. He couldn't return home until he'd killed every last one of their clan—Akila's father, the head of the djinn Council, had seen to that. What a guy.

I arranged Ian's good arm around my shoulders and lifted. He came up slowly, gained his feet, and motioned me away with murmured thanks. After a beat, he said, "What did the Morai say to you?"

"Um." I hesitated. Wasn't sure Ian should hear about it, especially the last part.

"Did you not understand him?"

I didn't answer.

"It may have been important." Ian had that determined look in his eyes, the one that said he'd stop at nothing to destroy every last Morai in existence no matter what the cost—to himself, or anyone else. "Can you recall any of the words?"

"Yeah." I stared at the ground. "He said, 'Foolish apprentice. He knows not what he sees. Die in service to your master's madness.'"

Ian recoiled like I'd gut-punched him. "You do not believe him . . . do you?"

"No." I sighed. "I think you're right. We'd better get out of here." The stench of burned flesh and spent blood hung in the dead air. If we stuck around much longer, I'd have to become a vegetarian, because the idea of cooked meat would stage a revolt in my stomach.

Ian limped out the way we'd come in. I followed him, and tried to ignore the whisper that insisted the deceiver the Morai warned about could be anyone. Even Ian.

Chapter 2

After we'd put some distance between us and the cave, the terrain changed from mostly rock to mostly trees. Ian stayed ahead of me and trudged along at a steady pace, ignoring the arm dangling lifeless from its socket, the massive burn on his chest, and his likely broken ribs. Immortality and stubbornness weren't the best combination.

I jogged to catch up with him. "Don't you think we should stop for a few minutes?"

He ignored me.

"Ian." I grabbed his good arm. "Stop."

"It was not right." He looked at me like he'd just realized I was still there. "He should not have been free of the tether. Akila's vision has never been wrong before."

Ian's wife was Bahari—the hawk clan—and had a knack for air magic, especially flying and illusions. She did the scrying beforehand and found tethers so we could go on our little killing sprees. "Uh, there's a first time for everything?" I said.

Ian shook his head. "There is something else here. Magical interference. This mountain is rife with it, and I do not like it. We must keep moving."

"Come on, Ian. We'll never make it back to town walking. Especially not with you beat to hell." Despite my protest, unease coiled in my gut. Anything that made Ian uncomfortable was bad news for me. Usually painful, bad news in the form of a vengeful Morai. But Ian could barely walk, much less cast any spells, and only time would restore his power. And mine. "Let's just make a quick pit stop, all right? Give it an hour. You can rest, and I'll stand watch."

He cast me a dubious look. And started walking again.

"Damn it, stop being a jackass!"

"I am fine." He staggered a little, took two more steps, and collapsed.

I cursed under my breath and went to him. "So we're resting," I said. "Right?"

"Apparently," he muttered into the ground.

"Glad you see it my way." I knelt beside him and tried to look through the trees. "I think there's a decent clearing up ahead," I said. "You gonna let me help you get there, or are you comfortable here?"

He let out a long breath. "Very well."

"You're welcome."

Somehow I managed to get him up and leaning on me. My burned hand let out a few shouts of protest during the struggle, and settled back to a persistent ache as we pressed awkwardly forward. The clearing that looked no more than fifty feet away took five minutes to reach, and it wasn't much of a clearing. Just a semicircular patch of ground covered in browning pine needles. At least there weren't as many rocks here.

"Okay," I said. "I'll let you down here, and—"

"You all just keep movin'."

The voice, not clearly male or female, came from across the

clearing. A shotgun protruded between two trees, with a figure in a wide-brimmed hat behind it.

For a minute my brain went blank. Why the hell would anybody else be on this oversize pile of rocks in the middle of nowhere? The only quasicivilization, the little mountain town where we'd rented a room, was miles away. But the shotgun suggested hunter, so maybe whoever this was had been hunting something they shouldn't have and didn't want to be discovered.

The sharp blast of the gun jolted me out of pondering. A cloud of dirt and pine needles burst from the ground near my feet. "Jesus Christ!" I yelled, dragging Ian back a few steps. "You can't just shoot people."

Brilliant. I sounded like a Sunday school teacher. That'd deter the nut with the gun.

"I said move. Get on outta here." The barrel came back up. "I won't miss next time."

Ian breathed in shakily. "I can walk," he whispered. "We will find another spot."

"Guess we don't have a choice."

The gun bearer moved forward and stopped just outside the light in the clearing. "You hurt?" The tone was a few degrees gentler, but no more welcoming.

"Yes. My friend's arm is broken, and . . . stuff." Rattling off a list of Ian's injuries didn't seem like it would help. I might have to offer an explanation, and I didn't have a lie handy.

"You ain't from town, or that militia bunch?"

Militia? "Uh . . . no."

"Saints and shitpokes. Dumb-ass tourists. You from up north too." The voice edged into feminine territory as some of the coldness wore off. "Were you climbin', or huntin'?"

"Climbing." I seized the innocuous excuse, hoping Ian had enough sense not to contradict me. "We were checking out the caves up there and lost our footing. He fell farther than me."

Ian stiffened, but he didn't say anything.

She—I was positive it was a woman now—sighed like I'd just confessed to not realizing the sky was blue. "S'pose you better come back to my place, then. It ain't too far. Your . . . friend can ride Zephyr. You'll have to walk."

I ignored the suggestive way she said *friend*. "What's a Zephyr?"

"My mule." She turned and moved back into the trees.

Ian shuddered and coughed. "A mule," he murmured.

"Sounds like fun." I suppressed a grin.

"Indeed."

"Come on." I led him across the clearing after the mystery woman. She stood about ten trees in, fitting the shotgun into a holster mounted at the side of a rich brown, wiry-looking animal laden with stuffed saddlebags. The mule glanced up at us, blinked slowly, and went back to munching on a clump of green leafy-looking things.

The woman kept her head bent enough not to show her face under the hat brim, and then she turned her back. She wore a thin black long-sleeved shirt, jeans faded to the color of mud, and men's work boots. A sheaf of copper brown hair hung down her sturdy shoulders. "Mount up," she said without facing us. "There's stirrups and a saddle, so even green slicks like yourselves can figure it out. You ain't got to guide him. He'll follow me."

It took a few tries to get Ian up on the saddle. Zephyr snorted once, when Ian wobbled and grabbed handfuls of stiff black mane to keep from falling, but he didn't buck or protest. I found the reins and wound them around Ian's hand a few times. "Better hold on," I said. "I don't know if I can pick you up again."

Ian looked down at the mule and blanched. "Are you certain about this?"

"Sure. It'll be fine."

"Jus' don't put your fingers near his mouth. They look like carrots to him," the woman said. "You set?"

Ian groaned.

"We're good," I said. "Thank you."

She made a sharp clucking sound and started walking. Zephyr swung from his feast and plodded along behind her with Ian swaying uneasily on his back.

I stayed next to the mule. Whoever this woman was, she obviously didn't want to get too friendly. I couldn't blame her. Ian tended to make people uneasy, and I wasn't much better.

"Name's Mercy," she said eventually. "You?"

"I'm Donatti. He's Ian."

"All right."

She lapsed back into silence.

At first glance, Mercy's place looked like a few acres of trees had exploded and fallen back to the ground in random piles. An open-face shack with a log fence growing out of it apparently belonged to Zephyr. Just outside the far end of the fence stood something that looked like three doghouses stacked on top of each other. Two smaller buildings, each about the size of two toolsheds pushed together, flanked a small but thriving garden.

The main house might have been a normal shape once, but irregular additions had been patched on until it resembled a deformed starfish. A wide, roofed porch ran the front length, where two screened windows flanked a rough plank door painted bright red. There was a small gray satellite dish on the roof. The huge, squat metal box on the right side of the house, with thick wires feeding in between logs, was probably a diesel generator.

On the left, a curtained shower ring had been fastened to the outside wall. The curtain was metallic silver, the stuff they made solar car windshield covers from. There were duckies embossed on it.

Mercy stopped the mule in the front yard and waved at the house. "Go on and get him inside," she said, still without turning around. "Just gonna get Zephyr unpacked, then we'll see about setting that arm up."

"Thanks," I said. "We really appreciate this."

She made a noncommittal grunt that could have been *You're welcome* or *Go to hell*.

I helped Ian down, who'd turned an unhealthy shade of green, and clumped across the yard with him. Hopefully he wouldn't need too much time to recharge his magic. I wasn't sure what Mercy intended to do with him, but I couldn't exactly tell her he'd be fine once he could turn into a wolf again. At least he'd be resting.

We made it onto the porch and through the door. The inside of the place looked a lot more organized than the outside. A pegboard just to the left of the door held a yellow rain slicker, a hooded sweatshirt, and a few empty hooks. There was a massive fireplace across the room, with the hearth and the inside grill swept clean and a few logs stacked in a metal basket beside it, and a sturdy three-foot cross mounted on the wall above. A couch and two chairs were arranged around a low coffee table on one side of the room, and behind the grouping stood bookshelves and a detached closet, with the folding door slightly ajar.

The other side of the room contained a table with bench seats next to a curtained window, and a set of countertop cabinets with a two-burner propane stove. A coffee percolator occupied one of the burners. Next to the cabinets were a water pump and a metal bucket. A desk in the far corner held a newer model desktop computer with a flat-screen monitor, complete with active modem. That explained the satellite dish. I guessed anybody could have internet access these days, even if they lived on a mountain in the middle of nowhere. Two open doorways led to other rooms, presumably the oddly shaped additions.

I settled Ian on the couch but didn't sit down myself. For some reason, the cross above the fireplace demanded attention. I moved in for a closer look. There were symbols carved on it. More djinn writing.

"Ian. You see what I see?"

He raised his head and grimaced. "Yes. It is a protection spell."

"What do you think? Should we make a break for it?"

He breathed in, and a coughing fit overcame him. A fine spray of blood flew from his lips and spattered the floor.

"Okay. I'll take that as a no."

"She is human," Ian rasped. "I do not perceive a threat here."

"Did you happen to perceive the shotgun?" Frowning, I paced back toward the chair. Maybe Ian was too injured to be paranoid, but I wasn't. First the cave, now this cabin. If whatever the cross had on it was a protection spell, it might've been against the Morai we'd just killed—but who put it there? I couldn't think of many reasonable explanations outside of Mercy knowing something about the djinn.

Ian seemed convinced she was human. But we hadn't seen her eyes. She'd made sure of that, and it was definitely deliberate. That was the thing about djinn. No matter how human they made themselves look, their eyes gave them away. They always retained the animal qualities of their clan—Ian's were rounder than a human's and ringed with black; Akila, like a hawk, didn't have any whites.

And all the Morai had slitted pupils, with swamp-mean hatred lurking behind a yellow-green gaze.

I opened my mouth to say something and heard scratching sounds. Claws on wood. They were coming from the closet.

My heart slammed a few times, and I tried to convince myself it was something domestic. Maybe a dog or a cat. I inched closer, cleared my throat.

The scratching stopped. A low chittering took its place, an alien sound I was sure no self-respecting dog or cat could ever make.

The front door flew open, and Mercy strode in clutching the shotgun. Her head turned toward the closet, where the disconcerting noise had grown louder. "You get outta there, Sister," she said. "And you better not've touched that blanket."

A small, black, furry hand, disturbingly human looking, poked out and folded the closet door open. The rest of the animal that lumbered out after it was a damned big raccoon. I'd seen smaller pit bulls. For a crazy instant I wondered if there were any djinn raccoon clans, but it didn't even glance at me or Ian. It went straight to Mercy and sat up on its hind legs, still making that weird chirring sound.

The thing was wearing a pink collar.

Mercy patted a pocket and produced what looked like a handful of dog food. She offered it to the raccoon, who took one piece in each hand, sniffed at one, and stuffed it in her mouth. "All right, Sister." Mercy put the pellets back and scratched the animal behind its ears, like a cat. "Go find your little ones. There's fresh fish outside."

Sister polished off the other nugget, dropped to all fours, and ambled away toward one of the smaller rooms.

"You have a pet raccoon?" I said. Like an idiot.

"Ain't you a bright one." Mercy racked the shotgun across two of the hooks on the board. She reached for her hat, hesitated, then pulled it off and dropped it on a peg. And stared at me.

Her eyes were human. But it wasn't hard to figure out why she'd hidden her face.

Her features were split almost exactly down the middle. One half of her face was tanned and healthy—and the other was dark red, the color of wine, from her hairline, down her neck, and across her ear. The eye on that side was distorted, the lid open too wide and pulled down at the outside corner so it appeared to bulge. Blood red filled in where the white should have been. Her good eye, a pale and pretty amber, dared me to say something stupid or pathetic.

"It must be a bitch finding the right shade of foundation," I said.

She struggled against a smile, and finally laughed. "Maybe you ain't all dumb," she said. "Donatti, you said your name was, and he's Ian. Right?" She cast a look at the couch and frowned. "He still alive?"

"Yeah. It looks worse than it is."

"Mm-hm. He gonna bug out if I check him?"

"I will behave." Ian smiled faintly without opening his eyes. "You have a lovely home, lady. We are indebted to your gracious care."

Mercy blushed a little. Most females seemed to have that reaction to Ian, even when he was bruised and bloodied. Especially then. But she shook it off fast and went back to being serious. She approached him, stopped. Frown lines furrowed her brow. "You're burned."

"Campfire," I said quickly. "That's what he landed on. I yanked him out." I held up my blistered hand for inspection and hoped I didn't sound completely unconvincing.

"Hmph. You two got no business up in these woods." A tiny smirk said she'd humor us anyway. "You sit. I'll be back quick. Need to get some supplies."

At once, sprawling in one of those cushioned chairs seemed like the best idea since the invention of room service. Even as

I sat down, I thought of a dozen things I should do instead of relaxing—call and check in with Jazz, figure out why Mercy had something with djinn writing on it, come up with a better story than "We fell into a campfire." I figured I'd just close my eyes for a few minutes and then worry myself into a good panic.

Consciousness fell away from me almost before I leaned back.

Eventually, a marginal awareness of someone patting my knee brought me swimming up from sleep. At first it was a dream. I was up against a wall, getting frisked—not a new experience for me, being a thief—but the cop's hands were tiny, like doll's hands at the end of regular-size arms. I asked him how he could hold a gun with those. He opened his mouth and chirred at me.

I snapped awake, and found a furry face with a pointed nose and a black mask inches from mine. The shout on the tip of my tongue came out a fuzzy, "Howza-wha?"

The raccoon standing on my lap was considerably smaller than Sister. I guessed he was a boy, because his collar was blue. He blinked bright black eyes at me, reached over, and started investigating one of the zippers on my jacket.

Low laughter drifted my way. "Do you often attract woodland creatures?"

"Yeah. Just call me Dr. Doolittle." I glanced around the raccoon and found Ian shirtless, bandaged and splinted, seated upright on the couch with his singed jacket and vest folded beside him. "How long've I been out?" I asked. "And where's Mercy?"

"Nearly an hour, and she has gone to pour out the water." He nodded at the open door. "I am sufficiently recovered," he said. "We can leave when it is . . . socially acceptable."

"I'm surprised you know that term."

A brief, bitter smile surfaced. "Well, I am a prince."

I grimaced in sympathy and looked away. It couldn't be easy for him, being the prince of a murdered kingdom. What the Morai had done to his clan, they'd done thoroughly. Ian was the last of the Dehbei.

Hence his relentless pursuit for revenge.

The little raccoon had gone from checking out my zippers to plucking at my shirt. I watched him for a few seconds, and tried to shift straighter in the chair. He flinched, freaked out, and grabbed handfuls of shirt—and hair—with a frightened bleat.

"Ow," I squeezed out, suspecting a yell would get me bitten. "Ease up there, little guy. That's quite a grip you've got. If you let go, I promise not to move anymore."

"Ernest. Behave y'self." Mercy's voice from the doorway sent the raccoon chittering again. He released my hair, settled down in my lap, and sent a hopeful look at the lady with the food. "You wanna feed him?" she said.

"Me? Uh, sure."

She came toward me, a hand in her pocket, and pulled out a few chunks of dog food. I held out my good hand, and she dropped them in. "Here you go, Ernest," I said, pinching one between thumb and finger and offering it to him. "Dig in."

He took it, blinked at me, and jumped down to saunter off to the back room.

I laughed. "What'd I do?"

"He's gone to wash it. The little ones wash just about everything they eat. Make a right mess of things." Mercy opened a plastic tackle box on the low table. She must've brought it out while I was sleeping. It was full of medical supplies—bandages, ointments, pills, a few disposable syringes, and a bunch of stuff I couldn't identify. She picked out a tube and a plastic-wrapped roll of white gauze. "Let's see that hand."

I held it out and tried not to wince while she smeared gunk all over it. "Nasty job you did here," she said. "Your friend's worse."

"Yeah." I forced myself not to babble on about campfires and falling off cliffs. The less I said, the easier it'd be to keep straight.

She put the tube down, opened the gauze, and started wrapping. "I know you're full of shit, you know. About fallin'."

Crud. My gaze flicked automatically to the shotgun. Still hanging by the door. I swallowed, but didn't say anything.

"Ernest likes ya, so you can't be too dangerous. Don't you worry none." Her hands flew with the gauze, wrapping individual fingers with ease. "I know what it's like. I got secrets of my own."

I managed a grin. "I bet you do. There's gotta be a reason you live up here in Nowheresville by yourself."

"You mean outside my dazzling beauty?" She tied off the end of the gauze and looked up at me with a smile. "Yeah, I got reasons. Wanna know why my name's Mercy?"

"Absolutely."

"It's the first word my momma said when I popped out." Uncertainty flickered through her smile, and for a moment it was bitter. "First and last one. To me, anyway." She stuffed the plastic wrap in a pocket and returned the ointment to the tackle box. "Either of you boys thirsty? I got a few beers chillin' in the back."

"I'd love one, if you're sure you don't mind," I said. "Ian?"

"Water would be most welcome," he said.

"Whatever floats you." She grabbed the box, headed for a back room, and returned in less than a minute with two brown bottles. She handed one to me, then looked at Ian. "Sure you jus' want water?"

"Please."

She shrugged and went to the pump. While she filled the bucket, I looked at the bottle label. The name printed on it was doppelbock. I didn't think I could even pronounce that. Maybe that meant it was good. I worked the cap off with my teeth, took a swig, and decided it was better than good. "Damn," I said. "Where do you get this stuff? It's amazing."

"It's local." Mercy filled a glass from the pump stream, stopped the flow, and took the water to Ian. "Pick it up in town now and again."

"You mean that bump in the road down the mountain? Resnik or Rickenback, something like that . . ."

"Ridge Neck." She popped her beer and downed a third of it without a pause. "Ignorance capital of Virginia. Might as well've called the place Redneck and been true about it."

I swallowed more beer to hold back a pained expression. Mercy didn't seem like the type to welcome sympathy. "You said something about a militia," I said. "Are they in Ridge Neck?"

She shook her head. "Crazy shits got themselves a compound, round the other side of the mountain. Ever'body in town pretends they ain't there. They got more guns than a county full of sheriffs, though, and there's somethin' wrong with them. Inbred, maybe. I seen . . ." She took another drink. "They ain't nice, is all," she said softly.

I glanced at Ian. He frowned slightly, but didn't say anything. After a moment's silence, I said, "Can I ask you something, Mercy?"

"Shoot."

"What's with the cross, there? It looks like it means something. All those symbols and stuff."

She blushed, a lot deeper than she had from Ian's flattery.

"It's Latin," she said. "Cal—a friend gave it to me. Supposed to protect me from harm. Bears and such, I suppose."

This time the look I exchanged with Ian held a lot more concern. Whoever Cal was either knew about the djinn, or was one himself. And Mercy apparently liked him quite a bit.

"That's cool," I said. "Like a spell, right?"

"Yeah, it's magic. I'm a witch. Watch out or I'll hex your ass into next week." She grinned, drank. "I wouldn't mind hexin' a couple rednecks. Mind you, just little hexes. Permanent hemorrhoids'd be a nice touch."

I had to laugh at that. Even Ian cracked a smile.

We made small talk for a few more minutes and finished our drinks. Finally, I stood and stretched. "I think we've imposed on you long enough," I said. "You have our eternal gratitude—especially for the beer."

"You're welcome."

Ian got up and gathered his clothes. Mercy walked us to the door. "I'm guessin' you got a way back to wherever you're goin'," she said.

"We do. Thank you, lady." Ian caught her hand and kissed it. She giggled.

I congratulated myself for not kicking him in the shin.

"You'd better get checked out soon," she said. "Both of you. That arm might not heal proper if you don't, and you're due for an infection." She looked at each of us in turn. "Drop by again if you want. You can bring me a beer and pay me back."

"We will." I smiled. Jazz would've absolutely loved her.

By unspoken consent, we headed back the way we'd come, up the mountain. Ian would have to heal himself completely for the next leg of our return trip.

Flying. My favorite.

Chapter 3

"**S**o I've been thinking," I half-screamed near Ian's ear, "wouldn't it be great to invest in a helicopter?"

"We've no need for such a contraption."

A lone bird zipped past my head. I lurched aside and watched my life flash before my eyes, which I'd squeezed shut to keep from glimpsing the ground half a mile below us. "Why not? It'd be just as fast, and you wouldn't get drained—"

"No. They are too loud. We would lose the advantage of secrecy."

"I hate you."

"Excuse me?"

I raised my voice. "I ate food. Ten hours ago, but I'm still gonna lose it if you don't land soon. Aren't we there yet?"

Ian didn't answer me. That could've meant we weren't even close, or we were but he was too stubborn to tell me. He knew damned well I hated flying. But short of a helicopter or a two-day hike through impenetrable mountains, there'd been no other way to get to or return from the cave where Akila had located the Morai's tether.

She could've flown this distance smoother than a Vegas

hustler and twice as fast, being part hawk and all. Unfortunately, Ian—and myself by extension—hailed from the wolf clan. The Dehbei weren't exactly suited to air travel. My personal flight ability rivaled that of a two-ton boulder, and Ian's wasn't much better. At least he could get off the ground. Still, he'd be exhausted again by the time we reached our hotel room, and we'd have to rest before we could open a mirror bridge to take us home.

Home was where the women were. His wife, my Jazz. We'd been gone two days and I already missed her, and our son. I'd lost out on the first two years of Cyrus's life and had spent the last year playing catch-up between Morai hunts. Now I couldn't imagine not being his father.

I risked opening an eye, and watched my sentimental thoughts vanish in favor of a deadly view. We'd passed the bulk of the mountain range and started over a stretch of jagged, rocky terrain. From our height the occasional flourish of vegetation looked like green bird shit dribbled across broken asphalt. Far ahead, beyond the wasteland and the rolling acres of forest that followed, a long whitish-gray smear represented Ridge Neck. We'd rented our usual Days Inn room. They had the biggest bathroom mirrors. If Ian gained a little altitude, we could be back on solid ground in fifteen or twenty minutes.

Just when I moved to suggest higher ground, I realized the bird shit below had sprouted leaves. An instant later I recognized the sinking feeling in my stomach as a literal sensation. We were falling.

"Ian! Quit fucking around." I gave him an awkward shake. It felt like tackling a mannequin. He rotated under me, and I caught a glimpse of wide, unblinking eyes and a rigid jawline. The same expression the Morai had worn when Ian cast a lockdown spell on him.

Then his head slipped through my arms, and he dropped like a bowling ball straight toward a fast and messy demise.

I must have screamed. Rushing air snatched the sound away, and all I heard was a thin whistling above the Niagara Falls roar of the wind. For a minute I considered flapping my arms like Wile E. Coyote, but a regrettably strong awareness of the laws of gravity stopped me. I had to try something, though. Ian might survive the fall, but my human ass would be on the next slingshot to hell in about two minutes—maybe sooner, if the shock stopped my heart before the ground splattered my flesh.

Ian's stiff form flipped wildly through the air, a good four feet from me and getting farther away. I had to reach him. Didn't want to find out what happened when a basically immortal being got torn to bits and lived through it, assuming I somehow survived to witness it. I decided to try air swimming. Dog-paddling wouldn't work, so I straightened my limbs as far as they'd go and headed in Ian's direction with a series of awkward flaps and spirited grunts, like a constipated angel.

I'd never been in a hurricane before, but the air slapping my face felt like at least category 4. The blinding wind made it almost impossible to get my bearings. Just keeping my eyes open was a challenge. I knew the big light blur was the sky, and the big dark blur was the ground. And the fluttering thing just ahead of my outstretched arm had to be the corner of Ian's coat. I executed a desperate, clumsy lunge and grabbed for him. My fingers closed around a fistful of hair.

That probably hurt like hell, but I figured he'd forgive me. Eventually.

I managed to drag him partway under me and wrapped both arms around his torso. Now all I had to do was stop us from hitting the ground. No problem. My frantic brain disgorged a handful of typically stupid ideas. I'd just turn those boulders rushing toward us into a giant trampoline, or transmute our flesh into feathers, or repeal the law of gravity. Maybe some passing astronaut would toss us a jet pack in the next five seconds or so.

Or maybe I should get serious and try to stop us from becoming hamburger.

I couldn't fly, and I couldn't release Ian from his frozen state. No time to consider who or what might've put him there. There was no handy lake or ocean to steer toward and hope for a soft landing that would only break every bone in our bodies. But I needed to survive—and the only thing in my favor was that djinn magic worked on the strength of need and the will of the user. No living being in that moment wanted to avoid hitting the ground more than me.

I closed my eyes, figuring I'd at least spare myself the anticipation and die fast if this didn't work, and concentrated.

I need to slow down. I need to keep all of my limbs attached to my body. I need to not land on those rocks.

I need a miracle.

Familiar pain balled in the center of my chest and surged hot through my torso. I welcomed the feel of the magic, let it take the lead and hoped it did something useful. For an instant I thought the descent slowed—but then pain eclipsed my awareness of everything except my own screaming nerves.

It had never hurt this much before. I couldn't even tell if I still had hold of Ian. Time suspended itself while the world vanished behind a solid wall of anguish. I stayed in tortured limbo for what seemed like both minutes and hours, and finally caught a single glimpse of fragmented green. My mind registered *tree* a split second after the image imprinted on my eyeballs.

My leg hit first, wrenched hard. The back of my head whacked something solid and produced definite nonmagical pain. I decided I'd failed, that the fluid trickling down my neck was my brains oozing from my shattered skull. My last thought before blackness took me was that Jazz would be pissed because I'd forgotten to put the laundry in the dryer before I died.

". . . caught us a couple of ugly-ass birds."

A round of disjointed laughter chased words that felt like spikes in my ears. I assumed I wasn't dead, because even purgatory couldn't hurt this much. Besides, I refused to believe demons talked like Boss Hogg from *The Dukes of Hazzard*.

"He dead?"

"Probably not this'n. See those tats on him? He's pure blood."

A cautious relief stole over me. They were talking about Ian, about the raised armband tattoos most of the djinn seemed to have. He'd lived too. But he was likely just as broken as I felt, and definitely unconscious, or he would've addressed these morons by now.

Still, the fact that they knew how to recognize and bring down a djinn suggested they weren't as dumb as they sounded. Young, low-level Morai, I thought. And more than one of them in the same place was never good news.

"What about that one up there? Want me to roust him down?"

I stopped breathing. Their attention would be on me now, and I suspected playing dead was my best bet at the moment. I wasn't in any shape to take on a djinn alone, much less two of them. I did have to wonder why he'd said *up there*, though. Where the hell was I?

"Leave him be." A third voice issued the command, and my gut clenched. Since when did the Morai travel in packs? This one had to be the leader. The steel in his drawl had instantly silenced the other two. "If he ain't dead, he's close," the leader continued. "And I want them both alive for a while."

"Think they got to the cave before we did?"

"That's what I aim to find out."

Crud. They must've come here to fetch the djinn we'd just killed. What beautiful timing we had. Even if both of us were completely fresh and unhurt, it'd be almost impossible to destroy three Morai at once—and that was assuming they had their tethers on them. Since we were dead anyway, I decided to risk opening my eyes.

They didn't notice. Probably because I'd landed in a tree, and the tops of their heads were ten feet below me.

Ian lay facedown on a flat slab of rock speckled with his blood. They'd stripped off his coat and tossed it at the base of my perch. The three of them stood around him and stared like they'd just brought down a gryphon. They were brown haired and muscled, sported deep sunburns, and wore similar clothing: nondescript T-shirts, well-worn jeans, and battered work boots. Slap cowboy hats on them and they could've stepped straight off some Texas dude ranch.

These assholes looked human. Had some of the Morai actually gotten smart and learned how to blend in?

One of them prodded Ian's shoulder with a boot. The motion shook the other two loose from their trances. Another lit a cigarette, and the third wandered over to the tree and hefted Ian's coat. "Hey, Lynus," he said. "Mind if I keep his duster? He ain't gonna need it."

The shoulder prodder shrugged. "Suit yourself." His gaze didn't leave Ian.

"Better be careful, Davie," the smoker said. "You don't know where he's been."

The remark produced a burst of yuk-yuk laughter from Davie. He gave the coat a shake, grabbed an arm, and yanked his hand back. "Aw, *shit*. He done got blood all over it."

Lynus looked up. "Then Val's gonna want it. Leave it be."

Davie dropped the coat and wiped his palm on his jeans. I closed my eyes and tried to silence my thudding heart, convinced they could hear it. Lynus's simple, sharp command had told me enough to kindle real fear. I'd taken him for the leader, but they were working for someone else. Someone who'd want the blood of a djinn. Definitely not good.

"Kit. Help me flip the sumbitch. I want a look at his face."

"Probably all smashed up now," the smoker grumbled. But he pitched the cigarette and crouched next to Lynus, and together they heaved Ian into a boneless roll that flopped him faceup. His open eyes stared directly up at me without seeing. A fat gash across the bridge of his nose leaked crimson down his face, so he appeared to be crying blood. His chest heaved once, then settled. He didn't move again.

"I'll be . . ." Lynus knelt and leaned over Ian. His breath left in a low whistle. "He's Dehbei," he said with something approaching awe.

"Damn. Ain't they all dead?" Davie shuffled over, but stopped when Lynus shot a hand out palm first.

Lynus tilted his head up to flash a grin that held more ice than Alaska. "All but one," he said. "We hit the jackpot, boys. This here's the prince himself." His gaze returned to Ian, and his voice dropped into a soft and lethal cadence. "Hey there . . . Gahiji-an."

Shit. Whoever these guys were, they knew too much. The one they worked for, Val, had to be a Morai too. They had themselves a nice little nest. Usually they kept to themselves, so they wouldn't have to share whatever power they managed to grab. Their clan wasn't exactly close-knit—they hated each other almost as much as they hated the other clans, and humans. If the Morai were banding together, the whole world was in serious trouble.

Lynus got to his feet and squinted up at me. "So that must be the thief. Not sure if Val wants him or not. I'm gonna ring in real quick." He pulled a cell phone from a back pocket and paced a few steps away to dial.

Now or never. If I could get near Ian, I might be able to get him moving again. He could amplify his power through direct contact with his descendants—namely, me. I held my breath, made a quick assessment of the biggest branches on the tree to use for bumpers, and rolled out.

My trip down was loud, fast, and punctuated with pain. I heard a few shouts from the thugs over cracking wood and the consuming agony of my right leg, which was almost certainly broken. One shoulder rammed the crotch of a thick branch near the bottom and flipped me wrong side up. I landed side first on solid rock, and something inside my rib cage snapped with an audible crack. My busted leg thumped to a rest on Ian's splayed arm.

The instant we made contact, he glowed. Just like I'd planned. Kind of.

All three Morai stood transfixed as the bright Ian shape changed—his body lengthened and thickened, his legs and arms thinned, his chest barreled, and his head elongated and flattened. Within seconds an oversize wolf stood where Ian had lain. His muzzle wrinkled in a threatening snarl. Black lips parted to bare huge, curved ivory fangs. I damn near laughed, mostly from relief. My, what big teeth you have, Grandpa.

Lynus rammed the phone in his pocket, stepped back. I got a good look at his face—and my worry about facing three evil djinn became shock. His eyes were human. No slitted pupils, no oversize irises. Just regular brown eyes, full of fury. Now I was really confused.

And then Lynus vanished.

I gasped aloud and tried to right myself. He shouldn't have been able to do that—unless he really was a djinn. Could they change their eyes if they wanted to? No time for that discussion with Ian now. He couldn't answer me anyway. Wolves didn't talk.

I managed to prop myself up against the tree. Davie and Kit had disappeared too. Terrific.

Undaunted by the lack of visual direction, Ian the wolf raised his head and sniffed the air. A low, constant growl issued from his throat. He tensed, drew back a bit, and lunged forward.

The sound of boots slapping rock rose just ahead, and a man-shaped ripple in the air moved to one side. Ian's leap missed by scant inches. "Davie!" Lynus's disembodied voice called. "Take the thief out."

I clenched my jaw and tried to think invisible thoughts. Nothing happened. Whatever I'd done in the air had drained me. My hands skimmed the ground, searching for a loose rock or branch to defend myself with. But without the senses of a wolf, my chances of deflecting an unseen attack were approximately none.

My search yielded nothing. I would have panicked, but a murmur of djinn words informed me that a weapon wouldn't have helped anyway—seconds before a flame curse hit me in the chest.

Ian whirled around at the sound of my scream. He bounded toward me, leapt past, and tackled a hunk of air that flickered into Davie. The fire in my flesh sizzled out and left me with only the throb of broken bones and massive bruising. I grabbed a low-hanging branch, hoisted myself up on my good leg, and pulled my short blade. Useless, but I felt better armed. Maybe I could carve a spear or something.

A horrible gurgling cry came from behind the tree. I swung around, suspecting the worst, and proved myself right. Ian had torn Davie's throat out. Blood stained his muzzle and sprayed across his heaving chest. Davie's open, glassy eyes—as human as Lynus's—stared at the sky, his expression frozen in eternal terror. Deader than Al Capone.

But Davie had used magic. And there was no tether. How could he be dead?

"Jesus Christ. Jesus fucking Christ, Lynus, he killed Davie. Lynus! You hear me? He ripped his fucking throat out. Jesus Christ . . ."

Kit's pitched babble came from somewhere to my right. A responding, inarticulate roar erupted behind me. I didn't need a wolf's senses to catch the grief in that cry, or the killing rage.

Ian shook his head. Droplets of blood flew from his snout in a fine mist. He bunched, turned, reached me in a single bound. He caught my shirt in his teeth and yanked hard.

My busted leg folded. I swore and stumbled, but Ian pushed under me and I landed draped over him like a hunted buck. He gave a rough bark, twisted, and snapped at me, missing my ass by half an inch.

Somehow, I understood what he wanted—but I sure as hell didn't like it.

The struggle to mount him lasted only seconds, though it seemed much longer. I managed to swing a leg over. My ribs howled as I pressed my body flat along his back and buried my free hand in the thick fur of his shoulder. I kept the blade handy, instinctively guessing I'd need it.

Harsh breathing arose to my right. The first words of a spell I didn't recognize slipped out between heaves. I listened hard, drew back, and threw the knife with all the strength I could muster.

The blade found its mark. A strangled yell interrupted Lynus mid-djinn. I couldn't tell whether I'd stuck him or just clocked him with the handle, and I didn't care. I thrust my fingers into Ian's fur. Muscles bunched and rippled beneath me, and then we were bounding across boulders at bone-knocking speed while Lynus's parting promise thundered through the crisp mountain air.

"Gahiji-an! I'll take my brother's blood from your worthless hide. You will die!"

Chapter 4

If my injuries didn't kill me, Ian would.

Every leap threatened to spill me off, and every landing sent new waves of pain through my body. The ground below raced by in a steady blur. Ian seemed to pick the most awkward patches of terrain he could find—sharp crags with mere inches of purchase, patches of loose rock that shifted and skidded under his paws, ledges so narrow they wouldn't hold a pencil. At one point he soared headlong across a five-foot gap, and I glanced down while we sailed over a yawning abyss that seemed to drop straight to Africa. After that, I kept my eyes closed.

I didn't dare look behind us. The two remaining thugs probably couldn't match Ian's speed, but I didn't want to find out I was wrong.

We finally reached the border of the thick forest I'd seen from the air. Ian raced into the fold without hesitation. His breathing came hard and fast under me, the human equivalent of an asthma attack. The third time he almost bashed into a tree, I decided we'd put enough distance between us and them—whether he liked it or not.

"Stop. We're clear now."

If he heard me, he showed no sign of slowing down.

"Damn it, Ian, stop! I can't hold on anymore."

A prolonged growl vibrated through him, but his ground-eating pace geared down to a jog, then a lope. Finally, he came to rest at the edge of a needle-strewn clearing and offered an impatient snort. I let go, thumped to the ground, and arched up with a yelp when my back collided with a softball-size rock concealed under the forest carpet. I spit out a curse and curled on my side, hoping nature didn't have any more surprises for me. Why couldn't any of the Morai hole up in a mall or something?

"Are you injured?"

I flopped faceup and glared at Ian, who'd returned to his natural state of asshole. "Are you stupid?"

"Where?"

"Leg, ribs, head, back. Pick a body part. It's probably broken."

Ian frowned. He knelt next to me, one hand hovering over the base of my throat like a priest about to push a baptism candidate underwater. "I've not much power left, but I may be able to heal your leg. Then, at least, you can walk."

"Terrific." I really looked forward to dragging through miles of woods with shattered ribs and a lump on my head the size of a small city. I exhaled, closed my eyes, and waited. The sharpest pain dissipated from my leg, but a bone-deep ache remained.

Ian gasped. I glanced at him. His skin had gone a ghostly sweat-slicked gray, and his eyes fluttered back in his head. "I cannot continue," he whispered. "My apologies, thief."

"Hey, it's okay. Think I can walk." Concern and urgency kicked my adrenaline into overdrive. I pushed up on my elbows, and finally noticed that Ian's neck and chest beneath the open vest he wore were splashed with blood. "What the hell happened? I thought transformation healed you."

He wiped absently at the mess. "It is not mine."

"Oh." An image of dead, mutilated Davie seared my brain. With it came the certainty that we needed to move before his brothers tried to claim their revenge. I had to assume Kit was related. "Any idea who those guys are? Because they can't be djinn," I said as I hauled myself off the ground.

Ian didn't answer for way too long. At last, he stood and stared back toward the edge of the woods. "Yes."

I waited. No explanation arrived. "Care to share with me?"

"They are . . ." He looked at me with unease stamped on his features. "Descendants. Like you."

"Excuse me?" The Morai had spent the last four hundred years hunting down and killing every last one of Ian's descendants. I'd been informed that my son and I were the sole survivors. And all djinn were magically infertile in the human realm—except for Ian, who had a little help from his wife. "You're telling me those bastards are related to you?"

Ian shook his head. "They are Morai."

"No." My automatic denial didn't stop the horror of acceptance that lodged in my chest. Impossible as it was, nothing else made sense. "Uh-uh. The Morai can't breed. If they could, they would've created an army by now. Take over the world, reign of terror and age of darkness, shit like that. Besides, they just looked like regular humans. How could you know they're Morai?"

The minute I asked, I decided against wanting to know. He told me anyway.

"I have tasted Morai blood before." His gaze flicked down to his gore-streaked torso. "However, they are . . . wrong. Tainted. I cannot determine why at the moment."

"Maybe they're inbred," I muttered. From what I'd heard, the Morai had a tendency to breed like rabbits back home just to increase their numbers—and any fertile female had been fair game, whether she liked it or not. Especially since female djinn could reproduce only once every three hundred years.

A frown creased Ian's forehead. "Perhaps," he said, sounding less than convinced. "We must move. They may attempt to give chase."

"Ya think?"

He shot me a sharp look. I decided to shut up.

We headed farther into the woods, me limping, him ambling like a reluctant zombie. I tried to listen for signs of pursuit, but our loud, clumsy progress drowned out any chance of staying undetected. I tried to guess how far it'd be to the town on the other side. My estimate wasn't encouraging. This stretch of trees had looked at least ten times as big as the cluster of buildings beyond. They'd catch up to us in no time.

At least Ian didn't have his tether on him, so they couldn't kill him right away. I enjoyed no such guarantees for survival.

I figured we must've walked halfway to China, but the damned forest refused to end. Still no sign of our pursuers who couldn't possibly exist. I was dying to know how the Morai had managed to produce descendants, since I only had Ian's word that they were sterile—and he'd lied to me before. Too many times to count. But I didn't think he had a clue this time. He'd seemed just as stunned as me.

We'd have to find someone who did know. Eventually. When we weren't limping for our lives.

I stared ahead at the ocean of nature and tried willing it to become civilization. Nature ignored me. But I did glimpse something in the distance that probably shouldn't have been in the woods. I nudged Ian and pointed. "Is that a pay phone mounted on a tree?"

Ian followed my gesture. "It appears to be."

"Great. Maybe we can call for a cab."

"You are joking." Ian glanced at me. "Aren't you?"

"Mostly." I moved toward the thing and wondered if it was somehow related to the Hillbilly Brothers back there. But I doubted it. The idea of a booby-trapped pay phone was a stretch even for the Morai. Besides, they hadn't expected to find us out here. They were looking for their recently exploded kin.

The metal case was a scratch-and-dent model, worn by time and what looked like the claws of large animals. The peeling, unidentifiable remains of a phone company logo clung to the outside. Inside, there was no phone, only a sturdy plastic utility box, held shut with a thick and rusted steel padlock.

The presence of this contraption in the middle of a wild, mountainous forest unsettled me. It was like digging up a dinosaur skeleton and finding a Rolex on its wrist.

Curiosity overcame my misgivings. I'd have no problem picking the lock. Despite my retirement from thieving, I'd kept my legally questionable skills as sharp as possible. Never knew when it would come in handy to open a lock, or hot-wire a car, or disable an alarm. I patted my pockets for a tool.

"Donatti."

Warning edged Ian's voice. I waved a hand in his general direction. "Know what I'm doing," I muttered. "Don't worry. I won't blow us up."

"Damn you, thief. *Look.*"

I looked. At first I couldn't tell what his problem was. Finally I realized that the strip of green about a hundred feet ahead wasn't more trees. It was a moss-covered stone wall, and beyond it stood a house. Not a rustic cabin, but a sturdy and sizable stone structure. Practically a castle. And from the soft light glowing in two of the upper windows, it appeared to be currently inhabited.

"Crud." I shifted reflexively to invisible, noting that even that simple trick caused more pain than it should have. I still hadn't recovered from my aborted midair braking. "They couldn't have passed us," I said. "Think there's more of them?"

"One might presume the possibility." Ian had disappeared too. His voice came from directly behind me. "We should investigate the situation."

I shook my head, forgetting that he couldn't see the motion. "You're crazy. We're both tapped. If there's anybody in there with more power than a twenty-watt lightbulb, we're dead. What if their leader is here—Val, or whatever his name was?"

"That is what I am hoping to find."

"No. Forget it, Ian." Again, I flashed back to the cave-dwelling Morai's warning: *Die in service to your master's madness.* Not going to happen. "I'm human, remember? You're safe as long as they can't get your tether. I'm not."

Ian sighed. "I am not fool enough to take on another djinn at this point. I simply want to ascertain whether this Val is here, so we can return in the future."

"What if we get caught?"

"We will not."

"And you're so sure about this because . . . ?"

There was a long pause before he said, "Are you not a professional thief?"

"No, I am not," I drawled. "I'm retired."

"So you are afraid, then."

"Don't do that." He was getting to me again, the bastard.

Impugning what little sense of honor I had left. "Look, we know where the place is. More or less. Can't we just go home and have Akila scry the place, find out whether there's a Morai in there?"

"Why should I subject her to the effort when we are already here?" I could practically hear him rolling his eyes. "Once we are inside the structure, I will be able to sense another djinn, if there is one present. And then we will leave."

I groaned. "Promise me you won't do anything stupid. I can't rescue you this time."

"Agreed." His tone implied exactly what I could do with the idea that he'd need rescuing.

"Fine. Let's go."

I turned and started toward the wall. When Ian didn't seem to be moving, I said, "Are you coming, or is this supposed to be a solo venture?"

"Yes." Pine needles crackled beneath his unseen feet. "And we had better move quickly."

"Why?"

"They are coming back."

I didn't need to ask who *they* were.

Chapter 5

We stopped when we reached the stone wall—at least, I did. I hoped Ian hadn't just charged on ahead. "You still here?" I half-whispered.

"No. I have gone to Starbucks."

"Now's a great time to develop sarcasm," I shot back. "Any idea how close they are?"

"Close enough."

"Well, that's helpful." I looked over the grounds for any sign of movement, and saw none. "We need a plan. We won't be able to talk to each other in there. So . . . how long, and where are we going to meet?"

"Fifteen minutes. And there, by that statue."

"What statue?"

"To your right."

I looked. At the far corner of the wall stood St. Jude, patron saint of lost causes. I knew because this guy had been a big deal at the Catholic orphanage where I spent most of my childhood. That's what we all were, lost causes—especially me, as the nuns reminded me daily. I had to wonder why a bunch of half-Morai thugs would want St. Jude hanging around.

Movement near the building caught my eye. A man in a dusky black robe emerged from a stand of trees at the corner of the walled property and headed for the building. Two more followed, dressed in the same fashion. Each of them sported a bowl haircut and a rope belt. I almost laughed. "Ian, I don't think we're going to find any evil djinn in here. It's a monastery."

"How can you be certain?"

"Because of the monks."

It took him a minute to see what I meant. When he did, he made an agitated sound and said, "We should still investigate. This could be a . . . blanket."

"A blanket." I practically had to bite my tongue. "You mean a cover?"

"Whatever you call it. I have no trouble believing those snakes would feign human purity to hide themselves, if they are breeding."

"Uh-huh. So, even though the rest of them go around flaunting their fangs and scales, this one might be posing as a monk."

"Yes."

"Right. And I'm Mary Poppins."

"Excuse me?"

"Never mind." If it'd get Ian to lay off the witch hunt long enough for us to make it home for a few days, I'd gladly spend a quarter hour poking around a monastery. Maybe the half-breeds on our trail would bypass this place and we'd lose them. "Fifteen minutes, at the statue. You want upstairs or down?"

"Up."

"It's yours. See you in fifteen."

I clambered over the wall. Behind me, I heard Ian do the same, and then his footfalls picked up their pace and passed me. He was practically running for the place. I hoped that didn't mean he'd sensed our pursuers closing in and had neglected to mention it to me.

Before I made half the distance to the monastery proper, a figure edged out from the shadows of an alcoved back door. Another monk, this one with shaggy blond hair and wearing a black robe. A beaded crucifix pendant hung around his neck— and his cane and dark glasses said I didn't have to worry about whether or not I was visible.

Still, being blind didn't mean he was deaf. I tried to walk quieter.

"Hello?" the blind monk called softly. His head turned in my direction. "Brother Justin? I thought you were working in the front gardens today. Is everything okay?"

I froze, hoping the monk would leave if he didn't hear anything else. He stayed put. After a few minutes, I started walking again. His demeanor shifted to wariness with my first step. "Who's there?" he said—not so softly this time.

Damn. I couldn't stand out here all day playing freeze tag with this guy. While I debated the merits of making a run for the other side of the building, the sound of footsteps infiltrated the silence. They weren't mine, or the monk's. The sounds were behind me. And they were getting closer.

I glanced back, expecting to see nothing. My expectations were disappointed. Lynus and Kit strode across the cleared ground, visible as billboards. I filed a mental note to break Ian's teeth for not telling me how close they were—if I lived that long. At least I had some mojo back. Still, I didn't dare move. I had to hope they wouldn't be able to find me, because I only knew spells that destroyed tethers, not humans, and I'd already thrown away my weapon.

But the half-breeds headed straight for the blind monk. "Hey. Old man," Lynus called as they neared him. "We're looking for a coupla dead men walking. They come through here?"

The monk went rigid as a rock. "Who are you?"

"Mother fucking Teresa. Answer the question." Lynus stopped in front of him, with Kit flanking his left. "Two guys. Beat-up, weird-lookin' assholes. You seen 'em?"

A sardonic smile flashed across the monk's face, and he tapped a finger on his glasses. "I haven't seen anything."

"Don't get smart, old man."

"Lynus, lay off." Kit elbowed him and stepped forward. "Look, mister, just answer him. We don't want no trouble with you."

The monk sighed. For just an instant he turned toward me, and I could've sworn he looked right at me. "No one at all has been here," he said. "No one but me, and the other monks. You do realize this is a monastery?"

"Yeah. It's also the only place to hide for miles in these goddamned woods, and we know they come this way." Lynus's hands clenched at his sides. "I think you're lying, Monk."

"I assure you I'm not. And I think you should leave."

"I think you should tell me where the fuck they are!" The enraged half-breed reached out and snagged the front of the monk's robe. Before I could even register that the bastard meant to kill someone over me, much less do something about it, Lynus jerked the monk forward and snatched the glasses from his face.

The second or so that followed refused to obey the laws of physics. Time distorted itself, stretching and folding, making out-of-order impressions on my brain. Lynus let out a breathless curse and dropped the monk's arm like it was on fire. He grabbed Kit, or maybe Kit grabbed him. Both of them vanished. Running footsteps sounded, then ceased abruptly in a rush of air. Like they'd taken off flying—but that was impossible. Snakes didn't fly.

Finally, my shocked system focused on the monk, and the gaze that returned unfailingly to the place where I stood. Those eyes weren't blind. They were reptilian green, with slitted pupils.

I couldn't move. No lockdown spell this time—sheer terrified indecision kept me planted in place. He was Morai, no doubt about that. But where were the fangs, the hairless dome, the seething and murderous hatred? There was nothing threatening about his appearance. He was tall and slender, with fair, almost feminine features. Lynus had called him an old man, but he didn't look that old. Late thirties—and since djinn didn't age the way we did, that probably gave him a couple of thousand years on Ian. Not good. The older a djinn, the more powerful he was.

I tensed, preparing to sprint for the building, find Ian, and get the hell out of here. I'd been set on fire enough for one day.

"So much for discretion." A small smile pulled at the Morai's mouth. He retrieved his glasses from the ground and put them on again. "I'd appreciate it if you didn't share this with the others here. My brothers aren't ready to know. They are human, after all."

He had to be talking to me. I was pretty sure there weren't any more invisible descendants out here—but then, how would I know? For the moment I didn't know a damned thing anymore.

He took a step toward me. "They won't come back," he said. "Please, show yourself. No harm will come to you."

I couldn't stand here and wait for divine intervention. Neither God nor Ian was about to swoop down and save me, and on the surface it didn't seem like I needed saving. But my limited knowledge crippled me. According to Ian, every time a Morai opened his mouth, a lie came out. And there were rules I didn't quite understand about the djinn killing humans. They couldn't do it directly, which was why the Morai had used humans to slaughter the rest of Ian's descendants. They could kill in self-defense—but only when they were in animal form.

Finally, I decided to take the risk and communicate. He wasn't a snake right now, and I was pretty sure I could outrun him. Still, I wouldn't let him see me yet.

"I take it you're not a monk," I said.

He looked startled for an instant. "Actually, I am," he said slowly. "I was ordained in 1692." He cleared his throat. "I never realized how disconcerting it is, speaking to someone who isn't there. I hope I'm correct in assuming you're djinn."

"More or less." I stayed invisible, not entirely convinced of his intentions. "Why couldn't those guys sense me? And if you knew, why didn't you tell them I was here?"

"For the same reason you can't sense me. These grounds are my haven, and they're protected from scrying spells. Though apparently they're not safe from random djinn who happen to be wandering in the wilderness." He frowned. "Who are you? Show yourself."

"In a minute." *Haven?* Who could a full-blooded djinn need protection from? The answer came like a kick in the teeth. Ian. And by extension, me. Feeling a touch queasy, I said, "Why didn't you turn me over to those bast—er, guys?" I couldn't bring myself to swear in front of a monk, even if he was a Morai.

"They seemed intent on shedding blood. I don't allow that here."

"Well, that's reassuring." I held back a sigh. If Ian knew I was standing here chatting with a Morai, he'd probably kick my ass. "All right. Here, I'm showing." I dropped the vanishing act.

The monk twitched. He paled a few shades. "You're human."

"Not exactly." I grimaced. He'd made *human* sound like a dirty word. "I'm—"

"I know who you are." His voice grew hoarse. "You're the thief Donatti. The slayer's apprentice."

My throat clenched tight. He knew my name, and apparently I'd acquired a title somewhere along the way. Not one I liked much either.

"The prince. Is he here with you?"

"He is indeed, snake."

Ian's voice came from the alcove behind the Morai. The monk whirled and held up a defensive hand. "Wait. *Rayan,* please listen—"

But Ian had already launched into a spell. The lockdown hit the monk in midsentence, and he stiffened and toppled to the ground.

"Jesus . . . creepers, Ian!" I shook myself loose and strode toward the building. "How long have you been standing there?"

Ian flickered into sight and regarded me with raised eyebrows. "Creepers?"

"Answer the question."

He made a vague gesture. "I happened to glance out a window and saw the half-breeds approaching. I could not determine why I failed to sense them—though I know now. His wards prevent detection." He glared down at the motionless Morai. "So I came to be sure you were safe. And found a snake in the grass."

"Really. Well, great job keeping me safe. You didn't do a . . . darn thing, except stand there and eavesdrop."

"I would have acted, had it become necessary. You handled the situation well enough." He gave me the look again. "Why are you speaking so strangely?"

"He's a monk. You don't curse around people of the cloth. Or djinn. Whatever."

His curiosity shifted to rage. "Are you mad? This is no monk!" He drove a foot into the Morai's ribs hard enough to flip him over.

"Ian!" I stepped between them before I could consider the consequences. "Stop it. He saved my ass. Probably yours too. The least you could do is hear him out."

"I will not entertain the couched falsehoods of a Morai." His eyes practically flashed fire. "If you do not plan to assist me, then get out of my way. I will destroy him myself."

The next words out of my mouth were the dumbest I'd ever uttered in my life. "I'm not going to let you do that."

"You—" Ian froze in place. I imagined that Caesar wore a similar expression when the knife went into his back. "Why?"

"Because he's defenseless. Let's start there. You just kicked a guy who can't move. That's like punching a quadriplegic." The shock of what he'd done was finally fading enough to let me think. I knew Ian would drag himself over broken glass with two busted legs if it meant he could kill just one more of them, and that was fine when every last one was a bloodthirsty murderer. But his obsession had blinded him to the fact that this guy wasn't. The monk hadn't even tried to defend himself.

Ian stared at me like I was speaking Klingon. "He is Morai."

"Yeah? And I'm Italian. I think. Does that mean I eat a ton of pasta and have at least one relative named Luigi?"

"I fail to see how this pertains to the Morai."

"Never mind. Bad analogy for a djinn." Behind me, the monk groaned and stirred. The spell was wearing off. If I couldn't make Ian understand in the next few seconds, he was going to do something I'd regret. "Look. You've spent four hundred years hunting these guys down, and you haven't even considered that they might not all be evil freak shows." My lip curled in disgust. "We had a human like that once. His name was Hitler."

Ian reeled like I'd slapped him. After a beat, a hint of anger resurfaced. "I am nothing like your Hitler. The Morai slaughtered my clan. They must be destroyed."

"Gahiji-an," the monk gasped. He pushed himself up and stood slowly, but made no move to attack, or even cast a spell. "If you won't show me mercy, at least consider my brothers and let us take this conflict out of their sight. They won't understand. They're innocent."

"As you are not, Morai." Ian's burning gaze fell on me. "Stand aside. Now."

"No." At least part of me hung back and watched in amazement while the rest of me practically begged him to hit me with a painful curse. Or a fist. "You're not doing this, Ian. The way it stands now, you can't kill him, and he can't kill you. Or me." *I hope.* "There's no reason we can't listen to what he has to say."

"If you expect me to give audience to this fork-tongued mockery of a—" Ian cut himself off with an audible click of his jaw. He closed his eyes, drew in a breath, and let it out slowly. "Very well. Let the snake speak, if you must. I will not interfere."

I didn't trust his sudden change of heart. Getting Ian to consider a new opinion was like suggesting that the pope toss the mitre and wear a baseball cap in public. "Why am I not buying this?" I said. "You're gonna do something stupid. I know you are."

"Do you wish my cooperation or not?"

I glanced back at the monk, who stood there like someone had stuffed a ticking bomb up his ass. "Yeah, I do. Thanks."

"Do not thank me, thief. Your ridiculous notions of innocence may lead to your death." He narrowed his eyes at the Morai. "Were I you, I would watch these so-called monks for signs of weapons."

"Please." The monk moved forward. His features contorted for an instant. "Come inside. We can talk in my study, and then . . ." He seemed to shrink a few inches. "Well, I suppose we'll see what happens next."

I stepped aside to let him lead. Hopefully, what happened next wouldn't involve pain—because if the Morai wasn't planning to double-cross anyone here, Ian probably was. And I'd have to get myself brutally savaged trying to stop him.

Chapter 6

Entering the monk's study was like stepping back in time a few hundred years. From the aged wooden shelves that held scrolls and leather-bound books with crackled pages, to the wall-mounted candelabra coated with years of wax drippings and the heavy velvet drapes drawn back from the windows, the room screamed *Why yes, I was alive during the plague, thank you very much.* A musty smell, not unpleasant, saturated the air and drove home the authenticity.

Two things refused to conform to the seventeenth-century-monk mold. The first was the oversize framed mirror on the right-hand wall, mounted a few inches off the floor. Last I checked, monks weren't into vanity. Djinn, on the other hand, used mirrors for transportation—and communication. Basically magic-powered webcams. I had to wonder if he was keeping in touch with anyone, since there shouldn't have been any other reason to have it in here.

And the second was the laptop computer on the surface of a carved wooden table by the window. Interesting. A technology-friendly monk.

After we filed in, the Morai closed the door. He removed

the glasses and put them on the table next to the laptop. "Let's start with introductions," he said. "I know who you both are. My name is Khalyn, but I'm known here as Brother Calvin."

Ian acknowledged him with a glower. I doubted he cared what his name was. To him, all the Morai were named dead meat. "All right, Calvin," I said. "I'm all for small talk, but I think you'd better give Ian a reason not to kill you pretty quick."

"Yes. I suppose I should." He closed his eyes and grimaced. One hand cradled the spot where Ian had kicked him. "I believe you broke my rib, *rayan.*"

"I will break more than that, snake, if you do not explain yourself."

I sent Ian an exasperated look. He ignored me.

"Well, you can just heal it later," I said to Calvin. "Right?"

He smiled a little, shook his head. "I don't use my power. For anything."

"Lies," Ian snarled. "You are attempting to put us at ease before you strike. It will not work. This whole place is enchanted, and you claim to not use your power?"

"I did place a scrying barrier on these grounds. Fifty years ago, when I built the monastery." He met Ian's furious gaze with calm. "That was the last time I did anything that didn't require manual effort."

"Why?" I said. "I mean, that seems a little extreme. Even for a monk."

"Because I did something that I regret. Something personal." His tone was layered with don't-go-there. "You have to understand. I've been in this realm for more than two thousand years. I was never involved in the wars, or any of the horrors my clan visited on yours. I'm a scholar."

My brain skipped a little on the part about two thousand

years. This guy could've met Jesus personally. That would've made me consider monkhood.

But Ian wasn't buying it. "All the Morai were brought back to the djinn realm after the havoc you wreaked here. The Council forbade your return, until your clan was permanently banished, all of you sealed in your tethers. You must have been sent here with the others."

"Really, Gahiji-an. You are familiar with the Council's corruption. Do you actually believe they were as thorough as they claimed to be?" Disgust registered in his face. "Besides, I didn't participate in that fiasco. I never really wanted to be a god."

"Your word alone will not absolve you." Ian folded his arms. "In fact, I cannot conceive of anything that would. You are wasting your time."

"So you would destroy me simply because I was born a Morai." Calvin stared at him. "I'd expected no less from you, *rayan*. What my clan has done to yours is unforgivable. But I hoped you'd at least entertain the idea that we're not all defined by our birthright. After all, your wife is Bahari."

Ian launched himself forward. He caught the monk by the throat and slammed him against the shelves. Books and scrolls shivered loose and tumbled down around them. "Never mention my wife, snake," he said through his teeth. "You are not worthy to think of her."

"Ian, let go!" I grabbed his arm and tried to pull him away. I might as well have been dead-lifting a bus out of a ditch. "We're listening. Remember? Being reasonable people. And djinn. Knock this crap off."

Calvin lifted a hand. "Understood," he croaked.

Ian pushed harder for an instant before he released him. He shrugged me off and treated me to a black-dagger stare. "I will listen, thief. But I assure you, I will not tolerate insults from the likes of him."

I failed to see anything insulting about Calvin's comment, but I wouldn't mention that now. I'd leave Ian to his denial of the truth in it. For the moment. "Look, there has to be some way to settle this," I said, and added quickly, "that doesn't involve breaking things."

Calvin rubbed his throat. The skin where Ian had throttled him was bright red and starting to bruise. "I'm afraid the prince is right." He made his way to the chair in front of the table and just about collapsed in it. "If I'm guilty until proven innocent, there's nothing to be done. I have only my word."

"Then you have nothing," Ian said.

"Wait." I tried to banish the visions of impending explosions haunting my mind. None of them ended well for me. "How about some information? Can you tell us anything about those descendants who were just here?"

Calvin's brow furrowed. "The scions? I thought they were after you."

"They were. But we have no idea who they are, or where they came from."

"Yes. Convenient, is it not, that they should have found us so close to your home?" Ian spoke calmly enough, but I recognized the threat in his tone. "Enlighten us, snake. I know they are Morai. Are they your descendants?"

"No. I've never seen them before today." Calvin's gaze flicked away for an instant. I was no lie-detection expert, but I thought he might be leaving something out of that statement. "And I was under the impression that you're the only djinn capable of reproduction in this realm, *rayan*. Logically, I would assume they're yours. How could you know they're Morai?"

The cold smile that wrenched Ian's lips didn't reach his eyes. "There were three of them."

"You . . ." Calvin went the approximate shade of soured milk. He wrapped a hand around the cross that hung from his neck and murmured a rapid string of Latin words. A catechism for the dead. When he finished, he cast a glare in Ian's direction. "Is murder your answer for everything, or do you reserve it for special occasions—like Tuesdays?"

The timer on my explosive visions started up again. "Hold on," I said. "That was self-defense. They attacked us."

"Of course it was. And what about all the Morai you killed while they were still bound inside their tethers? I suppose that was self-defense too."

Something inside me shivered and tried to crawl away. I suspected it was my conscience. I'd all but convinced myself we were right to kill them—but this guy was coming after my glass walls of denial with a hammer. Why did I ever think it was acceptable to destroy defenseless living beings? I would have screamed, or puked, if I'd thought it would accomplish anything outside of drawing the attention of two furious djinn to me.

Ian, on the other hand, wouldn't know regret if it nailed him in the balls. "You are extraordinarily well-informed for a sequestered monk who does not use his power." A sneer filtered through his frozen smile. "This does not bode well to convince me of your honesty."

Some of the flustered rage drained from Calvin's expression. "It's a logical conclusion," he said. "You've been hunting my clan for four hundred years. You've boasted dozens of kills. They couldn't have all been released—some of them must have still been bound and helpless." He made a weary gesture. "If I thought it would convince you, I'd subject myself to a truth spell."

Ian snorted. "Now I am certain you are lying. There is no such spell."

"Ah, yes. There's the paradox." Calvin shook his head. "I've been able to modify the *ham'tari*—"

"Enough, snake!" Ian blanched with fury, and I wished for something big and solid to hide behind. A mountain range would be great. "Even the Bahari have been unable to manipulate the *ham'tari,* and they created it. I will hear no more of your lies."

Bad move, Calvin. I remembered hearing about that particular spell. It had been used against Ian's father before the Morai clan leader killed him, and not in a good way. Most curses weren't intended to benefit the recipient.

"Believe what you will, *rayan,*" Calvin said. "And do what you must. I don't fear you as much as you'd like to think, since I know you won't find my tether."

The cold smile revisited Ian's face, and I resigned myself to running painful interference any second. "I do not require your tether to neutralize you," he said. "I will simply remove your deceitful tongue from your mouth."

The exaggerated sound of a creaking door came from the laptop on the desk, followed by a pop. An instant-message chat window appeared on the screen. I couldn't quite read what it said from across the room, but I made out the avatar the sender was using. It was a photo of a raccoon. With a pink collar.

"Mercy," I blurted. "Holy . . . cow. You're Cal."

Calvin moved between me and the laptop, wearing the same I'll-castrate-you expression Ian used whenever anyone mentioned Akila. "How do you know her?" he demanded. "If anything's happened to her . . ."

"Gifter of wards," Ian said with a sneer. "Tell me, Khalyn.

If you know nothing of these scions, what do you believe your Mercy needs protection from?"

Crud. He did have a point.

A bright and tingling ribbon of sensation wormed through my gut, raising gooseflesh and the hairs on the back of my neck. It took me a few seconds to realize it wasn't my nerves. It was magic. "Ian," I stage-whispered. "Does something feel different to you?"

Calvin reacted first. His eyes widened, and he snatched for his glasses and shot to his feet. "My wards," he said. "Someone's taken apart the spells. Only—" His entire body shuddered. "You have to leave this place. Now. Use the mirror, but don't travel to any place you want to stay undiscovered. Once you've arrived wherever you're going, leave immediately."

"What's going on?" I looked to Ian for an explanation.

"There is another djinn approaching. And not alone." A strange look shadowed his features—part rage, part resignation, and something else I couldn't identify. "Khalyn is correct. We must leave. We are too weak to face them."

Calvin made his way to the door. "Go quickly. I can't hold them off for long." With that, he slipped from the room and closed us in.

"Jesus Christ." I let out the breath I'd been holding. "I hope you know where we're supposed to be going, because I didn't follow any of that."

"Yes." Ian shook himself and approached the mirror, already drawing blood from a finger with his teeth. "We will return to the staging point, and travel on foot from there. We cannot go directly home. They may be able to trace the spell."

I decided to save my questions for later. The tingling ribbon had spread and invaded my limbs. Somehow I understood that whatever was out there, it was powerful. And extremely angry. "Hurry up," I said.

Ian had already opened the bridge. The mirror no longer reflected the study. Now it showed a shadow-drenched standard hotel bathroom, as viewed from above the sink. "Go," he told me. "I will follow you directly."

"You'd better." The brief idea that he might stay behind and try to take on the new arrivals left as soon as it came. Even Ian wasn't that stupid.

Or was he?

Before I could reconsider, my feet carried me through the mirror, and I emerged shivering in the hotel room.

I clambered down from the sink and felt for the light switch. By the time I flipped it on, the mirror had lost its reflection and Ian climbed through. I allowed myself a moment of relief before I realized he looked worse than I felt. The bridges shouldn't have taken quite so much out of him. That probably meant he'd cast an extra spell.

"What did you do?"

He perched on the edge of the sink, slumped in place. "A temporary ward," he said. "It should keep them from detecting us for a short while. I have not harmed the—Khalyn."

His grudging use of the name said more than his words. "Does that mean you're not going to destroy this guy?"

"We must keep moving." He didn't look at me while he slid to the floor and took a few unsteady steps. "The spell will not last long."

"You didn't answer me."

"No."

When he didn't elaborate, I said, "No you didn't answer, or no you're not going to kill him?"

"Blast it, thief! We have no time for this discussion." He pushed past me and into the main room, weaving like he'd just mainlined a bottle of liquor, and fell on his knees beside one of the beds. "Collect whatever you need, and give me a moment to recover."

I didn't like the dodgeball game he was playing. "Come on, man. Don't tell me you still don't trust him. He saved our lives twice."

Ian closed his eyes. "I am aware of this. Now move, unless you wish his efforts to have been in vain."

"Fine." I'd take it up with him later. I grabbed the bag I'd brought and considered changing, since I was filthy with dirt, twigs, dried blood, and God knew what else from our romp through the woods. But apparently we were in a hurry. I went back to the bathroom, washed as much of the crud from my face as I could, and finger-combed water through my hair.

"Donatti! We cannot wait any longer," Ian called. "We must leave."

"Coming." I sighed, shouldered my bag, and headed out to join him. My head pounded, my ribs ached, and my leg twanged every time I put pressure on it—but I was still alive. And I wanted to stay that way.

We left the key in the room and exited the building through a side door. Outside, a fine spring day in Ridge Neck, Virginia, refused to reflect the trouble we were in. Bright blue skies hung above tidy, whitewashed buildings tucked between flourishes of vegetation. The place would have made a great colonial postcard. Beautiful. And absolutely useless. No airport, no car-rental place, and if they had a bus station, I doubted they ran regular shuttles to the nearest cradle of modern civilization.

Not to mention that we stuck out like bikers at a tea party. I looked like something dragged up from a river, and Ian—

besides being almost seven feet tall with inhuman eyes—wore only pants and a tattered, bloody vest. We weren't going to get too far unnoticed.

"Damn," I said under my breath. "Now what?"

"Walk." Ian started toward the back of the motel. Away from the town. Headed straight for acres of wilderness.

I grabbed his arm. "Hold on. I thought we needed to make some miles here."

"Yes. And since you cannot fly and I have no power left, we will walk."

"Did you get hit on the head harder than me?" I let go and stepped back. "You're barely standing. I'm not much better. Who knows how far the next shitpoke town is through there? We won't last until sundown."

"We must—"

"Yeah, I know." I frowned and glanced back toward the mostly quiet village, this time with a thief's eye. It was doable. "We'll have to steal some transportation."

For once, Ian didn't disagree.

Chapter 7

As a personal rule, I never stole late-model vehicles in poor condition. People who drove cars like that couldn't afford to lose them. Robin Hood I wasn't, but I still had standards. However, since my only feasible options were a brand-new Mercedes sedan with more alarms than Fort Knox or a Chevy pickup that looked like it had survived the Depression, and we were in a hurry, I took the truck. My conscience and I could have it out later.

There was a grand total of one road leading out of town. I didn't breathe until the place was out of sight and we'd failed to pick up an entourage of whirling lights and sirens, or citizens with torches and pitchforks. Then I could concentrate on navigating the claptrap on wheels down the winding mountain road, with only a guardrail separating us from a thousand-foot roll down a rocky slope.

Beside me, Ian maintained a death grip on the oh-shit handle above his window while we bounced and rattled along. "Are you certain this vehicle is safe?" he half-shouted over the roar of a failing muffler.

"Sure," I said with more conviction than I felt. "Why?"

He pointed down between his feet. "I can see the road."

"Oh." I glanced over and looked through the rust-edged hole in the passenger-side floor at the dust gray asphalt rushing by. "Er . . . we should be fine. The floor's not important."

"Indeed." Ian slid back in the seat and tried to tuck his legs under him. It didn't work, so he settled for propping them on the dash. "I believe I would have preferred walking."

I decided not to let him bait me. The road dipped ahead, so I slowed to twenty and puttered down a steep incline that looked like it'd never end. "So, what's the plan now—hit the next town and find a mirror?"

Ian offered a weary nod. His eyes fluttered closed. "Wake me when we arrive."

Great. I thought about protesting. If I had to stay awake, he should too. But it made sense to let him rest. I still had some juice left, and if whoever was chasing us managed to catch up, we'd need everything we could get.

Toward the bottom of the incline, the blasted rock on the mountain side of the road gradually gave way to more trees. Twilight's shadow distorted them, made them a fairy tale woods that no self-respecting girl with a basket would be caught dead in. I flipped the headlights on against the gathering gloom, and wasn't surprised that only one lit up. The road leveled out a little, so I walked the protesting truck up to forty and held it there. Much faster and it'd probably shake itself apart. I pitied whoever owned this wreck, and not just because I'd stolen it.

Something vibrated against my leg, and I finally realized it was my phone and not the truck. I fished it out. The thing must've taken a hit at some point, probably during my tumble down the tree. A crack split the screen and spiderwebbed in a corner. The display flashed on and off, but between flashes

I made out the incoming number. Jazz. I thumbed the green button and said, "Don't worry."

"I hate it when you answer like that." The line crackled and echoed with distance. "You're late. I worried."

"We had to take a little detour."

"How little? I need to know when to start worrying again. And . . . are you driving?"

"Um. Yeah." No point in lying to her. She'd read it like a billboard.

"Funny. I don't remember you taking a car out with you."

"I had to borrow one."

She swore under her breath. "Okay, *now* I'm concerned."

"I know." I let out a sigh. "Tell you everything when we get back. Promise."

"And when might that be?"

"If I'm not there by midnight, cancel the pumpkin coach and send out the glass slipper."

"Gavyn!" She choked back a laugh. "All right. Just don't die."

"I love you too."

There was a long pause, and then she hung up.

My mouth turned down involuntarily. Jazz wasn't big on sentiment. It would've been nice to hear the words from her once in a while, but I understood her reservations. Our relationship hadn't begun on the best of terms—and the risks I took with Ian didn't help stabilize things. I wouldn't want to get too attached to me either.

I tried to slip the phone back in my pocket and missed. It landed on the seat, and the rattling of the truck slid it away toward the edge. I made a grab for it, but the tips of my fingers pushed it onto the hump between the footwells. Grumbling, I leaned over and snagged the damned thing before it could hit the floor and smash on the road.

When I straightened again, something big and fur covered filled the darkened view from the windshield. And it was getting bigger fast.

"Shit!" I slammed on the brakes and wrenched the wheel hard to the left, hoping to at least avoid flipping over the guardrail. The truck emitted an ungodly squeal. For an instant it rode on two tires before it dropped down and shot back into the turn, only to twist all the way back around. I hit the thing head-on at a good clip. My body bucked forward, and my skull met the steering wheel with a solid crack. Blackness followed instantly.

A groan penetrated the shell of my consciousness. I didn't associate it with me until a moment later when the pain hit. Wasn't sure I could move, but I cracked an eye open and realized I hadn't been out long. The living roadblock still stood outside, just beyond the crumpled and steaming hood, looking annoyed.

Apparently, we'd hit a hundred-point buck. On steroids.

"Ian." My tongue slurred the word, and it came out *eeng*. "That a moose?"

He didn't reply.

"Damn . . ." I gritted my teeth and pushed up slowly. Nausea rippled through me with the motion, and flashing lights danced in my vision. I tried to blink them away. When I shifted straighter, glass crunched beneath my feet. That wasn't a good sound. I made myself turn enough to get a look at Ian, for the first time actually hoping that he was just ignoring me.

He wasn't. The windshield had burst inward, and it looked like they didn't make safety glass back in 1900 or whenever this truck had rolled off the line, because a huge shard of it was embedded under Ian's sternum. Blood splashed his chest, painted the underside of his chin, welled along the sides of the glass, and oozed down his stomach. His head rested back at an extreme angle, and his half-open eyes rolled in their sockets.

Jesus. I knew he couldn't die, but how much abuse could his body take? It didn't look like he was even breathing. "Ian?" I half-whispered, and laid a hand on his arm. No glow. He'd told me once before that he couldn't amplify what wasn't there in the first place. He was still drained.

A tremendous snort drew my attention. Outside, the moose shook his massive head, lowered it, and rammed his antlers into the front grille. The truck rocked back an inch or so on creaking springs.

The motion must've shocked Ian back from wherever he'd retreated. He jerked stiff, his eyes snapped open. And he screamed.

His hoarse cry seemed to make the moose reconsider battling the truck. The animal turned and lumbered off into the trees. Ian drew a gurgling breath, and closed his eyes. "Hurts," he whispered. His lips barely moved. "Help . . . get it out." The arm closest to me rose a few inches, wavered toward the glass shard. Dipped and fell.

"Okay. Don't move, man. Let me . . ." I swallowed hard. It had to be in there pretty deep, or it would've fallen out already. I leaned over and tried to get a grip on a lower edge without slicing my fingers off. The first tug did nothing but elicit an anguished grunt from Ian and break my tentative hold. *Damn.* I set my jaw, grabbed the only protruding portion, and wrenched. The jagged edge sliced my palm, but the shard withdrew from Ian's flesh with an awful wet sound.

Gasping, I pushed the bloodied fragment away and squeezed my hand closed. "I'll try to heal you some," I said through teeth chattering like a San Francisco fault line.

"Nuh . . . *no*," Ian squeezed out. "Save it. Home. Akila."

"Christ, Ian." My stomach torqued more than it should've been able to, and I wondered if it had turned completely inside out. I knew what he meant—he wanted me to save my power for a bridge to get us home so Akila could heal him. "How am I supposed to do that? I mean, we're on a damned mountain. There's not gonna be a Seven-Eleven around the next corner, and moose don't use mirrors."

A corner of his mouth twitched. "Trust you . . . figure it out."

"Thanks a lot."

Ian failed to acknowledge my sarcasm. I held back a moan and felt for the door handle on my side. Maybe there was a pond nearby. Hell, I'd settle for a puddle. Mirrors weren't the only things that worked for transportation spells—any reflective surface would form a bridge, as long as it was fairly smooth. I'd never used water before, but I'd seen Ian do it. That would have to be good enough.

I popped the handle, swung the door open, and slid out in a creaking heap. Every inch of my body felt like George Foreman had used it for punching practice. The last rays of the dying sun burned a corona of light around the next mountain over, and I caught a pale shadow of my own battered face framed in the door.

Not a shadow. A reflection. The side windows weren't broken. I'd have to stuff Ian through, but it'd work.

I hauled myself back into the cab and shut the door. "Good news," I said. "We've got windows. Have us home in a second."

Ian murmured something completely unintelligible. I hoped he hadn't remembered anything important that he should've told me months ago, like making a bridge with a truck window on a mountain in Virginia always sends you to

Mars or something. He frequently neglected to mention the little rules. He claimed it was because they were instinctual for him, but sometimes I swore he left shit out just so he could laugh when I screwed up.

I was already bleeding, so I didn't need to worry about my missing knife. I swiped a fingertip across the gash in my palm and smeared Ian's symbol on the top right corner of the passenger window. Crescent, dot, squiggle. Picturing home, and my desire to be there, was easier than breathing. The words came quickly too. *"Insha no imil, kubri ana bi-sur'u wasta."*

The window darkened and showed part of a familiar blue couch. "Right," I said. "Try and cooperate with me here, Ian— or at least don't make this any harder." I slid an arm behind his back and pushed until he flopped against the window frame. One arm and part of his head went through before I couldn't move him that way anymore. I shifted, knelt on the seat and got both hands under him. With a lot of straining and cursing, I managed to get him most of the way through. Only his shins and feet remained. I shoved on his feet and heard a female voice shout something from the other side, just before the bridge closed.

I fell back and gave myself a minute to breathe. Still had to do that one more time, and I couldn't afford a mistake. I didn't have enough juice for a second chance.

Chapter 8

My ungraceful swan dive onto the living room floor confused me for a second. Then I realized something was missing. Ian. I should've landed on him. I pushed up on my elbows and battled a sudden surge of nausea while the room went disco ball around me. When the world stopped spinning, I spotted him lying a few feet away with Akila crouched beside him, already working a healing spell.

Jazz must've told her about our detour. The reflection spell only worked once, and then it had to be recast for the next transport. Usually, I came through here and Ian took himself directly to the apartment we'd built for them over the garage, so we could both have some private time. So much for that tonight.

"The pumpkin coach left. But I can probably dig up a glass slipper."

Jazz's voice shook a little. That meant she was mortally terrified. "No more glass," I muttered. "'Sides, we made it before midnight." I rolled onto my back and tried to smile up at her. It hurt like hell. But damn, was it good to see her face.

I still didn't know what she saw in me. She was gorgeous—her mixed blood gave her smooth coffee-and-cream skin, silky black hair, full lips. And her eyes were mesmerizing. One was a pale sea green, the other a deep and glittering brown. She hated them.

I adored them, and told her so even when she wanted to pound me for it.

"I could kill you," she whispered, and hunkered down next to me. "But I won't. What the hell happened in the last twenty minutes? You were fine. Weren't you?"

"Yeah." I closed my eyes and laughed, an action my ribs screamed at me for. "I hit a moose."

"You're kidding."

"Do I look like I'm kidding?"

"Oh, Gavyn." She reached out and grabbed my hand. She was definitely worried—she'd used my first name. Usually it was Donatti, or asshole. For an instant I thought there were tears in her eyes, but she blinked and the suggestion was gone. "Is anything broken?" she said.

"Don't think so. Well, maybe a rib or two." I tried to sit up, and pain lashed through me. "I'll just stay here for a few minutes."

"Good idea." Her hand tightened on mine. "I guess your bad luck is back, huh?"

"Back? It never left."

She frowned. "Maybe. But you've seemed pretty lucky ever since he came along." She indicated Ian with a half-hearted wave.

I started to protest—and realized she was right. More or less. I probably should've died a dozen times in the last year, or at least been seriously maimed. And before Ian intruded in my life, I'd never been able to catch a break. Random bad shit kept me constantly on the edge of survival. But once we destroyed Lenka, things kind of slid into place. I had a home, a family, and a purpose. Everything worked. Until today.

"It's a fluke," I said, more to convince myself than her. "Lots of people hit mooses."

"Sure they do."

A shadow fell over me, and a voice said, "You look terrible."

"Thanks." I twisted to look up at Akila's drawn features. She was a different kind of beautiful. Lithe and exotic, dusky skin, cascading black curls. Tall and willowy to Jazz's short and slender. Her eyes freaked me out a little, though. They were light brown all over, no whites, with pupils that could dilate to nearly fill them. Hawk eyes. "Same to you," I said. "How's Ian?"

"He has been better." She tried to smile. "He is sleeping. I have healed most of the damage, but he is still very weak."

Jazz looked at her, back to me. "So. What happened before the moose?"

"Moose?" Akila echoed. "I do not understand. An animal could not have done this to my husband."

I grimaced. "Long story. Any chance you have some of that healing left for me?"

"Oh! Of course. I apologize." She came down to my level, and her gaze skated over me with brisk assessment. "This will take a few moments."

"Fine with me. I don't have any pressing appointments."

Jazz cracked a smile, but a muffled thump from the vicinity of the stairs wiped it away. "What . . ."

"Mommy?" Cyrus sounded thin and distant, his voice full of sleep. "I gotta go *bad*."

"Damn it," Jazz muttered. "I shut the bathroom door. It's been sticking lately. Hold on, baby," she called a little louder. "I'm coming." She leaned down and brushed a kiss on the corner of my mouth. "You don't get out of telling me what happened. This is a temporary reprieve."

"Yes, ma'am." I would have mock-saluted, but my arms weighed a thousand pounds.

Jazz nodded and stood. "Call me if you need anything," she said to Akila.

I watched Jazz leave, and then turned a questioning glance on Akila. "Call?"

She smiled. "Jazz has given me a cell phone."

"Oh, good. Maybe you can talk your husband into considering a little technology too."

"I do not think he trusts your . . . gadgets." Akila held a hand over my chest. "Try to relax."

Relax. Yeah, right. I settled for closing my eyes and forcing my jaw to unclench. Akila whispered a few words in djinn, and the sensation of magic spread through my body, warm and pleasant, soothing the fire in my nerves like a dose of good Scotch. I wondered if the words helped. The few times I'd used healing magic, I had to run on instinct and need. The process was clumsy and unfocused, and took a hell of a toll on me. Ian said it was because healing was a strength of the Bahari. I wasn't so sure about that.

Soon I felt like I might live to see the sun come up again. I drew a deep breath and reveled in the absence of pain. "Thank you, Princess," I said. "I owe you one. That makes, what, fifty now?"

"You owe me nothing." She shuffled back and sat down on the floor. "However, I would like to know what has happened to you both."

"Yeah. All of us do, I think." I sat up slowly, at once wanting nothing more than to sleep for a month. "Maybe we should wait for Jazz, so we only have to talk about this once."

"There is nothing to discuss."

Ian's voice sounded like a blender full of gravel. I twisted around to find him trying to stand. He wasn't succeeding. He'd gotten one knee under him and a foot on the ground, but it didn't look like he'd get much farther without some help. Like maybe a crane or a forklift.

Akila rushed over to him and laid a hand on his shoulder. "*L'rohi,* you must rest."

"I intend to rest. In my bed." He wobbled, rose half an inch, and pitched forward. At the last second he thrust an arm out and managed not to smash his face into the floor.

"Gahiji-an!" Akila crouched next to him. "You should not move . . ."

"Help me stand, love. Please."

She frowned, but she wedged herself under his arm and got him on his feet. No doubt she understood it was pointless trying to talk him out of anything. It'd only taken me an hour or so to rub the wrong way against his stubborn streak when I first met him, and she'd known him for a few thousand years.

"Thank you," he murmured. "And you as well, Donatti. Good night."

"Hold up." As much as I sympathized with his current state of exhaustion, I couldn't quite let his comment go. "It sounded like you said we don't have anything to talk about."

"That is correct. There is nothing to discuss."

"Really? Because I thought having a Morai save our lives might be cause for concern about the whole kill-first, ask-questions-later strategy. Plus there's that bunch of Morai descendants to think about."

Akila went whiter than rice. She said something in the djinn tongue, too fast and quiet for me to make out.

Ian stiffened and glared at me. "They will die. All of them."

"You can't do that." I pushed off the floor and stood on legs that felt about as stable as cotton ropes. "This Calvin guy—"

"I do not care what he has pretended to have done!" No fire-and-brimstone preacher ever looked more fanatical than he did in that moment. "It matters only that he is Morai, and I have sworn to destroy them."

"Well unswear it, then." I managed not to flinch under his burning stare. "Maybe you really are losing it, Ian. Because if you honestly think he deserves to die, you're crazy."

He didn't say anything. Just looked at me like I'd spit in his face. Finally, he shook free of Akila and stomped off. His dramatic exit would've been more effective if he hadn't stumbled over his own feet twice on the way to the door.

"Akila," I said when he'd gone. "Any idea what all this is about? Seriously, he's not making any sense."

She blinked. Tears welled in her eyes. "It is ... not my place to tell you," she whispered, then walked out after her husband.

"It's gonna be somebody's place to tell me, damn it," I said to the empty living room. That somebody would have to be Ian. But I'd confront him tomorrow. Right now I was in desperate need of a shower, since magic didn't cure dirty. I made my way upstairs and heard a voice drifting down the hall—Jazz, talking to Cyrus. Probably reading him back to sleep. I decided to use the bathroom attached to the master bedroom, in case Cy needed to pee again.

Five minutes into the shower, the bathroom door creaked apologetically. "You all right, babe?" Jazz called.

"Yeah. You know, I bet they never run out of hot water in heaven."

"Huh?"

"Never mind." I arched my back into the spray and practically groaned with pleasure. "Cy go back to sleep?"

"Out like a light." A faint rustling sounded, and a cabinet opened. "Tory called earlier. He wanted Ian for something, and he got worried that you guys weren't back yet."

"Great." Tory was Bahari, like Akila, and an occasional pain in the ass, though he did try to help. He was young for a djinn—only a couple of centuries—and acted like a human teenager most of the time. He lived with Lark, an ex-partner of mine who dealt in gadgets and high-end art, and had more money than God. Lark had paid to have Ian's apartment built after we saved Tory's life. The two of them were lovers. They made a damned odd couple, but they were happy.

I didn't feel like dealing with Tory just now. "I'll call him tomorrow," I said.

"He'll probably freak out and come over by then," Jazz said. "So, I know you've got to be exhausted. You want to give me the short version?"

I snorted. "Sure. A Morai saved our lives today, and Ian still wants to kill him."

"Jesus." She paused, a little too long. "What are you going to do?"

"Not a clue. I've only figured as far as if he really wants to, I can't stop him. And I don't think that's good enough."

More silence. At last she said, "Maybe you should sleep on it. You know, things will look better in the morning, and all that . . . stuff."

"Maybe." I let out a sigh that ended in a yawn, and almost drowned myself when the water ran into my mouth. "I'll be out soon, okay?"

"Take your time." The door closed with a soft click.

I stayed put until the edge of a chill crept into the flow, and then turned the water off reluctantly. Jazz was probably right. With a hundred thoughts yammering for my attention,

I couldn't concentrate on a single one of them. I'd been more tired than this a few times in my life—but not by much. I'd be out the second my head touched fabric. I toweled off, threw on a pair of boxers, and plodded into the bedroom.

Jazz sat cross-legged on the bed, wearing a pale green silk robe. She smiled at me, reached up, and slipped the material from her shoulders. Her bare shoulders. That matched the rest of her underneath.

I decided sleep could wait for a while.

Falling dreams were never my favorites. Especially when I was falling off the wedged head of a seven-story-tall snake into a pit full of rabid wolves.

My eyes snapped open just before I could experience a close encounter with a set of long, sharp teeth. The falling sensation clung to me for a few long seconds, until my heart remembered to beat and my lungs remembered to breathe. I blinked in the darkness and let reality supplant the dream—toes to wiggle, fingers to unclench from sheets. Jazz breathing softly beside me. The bedside clock informing me of the time—5:19 A.M.— and the dissolving curtain of sleep fog telling me I had no chance of returning to slumber right now. What a rip-off.

I folded the covers back and disengaged myself from the bed. Might as well get something to eat. I scrounged a T-shirt that didn't reek from the laundry basket, pulled it on, and headed for the kitchen.

Where I found the back door ajar.

I skipped turning on the light and went invisible. My first thought was the half-breeds, that they'd somehow found us. Nothing in the kitchen seemed out of place—but then, if it was a bunch of Morai descendants, they wouldn't be looking for the fine china. And I wouldn't be able to see them either.

Movement through the window caught my attention. There was someone in the backyard. I crept toward the door and tried to peer through the crack. My vision was limited to a narrow sliver of grass, washed gray in the predawn, and a wedge of star-sprinkled sky just beginning to lighten. I toed the door and let it swing a little wider.

Ian sat on the picnic table. Drinking my beer. Three empty rings on the six-pack beside him. Two cans on the grass below his bare feet, and a third in his hand.

Not a good sign. Ian didn't drink.

I walked out and let the door close softly behind me. A slam would've woken Jazz. Ian either didn't hear the click of the latch or didn't care. I cleared my throat and said, "Enjoying yourself?"

No reaction. He didn't even flinch. After a few seconds, he took a long swig from the can and emptied it, then crumpled it with one hand and let it fall to the ground. His head turned in my direction with the approximate speed of erosion. "Do you often lurk about invisibly in your own yard?"

I dropped the vanishing act. "Only when some asshole steals my beer and leaves my back door open. And speaking of beer, it's not exactly a breakfast beverage." I moved to the table and helped myself to a can, thinking I might as well. I didn't feel like I'd gotten to sleep yet anyway, and it was still basically dark. "Thanks for the scare, though. I did have too much blood in my adrenaline stream."

"Did you." He gave me a flat stare, then grabbed another beer. "Allow me to impart some advice, Donatti. If you have come to plead a case for your new friend, you are wasting your breath."

"Whoa. Slow down, killer." I'd already decided a threatening approach wasn't going to work. I couldn't overpower him, physically or magically, and he knew it. "First, I didn't know you were out here. I was just hungry. And second—don't be an idiot. He's not my friend."

Ian arched an eyebrow, but said nothing.

"Come on. You can't seriously believe that."

"Why not? I am mad, after all."

"Damn it, Ian." I stepped up on the bench, sat next to him, and cracked the beer open. "Look. I'm sorry I said you were crazy—but you gotta admit, from where I'm sitting this doesn't make a lot of sense. Understand?"

"You understand nothing."

"Maybe I would, if you'd explain it to me." I took a drink, and my stomach informed me that I should've eaten first. "Something's going on here. Akila said it wasn't her place to tell me. Does that mean it's yours?"

Ian uttered a particularly nasty djinn swear. Something about my maternal relatives sucking off the devil. "I told you, I have sworn to destroy the Morai. Not some of them. *All* of them."

"And you can't make any exceptions—like maybe for the innocent ones who didn't destroy your clan?"

"There are no innocent Morai." His voice roughened, and he turned away. "There cannot be. I must destroy them."

"Why? I mean, it's not like you're going to spontaneously combust if you don't kill the handful of them who actually don't want you dead."

He looked at me then. I expected fury or disgust, maybe a sarcastic comment—but his expression was shattered. "It is exactly like that," he said.

"What?"

He didn't answer right away. Instead, he started on the fresh beer and drank until I was sure he couldn't breathe anymore. He finally lowered the can and stared out across the yard toward the red-stained horizon. "I have told you of my father, and the *ham'tari*."

"Yeah. Sort of." Akila's father, Kemosiri, apparently laid some kind of curse on Ian's father to swear his clan's allegiance. I was a little hazy on the details—mostly because Ian hadn't offered many. "What's that got to do with anything?"

"Have patience, thief. This is no simple matter." He paused, drew a breath, and continued in halting tones. "The *ham'tari* is a powerful curse. Few djinn are able to cast it, and none can dissolve it. Once laid, its conditions must be met—in this case, the complete annihilation of the Morai. Every last one." Ian closed his eyes. "Not even death can break the enchantment. The curse is passed on to the bearer's nearest blood relative."

A shiver raced through me with a vengeance. "I take it that's you."

"Yes." He refused to look at me.

"Okay. That . . . sucks." No wonder he'd been drinking. I was going to need a lot more beer, myself. "What happens if you leave this guy alone? Obviously you haven't destroyed them all yet, but you're still alive, so I guess it doesn't kill you. What does the curse actually do?"

"I cannot return to my realm until the task is completed. And . . ." He stared at his feet like he'd stuffed crib notes between his toes. "If I cease to pursue them to the best of my abilities, I experience a great deal of misfortune."

"So if you stop chasing these guys, you'll have bad luck."

He nodded. "Painful, debilitating bad luck. Such as being impaled by shards of glass." His shoulders slumped. "Khalyn saved our lives, but I cannot spare him in return. Things will only become worse."

I glanced up, half expecting to see a meteor flaming its

way toward Ian—and me, by proximity. I fought the urge to inch away from him. Hanging around someone with painful, debilitating bad luck would be hazardous to my health. I'd had plenty of personal experience in that area.

Something clicked in my head and refused to unclick. "Ian," I said slowly. "Does this curse affect me too?"

His expression said he'd hoped I wouldn't ask that question. His hand convulsed around the half-empty beer hard enough to dent the sides. "I am afraid it may."

"It *may*? Does that mean in the future, or is it a work-in-progress kind of thing?"

"Perhaps both." He practically coughed the words out, like they were bones caught in his throat. "I cannot be certain, since I knew nothing of your life before we met."

"But it's possible."

"Yes," he whispered.

My gut did a couple of barrel rolls. I flashed back to what Jazz had said earlier about my bad luck returning. Everything made sense, in an I'm-totally-fucked kind of way. My relentless misfortune had only stopped when I started helping Ian hunt down the Morai—and when I decided it was the wrong thing to do, Lady Luck walked up and bitch-slapped me again. With a moose. "Crud," I said. "I think I can be certain."

Ian finished his beer with a grimace. "This is horrible stuff."

"Yeah, but it does the trick." I drank some of mine. It was warm now, and starting to go flat. "Ian . . . I don't think I can kill an innocent man. Er, djinn. I can barely kill the guilty ones."

"Then I will."

I shuddered at the unforgiving cold in his voice. Sometimes I managed to forget what he really was—prince of an extinct warrior clan, general of its obliterated armies, and out for revenge as much as to end this curse. But he reminded me from time to time when he did things like rip a man's throat out with his teeth. "There has to be another way," I said. "What about Akila? Maybe she can do something, or she knows someone who can."

"Do you not think she has tried?" A brief sizzle of anger animated him, but he slumped back down fast. "There is nothing to be done. I must see this through."

A new thought hit me like a weighted fist. "What if you can't?" I had to force my mouth to form the words. "Jesus, Ian, what happens if you die before the Morai are destroyed?"

He looked at me with sunken eyes, and his voice emerged hoarse and hollow. "The full measure of the curse will pass to you."

I felt like I'd swallowed hot charcoal. If full measure meant I'd attract the kind of misfortune Ian had experienced, I wouldn't last an hour if he died. Painful and debilitating to a djinn was deadly to humans—like my parents, whoever they'd been. This curse had probably killed them. And if it took me out after Ian, Cyrus would inherit the damned thing.

I downed another mouthful of flat beer, trying to convince myself it was the taste that burned my eyes.

Chapter 9

Ian left for his apartment, pleading exhaustion. Not that I didn't buy it. I did, however, envy his ability to get back to sleep. There was no way I'd see the other side of consciousness for a while—unless someone brained me with a blunt object in the near future. Which was unfortunately a good possibility considering my change of luck.

I gathered the empties and the last full can, and headed back inside. An ordinary silence waited for me. Nothing ominous in the hum of the refrigerator or the soft slap of my feet on the linoleum. I opened the pantry to toss the cans in the trash, and the upper shelf didn't throw a bracket and dump canned goods on my head. No rabid raccoons hid in the shadows. I didn't even get a splinter or stub my toe.

Glowering at nothing in particular, I shut the pantry. This was stupid. I couldn't let a little bad luck—okay, a lot of bad luck, if the past was any indication—throw me off my game. I had bigger worries. Like a pack of murderous half-Morai who shouldn't exist, and being an accessory-by-omission to the impending murder of a monk. Imagining what might happen was pointless. Especially since reality was likely to outdo anything I could come up with in my head.

Though my appetite had fled some time around the revelation that I was cursed, I decided I should eat something anyway. I started a pot of coffee and contemplated breakfast in terms of available resources. Plenty of food, plenty of clean dishes, but a shortage of culinary skills limited my options to cereal or scrambled eggs. Since eggs would involve pans and spatulas and other hi-tech gadgets I didn't feel prepared to deal with on the bare side of dawn, I poured myself some cornflakes and settled at the table to wait on becoming caffeinated.

A few mouthfuls into my feast, Jazz entered the kitchen looking like a bear dragged from hibernation in February. She'd thrown on sweats and a frayed T-shirt, and her cap of dark hair lay pillow matted against her head. Her mismatched eyes peered at me with the suspicion of a cop reading a phony license. "You're not sleeping," she said.

"Neither are you." I smiled and flourished my spoon. "Want some breakfast? I make a mean bowl of cereal."

"Ugh. Coffee done yet?"

"Should be close." I pushed back from the table, went to the counters and fished two mugs from a cabinet. The pot was almost full. While the machine wheezed and hissed out the last dregs of water, I got the half-and-half out of the fridge. We were polar opposites when it came to coffee. She took a drizzle of lightener and just enough sugar to coat a wet spoon, or she'd drink it black in a pinch. I liked a little coffee with my sugar and cream. I fixed the cups and brought them back to the table. Jazz, who'd taken a seat, watched me with that same wary expression.

"I don't think things are going to work out for us," she said.

I froze halfway to my chair. "Come again?"

"You're a morning person." Her inflection suggested this offense was graver than murdering puppies or being a Jerry Springer fan. "I can't believe you never told me."

"Hey, nobody's perfect." I tried to keep my tone light so she wouldn't hear how much she'd scared me. She was the one thing I couldn't lose again. "I don't bag on you for your flaws."

"And what would those be?"

"For one thing, you don't wet your toothbrush. Freak."

She made a sound that could've been a laugh, and sipped her coffee. "Mmm. Okay, I forgive you." She folded both hands around the mug. One finger caressed the rim, an unconscious and idly sensual gesture. "Seriously, what's got you bright eyed at six in the morning? I figured you'd sleep until dinner, at least."

"I'm worried about global warming."

"Gimme a break."

"The rain forest?"

"Strike two." She flashed a concerned smile. "Spill. What's on your mind?"

"Well . . ." I toyed with my coffee cup and tried to find words. How could I tell her that I had a life-threatening curse, and that there was a good chance our son would suffer for it? *It's like this, babe. Cyrus inherited your hair, my eyes, your skin, and my drastically reduced life expectancy.* Somehow I didn't think that would go over well. "A dream woke me up. Bad one," I said. "Then I came down here, and Ian was drinking my beer."

"Oh, shit."

"Yeah." I slugged back some coffee, frowned. "So we had a chat."

"About that Morai you ran into?"

"More or less."

"What else?"

I stared at the table. It'd probably be better to just blurt it out, but I couldn't bring myself to do it. I decided to ease into the subject. "How's Cyrus doing?"

"He's fine. And that's not what I asked you." She glanced back toward the doorway. "But speaking of Cy . . . we need to talk."

I bit my lip. That was female code for *I'm unhappy about something and it's your fault.* "Whatever it is, I'm completely innocent," I said.

"Uh-huh." If the sarcasm were any thicker, she could've painted with it.

I opened my mouth to protest again, and the sound of small feet bumping down the stairs drifted in. After a minute, Cyrus stopped in the doorway and blinked blearily at us. "Hi, Daddy. Mommy, can I watch cartoons?"

"Sure, baby. I'll fix us some breakfast." She stood, caught my gaze, and mouthed *Talk later.*

I turned my attention to Cy. "Hey, big guy. Did I miss anything exciting while I was gone?"

He nodded solemnly. "I catched a snake."

"You did, huh?" I stifled a laugh. "Mommy must've enjoyed that."

"Aunt 'Kila said good job, but Mommy wouldn't come see."

"I'll bet." I grinned and winked at Jazz. She rolled her eyes. Her and snakes got along like salt and slugs.

Cyrus yawned wide enough to showcase his tonsils, then his face lit up in a beaming smile. "Daddy, watch this!"

Before I could say *I'm watching,* he disappeared.

When Jazz didn't scream, I assumed she'd seen this before. "So, this is what you wanted to talk about, right?"

She nodded. Her eyes didn't leave the spot where

Cyrus had been just seconds ago. "Can you see him?" she whispered.

"I'm right here, Mommy." Cy's voice, minus his visible presence, was a lot creepier than Ian's when he was invisible. "I'm all shiny. See?"

"Oh, boy." I moved closer to him and crouched down. "Cy, that's pretty cool," I said. "Does it hurt?"

"It feels funny."

"Yeah, it usually does." I held an arm out. "Can you grab my hand?"

"Sure, Daddy."

A quick intake of breath from Jazz marked the moment he made contact. Now I could see him, and the shimmer-haze that enveloped both of us. "Wow, Cyrus," I said. "When did you learn how to do this?"

"Dunno."

"Okay. Will you do something for me? I want you to let go of my hand, and take Mommy's. All right?"

"Donatti, I don't know about that. I mean, I'm not . . . like you guys."

I let go of Cy. Straightened, and smiled at her. "Trust me."

"Sure. Trust you." But she knelt down and extended her arm for the unseen Cyrus. "Okay, baby. Go ahead."

An instant later, Jazz popped out of sight.

"Whoa."

I had to laugh. "When he does that, you'll be able to see him anytime you're touching him. And no one else can see you."

"So I'm invisible."

"Yep."

At once, they both flashed back. Cyrus frowned. "What's ivin-zee-bo?"

"It means shiny." Jazz shot me a look, and I kept my mouth

shut. "Cy, why don't you go out and put some cartoons on? Breakfast'll be ready in a minute."

"'Kay."

We watched him wander in the direction of the living room, and I turned a skeptical look on Jazz. "Shiny?" I said. "Why didn't you just tell him what it means?"

"Because if he knows nobody can see him, he'll disappear when he's supposed to take a bath, or eat vegetables, or anything else he doesn't feel like doing." She exhaled and ran a hand down her face. "Other moms just worry about potty training and puberty. I get Invisible Boy."

"Come on, babe. It's not that bad."

She glared at me. Without a word, she turned away and headed for the fridge.

I watched her yank out a box of frozen waffles and tear the top open. She probably wished it was my head. "Jazz, I'm sorry," I said, though I wasn't sure what to be sorry for. "What can I do to help?"

"Nothing."

The single word was a bullet—and it hurt just as much. My mouth opened, but no sound emerged, so I closed it. I tried again. Couldn't think of a thing to say.

Jazz slammed the box down with a low curse and leaned on the counter, head hanging. "Look, Gavyn . . ." She drew in a sharp breath, and kept her gaze averted. "When I found out I was pregnant, and you were gone, I made a decision. I was going to raise my baby. I knew it wouldn't be easy. But I also knew it could be done. There's a lot of single parents out there—"

"Christ. Twist the knife a little harder, Jazz."

"Let me finish." She straightened, looked at me, and her eyes were diamonds. Glittering and hard. "I was ready for it. I understood the rules. Then you came back and broke them all."

"So you're saying you don't want me around?"

"No. Shut up and listen for a minute."

I just about had to bite my tongue, but I obliged.

She folded her arms and stared at nothing. "It's not you. It's the other stuff. All this . . . magic." Her mouth twisted around the word. "That part of him, of both of you, I'll never understand. I can't connect with it. There aren't any rules to follow." For an instant, her habitual iron confidence evaporated and she looked small and lost. "Things will never be normal for us. That's hard for me to face."

Something heavy lodged in my chest. I wanted to tell her she was wrong, assure her that everything would be all right— but a lie that big would hurt both of us. And I couldn't part with the truth either. I'd left her in the first place because I didn't want to let her down, the way I did everyone else I knew. But I'd screwed her over even more by coming back.

She must've read the devastation in my face, because she approached me and took my hand. "Don't," she whispered. "We'll find a way. I just need a little space right now, okay? Time to think."

"Yeah. Guess I do too." I swallowed hard. The lump in my throat stayed put. "I'm gonna step outside and smoke."

Jazz didn't object. No matter how much I wished she would.

I slipped out the back door and circled around to the garage, where I kept my smokes on the ground floor. Once again, I was fucking everything up without even trying. Donatti's Luck Strikes Back. With a vengeance.

Chapter 10

I wasn't sure how long I'd been sitting on the garage floor and staring out the open door, but it must've been awhile. Long enough to smoke four cigarettes that I didn't even remember lighting. If I'd been pondering the meaning of life, I could've arrived at a conclusion by now—but I wasn't thinking much. I couldn't get past the idea that I was completely screwed.

Finally, I decided sitting around feeling sorry for myself was counterproductive. I could be failing to sleep instead. I stood, indulged in a brief stretch—and only incurred a minor heart attack when I realized I wasn't alone. "Hey, Princess," I said after my pulse throttled down to a mild sprint. "Want my last beer? Ian drank the rest."

Akila wrinkled her nose. "I had wondered what that stench was." She approached for a few steps and stopped. "I assume he has explained the *ham'tari* to you."

"Yep." I lit a fresh smoke. Lung cancer was pretty low on my list of deadly possibilities right now. "Can't say it made me feel better, but at least I know."

"I hope you will not hold it against him. He is not at fault."

I shook my head. "You really do love the grumpy bastard, don't you?"

"I do." She smiled and touched her thumb to the base of her left index finger. A glowing gold band shone there briefly. Ian had the same enchanted ring. I'd gotten a crash course in djinn marriage from him—they bonded for life, and only death could shatter the rings that symbolized the bond. "For the sake of the gods I am sometimes not certain why, but I do."

"Yeah. I hear that." I'd given Jazz plenty of reasons not to love me. And I still had at least one more to lay out. It'd be a miracle if she didn't gut me after I finally managed to explain the damned curse.

Since envisioning Jazz pounding my face in didn't exactly lift my spirits, I tried for a change of subject. "How'd you and Ian hook up, anyway? I thought your clans didn't mix."

Akila's smile faltered, and her gaze flicked up to where Ian presumably slept above us. "Perhaps you should ask my husband," she said.

"I'm asking you." I gave her my best trust-me grin. "Come on, Princess. What happened to the lady who told her husband exactly where he could stick the idea of sending her back to the djinn realm without him?"

She laughed. "Very well. But it is a long story."

"I've got time."

Akila nodded and made her way to one of the lawn chairs near the garage door. She sat, and I leaned back on the hood of Jazz's Hummer. It took her a minute to get started. At last she said, "We were quite young. Not yet a century, either of us. Then, my father was considering a marriage proposal made for me by the cousin of a Bahari High Council member."

I frowned. "So the djinn practice arranged marriages?"

"Only among the nobility." She cast her gaze down for an instant. "His name was Nurien. He and his father had been living at the palace for several weeks. Though he was merely a century older, at the time he was twice my age—and I did not like him."

"Can't blame you there. It had to seem like marrying your grandfather."

"Yes. But it was not merely the difference in years. He was . . . wrong, somehow. I did not trust him. And he did prove himself to be most untrustworthy." She folded her hands in her lap, like she couldn't decide what to do with them. "A few days before my father was to announce his decision, a small band of strangers arrived at the palace seeking audience with the Council. They were Dehbei. Among them were their clan leader, Omari-el, and his son. The prince Gahiji-an."

I grinned. "Love at first sight?"

"Fascination, at the least." A slight blush rose in her cheeks. "My father had not yet permitted me to attend Council meetings, and I was not encouraged to leave the palace grounds. I had never seen any of the Doma before."

"You guys have too many names. I thought it was Dehbei."

Her flush deepened. "Doma means lower caste. Those who seat the Council are Pashi, and the rest . . . forgive me. It is not a pleasant term."

I shrugged. "No big deal. Humans have some pretty unpleasant terms too."

"They do indeed." Some of the color faded from her features. "My father was displeased, of course. Barbarians, he called them, and warned me not to speak with them. He could not refuse them audience, but he would not allow them inside the palace before the Council convened the following day. He forced them to make berth in the courtyard. Like animals."

"Your father's an asshole," I said. "Sorry, Princess."

She nodded agreement. "Despite the warning, I could not ignore their presence. I wanted to observe them. So I installed myself in a small outbuilding near the outlying border of the courtyard, and . . ." Her brow furrowed, and then a half smile pulled at her mouth. "Perhaps it would be better to show you. I am no storyteller."

"Uh. This won't involve time travel or anything, will it? I have a paradigm-shift phobia."

"Not at all." She raised her arms and whispered a few djinn words. Her hands slowly described a rough circle in the air. As they moved, her fingers left contrails of blazing light behind. She brought her hands together to close the circle, and the patch of trapped air shimmered and warped. An image resolved itself—a castle, gleaming white against a blue-violet sky. The building looked like it had been crafted from clouds. A small, dark shape that might have been a bird streaked across the backdrop.

I blinked, but the image stayed put. "Whoa. Djinn TV."

A delighted laugh escaped Akila. "It is a thought-form. An illusion of memory. Watch."

She gestured at me, and sounds filled my ears. A soft wind, rustling movement, murmured voices. The castle pulled back, and the image panned like a camera over a courtyard of lush grass and patterned flagstones. In the center was a floating tree, sculpted of flowing water with leaves of flame, turning slow revolutions in midair. I remembered hearing about it—the elemental fountain, representing earth, air, water, and fire. It was supposed to glow red at sunset.

On the far side of the fountain, a group of djinn sat on the grass or stood in twos and threes. Maybe fifteen altogether. All of them had the same shaggy, streaked hair and dusky weathered skin. And eyes like wolves. They wore vests and form-fitting pants; heavy boots; and long, hooded cloaks, all in shades of brown. Most of them had taken their cloaks off and spread them on the ground to sit or lie on, revealing hard muscle and the distinctive raised armband tattoos Ian sported.

They'd obviously traveled rough to get there. To the last one, they were dirt smudged, dust covered, and weary in expression and motion. More than one looked furious enough to eat raw iron and spit out nails.

One of them standing in a group bore a strong resemblance to Ian, though he looked older than Ian did now. I assumed he was Omari-el, his father. The clan leader seemed almost happy, and the faint lines at the corners of his eyes and mouth suggested perpetual cheer. Ian definitely hadn't inherited that from him. He gestured to a djinn sprawled on the ground a few feet away, who struggled to his feet and approached slowly.

Omari-el detached a cloth bag that hung from his waist and held it out. "Drink, Jai," he said. "I know you are empty."

The one called Jai accepted with a grateful nod. He held the narrow end of the bag to his lips and tipped the bottom up. Clear water dripped from the corners of his mouth as he drank. When he finished, he handed it back and jerked his head in the direction of the fountain. "A shame these pompous birds prefer form over function. Such a waste of perfectly fine water."

"Aye." Omari-el laughed and extended a hand. "Give me your skin."

Jai unhooked a similar bag. "Most of us are dry. And we've little food left." A brittle smile stretched his mouth. "Perhaps we should feast on falcon tonight."

"Easy, brother. It would be most impolite to eat our hosts."

"Hosts!" Jai snorted. "Omi, you are far too generous. These are jailers, and we are herding ourselves straight into their cells."

A shadow passed over Omari-el's features, but it cleared quickly. "We have come on our terms," he said. "If the Council will not listen, we will depart on them as well." The undercurrent of steel running through his words seemed to calm Jai. The clan leader turned and clasped the shoulder of the djinn nearest him. "Roan-el. Gather the skins, take Meiri with you, and go to the lodge we passed. Get water and food. And if you encounter a problem, tell them we will simply help ourselves to those fine, fat animals conveniently tethered in their stables, unable to escape our blades."

Laughter wound its way through the gathering. As the others moved to comply, Omari-el scanned the group and the grounds. A stern frown pressed his lips together. "Where is my son?"

"Off sulking, no doubt." Jai flashed a genuine grin. "The boy was most unimpressed with these windbags. I believe he expected golden stone and emerald grass, and a bit of a richer reception than the spit in the eye we received."

"Ah, well." Omari-el shook his head. "He will return when hunger bites his belly."

The view shifted abruptly, racing across grass to a small stone building on the opposite side of the fountain. The image flickered twice and resolved itself to show the inside of the structure, and a young Akila standing to the side of a window, watching the Dehbei with focused intensity. She was as breathtaking then as she was now. The gossamer dress she wore looked spun from silver spiderwebs, and strands of a similar material had been plaited into the long, silken sweep of her dark hair. Even her skin seemed to sparkle in the light streaming through the window.

The single spacious room contained a few strange long-handled tools along one wall, and a pile of pale dried grass that was almost hay, but not quite, in a corner. There was no door or flap over the arched opening on the back end of the building that served as an entrance. After a minute, a male djinn dressed in garish gold satin walked through and stopped in the center of the room. Sleek raven hair and impossibly round black-ringed eyes proclaimed him Bahari—and the sneer on his face said he wasn't nearly as impressed with the courtyard view as Akila.

"There you are, *rayani*," he said in throaty tones.

Akila gasped and whirled from the window. "Nurien. I thought you had gone on the hunt with your father."

"For those witless cattle? They bore me. I prefer a more exotic form of prey." He smiled, stepped closer to her. "Perhaps I shall hunt the wolf tonight."

Akila gave him a withering stare. "You would not dare."

"Why not? They are only Doma." His fake smile fell away. "You seem unusually interested in these barbarians, *rayani*. Shall I inform your father of your approval?"

"That will not be necessary." If her voice were any colder, she could've invoked an Ice Age. "Go and amuse yourself elsewhere, Nurien. I am weary, and not in the humor for company."

"On the subject of Kemosiri," he said as though she hadn't spoken, "he will announce his decision soon. I am certain he will agree to our proposal, and you will be my bride."

"I am not so certain." A slight tremor in her voice betrayed her lack of confidence, and she averted her gaze quickly. "My father would not force me to bond with a . . . a preening peacock such as you."

Nurien's jaw clenched. "Your father does not care who you bond with, so long as his personal accounts are fattened and his power is enhanced. We have made a generous offer, and he will not refuse." He closed the distance between them, grabbed her arms, and forced her against the wall. "Now. Let us celebrate our impending engagement."

"The lady asked you to leave. Peacock."

A figure materialized beside the haystack in the corner. Ian—smooth faced, painted with grime like the rest of his clan, more furious than I'd ever seen him. And I'd seen him killing mad. He moved toward the Bahari, one hand resting on a familiar ornamental dagger nestled in his belt. The dagger that now served as his tether in the human realm.

The wide-eyed look Nurien turned on him morphed into smugness. "So the Doma can speak," he said. "I thought you might grunt like pigs."

"Remove your hands from her."

"Or what? Will you poke me with your pig sticker?"

Akila bucked hard and rammed a knee in her assailant's gut. He staggered back. "I will never bond with you," she breathed. Concentrated points of color blossomed high on her cheeks. "You disgust me."

Nurien hissed sharply and raised a hand.

Ian moved impossibly fast. One leap carried him straight into the Bahari, like a torpedo, and knocked him to the floor. Ian straddled his chest, pulled the dagger, and held the edge to his throat. "Speak, and I will sever your vocal cords."

Nurien glared up at him. He held his tongue, but the fingers of one hand traced a complicated pattern on the stone floor, just beyond Ian's line of sight and on the side opposite Akila.

Seconds later, a horrified expression infused Ian's face as his arm moved away from Nurien—and plunged the dagger deep into his own shoulder.

A cry from Akila engulfed Ian's pained gasp. Nurien twisted hard to one side and sent Ian sprawling. He scooted back and stood against the wall. "Barbarian," he spat. "I will show you true power." His eyes rolled back for an instant, and he launched into a low and rapid chant.

Ian bounded to his feet, already drawing his uninjured arm back. His fist flew. A solid *crack* announced it connecting with Nurien's jaw. The Bahari, silenced in midspell, entered a boneless slide down the wall and slumped to the floor. "True power, indeed," Ian muttered. He turned his attention to Akila. "Are you hurt, lady?"

Akila shook herself. "No," she whispered. "But you are. Your knife . . ." She pointed.

Ian followed her gesture to the handle protruding from his bloodied flesh. "Ah, yes. I seem to be impaled." He wrapped a hand around the dagger and pulled, grunting when the blade emerged with a faint pop. "How unfortunate."

"Let me heal you." She approached him with hesitant steps. "Thank you. For stopping Nurien."

Ian nodded. He closed his eyes while Akila worked the spell, only daring to look at her when she'd finished. "You have my gratitude, *rayani,*" he said. A hoarse note crept into his voice. "I should rejoin my father. And you should take yourself elsewhere, before the peacock regains consciousness."

"Wait." She smiled at him. "How long have you been here watching me?"

"It was you who invaded my solitude," he said with the ghost of a grin. "I had entered this building, innocently intending to sleep, only to be encroached upon by a spy watching my clan."

"You do not look innocent."

His gaze could've melted boulders. "And you do not in the least resemble a peacock."

Akila caught a breath. "You . . . are in need of a bath," she blurted.

He laughed. "Aye. But unless you keep bathing water within the folds of your dress, I am not likely to have one soon."

"Come with me," she said. "I know of a warm spring near the palace."

"As you wish, lady."

The scene faded quickly, and reality filtered back in around the dissipating thought-form. I rubbed my eyes and stared at the real, present-time Akila. "Holy shit."

"What is the matter?"

"Your husband throws a helluva punch." I grinned at her. "I'm just glad I've never been on the wrong end of his fist."

She laughed. "I am glad as well."

"So . . . what happened to Nurien?"

"My father rejected the proposal, though my protest was not his reason for turning it down. He never did explain why." A look of almost pure hatred flashed in her eyes. "On the same day the Dehbei returned to their village, Nurien and his father disappeared. I have questioned Gahiji-an, and he insists it was not his doing, or his clan's. We assumed they left in shame due to the overturned proposal."

"Oh." I ran through a few mental calculations and came up short. "Wasn't this a long time before you and Ian got hitched?"

"It was. We stayed in communication with one another, and I used reflective magic to visit his village whenever I could escape my Council duties. Omari-el was far more amenable to our bond than my father." Sorrow crossed her face. "I loved him as well. He was the father I would have chosen, if there had been a choice."

I almost hugged her—but then I remembered Ian's right hook, and restrained myself. "Thanks for telling me this, Princess. I'll try not to call Ian a grumpy bastard anymore."

"No need to refrain from that. He certainly can be, on occasion."

"Yeah, like any day that ends with a *y*." I sighed and straightened. "Maybe I should head back inside, see if Jazz needs anything."

"All right. We will . . . see you later."

"Sure." I wandered outside and made my way to the front door. Slowly. I still had no idea what to say, and I wasn't sure I'd given Jazz enough space. Or whatever. But if she needed more, I'd be happy to crash for a while. My body insisted that not only could I sleep now, but I'd have no choice about it in five minutes or so, no matter where I happened to be.

Chapter 11

Jazz took one look at me and insisted I get some sleep. Not that I was going to stage a protest on that point. By the time I woke up, it was Cy's turn to go to bed. And somehow I got roped into bedtime story duty.

It wasn't going well.

Cyrus, seated Indian style on his bed, frowned at me. "No, Daddy," he said. "Do the monster voice. Like Mommy does."

"Uh, right." I cleared my throat, backtracked a few sentences, and growled, "We'll eat you up, we love you so." My growl sounded like an angry Muppet imitation, but Cy seemed okay with it. I finished the last few pages without interruption from the peanut gallery and closed the book. "Okay," I said. "Let's get you covered up."

He flopped back on his pillows with a sigh that clearly said *Daddy, you're doing it wrong.* "You forgot my drink."

"I did?"

"Yeah." He pointed to a bright yellow cup with a sip lid on the table next to his bed. "See? It's empty."

I reached over and picked it up. A few drops of liquid sloshed around inside. "I guess it is," I said. "We'll have to fix that. What're you drinking—mud? Worm juice? Maybe tequila."

He giggled. "Water!"

"Got it. One water, coming up."

I slipped out of his room into the hallway. Jazz was just coming up the stairs, carrying a pile of folded towels. I met her at the linen closet and opened it for her. "You didn't tell me about the monster voice," I said.

"Huh? Oh, right. The book." She smiled and stowed the towels on a shelf. "I'm sure Cy filled you in."

"Yeah, he did. 'You suck, Daddy. Do it like Mommy.' Thanks for the heads-up." I grinned at her. "So when do I get to hear your monster voice?"

"Growl," she deadpanned.

"Whoa, baby. That's sexy."

"You should hear my big bad wolf." She reached across, pulled the closet shut. "He all set in there?"

"Not quite." I shook the cup. "The boy's thirsty."

"Right. You got that? I'm going to say good night."

"Sure. I'll be—"

She'd already started for Cy's room.

"Right there," I mumbled. I held back a sigh and went into the bathroom. It wasn't hard to tell she was distracted at best, and probably still pissed off. Couldn't really blame her there. And I hadn't even given her the good news yet.

I filled the cup and made my way back to find Jazz drawing a blanket over Cyrus. She leaned down and kissed him, then stepped back to let me through.

"Thank you, Daddy." Cyrus accepted the cup and took a quick drink. "Wait! We hafta make a wish." He sat up, pushed the blankets back, and swung his legs over the side. "Mommy, can Daddy wish with us?"

"Sure, baby."

I raised an eyebrow. "What are we wishing for?"

"Whatever you want. It's a secret when you wish on a star. Right, Cy?" Jazz scooped him up and carried him to the big window. She pulled the curtains back. Outside, only a faint line of light remained on the horizon, and a handful of bright stars dotted the sky. "You ready?"

"Uh-huh."

They spoke in the same breath. "Star light, star bright . . ."

I listened to the familiar poem, but couldn't bring myself to join in. This ritual belonged to them. The simple harmony and comfort in it, the unconscious intimacy, the small gestures—a point and a laugh from Cyrus, Jazz's answering smile—almost made me feel like a voyeur. When they finished, Cyrus scrunched his eyes shut tight.

I concentrated on the brightest star I could see. *I wish this curse will never touch my son.*

"Okay, little man." Jazz carried him back to the bed. "Time for sleep."

After she settled him in, I went over and ruffled his silken curls. "Sleep tight."

He rolled onto his side and looked at me. "What'd you wish for, Daddy?"

"I thought it was a secret." I smiled, and whispered, "A pony."

"Really? I'm gonna wish for a pony tomorrow." He yawned. "G'night."

"Good night, Cy."

I slipped out and left the door ajar, like I'd seen Jazz do. She waited at the top of the stairs. "Akila and Ian are on their way over," she said. "I guess Ian wants you guys to head out again tomorrow."

"Terrific. Can't wait." I sighed and plodded over to her. Might as well make her completely pissed at me. "Jazz, I need to tell you something you're not going to like."

"You mean about the curse?"

"Uh . . . yeah." I didn't have to add *How'd you know*—my expression said it for me.

She smirked. "Akila told me. While you were sleeping."

"Great. Guess I should be glad you two are getting along so well." I followed her down the stairs, toward the living room. "So what's next? Are you gonna start painting each other's toenails and going out to strip clubs together?"

"Been there, done that."

I stopped. "You're not serious."

"Wouldn't you like to know." She turned, and a teasing smile flitted across her mouth. "You're still cute when you're jealous, Houdini."

Some of the crushing weight on my shoulders eased. She hadn't used that nickname in months. I wasn't sure why she'd suddenly lightened up, but I didn't want to risk dampening the mood again. "And you're beautiful when you're screwing with my head," I said.

"Which one?"

I gave a desperate moan. "Not fair. We're having company."

The front door opened right on cue, as if my life were a crappy television sitcom. I half-expected to hear a canned laugh track. Instead, I got a low chuckle from Jazz and a whispered promise of *Later*. It'd have to be enough.

Akila entered first. When Ian came in behind her, for an instant I thought I was seeing a ghost. Wearing only a vest, pants, and boots, he looked just like his father in Akila's vision—but scrubbed clean of dirt and any trace of good cheer.

Exhaustion lurked in his stance and his eyes. A good wind could've carried him off to the next county.

I would've felt sorry for him if he had better timing.

Watching Akila make a thought-form the second time was just as fascinating as the first.

She sat on the couch, her back to the big folding mirror we used for bridges, with Ian beside her watching intently. Jazz and I hung back. Inside the circle she'd formed hovered a bird's-eye view of rolling, forested mountains under a full and blazing moon. I had the vague impression I'd seen this before—but I couldn't be sure, since at the time I'd been falling a zillion miles an hour toward certain death.

"So, Princess," I said. "You going to teach me how to make these?"

She laughed. "You are not Bahari."

"I'm not Dehbei either. Not really. So maybe it'll work for me." Some kind of bird soared across the image—a big one. It might've been an owl. "At least tell me how you're doing it," I said.

Akila shrugged. "I am scrying, and projecting an illusion of what I see." The image wobbled, flickered, and solidified again.

"Donatti." Jazz elbowed me. "Let her concentrate."

"Sorry, Princess." I shut my mouth and watched. This was the first time I'd been involved in the actual search for a tether. Usually Ian just told me where we were going and what we were looking for. He hadn't offered an explanation for this, but I suspected it was the closest he could come to an apology. That, or he just wanted an extra pair of eyes in case he missed something.

"There." Ian pointed to a deep canyon that scored the face of a mountain. "We crossed this. It should be close."

Akila nodded, and the view zoomed across the canyon to skim the tops of the trees beyond. "I do not sense anything here," she said quietly. "He may have replaced his wards."

"Keep searching."

I resisted the urge to smack Ian in the back of the head. The trees grew closer, until it almost seemed we could reach out and touch them. A few patches of wobbly bare ground appeared between the branches rushing past. The overall effect was like someone had strapped a webcam around the neck of a geriatric bat and kicked him out of his cave before he'd woken up for the night. Apparently, Akila didn't have as much control over live thought-forms as remembered ones.

"Is anyone else getting dizzy?" Jazz murmured.

I nodded agreement while the woozy bat-o-vision sluiced by a small stream, a massive deadfall, and a big furry something that probably had sharp teeth. Nothing looked familiar to me, but if this was the right place, I'd covered most of this ground trying not to fall off the back of a running wolf. I didn't expect any landmarks to jump out.

The image canted drunkenly to the right and skimmed across a spacious clearing with flashes of gray stone. It slowed, zoomed out, and backtracked. "Here," Akila said. The vision centered on the clearing, and the familiar building it contained. "This is your monastery, yes?"

"Yes." Ian leaned forward. "Is his tether there?"

Akila rolled her eyes. "I am not that fast, my heart. Give me a moment."

He opened his mouth, and with a sharp look Akila made him shut it.

Jazz grinned. "Now there's a trick I wouldn't mind learning. Nice death stare, Akila."

"Thank you, Jazz. I will teach it to you."

I let out a groan. "Do I get a vote in this death-stare thing?"

"No," both women responded at once, and then laughed together.

After a minute, Akila frowned. "I feel nothing here. No magic at all."

Ian released a frustrated snarl. "Then we will go there, and force him to reveal his tether."

"Come on, Ian. He already said we'd never find it. It's probably nowhere near the place." A shudder snaked down my spine. "And I'm really not into torturing monks."

"Blast it, thief! I have explained this. He must be destroyed, or we will—"

"Wait." Akila gestured at the thought-form, and the image started moving again. "I sense . . . something. Not far from here."

At least her statement shut Ian up for a few minutes. The view rushed across the mountain, direct and purposeful. It passed over thick patches of evergreens, deep and tangled thickets of underbrush. Finally, the rapid motion slowed and focused on a gated chain-link fence—complete with a couple of armed guards. Beyond the fence lay a collection of wooden buildings arranged in three straight lines. Something about them didn't look right, but I couldn't quite decide what it was. If the guards had been in uniform, I would've thought military base. But there were no flags, no insignia of any kind. And last I checked, the military didn't issue sawed-off spearguns.

"Holy hell," Jazz said. "Whatever this place is, these guys're some serious fuckers."

"Yeah." My voice wasn't exactly steady. This must be the militia Mercy had mentioned. Fenced on three sides, the area butted against a sheer rock face carved from the mountain. Distinctive snarled lines of barbed wire ran along the top of the chain-link fence, and a watchtower rose above the center of the fence opposite the cliff. The only path into the compound led directly to the guarded gate. Rock-strewn ground dropped sharply away from the rest of the fence line. Whoever they were, they didn't want company.

Akila shivered. "This place feels wrong."

"Is the tether here, then?" Ian regarded the image with predatory expectation. "He is a fool if he believes gun-wielding humans will stand in my way."

"Hate to point this out, Ian, but gun-wielding humans have stood in your way before. Remember Skids?" I said. "I remember Skids. And Conner, and Pope—"

"Enough." Ian glared at me. "I do recall what transpired, thief. And I will not make the same mistakes."

Akila said something in djinn. I hoped she was calling Ian a nasty name, but whatever she'd done added sound to the image. At first there was little outside a vague hum—a small breeze, distant traffic, the electric murmur of the perimeter lights. A branch or a twig snapped somewhere, and one of the guards sent a glance toward the sound. "Ain't nothin'," he said after a minute.

The other one didn't move. "I know."

"Shit." The first guard's drawl warped the word into *sheeyit*. "Don't know why I gotta stick out here. Everybody knows you can handle this, Billy. I got a girl waitin' on me."

"Paul."

"What?"

"Shut up."

"Fine." The one called Paul leaned against the fence and lit a cigarette. But he shut up.

A chill stole through me. The cadence of their speech matched the half-breeds we'd run into—and this place was practically within spitting distance of the monastery.

Another gesture from Akila, and we were moving down one of the corridors between buildings. The closer look helped me figure out why the structures looked wrong. None of them had windows. Not even in the doors—everything was solid wood.

Toward the end of the row, light spilled from an open door. The view moved inside. Six figures were seated at a round table. Everyone was armed with a weapon designed to blow large holes in flesh. The nearest, a blond dressed in white, sat with his back to the thought-form. Flanking him were faces that completed the freezing process in my blood. Kit and Lynus.

"Jesus, Ian. They've got a goddamn army."

"They?" Jazz frowned. "You know these people?"

"They're not exactly people. At least two of them are part djinn. Like me—only they're Morai." I kept my voice low. "Can they see us?"

Akila shook her head. "The Morai are not skilled with air magic."

In the vision, Lynus shifted and scowled. "How long's this gonna take?"

"Patience." The voice came from the blond. And it sounded damned familiar. "We'll find them eventually. You know they're not our priority now."

"But they killed Davie!"

"Yes. And they'll pay for it. Now hush, child."

Jazz muttered a curse. "Let me guess. 'They' is you two," she said.

"Uh." I rubbed the back of my neck. "Yeah."

"And you were going to tell me this when?"

"I was getting to it."

The image wavered. "Gahiji-an," Akila said. "Something is not right. I cannot scry further in this room."

"Perhaps they have set a ward. But if they have, it is weak. We should attempt to learn what they are planning."

"I do not think—"

A male voice from the vision interrupted her. "We have company." The voice hadn't come from anyone at the table, but the blond turned in the chair. It was Calvin.

"Well, now," he said. "We've been looking for you."

He was definitely talking to us.

Ian stood like his ass was on fire. Akila followed suit. She made a frantic gesture, and the thought-form vanished. "No," she breathed. "Impossible. The Morai cannot manipulate illusions. Their strengths lie in fire, not air."

"I think they just did." I looked at Ian. "Now what?"

He blinked. "I—"

"Gavyn." Jazz's fingers dug into my arm. "The mirror!"

I knew what was happening without even looking. Reflective magic only worked when you knew what the place you were aiming for looked like—and of course, the biggest mirror in the house was right behind us. If they'd seen us, they'd definitely seen that.

I turned toward it, and everything south of my throat liquefied. The reflection was gone. In its place stood the scene we'd just been watching, from another angle and with an important difference. The armed and angry guys were on their feet, headed straight for us.

Before I could even remember my own name, much less do a damned thing, a hand thrust through the mirror frame holding a snub-nosed .357 Colt at the ready. And fired.

Chapter 12

When Akila flew back and hit the floor, my brain cried foul. That didn't make sense. Why would they shoot Akila, when Ian was right there?

The guy attached to the gun stepped through and drew a bead on Ian, who looked just as shocked as I felt. But the mirror didn't change back behind him, and another man came through. Then another. The bridge wasn't closing.

How the hell could it stay open?

A second shot thundered from the Colt, deafening in close quarters. This one slammed Ian against the wall hard enough to crack plaster and spray puffs of dust. Akila, half risen from the floor, with blood soaking the front of her shirt, made a weak gesture at the lead man and tried to cast a spell that ended in a garbled, choking cough.

My ringing ears prevented me from hearing the second guy fire—but I felt it when the bullet carved a hot furrow into my shoulder.

The pain sharpened my focus. *Jazz.* Had to make sure she got out of here. I whirled and spotted her just in time to back away so the ceramic pig she'd launched like a missile wouldn't hit me. It struck the guy with the Colt square in the head. A dull, sickening crack suggested he wouldn't shoot anyone else for a while.

In the meantime, two more had pushed through the portal. The last was Lynus, sporting a speargun and a lethal expression.

Thug Number Two stepped over his fallen comrade and squeezed off two shots. Both hit Akila at almost point-blank range. A terrible, wounded roar from Ian drew the invaders' attention for an instant, and held it when he started to glow.

I took the opportunity to launch the nearest piece of movable furniture at them, an end table with a glass top. It caught Three in the chest, cracked, but didn't shatter. He stumbled back into Four and tripped them both. The mini-pileup wouldn't stop them for long, though. And Jazz was still here.

"Jazz," I panted, already looking for another makeshift weapon. "Get Cyrus. Get your gun. Tell him to be shiny and don't come back down. Shoot anyone who's not me."

"I can't—"

"Goddamn it, go!"

She hesitated for half a second, then turned and ran for the stairs. I'd probably regret that later. But I had a better chance of surviving this than she did. The instant she was out of sight, I made myself vanish and tried to take a few seconds to assess things.

I couldn't see Ian anymore, but I could see the mirror and the impossibly open bridge. Calvin stood on the other side, watching the action here. The white thing he wore was another hooded robe like his black monk's costume.

There was something else different about him too. I couldn't put my finger on it. But at this point, it didn't matter.

To the side and just behind Calvin stood a figure in the same kind of robe, but the hood was pulled up to bathe his face in shadows, like he'd just dropped by from the Ku Klux Klan.

He appeared to be holding a spell. If I had to guess, I'd say he was keeping the bridge open. More troubling was the growing crowd of reinforcements in the room with them. How many of these assholes did they have hanging around? Were they all descendants?

A hundred or so pounds of fur, muscle, and fang exploded over the back of the couch, on a direct course for Two. Lynus, who'd managed to clear the body jam, fired a spear. The shot kicked Ian aside in midair, and the deadly silver shaft passed through the wolf's body and kept going. Something shattered across the room.

The sound galvanized me. I knew what I had to do.

Ian landed hard on his side, half a foot from me. I crouched and laid a hand on his heaving flank. The glow that infused him was brighter than before, and I felt something pass from me into him. That was new. But I didn't have time to wonder what the hell he was doing. I left him to fend for himself and concentrated on getting to the mirror.

Two and Three climbed over the couch, headed for the fallen Akila. Lynus chambered another spear and set his furious sights on Ian. That left One still unconscious but stirring, and Four with a big-ass cannon pointed in my direction. He couldn't see me—but if he started firing, he'd probably get lucky.

I cut left, hoping to get between the thugs and the mirror without incident. At the same time, Lynus fired and missed. The spear thunked into the floor and buried itself, all but the last two inches or so. I heard Ian start a spell. Hoped it was a good one.

Finally, I reached the mirror—and a sick sense of futility washed through me. I'd never realized how big the damned thing was. I had a better chance of winning the lottery in the next five minutes than breaking that glass with my fists.

While I sent a panicked gaze around the immediate vicinity for something heavier than a couch cushion, an awful liquid sound behind me demanded attention. I risked looking back. The noise came from Lynus. Thick black gunk oozed from his nose and mouth, trickled from his eyes like demented tears.

Shit. I'd kind of hoped that soul-drain thing wouldn't work on part-humans.

Four swung his cannon around. He blasted away until Ian dropped, then moved to help the spluttering Lynus.

The sight of Ian's mangled, motionless body made my throat hitch. He'd been hit at least four times, and one of the shots had obliterated half his face. No one who looked like that should be alive. *He can't die, but you can. And Jazz and Cy can,* I reminded myself. I couldn't get to him now. I would have to try and heal him later—if there was a later.

In the mirror, Calvin turned to the other robed figure. "Send them help," he said. "We have . . . business to attend to at the monastery." The figure nodded in response.

I had to get that bridge closed. Now.

It was still a mirror on our side, and it'd break if I could hit it with something. But no solid objects, blunt or otherwise, presented themselves in my range. I'd have to make one. Nothing like a little pressure to spark inspiration. I yanked a shoe off and concentrated on willing it into something useful, hoping I wouldn't end up with just a bigger shoe. Transformation worked best when the thing being changed resembled the desired result. Unfortunately, shoes didn't have much in common with sledgehammers.

I held it sideways and didn't so much attempt magic as demand it. Heat flared in my chest and shot through my arms, as if it were eager to escape. I passed a hand over the sneaker and felt it grow heavier, watched the tongue stiffen and elongate. In a few seconds, I had a solid iron shoe mounted on a three-foot curled wooden tongue.

That'd work.

I gripped the tongue with both hands and drew back. The first of the new recruits had a foot through when I swung. Something in me cringed—I knew from experience what happened to body parts stuck in a bridge when it closed—but I didn't stop. Couldn't have if I'd wanted to. The hammer struck dead center. Glass shattered, sprayed shards, rained fragments. Warm wetness sprayed my arms along with the slivers, and my gut rebelled when I realized it was blood jetting from the leg stump on the floor.

The breaking noise got Lynus's attention. He loosed a frustrated shout, and I froze to stare openmouthed at him for so long that if I hadn't been invisible, I'd be dead. He looked like he'd aged fifteen or twenty years in the last minute. His features were sharper, leaner, and harder. Practically weathered. White streaks marbled his hair, which had grown out from buzz to shag.

Now I knew what a soul drain did to descendants.

"Goddamn thief!" Lynus wiped the last smear of black stuff from the corner of his mouth and glared in my general direction. "Get Theo up," he said to the thug who'd been helping him. "Get him over here."

The guy with the cannon came around the couch. Him and Theo, the first one, were both out of sledgehammer range, so I moved away from the mirror in case Cannon Boy decided to take a few potshots. While he maneuvered his groggy comrade up from the floor, the other two resurfaced from behind the couch, bearing Akila's limp form between them. They'd bound her hands and feet with some kind of moving rope that almost looked like headless snakes. Thick coils of a blue-black fleshy substance wound in slow circles around and between her limbs. A triple band of the stuff encircled her bloodied throat.

Lynus pointed at the picture window across the room. They

carried her toward it, and I realized they meant to take her somewhere. Probably to their base. Why the hell weren't they taking Ian?

Theo managed to stand on his own. "Ray," Lynus said. "Drag that ratty-ass carcass over here. They want him left alive, but he'll live through 'bout anything. And I know you're listenin' to this, thief," he said with a sneer. "You won't be hiding—or living—much longer. You owe me a life, and I aim to see that debt paid in full."

Lynus launched into a spell before I could say *Can't we talk about this?* I didn't know what he planned to throw at me, but instinct strongly suggested I get the hell away from these guys without finding out.

I rounded the nearest corner, the short hall that led to the guest bedroom, and discovered that for once, my instincts had served me well. Three steps down the hall, I got walloped by a force that felt like someone had jammed a live wire up my ass. No smoke from my hair or sparks from my fingertips, but electrocution might have been preferable to the actual side effects.

The shimmer that said I was invisible vanished—and no matter how badly I needed to not be seen, it refused to come back.

"You gonna find that asshole and kill him. Make sure you get his woman too."

I had to fight hard to keep myself from rushing out there and trying to brain the country-fried bastard with my shoe hammer. If I did that, the other two'd blast my vital organs into next week. All I could do was stand there and try to figure out how the hell to get upstairs before them without being seen.

A rough *shurr* sound indicated something heavy being dragged across the floor. Probably Ian. "Lynus," one of the thugs said. "Thought you laid down a snare."

"Yeah, I did."

"So where's the thief?"

"Not in this fucking room no more. Here, hold him up." There was a thud, a pause. The metallic snap-hiss of the speargun firing. A nasty wet crunch that had me shoving a knuckle in my mouth to keep from heaving. That had definitely gone through flesh and bone, and probably wall. "All right," Lynus said. "This more like it." A click signaled a reload, followed quickly by another firing, another muscle-tearing crunch. I had to wonder if Ian could even feel anything at this point. "I'm headed back to see if Val can fix this mess. Somebody open me a goddamn window. I'm tapped. You two clean house—and find their fucking lamps, if they're here. Trash the place. We get those, we have 'em nailed."

I couldn't wait around to hear the rest of their conversation. Couldn't even pause to puzzle out what the hell all of that meant. If this snare thing affected invisibility in general, and not just me, Jazz and Cyrus couldn't hide anymore. My brain took a backseat, and I moved automatically to the guest bedroom and the window I knew was there. My awareness of the layout here was my only advantage. I intended to use it.

I got the door closed and locked with minimal sound, thanks to years of practice. The idea to head outside, up the chimney and in a second-floor window occurred first, before I remembered there was an easier way. It involved blood. I'd lost my knife and I hadn't mastered Ian's self-biting trick yet, but my shoulder was still bleeding some. I traced the familiar symbol on the corner of the window and whispered the incantation to open a bridge, concentrating on the upstairs bathroom. The faint moonlit reflection vanished, and near darkness took its place.

I slipped my remaining shoe off before I went through.

Walking around upstairs was risky enough without the added noise of a clomping sneaker. I held the shoe-hammer against my body and climbed through onto the sink. One knee ground painfully against the faucet when I landed. I slid sideways, bit back a yelp—and felt the wind of a bullet pass about a millimeter over my head on its way to blasting the mirror.

I was almost thankful for the shards that sliced at my face and arms. Better than decorating the wall with my brains.

"It's me," I breathed after my ears stopped ringing, hoping like hell it'd been Jazz on the other end of the gun. If it was, we'd have about thirty seconds until unwelcome company. And if it wasn't, I was probably dead anyway.

There was a scant pause, then a whispered, "Oh shit. Did I hit you?"

"Not this time." She was in the bathtub. Presumably with Cyrus. Most three-year-olds would be screaming bloody murder, but Cy was used to staying quiet when "bad guys" came around. It was a behavior I desperately wished he'd never had to develop—but it had saved his life, and ours, more than once. "Are you guys still . . . uh, shiny?"

"No. Cy said it went away."

"Damn." That snare thing had to be a total anti-invisibility package, then. "Don't move for now. I need to listen a second."

"Right."

I dropped to the floor as quietly as possible, forgetting about the shattered mirror right up until broken glass crunched under me and bit through my socks. A whimper caught in my throat. With no choice but to keep going, I moved to the door and tried to ignore the thousand-cuts Chinese torture my feet received. By the time I reached it, my socks were soaked with blood. I stopped and cupped both hands on the wood, then leaned in to listen. There was movement downstairs. A lot of it. Bangs and thumps, things breaking. The bastards must've heard the gunshot up here, so they'd probably decided to start on phase two of their orders, then come and kill us when the shooting stopped.

Find their fucking lamps. Trash the place. I knew what they wanted—tethers. Ian's and Akila's. If they got them, it'd be game over for all of us. At least they weren't close to finding them yet. I was pretty sure Ian's was out in their apartment. Akila had never mentioned what hers was, but they must've stashed it just as carefully as Ian's.

I fell back a step. My throbbing feet protested louder than a rally leader with a megaphone. "Okay. Brief," I whispered through gritted teeth. "Two guys. Armed. Shoot-to-kill orders. They saw you. Not sure if they know Cy's here, but I don't think so."

"Here." The curtain rustled, and a hand thrust through holding a gun butt first. Her Sig Sauer. Heavy shit.

"Keep it. I want you guys safe."

"I've got three in here."

"Course you do." I took the gun and held back a laugh. That was Jazz—always prepared. "Listen. Stay right there. I'm going to draw them away—"

"Don't." Her whisper wavered a little. "Can't you just hole up here? Let them come up and we'll pick them off."

Steel bands tightened across my chest. I wanted nothing more than to stay right here and protect my family—but I knew it wouldn't work. If they cast a lockdown on me or something, Jazz and Cy would be sitting ducks, no matter how many guns she had. Getting them to engage me alone, making sure the thugs couldn't even find them, much less take a shot, was our only chance. And I had no time to explain. At least not with anything that resembled tact.

"Please stay there," I repeated, already working on the full-length mirror that hung on the inside bathroom door. "I've got to take them on. They have magic." *And you don't,* I kept myself from adding.

The fact that she didn't respond said she understood, but she didn't have to like it.

This time I bridged to the mirror in the master bathroom. "Shoot anyone who tries to come in," I said. "I won't come back unless they're finished. Marco Polo, okay?"

"Fine."

Crud. I really hated that word, especially coming from Jazz. She got what I meant—but things were not even close to fine, and I'd hear all about how not fine she was with this if I lived long enough. "Babe . . . I love you," I whispered, then plunged through the mirror knowing damn well she wouldn't say it back.

I thought she called something after me anyway. It probably involved the threat of bodily harm.

The cold that engulfed me on the passage through was brief. On the plus side, the other end was a full-length model too, so I didn't have to crawl over anything. But I still had to walk.

A single, agonizing step told me I wasn't going any farther until I got the glass out.

With a silent curse, I sat on the floor and stripped off the bloodied socks. Pain shagged up my legs when the motion shifted the shards embedded in my flesh. I tried to pull one of the big ones out, but only managed to elicit a supernova of hurt. I damn near passed out. Startled tears scalded my eyes, and I pressed back a frustrated scream. This wasn't going to work. It looked a lot easier when Bruce Willis did it in *Die Hard.*

I closed my eyes and told myself I had no choice. No matter how much it hurt, I'd have to yank out as many fragments as possible. If I sat here much longer, I might as well pull the trigger on Jazz and Cy myself. I needed to walk. Right fucking now.

For an instant I failed to associate the blossom of heat in my chest with the clink and patter of glass on linoleum. By the time I realized I was magicking them out, it was done.

Meanwhile, I'd lost precious minutes while the glorified frat boys downstairs plotted my demise. I levered to my feet and walked as fast as I dared. It still hurt like hell, but at least it didn't feel like a hundred sword-wielding cockroaches were attacking my feet. The dim glow from the emergency light above the sink revealed bloody smears, not quite foot shaped, as I hobbled across the floor. Actual healing would have to wait.

I made it out and crossed the bedroom. Carpet proved kinder to my shredded feet, even if I was staining it beyond salvation. I stood on the wrong side of the door and pulled it open slowly. The party on the first floor sounded like it was winding down. An occasional halfhearted thump, the casual crunch of a shoe on household debris. Voices, but far enough away that I couldn't make out words. At least it sounded like they were both still down there.

Just when I'd convinced myself I had a few seconds to think of a plan, I heard the distinctive creak of the bottom stair. Time to wing it.

The main bathroom was almost directly in front of the stairs. If they searched room by room, they'd look there first. I fired a shot toward the window that overlooked the garage. And missed by a foot. But the crack of the gun was loud enough to draw attention, even without breaking glass. I'd have to hope they took the bait.

And if they did, I'd have to shoot them. Or try to. I was a lousy shot, and I'd never actually killed a human being—or part-human, anyway. At least, not directly. But I was pretty sure I wouldn't have a problem cutting down anyone who wanted to kill Jazz. I decided I wouldn't miss if I held the muzzle against something vital and fired. Which meant getting them close enough to manage that, without getting shot myself.

No problem. And after that, I could talk good ol' Theo and Ray into forgetting the whole kill-the-thief idea and playing poker instead.

A full minute passed without sound. At least one of the other stairs should've creaked by now. I had two choices. One, wait some more and hope they hadn't managed to get quieter, and weren't already opening Door Number One. And two, make damn sure they knew exactly where I was through an act of daring and outrageous stupidity.

My mouth opened before my brain could argue that option two was assisted suicide.

"Hey, assholes!" I yelled through the open door. "If you're supposed to clean house, you missed a spot."

Nothing. Not a step or a rustle. I'd visited louder graves.

"Come on, shitheels. The party's up here now."

Still no response. I imagined Jazz huddled in the bathtub with Cyrus, dreaming up inventive and painful ways to cure me of stupid. She'd never approved of the direct approach. But I'd have to make a move soon, because my butchered feet weren't going to carry me more than a few steps—and it was damned hard to crawl out of gun range.

I decided to go in a personal direction. "How's your head, Theo?" I called. "Must've been a bitch getting laid out by a knickknack. Did you learn your best moves from Martha Stewart?"

This time I heard something. A soft rasp, like a hand running along a wall. The sound was close. Practically right outside the door.

I held my breath and gripped the gun in both hands like a bad actor playing the expendable cop in a horror flick. Moving fast, I leaned out partway and squeezed off three or four rounds in the direction of the sound.

The hall looked empty. But an answering shot punched a hole through my forearm.

"Fuck!" I hit the floor and kneed the door shut, knowing there'd be more bullets. In the space of a breath, a prolonged volley battered the door and showered me with splinters. I dragged back, gasping and cursing, and tried to figure out what the hell had happened. They couldn't be invisible—could they? I didn't know much about magic, but a spell that only targeted Dehbei blood would've taken a fuck of a lot longer. The snare Lynus cast had to be a general no-disappearing thing. So why hadn't I seen my assailant?

Finally, I realized the bullet had gone through my arm top down. The bastard was above the door.

An abrupt halt to the gunfire left ringing silence behind. I set my jaw against anticipated pain and stood on feet made of needles and fire. Somehow, I'd managed to hold on to the gun. Score one for Donatti. That made the odds about as even as a three-card monte street game.

I reached for the door and stopped. Couldn't have a repeat performance this time. One more hole in me and I'd bleed to death before Jazz could have the pleasure of haranguing me into an early grave for leaving her out of this. I switched the gun to my injured arm against strenuous self-recriminations that I was an utter bonehead, then yanked the door open and reached out and up.

My hand encountered flesh. I clamped on hard. A surprised shout preceded another shot that burrowed into the floor at my feet. I looked up to find Theo floating near the top of the door, with my fingers digging into the arm that held his weapon.

He tried to pull back. "Son of a—"

I yanked down on him midepithet. He came toward me easier than a balloon on a string. I brought the Sig up, pushed the muzzle against his chest, and pulled the trigger before my internal morality police could handcuff my intentions.

He thumped to the floor. "Bitch," I finished for him. "Don't you know snakes can't fly?"

Theo didn't answer. He must've figured it out for himself.

Panic manifested in my gut and reminded me that there was still another guy with a gun out there, and I was losing enough blood to stock the Red Cross for a month. I scanned the ceiling in case Ray had developed Superman delusions too. Nothing but unarmed drywall up there. Down the hall, the bathroom door remained closed and untouched.

"Theo. Goddamn it, you get him?"

Still in the living room. I dropped so my head wouldn't be an easy target through the rails, and crawled toward the stairs with the gun directed out. I'd have to take any opportunity I could get to fire on him.

"Jesus jumpin' Christ." Footsteps crackled on fragmented things, growing closer.

I made the top of the stairs and waited.

"Theo? What the . . . " Ray stepped into the clear. "Fuck!"

He sprinted for the kitchen, ducking low. I fired, he fired. We both missed. I couldn't let him get out of the house—if he hung around here long enough for shit to calm down, he could just come back invisible and pick us off one at a time. But I couldn't take the stairs fast enough on foot.

So I slung myself over the banister and slid down.

At the bottom, I managed a clumsy dismount and roll that would've earned me a negative score at the Olympics. But I reached the kitchen doorway while Ray was still trying to scramble past the table to the back door.

With a mental promise to my feet that if I lived, they'd spend a week soaking in warm and expensive champagne, I wrenched myself from the floor and kicked off a shot that caught Ray—though not in a place I expected. He screamed and hit his knees, a few feet from the door. "My ass!" he bellowed. "You shot my ass, you dirty no-count fuck."

"I can count just fine," I said through clenched teeth, trying to aim somewhere more lethal. Sweat drenched my shirt and trickled from my temples. Black spots pulsed a gruesome kaleidoscope across my vision. *Just a few more seconds. Please . . .* "One, two. I win."

"Don't bank on it, wolf-boy."

A bullet grazed my hip before the sound of the report whip-cracked over my eardrums. I buckled, hit the door frame hard, and sank to my knees. The Sig in my hand weighed a thousand pounds. I couldn't lift it again.

Ray stood and flashed two grins—his teeth, and the black hole of death at the end of his gun. "Y'all say hey to Lucifer for me," he said.

When the back door banged open, for an instant I thought the silhouetted figure outside was Satan himself, come to collect me personally. But I didn't think the devil spoke djinn. And even if he did, I doubted he knew how to cast a locking spell.

I tried to tell the new arrival that he didn't have to bother. I couldn't have moved if he paid me. But the swirling blackness coalesced over my eyes before my tongue would obey.

Chapter 13

"Donatti."

The voice that dribbled through my fuzz-blocked ears sounded familiar. That didn't necessarily translate to good news. I had far more enemies than friends, so the odds were stacked in favor of someone who'd happily finish the job Ray and Theo had started.

"—the fuck's going on?"

I flexed a hand. It moved accordingly, and surprised me enough to crack an eye open. A dark-haired figure dressed in black kneeled next to me. I couldn't make out his face, but he made no move to kill me.

"Come on, man. Don't pass out on me again. Where's Ian?"

At last an identity paired itself with the voice, and I realized I'd get to live at least a few more minutes. "Tory," I croaked. "You finish that other guy off?"

"You know we can't kill humans."

"He's not all human."

"Shit." Tory shot to his feet. "He's still locked down. But I can't—"

"Handcuffs. Top cabinet, left of the door."

He shook his head. "I don't even wanna know."

"And hit him in the head with something too. Make sure he's out for a while. He might know a handcuff-opening spell. These guys can do some weird shit."

"If you say so."

I allowed myself to relax a little while he secured the thug. Tory would be glad we were even now; I'd saved his life a year ago. More or less. But he wouldn't be so thrilled to find out what had happened to Akila. He was supposed to be some kind of royal protector for her, though he'd left most of the protecting in this realm to Ian. Not by choice. Ian had insisted, and he had a few centuries on Tory. Not to mention that she was his wife.

My eyes must have closed again, because I felt Tory working a healing spell before I saw him come back. I decided to leave them shut for a minute and savor the shrinking pain. "Why'd you come here?" I said. "You psychic now, or what?"

"You know that alarm system I set up for you?"

"The wards."

"Yeah. Those." He glanced toward the now silent thug. I really hoped he'd knocked him out. "Well, they went crazy. And then they fell apart. I tried to come through your mirror, but nothing happened."

"It's broken."

"I got that impression. So I used Ian's instead. And then I heard a gunshot in here."

"And then you saved my ass." I opened my eyes. "Thanks."

"Sure." A deep frown etched furrows in his mouth. "I shouldn't have had to, though. There's only one guy here, and he's not even djinn. What happened? Where're Ian and Akila?"

I really didn't want to answer that last question. I sat up slowly and nodded in Ray's direction. "There were five of them," I said. "He's the last. I killed one." Saying it out loud sent a wave of revulsion through me. "The rest . . . well, they're gone." I couldn't bring myself to tell him they'd taken Akila. Not yet. There were too many things we still had to figure out, and either Tory or Ian would rush off to save her without a plan—and get themselves caught or killed in the process. Alone, I wouldn't be able to get them all back. "They're descendants, like me. Only they're Morai."

"Impossible."

"Everybody keeps saying that, but it's not going to change the facts." I grabbed the door frame and hauled myself to my feet. "They're Morai. There's a shit ton more where those came from. And Ian . . . is in bad shape." I had to drop my gaze. "He's in the living room. I think."

Without a word, Tory whirled and ran for it. I took my time. Besides feeling like a pile of shit caught in an elephant stampede, I already knew what he looked like. And I was in no hurry to see it again.

Tory's anguished cry tore through me when I stopped at the bottom of the stairs.

"Marco," I called up after giving him a minute, hoping Jazz could hear me. I didn't think I could climb all those steps. A few muffled thumps later, the bathroom door slivered open.

"Polo."

It was the most beautiful word I'd ever heard. Relief convulsed my throat, and it took a few seconds for my voice to squeeze through. "It's safe," I said. "But I don't know if you should bring Cyrus out of there yet."

Jazz opened the door farther. "How bad is it?"

"Remember Buffalo?"

"Yeah."

"Worse than that."

"Great." She let out a long breath. Back when I was a full-time thief, and Jazz drove getaway, we'd been in on a job that overlapped a mob operation. Nobody told us that little detail, and we'd accidentally busted up an informant torture party. It was the only time I'd seen her close to puking. "Well, I can't keep him in here for long, and he sure as hell isn't going to sleep. I'll give you a few minutes, but we have to come down soon."

"All right." A few minutes wasn't going to be enough time to put Ian back together. I wasn't even sure if Tory and I combined could fix him.

I headed reluctantly to the living room, barely taking note of the destruction they'd caused. At first I didn't see Ian—only Tory, standing motionless in front of a wall. Finally I realized Ian was there too. But it was an image my mind didn't want to recognize.

Lynus had crucified him.

Arms spread, legs together, spears tacked him to the wall like a gruesome life-size poster. One in each wrist, one through both ankles. Another silver shaft protruded from his chest. I guessed that one had been to anchor him in place, since pinning his limbs alone wouldn't have kept him upright. His bowed head wasn't quite enough to hide the damage he'd taken from the bullet in the face. In the few places he wasn't drenched in blood or blasted apart, his flesh looked dirty gray tinged with blue. Like a corpse fresh from the morgue.

Tory turned toward me. His eyes practically glowed. Tics and spasms contorted his features with an irregular rhythm. "Akila," he ground out. "She's stronger than me. Might be able to heal him."

I stopped myself from blurting out the rest of the bad news right away. "Let me try and help him first," I said. "He can draw power from me. Sometimes. We're gonna need that asshole in the kitchen. Can you bring him in here? We should keep an eye on him."

"Damn it, Donatti. What happened to Akila?"

So much for stalling. "She's . . . not here."

"Where is she?"

The ferocity in his voice shook me. He sounded so much like Ian, I started to wonder if he had some wolf in him after all. I'd have to hope he didn't decide to shoot the messenger. "Listen, Tory, don't get crazy on me. We've got to think this through, or—"

"*Tell me!*"

I could barely get the words out. "They took her."

"They . . . what?"

"Jesus Christ. They fucking took her!" I wanted to scream, hit something, rip things apart. "They shot her. Tied her with some magic goddamn rope or something and took her back to their compound. I don't know what the hell's going on, why they wanted her. So go get that fuckwad and bring him in here. And we'll ask him."

For a second I was convinced he'd take a swing at me. But he started for the kitchen—slowly at first, moving in jerks and hitches, picking up speed on the way.

I made myself approach the monstrous tableau on the wall. "Ian." I sounded like a rusty hinge. "Come on, man. Breathe. Twitch. Do something . . ." I laid a hand on his chest. Nothing beat or moved beneath his cold skin. "I can't get more direct than this. Damn you, take it!"

No effect. He wasn't dead—couldn't be—but he wasn't exactly alive either.

Ian has left the building. Desperate laughter tried to claw its way from my throat. I choked back on it, knowing I couldn't lose control now. We weren't safe here anymore. Those bastards had been here once, and I had no doubt they could find their way back. Maybe not as fast without the mirror, but they'd be back sooner or later. I was betting on sooner.

If I couldn't revive Ian, at least I could try to get him down from the wall. I grabbed the shaft of the spear in his chest and almost pulled before I realized the other end was probably barbed. I pushed on it, but it didn't budge. No surprise there. Brute strength wasn't an option, and I didn't have a blowtorch, or even a hacksaw.

I took a closer look at him. The protruding ends of the spears were straight, except for the notched needle-eye holes at the top where towlines were supposed to be attached. Though the idea did unpleasant things to my stomach, I could probably wrench him off. I grabbed an arm and pulled. It didn't glide over the shaft so much as squelch and crunch. Dark blood pulsed from the hole and spattered on the carpet. If he'd been human and somehow still alive, this process would've finished him.

I freed both arms. His ankles were harder, nastier, but they came away eventually. I had to grab him in a demented bear hug and push back against the wall with a foot to torque his body over the last spear. Once the end cleared him, warm liquid gushed against me and soaked my shirt. I didn't know how he could still have enough in him to bleed.

Ian unconscious had all the weight and maneuvering ease of a grand piano. I staggered toward the couch with him and managed to pile most of him on it. My muscles shivered with exertion, and I fell back to catch a breath or two.

After a minute, Tory stalked back into the living room, dragging Ray behind him by his cuffed hands. He stopped and deposited the thug beside the couch, then nodded in Ian's direction. "Anything?"

"No."

"Fuck!" Fury twisted his face, and he launched a kick at Ray. A muffled hiss indicated the bastard was conscious, or on his way there. Tory leaned down, hauled him up with one arm. And backhanded him. "Where is she?" he shouted.

Ray opened one eye. He gasped, drew breath, and let out a grinding laugh. "You gonna torture it outta me, are you?"

"Damn right we are." Tory shook him hard enough to pop a few joints.

A cancerous grin spread on his face. I'd seen expressions like that too many times before. They usually preceded unpleasant surprises, like spare guns or spring-loaded blades hidden in sleeves. "Tory," I said. "Watch his hands."

"Oh, you ain't gotta worry about my hands, hoss." The grin widened, and his lower jaw worked back and forth like he had something stuck in his teeth. He bit down. A faint crunch sounded in his mouth, and he swallowed with a wince. "Bring it," he whispered. "You got twenty seconds to get somethin' outta me."

"Shit! Tory, heal him. Now."

Tory glanced over at me. "What the—"

"He popped a suicide cap. Poison. Just fucking do it!"

Ray's eyes rolled back in his head. His body jerked and jittered like a puppet controlled by a speed freak. Saliva bubbled from his mouth, foamed at the corners, and a series of strangled half-formed sounds emerged from his throat. It sounded like laughter.

He was dead before Tory spoke a single word.

Tory dropped the body and stepped back fast, as if suicide were contagious. "I'm sorry," he said. "I couldn't . . . damn it, why would anyone do that?"

"Hard-core fanatic fucks," I muttered. "They're

brainwashed." And more dangerous than I'd ever imagined. If these assholes were willing to die so easily to protect whoever ran them, we didn't stand a chance of getting Akila back. We'd be lucky to live through the end of the week ourselves.

And Ian and I were both fresh out of luck.

"Buffalo was an understatement. I'd have gone with Hiroshima."

Jazz's soft statement knocked me out of doom-and-gloom contemplation. She lingered at the far end of the room, holding Cyrus against her like he might float away if she let go. Her gaze locked on me, and she shuddered briefly. "Shouldn't you fix that?"

I glanced down at my soaked shirt. "It's not my blood," I said, and made a weak gesture toward the couch. She couldn't see Ian from there. That was probably a good thing. "Um . . . you really shouldn't have brought him down here."

"Like I'm going to leave him alone right now." Her head swiveled in Tory's direction. "I don't know how you got here, but I'm glad you did. Anyone have a clue what the hell's going on?"

Cy shifted and looked around, wide eyed and solemn. "No more bad guys."

"That's right, baby. Daddy got them all." She offered a faltering smile.

Not exactly. I couldn't tell her yet that things were worse than ever. Instead, I concentrated on the most immediate problem. "Ian's out cold," I said. "He's not responding to anything."

Jazz frowned. "What about Akila?"

I shook my head. Jazz went paper white, but she didn't say a word.

"I'll try to heal him." Tory's voice was taut as a trip wire. "We're going to need him fast. We can't wait much longer."

"Wait for what?" Jazz whispered.

"To get Akila back."

"Jesus. They took her?"

"Hold on." I started around the couch with memory sparking a crazy idea. The last time Ian dropped in a gunfight, it'd been Cy's touch that had brought him back. Maybe it would work again. "Jazz. Remember the thing about descendants and direct contact?"

"I guess."

"Okay. It's not working with me, but I'm beat. And I think Cy can help Ian."

Her eyes narrowed. "How?"

"He only has to touch him." I stopped in front of her and looked back. Didn't really want to expose Cyrus to more death and destruction than necessary. "Tory. Can you get that sack of shit out of the way?"

"My pleasure." He snagged Ray's corpse and dragged it toward the far end of the room.

I faced Jazz again. "I'm sorry, babe," I said. "I don't like this either, but it's the only option left right now."

Some of the fierce light left her expression. "You really think Cy can heal him?"

"Yeah. He's strong—like his mother." I smiled and touched the side of her face.

"Uh-huh. Lay it on thicker and you're gonna need a shovel."

"So is that a yes?"

"What do you think, Cy?" She rubbed his back, cocked her head to look at him. "Do you want to help Uncle Ian?"

"Okay."

"Sweet. Come on, little man." I carried him over to the couch and stopped before Ian's mangled body entered his line of sight. "Cy, I think it would work better if you closed your eyes real tight," I said. "Can you do that?"

"Uh-huh." He squinched his eyes shut. "See?"

"Good job. Keep 'em just like that. Okay?"

"Okay, Daddy."

I knelt on the floor and took one of Cy's hands. A sharp gasp drew my attention. Jazz stood a few feet away, rapidly turning a pale shade of green. One shaking hand flew to her mouth. She made a thick sound and looked away. "Jesus . . ."

Tory came up behind her. "He'll be all right," he said, steering her gently away. "Come on. This won't take long."

I gave him a grateful nod. "Ready, Cy?"

"Yep."

With a silent prayer to whatever god might be listening, I guided Cy's arm out and pressed his small palm against Ian's skin. A shiver wracked his body on contact. "Uncle Ian doesn't feel good," he whispered. "He hurts inside."

The words blazed a trail of gooseflesh down my back. "I'll bet he does," I managed through teeth that wanted to chatter like a wind-up toy. "But you're doing great. Just keep—"

A burst of intense cold spread through me and stole my breath. Cyrus whimpered a little, but he kept his eyes closed and his hand resting on Ian. A faint glow traced Cy's fingers, intensified, spread over Ian in undulating waves, hard and bright as a winter sun. I felt energy being pulled from me and passed through Cyrus—as though he were a living suncatcher, filtering and magnifying the light.

Cy drew back on his own before I could snatch him away. I rocked back, tried to stand. I couldn't make my legs move. My arms trembled under Cy's slack weight. "Jazz," I croaked. "I can't hold him . . ."

She rushed over and scooped him up. "Mommy," he murmured. "I'm sleepy now."

"Okay, baby. You rest awhile." She moved away with him,

her gaze riveted to the increasing brilliance that enveloped Ian, the changing shape just visible inside the glow.

I stayed on my knees, shivering like a shaved Chihuahua. The transformation took longer than usual. Finally, the light faded and left the wolf, sides heaving, eyes closed. He slid to the floor and landed hard with a thump and a whine. One back paw scrabbled weakly on the carpet.

"Ian." I moved to stand and fell back on my ass. On the second try I managed to gain my footing, but my legs wavered and carried me backward—not the direction I'd intended. "Ian," I repeated. "Can you get up?"

The wolf's eyes opened. His head lifted, and a steady growl rumbled deep in his throat. Black lips peeled back from curving ivory fangs. He rose on his haunches, the growl spiraling into a prolonged snarl.

With a vicious bark, Ian sprang straight at me.

Chapter 14

I went down under Ian's weight. Powerful jaws snapped shut inches from my face. I threw an arm up—and Ian sank his teeth into it.

A buzzing white noise filled my head. Dimly, I heard Jazz scream at Tory. Something about getting Ian off me or she'd shoot him some more. But I understood what he was doing. I tried to wave my free hand, to let her know I was all right. I wasn't sure if I succeeded in moving.

Blood magic. A disgusting but effective way to amplify power outside of having a handy descendant. Good for any clan vile or desperate enough to use it. Drink the blood of a djinn—or part djinn—and get a temporary mojo boost. Ian didn't have enough power to transform back from his wolf state, so he'd gone for my blood.

One of these days, I was going to bite him back. Just for the hell of it.

Ian wrenched his fangs free. A rough tongue lapped the wounds he'd made, and I swallowed bile at the awful sensation. "You son of a bitch. Warn me next time," I said. "Had enough, or should I go find a razor and open up a vein?"

The wolf backed off me, growling. Light rippled along his spine and spread to swallow him. It faded and left Ian on hands and knees, head bowed, gasping like an asthmatic after a mile run. "Akila," he said between pants. "She is injured."

"Ian . . ." I sat up, wishing there was something big and impenetrable between us. Like the heart of an African jungle. Tory's reaction had been a Fourth of July sparkler compared to the erupting volcano Ian was about to become. "Those guys didn't come here for you."

His head came up slowly. A jagged red scar blazed a path down his cheek where the bullet had opened his face. Barely controlled fury burned from his eyes. "Explain."

Chills raced through me at the sight of him. I knew there were some things djinn magic couldn't heal in this realm, but I didn't think that included gunshot wounds. "Lynus said they wanted you left alive. Whoever they are. But—"

"Akila." The word was at once demand and broken plea.

I closed my eyes. "They took her."

He said nothing. I dared to look at him, and wondered if he'd somehow slid back to near death without falling over. He'd stopped moving. Stopped breathing. His eyes were on me, but they weren't seeing anything.

"Ian, listen. I overheard a few things that I think will help. If we take a little time to regroup—"

"You." He pushed up to his knees, and his hands clenched in tight fists. "You let them take her."

"Whoa. Hold on a minute. I didn't—"

"Why did you not stop them?" His voice rose, coarse and heavy. He struggled to stand. "We must bring her back. She is not . . . gods curse you, thief! How could you let them?"

"You bastard." If Ian's tether had been at my fingertips, I might've destroyed him right then. "There were five of them, and one of me. They had guns. What the fuck was I supposed to do? And you didn't exactly stand in their way either."

"You were not immediately injured. You could have protected her. Even if you were shot, you could have been healed."

"Goddamn it, Ian, I'm human!" It took all the willpower I had left not to break his jaw. "If I get shot in the wrong place, I don't get a do-over. I just die."

"You still should have stopped them!"

"That's enough, Gahiji-an." Tory stepped up beside me and fixed Ian with a warning stare. "He did everything he could. He was just about dead when I got here."

Ian blinked. "Taregan? How . . . we must find her. She is in danger."

"We're all in danger." Pissed as I was, I decided to let it go for now. Ian dropping the blame game was the only apology I'd get. "There's a hell of a lot more than five of those bastards. Besides the guards we saw first, at least a dozen crowded in there toward the end."

"Damn," Tory said. "Are they all scions?"

"I'm not sure. But we should probably assume they are." I glanced back to see how Jazz was taking this. Cyrus lay slack in her arms, and she paced in slow half circles with him, ostensibly ignoring us. The set line of her jaw said she was listening anyway, and not liking what she heard. "We know there's at least one full-blood Morai."

Ian spat a curse. "Khalyn."

"Yeah. Him." I couldn't decide who I was more furious with—Calvin for being a damned good liar, or Ian for being right. Part of me realized that I should've been angry at myself. After all, I'd been dumb enough to fall for the monk routine.

I ignored the internal debate and gave Tory the short

version of our encounter on the mountain. "Calvin said he was going back to the monastery," I said after the explanation. "Said he had business to attend to, or something."

"I do not care what that lying snake does. I am going to get my wife." Ian took two steps and went down on a knee. He gasped, and started to crawl across the floor. "The mirror. What happened?"

"Ian, stop!" I moved in front of him. "I had to break it. They were keeping the bridge open somehow."

He slung an arm over the edge of the couch and pushed to his feet again. "We will use mine, then," he panted. "I assume you have not broken that as well."

"We're not going anywhere right now."

"We must! Akila—"

"—is going to have to wait. I'm sorry, Ian." My own words felt like they were coming from someone else. Someone a lot smarter than me. I'd never been the voice of reason. "You can't even stand up. I'm not much better. And there's no way we can take on a two-thousand-year-old djinn in this shape, much less who knows how many descendants. She'll make it, as long as they don't have her tether. Right?"

A visible shudder wracked Ian's body. He didn't reply.

"Right, Ian?" I repeated, knowing damned well he'd heard me.

He closed his eyes. "They do have her tether."

"What?"

"When she crossed to this realm, she had no time to prepare." He shivered again, and leaned hard on the couch. "She was forced to bind herself to something close at hand." A harsh bark of laughter escaped him. "Very close."

"No." Tory blanched, at once looking just as bad as Ian. "Please tell me she didn't . . ."

Ian touched his index finger. The band of gold light pulsed

in response. "Akila's tether is with her always," he said. "She is bound to her ring."

Under strenuous protest, Tory half-carried Ian off to the guest bedroom for a short rest, and to try healing him a little more.

And I prepared to make Jazz hate me.

When we had the wrecked living room to ourselves, she laid Cyrus down on the couch and let out a sigh. "He's getting heavy," she said.

"Yeah. He's a solid little guy." I moved toward her, wanting to hold her, afraid she'd slap me if I tried. I'd already fucked up her life beyond repair, and I was about to make things worse. I had no idea how to start telling her she had to leave her own place. Leave me. Maybe for good.

"Gavyn." Her voice was flat, her expression wooden. "There's a dead body in my house."

I had to look away from her. "Actually, there're two," I said. "The other one's upstairs by the bedroom."

"You killed two of them?"

"No. That one popped a poison cap to keep Tory from torturing him for information." I gestured at the feet protruding from behind the television. "But I shot the one upstairs."

"You actually killed someone."

"Jesus Christ! Yes, I did. It's official. I'm a murderer." I didn't feel any better admitting it the second time. "I had to. He would've killed me . . . and then you and Cy."

Jazz crossed her arms as if she were cold. "What do we do now?" she whispered.

"Now, you take Cyrus and get the hell out of here."

The words left my mouth before I realized my intention of saying them. She stared at me. Her eyes glittered, and her lips thinned. "And do what, exactly?" she said. "Live in the goddamn truck?"

I refused to register the sarcasm in her voice. "Stay with Lark. Tory's got a shitload of protection on that place, and these assholes don't know he's involved."

"Stay with Lark," she echoed in a tone that suggested I was dumber than a dirt sandwich. "Just show up at his door and say hey, Lark, me and my kid are gonna live with you while the other guys go get themselves killed. That about right?"

"I'll call and tell him you're coming." She was being logical again. I couldn't let myself pay attention to the facts, because djinn affairs tended to overrule the real world. Jazz always had trouble factoring that into the equation. "You need to go. I don't know how long it'll take them to find this place again."

"This is my house. I'm not letting a bunch of thugs drive me out."

"Damn it, Jazz, they're not garden-variety goons!" I knew she could be just as stubborn as Ian when she wanted to, but this time I couldn't let her win. No way in hell I was going to end up saying *I told you so* to her tombstone. "Being a badass doesn't make you bulletproof. Or magic proof."

Her jaw twitched. "They aren't bulletproof either. I shoot them, they die."

"How are you going to shoot something you can't see? Something you don't even know is there? What about when they cast a lockdown on you?" Desperation flattened my voice. If I thought it'd help, I would've gone on my knees and begged. But I knew her pride, her need for independence. She wouldn't go just because I asked.

I had to make her want to leave. *Need* to leave. If it was her decision, she'd stick to it.

"All right, genius." Anger sizzled through her, practically sparking along the rigid lines of her body. "Say we go to Lark's place. Then what? We wait for you to die, and come back here, and maybe these freaks come after Cyrus? Or maybe you think you've actually got a shot at wiping out the whole circus, and then everything goes back to the fucked-up mess we keep pretending is normal."

"Hey, keeping me around was your idea, remember? I told you it wouldn't work. This is what I do now, so deal with it." Christ, I couldn't believe this shit was actually coming out of my mouth. "And we've got a better shot without you and the kid hanging around."

For just an instant, her shield lowered and I caught the devastation in her eyes. I'd been expecting that—but it hurt more than I could have imagined. It would've been easier to withstand a week of constant torture and starvation than to take that look, the pain and the betrayal in it, knowing I'd intentionally caused it.

And I couldn't stop.

"You're just in the way." Somehow I managed to keep my voice from shaking. "You can't compete at this level. You'll never be able to. All you can do is slow me down." Every word I spoke was a knife that turned back on me and slashed a new wound. But I couldn't let her see me bleed. I had to convince her I meant this bullshit. "You're useless here. Get out."

She didn't respond for so long, I thought I'd taken it too far. Finally, the controlled vacancy broke into fury. "Big, bad Donatti," she said with a sneer. "You know, I expected a line about having to protect Cy. But this is shitty even for you."

"Since when is being honest shitty?" *Damn it, just go.* "You said it yourself. You don't understand this magic stuff."

"No, I don't." She glared at me—no tears, no trace of hurt.

No forgiveness. "You know what else I don't understand? Why I ever . . ."

My breath caught. I had to force the sharp intake into a longer draw, push my expression from anticipated pain into disgust. If she finished that sentence, I was done. Game over. I couldn't bear to hear her say the words she always left out now, to have her take them back without even giving them to me first.

"Forget it." She stalked over to the couch, picked up Cy, and carried him to the door. "You and your goddamned conscience have fun. If you don't get killed, maybe we'll be at Lark's when you're done. And maybe we won't. I'm through promising anything to you."

She didn't slam the door shut.

The soft snick of the latch felt more final than a bang. An explosive end, an exclamation point to her declaration, and there would've been a chance for the heat to die down. For emotions to clear and hint at the truth I hadn't been able to give her. But this was a period. A quiet confirmation that while I'd bullshitted her, she hadn't erected a similar front. Her good-bye was real.

I managed to wait until the Hummer's engine started before I dropped to the floor and wept.

Chapter 15

Bereft. People tossed that word around at funerals and fires and other disasters. A sense of loss, an empty ache. It didn't begin to cover what I felt. If Jazz and Cy had died, this would've been easier to take. Knowing I'd improved their chances of survival was about as comforting as a drop of water on a third-degree burn.

"You were right to drive her away."

The sound of Ian's voice produced instant irritation, despite the genuine concern it contained. I kept from lashing out at him by reminding myself that his woman was gone too—and nowhere near safe. But I still didn't feel like having a heart-to-heart with him. "Drop it," I said without moving. "We've got other concerns."

"Very well."

I got up, thankful that at least I'd stopped blubbering, and turned around silently, daring either of them to make a smart-ass comment. Not a word. Ian stood more or less steady, not leaning on anything but ready to drop anyway, and Tory slouched a few paces behind him. They both looked like I felt. Worn down harder than a neighborhood football.

And we were still going after these bastards. Brilliant strategy. It was like David and Goliath—if David had a broken leg, wore a blindfold, and hadn't slept for a week before he went to the valley. Hell, we didn't even have a lousy slingshot.

"We've got to ditch the bodies before we take off," I said. "The rest of this mess'll have to wait. So I guess we bury them. Tory, can you—"

"No need for that." Tory crossed the room to the picture window. "I've got just the place to send them." He nipped a finger and went through the bridge-opening bit. The glass shivered into a view of rusted, wrecked, and battered vehicles on a vast dark lot. It was a familiar junkyard. We'd been there a year ago, hiding out from a different threat to our lives.

Apparently, some things never changed.

I helped him heave Ray's stiffening corpse through, and we headed upstairs to repeat the process with Theo. We had to drag him through the bedroom into the adjoining bath. There was blood everywhere—splashing walls, soaking carpet, smearing tile. Too much of it was mine. The flat copper smell tainted the air like the remnants of a recently burnt meal. I suspected that no matter how much this place was scrubbed and freshened, I'd always catch the scent of blood here.

"All right," I said when we'd sent Theo tumbling through the mirror after his buddy. "Do we have anything resembling a plan?"

Ian tore his gaze from his feet. "We will go to this compound," he said.

"Ian, we can't." I hated having to say it, but somebody had to think with his head right now. "We'll just get slaughtered. There's too many of them, and that place is a fucking fortress."

I expected him to rip me a new asshole. Instead, he closed his eyes and said, "The monastery, then. Khalyn said he was returning there. He is one, and we are three. We will force him to help us retrieve Akila."

My shock at having him agree with me gave way to suspicion. He never gave up that easy. But right now, I'd have to trust him. It was possible that he'd actually try the approach that didn't guarantee death, just because it was Akila's life on the line, and not his. Or mine. I was apparently expendable in the name of killing the Morai.

I let it go for the moment, since I had my own stake in this game. Besides, there was another concern. "You sure we're three?" I glanced at Tory. "I don't think anyone asked if you wanted to get involved with this shit."

A stricken look passed over Tory's face. Determination replaced it. "I'll go," he said. "Just give me a minute to call Lark."

I nodded. "Do me a favor. Tell him Jazz and Cy are coming to visit."

"I will." He walked out of the room reaching in a pocket.

Ian resumed his Olympic floor staring. I had the distinct impression I'd be the only one thinking tonight. I'd done enough of that already. So much that my head wanted to split right down the middle and grant me the mercy of spilling out my hyperactive brains. There were some things I just didn't understand—and wouldn't no matter how hard I tried to figure them out. "Ian, I'm gonna need you here for a few minutes," I said.

He looked up, and his dazed expression pulled itself together a little. "Those marks on the floor," he said. "What happened in here?"

"No shoes, broken mirror. Long story. And thanks for the reminder." Didn't want to go tromping around in the woods barefoot. I slipped into the bedroom, threw on socks and an old pair of work boots. When I returned, Ian stared at me like he'd never seen me before.

"You did attempt to stop them."

I gave myself a mental pat on the back for not exploding at him. "Yeah. Didn't work out so great, though."

"I apologize for my reaction. I . . ." His eyes closed briefly. "I cannot lose Akila. I have no clan, no homeland. She is . . . everything."

"I know." More than I cared to admit. I had no family, no place of my own. I never had until Jazz. And now I was back to square one. "So let's make sure we get her back. All right?"

He nodded. And offered nothing more.

I let out a sigh. "You know, make Calvin bring her back isn't exactly what I'd call a good plan with a high probability of success."

"Perhaps you have a better idea?"

"Not really."

"Then we will proceed with this."

"Terrific. Well, this David isn't going in without a slingshot."

"Excuse me?"

"I'm bringing a gun." I started for the door, stopped. "Lynus told these guys to look for the lamps. You know what that means?"

Ian's lip curled. "My tether."

"Yeah. It's not safe to leave it. They can find this place again."

"It is in my apartment." He straightened and came toward me. "You and Taregan meet me there. We must move quickly."

I let him go first. "Ian . . . any idea why they took Akila?"

His eyes met mine. "I do not know. But they cannot wish to use her as a threat against me. If it were my life they wanted, they would have taken me as well. I could not have stopped them." A gray pallor washed over his face. "I fear they have no use for her. If that is the case . . ."

He didn't have to finish the thought. I'd already had the same one.

Just like the old days.

I loaded up. Strapped on a shoulder holster and ankle blade bands, grabbed a military vest and stuffed the pockets with extra ammo, cutters, wire, picks, Maglites—anything I thought might come in handy. Probably should've retrieved the cuffs from Ray before we heaved him, but Jazz had a spare set in a dresser drawer. I took them, and the key, then tossed a jacket over everything. More pockets always helped.

I headed downstairs for the Sig that Jazz had given me. Should be in the kitchen somewhere. On the way through, I heard Tory's voice from the living room.

"—told you before. *Adjo,* I can't. I'm sworn to protect her. I *want* to protect her . . ."

I grimaced and moved out of hearing range. Lark wasn't taking the news well. I couldn't blame him. At least he and Jazz would have a lot to talk about. They could swap notes on the stupidity levels of their respective lovers.

The gun lay under the table. I snugged it into the holster and meandered back toward the living room, just in time to catch Tory terminating the call with a troubled frown. "I don't suppose you have any idea what the hell these guys want," he said.

"Not a clue." He didn't mention Lark, I wouldn't ask. "Ian's waiting in the garage."

Tory fell into step with me. "This just doesn't make sense. The Morai are breeding? They can't. We're all infertile here, except Ian. And they want Akila?" He shook his head. "They didn't take Ian, so that leaves out the hostage possibility. Unless they're stupid."

"Which they're not."

"Yeah, I gathered that." He glanced up, as if the stars might spell out a reason. "I'd say that maybe they wanted her to break the fertility bind, like she did for Ian, if they didn't already have scions. How the *fuck* did they get scions?"

"Funny," I said. "Calvin used that word too. *Scions*. Never heard you say it before."

"The Morai we're going after?" He shrugged. "Well, it's a common enough term. Most of the Doma don't use it, but that doesn't mean . . . oh. You don't know about that. The Doma are—"

"Lower class."

He looked surprised. "Yeah. That's it."

"Akila told me." I had to wonder if Tory even recognized casual racism—or clanism with the djinn—when it came out of his mouth. At least the princess had the grace to blush. "So, you have any more theories?"

"Just one."

"And that'd be . . . ?"

"We're fucked."

I stared openmouthed at him for a second. Then I laughed hard enough to crack a rib. Almost couldn't stop, especially when Tory joined in, leaning against the side of the garage to keep from falling over. I forced myself to sober up out of respect for Ian, who might be within earshot, but the occasional snort still dislodged itself from my throat. A corner of my mouth twitched. "Damn," I said. "You've been hanging around humans too long."

"What can I say? Your species is a bad influence." Tory straightened and ran a hand through his hair. "Let's get this over with."

We climbed the wooden plank stairs at the back of the

garage. The door stood open at the top. I hadn't been up here in a while, long enough that I'd missed the subtle but definite transformation of the place that bore Akila's hand. There was a flow to things, a breezy note worked through fluid furnishing arrangements and draped fabric. Lush and thriving plants at the windows, candles clustered intimately in nooks and on tables. Even the air seemed cleaner and fresher than any interior space had a right to be.

Ian stood beside the tall gilt-framed mirror. He'd stuffed the dagger—his tether—in his waistband like it was an afterthought. "Come," he said. "I will go through first."

I pointed at his tether. "You probably shouldn't carry that around. Maybe we should take a detour, conceal it somewhere."

"I will not delay any longer."

I glared at him. "How're you going to get Akila back if you're dead?"

"Blasted—" He grabbed for it and held it out to me handle first. "Then perhaps you will carry it for me."

"This is your life. You're going to trust me with it?"

"What choice do I have?"

I took the dagger without a word and secured it in a zippered pocket. Ian wasn't himself, so I'd let the caustic comments slide.

Ian turned to the mirror. "Remember, Donatti, you must create a bridge for Taregan before yourself. He cannot reach the place alone." He went through the motions—painted the blood symbol, spoke the spell.

Nothing happened.

"What . . ." Jaw clenched, Ian repeated the incantation. The mirror stayed unchanged, throwing back only his furious reflection. "Gods take this! Perhaps I am unable to concentrate. You try it, thief."

"Uh, right." Ian's blood was still on the mirror, so I wiped it away with a sleeve. Didn't know if it'd work for me. Producing a switchblade from a pocket, I sliced a finger and did the blood-writing thing, then called up a memory of Calvin's study, of the mirror there that had struck me as out of whack, and let the words fly.

I stared at myself—unchanged, perplexed. "I'm not getting anything."

"Try again."

"Ian. It's not gonna work." I stepped back, folded my arms. "You think maybe he broke it after we used it or something?"

"Perhaps. More likely, he has placed a barrier spell on the mirror to protect himself from me."

"Whatever. Look, the important thing is, the direct route isn't an option anymore." This'd probably be a bad time to remind him that I'd said we should get a helicopter. "We'll have to get there another way. Maybe we should just drive. If we pushed it, we could make it in eight, nine hours."

"No," Tory said. "That's not fast enough. We should fly."

I shook my head. "Ian can't go that far without exhausting himself, and I can't fly at all. I know you're good, Tory, but you can't carry us both all the way to Virginia. We have to . . . wait." I fished out my cracked cell phone and caught a glimpse of the time on the flashing screen. Just after midnight. "The hotel we stayed in wasn't that far from the monastery. We could bridge there. And it's a small town, so maybe the room's still empty."

"Yes." Something resembling relief eased across Ian's features. "That may work."

"Course it will. But I'll go first." At this point, I doubted Ian cared how many humans we scared or pissed off. But I didn't want to create unnecessary confusion. The compound was close to the town too—and the harder we made it for them to find us, the better. People would remember a bunch of strange men turning up from out of nowhere in a hotel bathroom. And they'd talk about it.

Ian nodded his assent. I turned back, concentrated on the hotel mirror, and said the spell. It worked this time. Gleaming silver resolved to a shaded view of shower curtains and undisturbed towels. I hoped that meant the room wasn't occupied. With only a second's hesitation, I crouched and stepped through.

Chapter 16

It didn't take long for the novelty of walking through the forest at night to wear off. I'd had enough the second time I tripped on an exposed root, and long before the fourth time I got a stinging faceful of branch.

We'd gotten lucky and slipped out of the hotel unnoticed. Maybe because we'd both decided Calvin needed to die after all.

Or maybe because the universe was saving all the bad luck for the woods.

I played the beam of my Maglite ahead on Ian and Tory, who forged through like there weren't a thousand sticks clawing for their eyes. The bastards. Ian turned in response to the light and frowned back at me. "Can you not move faster, thief? We have much ground to cover."

"Sure, no problem," I retorted. "You move all these goddamned trees out of the way, and I'll start running."

"You have a light."

"Yeah, but I don't have wolf vision. Or depth perception." I stumbled along a little faster and narrowly avoided walking smack into a protruding limb that would've lumped my head nicely. "Any idea how much more nature is between us and the monastery?"

"Mile and a half, maybe a little more," Tory said. "I think."

"You think?"

He gave a careful shrug. "We're following the only magic we can sense, but it's faint. He must've put up more protections. They just aren't as solid as the first time you guys came across the place. Otherwise, we wouldn't be able to find it at all."

"Great. So how do we know that whatever you're sensing is actually Calvin? That compound of theirs is around here somewhere too."

"We don't."

The distant, hackle-raising cry of an animal broke through the trees, as though the forest wanted to punctuate his statement. I tried to shake the chills that clung to my arms and the back of my neck. If I believed in premonitions, I would've thought I'd just had one—that we were headed into something we didn't have a shot in hell at walking away from.

The brief conversation strangled itself on urgency, and we got moving again. Ian and Tory could've been ghosts for all the noise they made. But I produced enough racket for all three of us. I tromped on twigs, broke branches, and cursed every stick and thorny weed that tore my clothes and skin, right along with the ones that didn't just for thinking about it. The wildlife chorus didn't help either. The more I tried to tune out the various hoots, chirps, squeaks, and howls that punctuated the air at irregular intervals, the louder they seemed to get, until I was convinced we'd been surrounded by an army of rabid wolverine-mounted squirrels. A low and ominous rumbling almost solidified my delusions before I recognized the sound as thunder.

I had a few seconds to reflect that rain sizzling on leaves sounded like fire before the downpour penetrated the branches and soaked me.

With a mental note to refrain from saying things couldn't get worse, I hustled to catch up with Ian. I'd closed half the distance when I discovered that water makes leaves and pine needles slippery. My front foot shot forward like a rabbit at a greyhound track, and I plopped on my ass in a puddle of muck.

I groaned and looked around for the flashlight. A feeble glow to my left revealed that I hadn't killed it, but it had landed half submerged in forest floor slime. I made a grab for it. My fingers closed around the barrel—and something in the mud slithered against them.

I drew back and shouted. What emerged from my mouth was something like *yee-urgle-eck*. Footsteps approached me, but my attention stayed on the slender, sinewy shape making its lazy way across the damp patch of light. At least it was headed away from me.

"What are you doing?" Ian demanded.

"Taking a mud bath," I said weakly. "I slipped. And there's a snake."

"Where?"

I pointed. After a few seconds, Tory laughed.

"Well, it's not a Morai, anyway," he said. "Do you want us to save you from it, Donatti? That thing's gotta be, what, a whole foot long. A truly terrifying specimen."

"I hate snakes. And I hate the damned woods. When we get home, I'm going to shoot an environmentalist."

I thought Ian might've smirked, but it was too dark to tell. "Perhaps you should stay closer," he said. "There may be frogs here as well."

I glared up at him. "Ugh."

"Here." Ian held out a hand. "We should remain together. This is no night for—"

He broke off and stared down. A faint shimmer of light

pulsed into existence around the index finger of his extended hand. The narrow band grew brighter by the second, until an intense golden light poured from it to throw angular shadows in every direction and illuminate the horror etched into Ian's features. For a moment the ring appeared cast in molten flame, impossibly bright, like a miniature sun.

And then it shattered.

I couldn't even hear the rain anymore.

The glowing fragments of Ian's ring drifted in the air, fading slowly, like ashes scattered from a fire. No one moved, no one spoke. The frozen tableau stretched on forever, until I let out an involuntary gasp when my body realized I'd stopped breathing.

Nobody had to say what this meant—only death could shatter the bond. They'd killed her.

Tory dropped to his knees. Ian remained stiff and silent, slightly bent, his hand still outstretched, as though he could take it back if he didn't move.

A thousand things I couldn't say battered through my head, trying to reach my tongue. I refused to speak. Nothing would matter. There were no words that wouldn't feel like salt on an open wound—especially coming from me. My woman was still alive.

The rain kept falling. Eventually I heard it again, a thousand cold teardrops beating down on the world. Heaven mourning. With a shaking hand, I reached for the flashlight and made a halfhearted attempt to mop away some of the mud. If I stayed busy with pointless tasks, maybe I wouldn't scream.

"Gahiji-an." Tory's voice. A mere scrape of sound.

Ian gave no sign he heard, or cared. He didn't even blink against the water beading and dripping down his face. His eyes were blank, his pupils constricted to hard black pinpoints.

Immobile in the dim backwash of light, he appeared drained. Lifeless. A cadaver shocked upright.

Tory coughed out a hoarse sob and lurched to his feet. "Gahiji-an," he repeated without strength. "My prince. What can I do?" He laid a hand on Ian's shoulder.

At his touch, Ian snapped.

He straightened like a shot and stumbled back. A sound somewhere between a growl and a wretched cry issued from his clenched teeth. In a blink, he lobbed a fist at Tory's jaw that stopped a hair shy of connecting. Tory didn't even flinch. Ian's arm remained there for long seconds, the muscles twitching in visible erratic spasms beneath his skin. Finally, he lowered it and whipped around to face me.

The sheer madness in his eyes robbed my breath.

"Leave." It was a command, fortified with an unspoken threat. "Go back. Survive. The barrier must be maintained."

I shook my head and loosened my reluctant tongue. "Fuck the barrier." He'd told me before that living Dehbei blood was the only thing preventing the Morai from returning to the djinn realm, that if he died, Cyrus and I had to stay alive. A spell the Dehbei had managed to cast before the Morai finished them off. "Let them deal with the bastards. I can't just leave—"

"You will go back." Something deep and vicious laced his words, as though the wolf in him had seized control of his vocal chords. "Taregan. *Kesura lo ani esa q'rohi ka-et.*"

My spine crawled at the translation my mind offered. *Bind his small soul to me.* I didn't know exactly what that meant, but I was pretty sure I didn't want it to happen.

Tory blanched. "Maybe you should reconsider."

"Do it!"

"I . . . I don't think I can. It's a big spell."

Ian vibrated with fury. He sank his teeth into the meaty

part of his palm, drew them out dripping with blood, and held his bleeding hand out to Tory.

"Jesus," Tory whispered. Shivering, he took Ian's blood offering without another word.

"Ian, what the hell?" I scrambled back in the mud, trying to stand, convinced I couldn't let them go through with whatever this was. "Don't. You're not thinking straight."

Tory finished and wiped a crimson trickle from his mouth. He advanced toward me. "I'm sorry, Donatti."

Stop. The word failed to materialize beyond my thoughts. He'd cast a lockdown on me. He knelt, put a hand on my chest, and beckoned to Ian, who edged close enough for Tory to touch him at the same time. Tory closed his eyes and murmured a chant, barely audible above the sweep of the rain and the soughing wind.

A strong tugging sensation bloomed in my gut. Pain drove up from there to my chest, and I could almost feel a lump of something that was purely, vitally mine pass through my breastbone into Tory's hand. He shuddered when it happened, and again seconds later when I guessed the thing left him and entered Ian.

At once, I felt like I'd sprinted a hundred miles uphill. It took everything I had not to pass out in the muck.

Tory dropped his arms, gasping, and gestured at me. My motor control returned, and with it came an overwhelming dose of nausea. I managed to turn my head before I could throw up on my legs. What came out felt like a gallon or so of superheated motor oil—thick, smooth, and odorless, scalding every inch of flesh it touched.

I knuckled a drizzle from the corner of my mouth and moved my hand toward the beam of the dropped flashlight. Viscous black fluid glistened on my skin. The same stuff that had leaked from Lynus when Ian drained his soul.

"What the fuck did you do to me?" My voice sounded papery and ancient, a wheedling scrawl. "You can't do this. You can't . . ."

Lines of crackling light crawled around Ian like trained lightning. "Forget the monastery. I am going straight to their nest. I will tear them all apart," he grunted. His upper lip lifted to reveal lengthening eyeteeth, and he struggled visibly against the transformation that seemed to grip him involuntarily. "As many as possible, before they bring me down. You will know when I am finished." His hair thickened, formed rough points. He shook his head with a snarl. "And you will end me then. Destroy my tether. You must survive."

"Ian! Goddamn it, don't be an idiot. I don't know anything!"

The glow consumed him. He bent and warped, and became the wolf. For an instant his eyes met mine—and the anguish in them filled me completely, turning my blood to liquid fire. Then he whirled and ran.

Tory stood a few feet away. "Do what he's told you to," he said. "I have to help him. I've got just enough left to transform."

"Wait," I croaked. "This is stupid. I can help too. He's stronger when I'm around—he said it himself."

"Didn't you feel what happened?" Tory shook his head. "He's taken part of you with him. Your presence won't boost him any more than what he's carrying now. He wants you to live . . . because he can't. Not without her." The rain had slowed to a drizzle, but moisture still streamed from Tory's eyes. "Tell Lark I'll return if I can. Don't let him come after me."

I shivered. Before I could lodge another weak protest, the light of Tory's transformation blazed from him. The hawk rose above the trees with a mournful cry, leaving me with the most important question unanswered.

If two djinn and a descendant couldn't best five of these bastards, how was I supposed to survive them alone?

Chapter 17

We'd lost the war before the first real battle ever started.

Akila was dead. Ian was about to join her. Tory . . . I didn't even want to think about how he'd end up. One of his clan, Shamil, had been held captive and tortured for years by the Morai clan leader so the bastard could have a constant supply of fresh djinn blood to amplify his power. We managed to rescue him and send him back to the realm—eyeless, forever tormented, but still alive. But that had been four of us against one djinn and his psychotic human puppet. Now, it would be me against an army.

And I was supposed to just go home and forget about it.

I'd have to destroy Ian. Jesus. Every Morai hated him, with good reason, and I couldn't leave him in their hands. Even if they had his tether, I doubted they'd kill him anytime soon. They'd torture him forever. And they'd use him to track me down. Still, I had no idea how the hell I would know when he'd done all he could. I didn't know a goddamned thing, and there were no djinn left for me to ask.

Except Calvin. And I sure as shit wasn't asking him.

I groped for the flashlight and shook some of the mud from it. At the least, I had to get up. Couldn't sit here all night—if the descendants didn't find me, the animals would. I hunched forward and pushed off the ground. Standing wasn't too bad. I was sore and a little queasy, but otherwise solid. Apparently the side effects of that soul spell were temporary.

That didn't make me feel any better about being subjected to it.

A quick gust of wind forced a miserable sneeze from me. I trudged over to the nearest tree and leaned against it while I wiped rainwater and dirt from my eyes.

Playing the beam around the area didn't exactly lift my spirits. The soaked forest seemed even more confusing and impenetrable than before. With every tree and branch and bit of ground the same slick, dark color and consistency, I had no clue how to get out of here—or what I'd do when I did. *If* I did. I couldn't even tell which way Ian and Tory had gone a minute ago. The thought of leaving them for dead and spending the rest of my life running from Calvin and his crew held about as much appeal as eating a bowl of thumbtacks. But it looked like I had no other choice.

In less than twenty-four hours, I'd lost everything that mattered to me. I almost wished I'd get mauled by a bear or struck by lightning, but if I died, Cy would inherit the curse. And there was no way in hell he'd survive it.

I sneezed again. My stomach cramped with the force, and gooseflesh tightened my shoulders and made my arms crawl. It'd be just my luck to catch pneumonia or something on top of everything else. I considered climbing a tree and waiting until dawn to look for a way out, but I couldn't risk staying in one place for that long, and the damned woods wouldn't look any friendlier in the morning. Besides, I'd probably fall asleep, do a header, and break my neck.

I picked a random direction and walked, trying to stay in a straight line. The woods had to end eventually. For the first few minutes I moved the light in a sweep pattern and checked as far as it would reach, hoping for a big puddle so I could try to get myself through a mirror somewhere. But the natural forest floor covering refused puddles in favor of big piles of mush and little patches of muck. Unless I happened to trip over a stream, I was stuck slogging on foot.

Eventually, the misery lodged in my gut gave way to cold panic. The endless unchanging landscape smothered me—tall black trees, somber sentinels determined to imprison me; the clutch and splash of sopping, lumpy mud beneath my plodding feet; the unrelenting stench of wet dirt and decaying leaves. My heart picked up the alarm and pounded light and fast. My pulse fluttered in my throat.

I stopped thinking. And ran.

Dark, rain-slicked shapes blurred past. Somehow my feet planted themselves on solid patches of ground. I failed to plow face-first into a single unyielding trunk. Part of me realized I'd dropped the flashlight somewhere, and the rest of me recommended that I not think about that. My vision made adjustments to the darkness. I ran, and my breath pistoned in and out of my lungs, short pants instead of long gasps. I sailed over roots and ducked under branches without seeing them until I'd already made the motions to avoid them.

I wasn't sure how long the reckless sprint lasted, but my pace slowed when my calf muscles started to burn. I reined myself in and targeted a tree to rest against. When I jogged over and threw an arm up to catch my breath, my hand encountered something cold and smooth where I expected rough bark.

It was a pay-phone booth.

I went invisible before my brain could sort things out.

Not far ahead, dim light shone from a few windows of the monastery. Three shadowed figures stood in a loose cluster in the yard. The orange flash of a cigarette illuminated one of them briefly and cast a glow around the rest. They weren't monks, unless someone had changed the dress code to denim and guns.

While I stood there weighing my extremely limited options, a muffled and prolonged scream rolled from the shadow of the building and made a decision for me. I drew my piece and sprinted for the bastards.

They weren't taking Ian without a fight.

I brought one of them down before I crossed the wall.

The Sig handled beautifully. I issued a silent thanks to Jazz for giving me her best weapon, and drew a bead on the next one. The few seconds they engaged in looking around for the source of the shot were enough for me to fire again. One of them flew back and hit the ground.

The last one vanished.

I went still, determined to hear him first. It was hard to listen over the blood pounding in my ears, the sick adrenaline rush of the kills. I made myself concentrate and finally heard footsteps on wet grass.

They were moving away from me. Toward the monastery.

I vaulted over the wall. When I touched down, the sounds ahead stopped. He was probably looking for me. I crouched low in case he decided to try for a random shot, and stared in the direction I thought he'd gone. A thread of pungent odor invaded my nostrils—sharp and sour, distinctly human. I could smell his fear.

And I could follow it. Right to the flattened patches of grass beneath his unseen feet.

I hammered out four shots in rapid succession. He flickered into view with the second, dropped on the third. I froze again and waited for activity from the building, expecting reinforcements to rush out and throw spells at me until I exploded.

Nothing happened.

The silence unnerved me. There had to be more of them. The scream I'd heard was pure pain, definitely not self-inflicted. So why weren't they responding to the gunfire?

I stayed low and took a few hesitant steps toward the place. Still nothing. Keeping the gun ready, I moved closer and tried to scope things out. A slight movement to the left of the back-door alcove drew my attention. I stopped again, waited.

A dark shape exploded from the shadows, straight up to the roof. A cloaked and hooded figure in white, possibly the one I'd glimpsed behind Calvin in the mirror. Or maybe Calvin himself. The figure hovered for an instant, facing me, then turned and flew like a dart into the night.

I approached the spot he'd left. A shallow moan drifted up from the ground, and I searched my pockets until I found the spare flashlight. Whatever they'd done, I had to see it to help. And I'd have to hope there weren't any more of them waiting in the wings. I switched the light on, and the beam found a crumpled heap lying on the ground along the wall of the monastery.

But it wasn't Ian. It was Calvin.

He'd put on the black robe again. Bruises and cuts marked his ashen features, and his left arm flopped at a disturbing angle. The front of his muddied robe was torn open, revealing a bloody gash crusted with dirt.

I had to wonder why his mystery pal had gone after him like this, though his condition failed to generate sympathy. I wanted to plug him a few times myself. I couldn't destroy him, and I wasn't ready to get into the torture racket—but maybe I could scare some information from him, and then leave him crippled enough for me to escape.

I knelt and pressed the muzzle against his throat. "You won't die, but it'll be really fucking painful," I said. "And if I hear one word that isn't English, I pull the trigger."

He stirred, but made no effort to get up or look at me. "I won't help you." A cracked whisper, barely audible. "You had no right . . . to kill them."

"And you had the right to kill Akila?"

Calvin flinched. After a long moment, he turned his head and looked at me. "Donatti."

"Yeah. Surprise."

"So it's true. They destroyed the princess." He closed his eyes again. "I thought you were one of the . . . other scions. They killed my brothers too. Shot them like dogs."

"You can drop the bullshit monk routine." I pushed harder with the gun. "Where's Ian? Did he come here?"

Calvin shook his head. "Please. My brothers. If you just look, you'll see them . . ."

"I said drop it!" Christ, he sounded convincing. I could almost believe there were piles of dead monks inside somewhere. The ones we'd seen before were probably descendants, too. Window dressing for whatever it was he did up here. "I know you're working with them. I saw you, when you sent those assholes to kill me."

"I sent no one."

I came real close to firing. Only stopped because he wouldn't be able to talk anymore. "Do you think I'm stupid? Changing your clothes doesn't change your face. I'm a criminal, remember? I've seen through better disguises."

He shivered. "I can explain . . ."

"I don't wanna hear it." I set the flashlight down and freed one of my blades from an ankle holster. "What I want to hear is what the fuck's going on. I swear to God, I'll—"

Pain ripped through my shoulder without warning and knocked me to the ground. It almost felt like I'd been shot. I scrambled to right myself, tried to aim a shot at Calvin. He hadn't moved or spoken. How the hell was he doing this? Another blast of agony exploded in my thigh. I made myself invisible, hoping he wouldn't be able to target me, and touched fingers to my shoulder. No blood. No injury of any kind.

"Son of a bitch," I said. "I know you can't kill me like this." I lifted the Sig—and a phantom bullet hit between my shoulder blades, knocking me to my hands and knees. I tasted blood that wasn't there. "I'm gonna blow your fucking skull apart," I said through my teeth.

"Wait. Please listen. I'm not . . ."

The rest of his statement escaped me when new pain filled every cell of my body. Everything around me dissolved, like a chalk drawing in the rain, and I was facedown on packed dirt, surrounded by shifting shadows. A bloody, battered shell. One of the shadows kicked me. I felt it connect, tried to move out of the way. But my muscles wouldn't respond.

Then I pushed up without any effort or thought. I wasn't controlling the movements. Slowly, I realized I was wearing a vest. And glowing.

This body wasn't mine. Somehow, I was inside Ian.

Skin crawled and shivered while fur forced itself through pores. Jaw stretched, teeth lengthened. A mindless, crazed fury replaced thought and awareness. Murderous intentions. A lunge into the shadows. Blinding light swallowed the world.

I opened my eyes, and Calvin was kneeling over me. "Ian,"

I gasped. "How . . ."

Searing pain filled my head. It lasted for long seconds, and then at once I returned to normal. My hands were empty. The bastard must've disarmed me during whatever the hell that was. I glared at him. "You might as well get it over with," I said. "If you try to draw things out, I'll get away."

"I'm not going to kill you." Calvin leaned back on his haunches and sighed. "It wasn't me you saw before. It was Vaelyn."

"Who?"

He bowed his head. "Vaelyn," he said in a whisper. "My twin sister."

Chapter 18

I almost wanted to believe him. If it was true, I'd probably live longer.

On the surface, it kind of made sense. Lynus had definitely referred to a Val among them. And something had seemed off when I saw Calvin in white. The face was a little rounder, a little softer. The eyes were intensely murderous. But damn, if that hadn't been him in the mirror, his sister wasn't a twin. She was a clone. And she made one ugly female.

My gun lay on the ground just beyond my hand. Maybe I'd just dropped it—but I wasn't taking any more chances. I grabbed the gun and rolled away from Calvin to stand out of his reach. "Convince me," I said. "Or I'm putting you out of commission."

He stayed put. Didn't even try to look at me. "You know I can't."

"Try."

He sighed. "Among the djinn, twins are always one male and one female, and always identical. Each possesses a slight leaning toward the opposite gender. I am . . . shall we say, less rugged than most males of my clan, with more hair. Vaelyn is stocky and rough voiced for a female. She is my sister." Calvin made a weak gesture and sank farther down. "And she was . . . my mistake. I should never have released her."

"From what? Her tether?"

"Yes." He stared up at me. "I've regretted it for fifty years."

"So she's the reason you don't use magic anymore."

He nodded. "Vaelyn is insane. I'd hoped two thousand years of quiet reflection had served to restore her to sense, but it only made her worse. As you can see, she has no reservations about violence."

"Wait." I glanced back across the yard to the dark heaps that were dead scions. "The guy—er, whatever, in the cloak who flew away when I shot those assholes. That was Vaelyn?"

"It was."

So he was the business she had to take care of here. "Why'd your sister kick your ass?"

"I told you. She's insane." Calvin stood slowly, grimaced, and cradled his lopsided arm. "She can't destroy me, so she had her disgusting half-breeds slaughter my brothers instead."

I decided to ignore the disgusting half-breed comment for now. "Let me guess. That's a twin thing, right? If you die, she dies."

"Yes, but not because we're twins." He flashed an expression that suggested he hadn't meant to say that. "You see, Vaelyn developed a method to transfer tethers. She bound herself to mine in order to prevent me from destroying her."

"Jesus Christ. There's no love lost between you two, is there?"

He gave me a pained look. "Please don't take the Lord's name in vain."

"Holy . . . uh, crud. Sorry." Memories of ruler-wielding nuns zipped through my head, and I thrust my free hand reflexively behind my back. But the Sig stayed pointed at him. "It does seem kinda funny that a guy who says he's a monk, and is opposed to murder, would want to kill his own sister."

"She's dangerous," he said flatly. "Still, I have no wish to destroy her. And even if I wanted to, I couldn't. Djinn can't destroy their own tethers."

"Really." Another little fact Ian must've forgotten to mention. "Well, I—"

Whatever I'd planned to say got swept away under a tide of sudden pain. There was no distinct sensation of gunshots or punctures this time. Only pure, unrelenting agony that drove me to my knees.

Destroy me. Damn you, thief. What are you waiting for?

The pain vanished when Ian's voice in my head stopped. "What the *fuck* is going on?" I blurted out. As if Calvin had a clue. I clenched my jaw and stood, expecting to be knocked down again any second. I almost wanted to fulfill Ian's request and kill him right then for whatever the hell he'd done to me. But I couldn't bring myself to do it. Not yet.

Calvin's brow furrowed. "Are you all right? Have you been injured?"

"No." I scowled at nothing in particular. "I'm hearing Ian's voice. And feeling his pain. I think."

"That's . . . unusual."

"Can't argue there." I rubbed my pounding head and tried to block all the thoughts that demanded attention. My brain didn't have enough circuits to deal with everything at once. "It's probably because of what he did to me on the way out."

"And that would be . . . ?"

"I don't know. It was a spell. Something about binding my small soul to him."

"The *rohii'et*." Calvin lost a few dozen shades of color, took a stumbling step back—and genuflected.

Seeing a Morai make the sign of the cross froze my blood. "I take it that's a bad thing."

"It's evil. He's stolen part of your soul."

"Er. When you say 'stolen,' does that mean I'm not getting it back?"

"Yes. It does." He leaned against the wall of the monastery like his legs couldn't hold him up anymore. "The *rohii'et* lets him tap into your power. He can use you like a battery. And since you're bound to him, his intense feelings are reflected in you—particularly if he's thinking of you at the time." Calvin closed his eyes. "Why would he do such a reprehensible thing?"

The disgust lacing his tone pissed me off. "Maybe because your crazy-ass sister murdered his wife," I said. "This isn't supposed to be permanent. He went out to their compound to kill as many of the bastards as he could, and now he expects me to destroy him so they can't torture him for the next few centuries."

"Compound?"

"Yeah. The bitch has herself an army, in case you couldn't tell from the reinforcements."

"The scions." Calvin straightened a bit, winced. "I take it you killed the three she brought here."

My conscience made a spirited attempt to induce vomiting. "Thanks for reminding me," I said. "Got any idea where they came from? They can't be hers—and they'd better not be yours."

"I had nothing to do with them." His voice cracked, and I suspected he was lying. At least in part. I doubted he'd fathered the bastards, but he knew more than he was letting on. "How many are there?" he said.

"I'm not sure, but I know that wasn't all of them. I think they have women too."

"The djinn were never meant to breed with humans." Calvin's eyes narrowed, and I felt his passive condemnation of me in that stare. "You should honor Gahiji-an's wishes. Destroy him, and walk away. You can't defeat Vaelyn."

"No, I can't." I glared back at him. "But you can."

He didn't say anything for a long time. Finally, he turned away and limped toward the monastery. He froze after a few steps and spoke without looking back.

"Perhaps I could, if she were alone," he said. "But I won't."

I didn't follow him right away. I couldn't. Ian's consciousness dragged me off again, and I found myself locked in his pain-riddled body, chained upright, bleeding from everywhere. Unable to see beyond vague, smudged shapes that may or may not have been moving. What I felt from him was more than physical. The anguish of his soul exceeded the torture a thousand times over.

Destroy me. Please. For the love of the gods . . . release me.

A raw sob lodged in my throat. I couldn't tell if it came from him, or me. Blurred patchwork vision shifted up a few inches—Ian lifting his head. A cloaked and hooded silhouette stood before him. Fire consumed his blood.

His scream drove nails into my heart.

Silence. Another figure stepped from behind the first. The hooded one raised an arm, and the new arrival mimicked the movement with a long, curved blade clutched in a hand.

No! Taregan . . .

For an instant I caught a clear glimpse of the face behind the knife. Tory, bloodied and bruised, stricken with horror as his arm betrayed him and plunged the blade into Ian.

I crashed back to my own awareness, sprawled on the grass beside the monastery. He must've stopped thinking about me. Probably wasn't thinking anything right now. Echoes of pain lingered in my gut where he'd been stabbed. Hot tears bathed my face.

I couldn't let him suffer anymore. I had to honor his wishes.

If I did it fast, maybe I wouldn't have time to talk myself out of it. I pushed up to my knees and extracted Ian's tether. My hands shook when I drew the blade, and I almost dropped it. *Oh God. I can't do this.* My body moved without input from my brain, slicing the keen edge of the dagger across my palm. Blood pulsed and drizzled on metal.

Crimson-tinged light blazed along the surface of the blade where my blood coated it, forming familiar symbols. Djinn writing.

That wasn't supposed to happen.

Only Ian's blood should've had this reaction. I'd seen it when the Morai leader tested Ian—we'd made decoys to try and keep him alive, but things hadn't exactly gone according to plan. This was a blood tell. The glowing symbols insisted this was my tether. Which was impossible.

I spoke the spell anyway. The dagger failed to burst into flames.

There was no way I could summon the nerve to try again. I wiped the blade clean on the grass, replaced it, and headed in search of Calvin. The back door stood open. I walked in and immediately discovered proof that he'd at least told the truth about his brothers.

Two bodies in brown robes lay faceup on the floor in the hallway. Each of them had been shot once in the head, at point-blank range. Their contorted, frozen stares were almost a mercy to look at compared to the exit wounds that were thankfully not visible. These descendants really were monsters. There had to be a special fiery lake in hell reserved for people who slaughtered monks.

I edged around the carnage and made my way to Calvin's study. He was there, searching his shelves of scrolls for something. "I told you I'm not going to help you," he said without looking at me. "Just leave. Or shoot me and then leave, if it makes you feel better."

"I can't destroy Ian," I said.

Calvin shook his head. "I know he's your ... friend." He lifted his good arm, moved a few scrolls aside, and frowned into the space. "Honestly, though, he'll be better off if you do. You can't save him, and they will torture him for a very long time. He's Gahiji-an the Slayer. He's killed their kin without remorse."

"You don't get it." I moved farther into the room. "I literally can't. I tried."

His gaze swung in my direction. "What?"

"You said djinn can't destroy their own tethers, right?"

"Yes."

"Well, the damned thing's acting like it's mine. I started the spell, got my blood all over it, and it lit up with djinn writing like it does with Ian's blood."

"Of course," he breathed. An expression of wonder spread on his face. "You're his scion."

"Uh ... yeah. So?"

"The *rohii'et.* It must work both ways with you." He went back to shuffling scrolls, faster this time. "Not a theft, but a true bond. A sharing of souls. Have you noticed anything different—abilities you didn't have before the spell?"

"I guess," I said slowly. "I can hear better, smell better, see in the dark. Like a wolf. I never could pull that off before, but Ian can."

"Yes. Don't you see? As he can draw from you, so you can from him. Ah, here it is." He pulled a tightly wound parchment from a shelf. "I have theories about scions, but of course I've never been able to test them."

"Wait a minute. I thought you hated the idea of half-breeds."

"I wasn't always opposed." His good humor faded visibly. "One tends to change one's views after two thousand years of observation."

"Oh. Right." I glanced around the room, suddenly uneasy. Something felt wrong in here. "So, does that mean I have a tether now?"

"It would seem that way. But I can't be sure. Your situation is unique." He worked one-handed at the leather tie around the scroll. "I don't suppose you'd let me see it."

"Hell no."

"Well, I had to ask."

I made a vague noise and moved toward the window, still searching for the source of the wrongness. Maybe they'd sent more goons out. "You know, you should really consider healing yourself," I said. "You're going to be permanently crippled or something."

"I won't use my power."

"You're an asshole."

He raised an eyebrow. "Excuse me?"

"How can you stand by and watch your sister murder innocent people?" I wanted to shake him, or maybe tear his throat out with my teeth. That was a new urge. "I'm sure this isn't the first time she's done it. Did you even try to save your so-called brothers?"

"I . . ." His face crumpled. "I couldn't. Vaelyn held me back."

"Uh-huh. And if you'd done something about her years ago, maybe it never would've come to this."

"You have no right to judge me." For a minute Calvin took on the qualities I'd come to expect from the Morai—vicious, seething hatred; a barely restrained animal gleam in his eyes. "You're *his* apprentice. The innocents you killed didn't even have the chance to defend themselves. I won't be condemned by the likes of you, thief."

Something inside me cracked. Only Ian called me thief, and he'd earned the right. I grabbed the front of his robe and yanked him toward me. "My name is Donatti. And I learn from my mistakes. Are you gonna do that, or just keep hiding in your little sanctuary behind your man-of-the-cloth act like a sniveling coward? Because if you are, then your brothers died for nothing."

His fury deepened, and I realized I was holding a two-thousand-year-old djinn by the scruff like a misbehaving dog. Not the most brilliant idea. Before I could say *Sorry, my bad,* his anger switched to astonishment. "Have your eyes always looked like that?"

"Like what?"

"Well, they're . . . not exactly human anymore."

"Huh?" I let go of him, and my hand moved automatically toward my face, as if I could see with my fingertips. "They were human last I checked. What's wrong with them?"

"Go and look." He gestured at the other end of the room, where the mirror still hung on the wall.

I turned slowly and approached with caution. My uneasy feeling grew the closer I got to the mirror. From a few feet away, I could tell something was different. My eyes had always been blue, deep blue, like new denim. But now they were pale and wintry, and the irises took up a hell of a lot more eyeball. Add the pinpoint pupils and black rings lining the lids, and it looked like I'd gotten an eye transplant from a Siberian husky.

Terrific. I had permanent guyliner. Jazz was going to love this.

I pushed away the pain of thinking about her and stared at my alien reflection. Just another side effect Ian hadn't foreseen. "Oh, man," I groaned. "This is some weird shit. Do you think it's—"

Something moved in the mirror. A silhouette-shaped distortion rippled the image, then settled. That was probably a bad thing. I backed away and grabbed for my gun. "Calvin," I said. "Any idea why your mirror doesn't work for bridging anymore?"

"What do you mean, it doesn't work?"

I kept watching it. "We tried to come through here first, but it was blocked or something. I think your sister might be fucking with it."

"How clever of you, Gavyn Donatti."

The voice came from the mirror. The reflection vanished, and Vaelyn took its place.

Chapter 19

I wasn't waiting for an insurgence this time. I shot the glass with zero hesitation.

Unfortunately, the bullet bounced off the surface like I'd fired a cotton ball.

Vaelyn grinned. "Now, child. There's no need for that," she said—and it was Calvin's voice, Calvin's inflections that emerged from her mouth. I had to glance back to make sure he was still standing behind me. If I had any lingering doubts about the twin-sister bit, they were crushed now. "We aren't going to kill you yet," Vaelyn said. "You are no threat . . . weak, diluted, tenth-generation scion of Doma that you are."

"Yeah? Well, this Doma just took out three of your wonder boys."

"Yes. We know. All the more reason for prudence and patience on our part." Her smile stretched farther, baring an impossible number of teeth. "Khalyn won't turn on us, Gavyn Donatti. He can't. You're wasting your breath, when you should be saving it to run."

"Blast you, Vaelyn!" Calvin took a menacing step forward, despite the quaver in his voice. "How long have you been spying on me?"

"Your bluster is amusing, brother." The grin fell away, suggesting that she was decidedly not amused. "You will give us what we want. You will perform the *ba'isis* for me."

"I won't."

No translation came to me for that word, but I doubted it was a spell for world peace or eternal sunshine and rainbows.

"Time grows short. We will not be patient much longer." Vaelyn sneered and raised a hand. "Think there is nothing left we can take from you, brother?"

"It doesn't matter. I won't help you."

She cut her gaze to me, and the lunatic grin resurfaced. "Run, Gavyn Donatti," she whispered. "Run and hide, little mongoose. We will enjoy the chase."

My mouth disengaged from my brain. "Make me, bitch."

"Very well."

Her lips moved, and the mirror shivered like a lake in the wind. She reached forward. Her hand broke the surface and extended into the room.

So I put a bullet through it.

Vaelyn showed no sign of pain. She didn't even flinch. Her smile stayed put. "*Ela na'ar,*" she said, and withdrew. I knew that one. *Fire.*

Behind me, Calvin screamed.

I whirled to find him engulfed in flames—real ones, not the psychological burn of a flame curse. And I didn't know any putting-out-fire spells. "Shit! Now'd be a good time to start using your magic," I yelled. "Stop, drop, and roll, damn it. Do something!"

He gibbered a few words between screams. They weren't English, or djinn, and they didn't change anything. He just stood there burning.

"Fuck, fuck, *fuck.*" I scanned the room looking for

something wet. Fat chance. I had a better shot at finding a stripper in his closet. My gaze landed on the heavy velvet drapes at the window. I grabbed them and yanked hard. The curtain rod detached along with them, pulling a few chunks of plaster from the wall.

I tossed the drapes over the burning djinn. When he was covered, I wrapped both arms around him and dumped him on the floor. The heat seared my skin, practically melted my chest and arms. Trying to ignore the pain, I beat at the fabric with my palms until smoke squirted from the folds. I rolled him twice, gave him a few more whacks just in case, and pulled the drapes off.

At least he wasn't on fire anymore.

The sight of him did unpleasant things to my stomach. So did the stench. I crouched next to him, hesitant to touch any part of his charred, smoldering body. "Hey. Calvin. If you're conscious, you should try and get up. We've got to get out of here, before—"

Too late. I could feel the heat at my back, hear the ravenous crackle of flames. All those books and scrolls made great kindling. I glanced over my shoulder. The fire already licked at the ceiling, and it was spreading fast.

No sign of awareness from Calvin. I'd have to carry him out. Lucky me.

I slid one arm under his knees, the other under his back, and tried to lift him. Only managed a few inches before I dropped him. He was damned heavy, and the crinkle-slick feel of his ruined skin didn't help. Jaw clenched, I heaved him into a sitting position and managed to sling him over me in a fireman's carry.

It took forever to get on my feet. With Calvin across my shoulders like a freakish stole, I traced the path back out of the monastery and started across the yard. I wasn't sure how far away we should get from the place. Maybe the South Pole.

But I wouldn't be able to carry him too much longer, so I settled temporarily for the phone booth tree.

There, I set him down as gently as possible and propped him against the trunk. He groaned. I hoped that meant he was conscious. "Calvin," I said. "You've got to heal yourself. We aren't safe here. We've got to move, soon."

His lips parted slightly. "Can't," he whispered.

"Why not? You haven't used magic for fifty years. You should have enough juice to make a whole new planet or something."

"Please . . . help."

"Damn it, I can't heal you. I'm mostly human. I don't have enough power for that. You have to transform, remember?"

He drew a rattling breath. "Blood," he gasped.

"Shit." I really didn't want to do that, but there were no other options. I knelt and fished out a switchblade. Since I'd already sliced my palm earlier, I reopened the cut and held it to his lips with a wave of disgust. Blood drizzled into his mouth, a demented communion.

When the flow stopped, I pulled back and hoped it was enough. A faint glow outlined him and grew stronger. His body shifted, constricted, bowed forward with looping and fluid grace until his head touched the ground. He vanished into the light. Finally, the biggest goddamned snake I'd ever seen lay coiled at my feet.

My brain chose that moment to remind me that a djinn in animal form could kill humans. I decided against climbing the nearest tree or running like hell, but my hand went to the butt of the Sig and stayed there.

After a minute, he changed back into sitting, exhausted Calvin. He studiously avoided looking at me. "You could have left me in there," he said.

"Maybe. But it would've cost me a billion Hail Marys,

and I haven't said those since grade school." I frowned. "Why couldn't you heal yourself? I mean, you didn't do anything magical in there. You should've had plenty of power."

"I'm not as strong as you believe. There are . . . complications."

"Whatever." I held a hand out to him. "Come on. I don't know how far that fire's going to spread. We should really go somewhere else."

"Why did you do that?"

I sighed. "Look, let's save the incredulous chitchat for when we're not close enough to roast marshmallows, okay?"

"It won't burn farther than the monastery." He took my hand anyway, and levered himself up. "But you're right. We should get away from here. Vaelyn may still be watching."

"Terrific." I glanced around at the impassable, directionless forest. "Which way do we go, Columbus?"

"Follow me." He started off in a direction I was pretty sure led up the mountain.

I fell into step with reluctance. One way or another, I'd have to try and get to Ian soon. I couldn't destroy him—didn't want to anyway, damn it—and I couldn't take many more unexpected voyages into his personal hell. Unfortunately, I suspected things were about to get worse. I was hanging around with a Morai, and I had no desire to kill him. Hello, bad luck.

"All right," I said. "I'm almost afraid to ask . . . but what's a ba'isis?"

He took his time answering. "It's a fertility spell," he said slowly. "Vaelyn is coming into her reproductive cycle, but she's unable to conceive in this realm because of the tether bond."

I nodded. Ian had more or less explained that. Part of the spell that bound them to their tethers screwed with their blood, exactly so they couldn't do what Ian had done. Breed with humans. But Akila had been able to break it for him because tether spells were a Bahari thing. "So she's going to get one of her studs to impregnate her," I said.

Calvin shook his head. "She wants a child of her own. But she doesn't want a scion."

My head pounded sickly, and I connected the rest of the dots before he continued.

"Gahiji-an is already fertile. She intends to force him to breed with her."

It took me a few minutes to react to the news. I couldn't imagine how she'd possibly get Ian to screw her. Then I decided that I didn't want to know. But I had to wonder how she knew about this fertility spell—and why she needed Calvin to do it, instead of just doing it herself.

I suspected he'd used his magic at least once more after he released Vaelyn.

"So, about those Morai scions," I said.

His back stiffened while he walked. A good sign he was about to lie. "What about them?"

"Who's their father?"

"I don't know."

"Wrong answer." He was moving pretty fast for a guy who'd been on fire twenty minutes ago, but I didn't have any trouble keeping up with him. "You wanna try again?"

"A Morai, apparently."

"Don't bullshit me, Brother Calvin. You know a hell of a lot more than you're saying."

He stopped midstep. After a few seconds, his shoulders slumped. "Maybe we should rest for a few minutes, and have that chat you mentioned."

"Good idea."

"Here. We'll have a seat." He made his way to a fallen

log, brushed a few pine needles from the surface, and settled on it.

I hung back. "What are the chances of bugs crawling on my ass if I sit there?"

"Slim to fair."

"I'll stand."

"Suit yourself." Calvin let out a breath and absently fingered the wooden crucifix around his neck. "It was an experiment," he said at last. "When I first released Vaelyn, she seemed . . . sane. Grateful. And she was curious about my work, about my discoveries regarding djinn magic in the human realm."

"And her being your sister, you weren't suspicious."

"Yes. I believed she'd found some balance." He blinked slowly. "I had long ago accepted the fact that I'd never return to our realm, and worked to carve out my place here. Vaelyn told me that she wanted the same thing—only her vision of staying in the human realm included a family. More than that, a community, separate from humans but at peace with this realm." A quick sigh escaped him. "It seemed like a good idea at the time."

"Yeah. Road to hell, right?"

"Excuse me?"

"Never mind," I said. "So you were trying to give your sister a community. Does that mean they're your scions?"

He shook his head. "I'll get to that. In the first few years, she would disappear for weeks at a time. Exploring the new world, she said. Each time she returned a little more confident, and just a bit . . . harder. Hungry, and anxious. I didn't want to see the decline. Finally, after a two-month absence, she came back with a companion. Another Morai. She said she'd found him in London, living as a museum curator."

"Who was it?"

"His name was Barzan. I had never met him before, but Vaelyn claimed he sought peace among humans, as we did." Calvin frowned. "Once she'd found him, she pressed me relentlessly to attempt the fertility spell with him. One child, she told me. She wanted them to raise a child, her and Barzan. She'd made arrangements for a human surrogate. A young woman, she said, living in poverty, whom she intended to pay enough money to start a new life."

"How noble of her," I muttered.

He hesitated for a minute. "I wanted to believe her," he said. "Allowing her this gift, this opportunity to become a mother of sorts—I hoped it would smooth the rough edges I saw resurfacing in her. And so, I relented. I performed the *ba'isis*. Since the binding spell that creates our dormancy in this realm is one of air, I was only able to undo it temporarily. Three days," he whispered. "Seventy-two hours. Plenty of time to impregnate one woman. Or dozens."

I shivered. Ian had done the same thing a century or so back, when Akila undid his fertility bind permanently. But he'd done it to stay alive, to keep the Dehbei-powered barrier between realms running and make sure the Morai stayed trapped. I suspected Val and Barzan had slightly different motivations.

"Vaelyn had already built her community. Her compound, as you called it. She'd recruited young, fertile human women with the promise of wealth and power. She had formed a cult. And Barzan seeded them all."

I decided I should sit down after all. "So now those two are running the army down there," I said. "What do they really want? Besides Ian and Akila, I mean."

"I don't know. But Barzan isn't with her anymore."

"You sure about that?"

He nodded. "Shortly after the *ba'isis* expired, he went mad. I'm not certain whether it was a side effect of the spell, or Vaelyn, that drove him insane. She may well have, just to get rid of him—since it was obvious she wanted complete control. After the scions were born, she had their mothers slaughtered. She recruited human males to do it." He closed his eyes, crossed himself. "Barzan fled into the mountains. Lived in caves, sealed himself away from all contact. Until . . ."

"I destroyed him," I said through numb lips.

"Yes. Quite a feat, considering how powerful he must have been."

"He was powerful?"

He looked at me like I'd just asked if water was wet. "Living scions increase a djinn's power in this realm. Surely Gahiji-an told you that much."

"Oh. Right." I frowned at him. "But he really wasn't that strong. I mean, we had a lot more trouble with Lenka, and he didn't have any scions."

"Maybe he wanted to be destroyed," Calvin said.

"Or maybe the guy we found up there wasn't Barzan."

He offered a dry laugh. "How many djinn do you think there are in these mountains?"

"I don't know, but I saw someone with Vaelyn when they attacked my house." *Jazz's house,* a little voice reminded me. I told it to shut the hell up. "A guy in a white hooded cloak, like the one she wears. I'm almost positive it was another djinn."

"It must have been a scion."

"Could a scion keep a single bridge open long enough for five guys to pass through?"

All the color fell out of him. "No."

"I think your sister pulled a fast one on you. There're two of them."

He folded his arms as if he were cold, or in pain, or both. He didn't say anything, but I figured he was thinking the same thing as me.

We were screwed.

Chapter 20

The rain came back like God ordered a second flood.

I stood and sent a few curses skyward. Sheets of water pelted me, and the stinging pain in my chest and arms reminded me that I still needed to heal myself from the burns I'd sustained. If that was even possible. I'd always had Ian or Akila to do it for me.

"We have to get out of this." A violent whole-body sneeze sent me stumbling and punctuated the urgency of escaping the elements. "Any ideas?"

"Not in particular."

Thunder pounded over the tail end of his statement. I blinked some of the rain out of my eyes and tried to look around. There were a lot of trees. A blinding flash of light burst almost directly over us. For half a second I thought about how I'd never seen lightning so close before.

In the next half, I was facedown on the ground, feeling like someone had swung a baseball bat into my back. And then zapped me with five or six Tasers at once.

"Apprentice!"

I barely heard Calvin's shout. My ears felt plugged—or

maybe shattered—and I smelled something burning. Not a single muscle wanted to move.

Jesus Christ. Save a Morai and get struck by lightning. What a fun curse this was.

Calvin rolled me over, and I yelled something incoherent when the motion hammered pins and needles through every inch of my body.

"You're alive," he said.

I glared at him. "Lucky me," I muttered, moving my mouth as little as possible.

"Can you walk?"

"Ugh." I curled and uncurled a hand. It hurt, but at least it responded. Groaning, I boosted myself up on my elbows and managed to sit. "Not much choice there," I said. "Unless you're gonna carry me." I stared at my feet. Something wasn't right there. Finally, my spinning head put it together—the toe of my left boot had blown out, and shreds of charred sock poked through.

I never knew lightning left exit wounds.

Calvin held out a hand. I sighed, took it, and let him help me on my feet. "There're a few caves not far from here," he said. "Come on."

I limped after him up a slight incline and into a crumbling slit, curtained by tree roots, in the mountain. By the time we pushed inside, most of the buzzing sensation had dissipated and I merely ached everywhere.

The cave was completely closed in. Even with the changes in my vision, I could only see about six inches of lighter blackness in front of me. And I'd left the spare flashlight on the ground at the monastery. "Got a light?" I said.

A ball of blue flame blossomed in Calvin's hand. He stared at me, half smirking. "I must say, I've never known anyone who was struck by lighting before. Does God not like you?"

"Not especially," I mumbled, barely registering his words. I was busy gaping at the cave walls.

Someone had had a lot of time on his hands. I was guessing Barzan. Djinn writing covered the walls, marked in heavy charcoal black and a dark, inky substance that used to be blood. I couldn't read it, but it still creeped me out. I doubted he'd been recording his mother's recipes for mouse pie, or whatever the Morai liked to eat back home.

Calvin followed my gaze. When he noticed, his mouth opened wide enough to drive a train through. "I knew he was mad," he said. "But I'd never suspected how much."

"So what's it say? Besides 'Beware the deceiver.'"

He gaped at me. "How did you know?"

"We found a little of this when we . . . uh, set Barzan free. But it was mostly smudged out."

"I see." His lips thinned for an instant. "Most are protection spells. Wards and seals. But it does say 'Beware the deceiver' several times. And there's something else. Here." He carried the floating flame ball closer to a wall and ran a finger across a series of symbols that repeated itself several times. "'He of two worlds will destroy all.'"

"That's it?"

Calvin nodded.

I threw my hands up. "Great. Let's play 'Which descendant does the crazy guy mean?' It could be any of them. Some warning. Doesn't any of this stuff say anything . . ." I blinked. He was looking at me like I'd just confessed to being Jack the Ripper. "What?"

"Perhaps he doesn't mean the Morai scions," he said. "There's only one of you."

"Oh, come on! Do I look dangerous to you? Besides, I never even met this guy until—"

He raised an eyebrow.

"Okay. You got me there. But like I said, I'd never seen this guy before, so he couldn't have meant me."

Calvin looked less than convinced. He whispered something and moved his hand away from the flaming ball. It stayed hovering in the air. "You should heal yourself," he said. "Those burns look painful."

"Yeah, well, I can't exactly transform. But I'll try the healing thing, I guess."

"Try?"

I shrugged. "I'm not very precise with healing. When I have to do it, I pretty much run on instinct. It usually works. I've just . . . never done it on myself."

"I see." He folded his arms. "Didn't Gahiji-an teach you how to focus a healing spell?"

"I didn't think you could do that. Ian doesn't seem to know how, anyway."

"But you can still use healing magic? Interesting."

I wasn't sure I liked this conversational direction. "What's interesting?"

"Nothing, really. A stray thought." He closed his eyes for a moment. "If you like, I'll explain healing focus. There's too much to cover at once, but I'll give you the basics."

I still wanted to know what was interesting, but I'd let it pass for now. If this guy was anything like Ian, he'd tell me when he was damned good and ready. "Go for it," I said.

He nodded. "The body contains energy points. Each is associated with different aspects of life, health, and soul. The strongest of these points are located at the base of the spine and the throat. It helps to know which point controls the area you're trying to heal, but in general these two are sufficient. Understand so far?"

"Yes. Wait . . . no."

"All right," he sighed. "By way of an example, your burns. Skin and muscle are linked to the throat base point. So you would focus the healing spell on that point and draw it down through the body to the damaged area. Like threading a needle."

"I think I get it." Maybe not exactly everything, but I figured it'd be clearer when I actually tried it. "Okay. Here goes."

I held a hand out flat just above my throat, just like Ian usually did. It might've been instinctual for him—but maybe he knew more about healing than he'd bothered to tell me. That wouldn't be much of a shocker.

My own magic came easily enough, and with the expected pain. I looked down and tried to visualize directing what I had there. *Heal.* I blinked once. A brief afterimage showed a bright spot right at my breastbone, so I closed my eyes to see if it would help.

The energy point glowed like a beacon behind my eyelids, a warm and pulsating red. Part of me wondered why I could see so much better without actually looking, while the rest carried on channeling the spell through the red light. The usual searing pain that accompanied all my attempts at magic lessened and left my thoughts clear. I had no trouble drawing the spell through myself, guiding it through my chest and arms. I could feel skin coming together and knitting itself whole.

I pulled back and opened my eyes. "Holy hell."

Calvin stared at me. "Holy hell, indeed," he said. "You learn quickly, Donatti."

"Something like that." I cleared my throat and turned aside. This little exercise brought up a whole new wave of questions.

But before I could ask any of them, I was plunged abruptly back into the Ian Horror Show.

Burning. No flames, no smoke, but his body was burning all the same. There were too many broken bones to count. The wisp of consciousness Ian had left repeated two words in an uneven stream: *Kill me kill me killmekillmekillme kill. me. Killme.*

A cold shock doused the fire and awakened new pain— saltwater on open wounds. Swollen eyelids pried apart to reveal a blurred sliver, a glimpse of a hood. Cracked and bleeding lips parted in a snarl.

"Rayan." Calvin's voice, mocking and cruel. "We have a task for you."

"Khalyn . . . fool." Raw sound, barely forming words. "I will do nothing. For you."

Vaelyn laughed and didn't correct the mistaken identity. Of course she wouldn't. This hurt him more. "It is a small matter. We desire a child of royal blood, and you will impregnate one of our choosing. In two days' time you will begin."

"Will not touch . . . Morai whore."

"Your reward will be your destruction."

I felt him consider it, beg for it in silence. *Please destroy me. Please.* "You cannot."

Another laugh. "We know who holds your tether. It will be delivered to us when he comes for you. And he will come."

No. Donatti . . . A shudder wracked him.

"When the time arrives, you will give. Or we will take, and take, and take for all eternity, and you will live in agony while your seed burns this realm into oblivion."

White-hot pain exploded in his wrists and ankles, his head. His screams drove me out.

I opened my eyes with a gasp. Cold stone floor beneath me. Calvin hovering above me, his face pinched with concern. "I can hear them," I said. "And I don't think they know."

The storm outside the cave slacked off while the one inside raged on.

"I won't help you," Calvin said again. "You pulled me from the fire, and I thank you for that, but I would have survived. And you're still his apprentice. Still a murdering thief." He paused for a breath. "As for Gahiji-an, I believe you humans have stated my feelings for him best. I wouldn't spit on him if he were on fire."

"He is on fire, you son of a bitch." My hands clenched and unclenched, longing to crack his jaw. I considered putting a bullet in him for shits and giggles. Hell, like he said, he'd survive. "Your freak show of a sister likes her flame curses. All you Morai do."

"All Morai are not the same!"

"I thought that for a few minutes. But you're changing my mind."

He whirled on me. "All right, apprentice. Let's play your master's game." A cold smile settled on his face. "Give me a reason. Why should I help you?"

"Because—" Damn. I couldn't think of one. Technically, he didn't owe me anything except half a pint of blood, and I didn't want that back. He didn't know me, didn't know Ian or Tory, and apparently didn't care what his sister did as long as she left him out of it. I shuffled back through the last few torturous days and seized on the one thing he'd seemed interested in. "Your scion theories," I said. "Whatever they are. You can test them."

"With you?" He managed to make *you* sound like *the most disgusting creature to have plagued the earth since Attila the Hun.*

"Yeah, with me. I don't see any other scions volunteering for the job."

It took him a minute to reply. "Tempting, but no."

"Why not?"

"Many reasons. Not the least of which is the trifling matter of your tendency to kill any Morai you come across."

"I haven't killed you. Yet."

"And there you go proving my point."

I stifled a breath that would've been a scream. "Fine." I'd have to try the subtle approach. Unfortunately, I possessed all the subtlety of a goon with a pipe wrench. "Can you at least tell me about your theories?"

He shrugged and looked away, but not before I caught the gleam in his eyes.

"Come on, I'm curious. Why is it interesting that I can use healing magic?"

"Because it's not instinctive, except to the Bahari. Transformation is instinct, but that type of healing is basically a side effect of shifting form." His sigh suggested he'd just lost some internal battle. "You're a Dehbei scion. You shouldn't have been able to heal anyone before you learned how it worked—and even once you knew, it should have been harder than it was for you just now."

"So why could I do it before, then?"

"I don't know. However, it does fit with my theory."

"And that'd be?"

He frowned. "I'm not sure I should tell you."

"Why? Do you really think I'm going to learn this big secret and then destroy you or something?"

"Yes."

His soft, drawn tone sent a shock through me. That wasn't sarcasm. He was actually afraid of me. Me, the bumbling idiot who'd been a half step away from getting myself and Ian killed a hundred times in the past year, who could barely squash a spider without an ocean's worth of guilt, who'd probably obliterated half of my own soul because every time my hand was forced and I had to kill or be killed, a piece of me died with my victim.

For the first time, I considered what I must have seemed to him—Ian's partner in slaughter, his willing trainee. The mad prince's lackey. The Slayer's apprentice. Nausea knotted my gut, and I drew a deep breath to try and ease it. "Look, man," I said. "I'm not going to hurt you. I hate destroying anyone, human or djinn. I never wanted any of this. But with your clan trying to kill me and Ian every time I turn around, and the whole *ham'tari* thing, it's been hard to get around."

His eyes widened a bit. "What *ham'tari* . . . thing?"

"You don't know?" I held back a minute, not sure why I'd thought it was common knowledge to the djinn. But it made sense that it wasn't. Obviously, it was a dirty spell, and that bastard Kemosiri wouldn't have bragged about using it. Ian probably didn't want anyone to know either. He'd only told me to make me stop nagging him about destroying Calvin. But if telling him would convince him to help me get Ian the hell out of the compound, I'd risk Ian's eternal bitching and moaning. "I'm not entirely clear on everything," I said slowly. "Basically, Kemosiri—you know who he is, right?"

Calvin made a disgusted sound. Yeah, he knew.

"So Kemosiri laid this curse on Ian's father to force him to wipe out the Morai. His father was killed, and the curse got passed on to Ian. And since I'm his descendant, I get echoes of it. I've had shitty luck all my life. I guess it's because of the *ham'tari*." I looked at my feet, suddenly feeling like I was stuck in a confessional booth with glass walls. "The only time things have gone right for me was after I met Ian, when we started going after your clan together. I'm sorry for what I've done. But if Ian dies, I get the whole curse. And I have a son."

I waited. Calvin didn't say anything. His expression had gone blank.

"Don't you get it?" I said. "Come on. You've seen it yourself. I pulled you from a fire and got struck by lightning. That wasn't God. It was the damned curse."

He frowned. "That was definitely unusual."

"No shit. And besides," I said, "I don't think I could hurt you even if I wanted to. You're two thousand years old. I'm just a watered-down descendant, ten times removed."

"You have more power than you realize."

I snorted. "Yeah. You should see what I can do with a sneaker."

"You don't understand." With a tired gesture, Calvin sat on the nearest rock. "Djinn grow more powerful as we age, but our life spans are a bit longer than yours. And our magic is drawn from the djinn realm. We are limited here, weakened by our tethers and the spells that bind us to them." He looked at me. "I believe the reverse holds for scions."

"I don't get it."

"The power still builds with time," he said. "But because human lives are shorter, it builds along the line of descent, rather than the individual. Each generation of scion has greater potential power than the last."

I started to laugh that idea off. But then I remembered Cy, and how he could control his invisibility already. At three years old. I didn't recall much of my childhood, but I knew the nuns at the orphanage would've burned me at the stake or something if I'd ever vanished in front of them. "Okay. I might buy that," I said. "But why are your sister's goons so much stronger than me? I mean, they've gotta be first generation, second at best."

"Because magic adapts. The power of the early generations, the first scions who are direct children of a djinn and a human, still comes largely from the source tied to the djinn realm. And those with Vaelyn have been trained to use it by a djinn, one who, regrettably, knows almost as much as I do about how our magic works." A pained expression crossed his face. "But later generations—your generation—are almost entirely dependent on earth magic. The further along you are in the line of descent, the more power you draw from this realm. From the earth itself."

"Uh-huh. You know, most people would disagree that there's any magic on earth. Outside of Disney World and the Bermuda Triangle, that is."

"There is power here. Vast, untapped power. Humans have forgotten how to use it." He flashed a small smile. "When we first came to your realm, magic was embraced. There were human sorcerers then, with talent and skill that rivaled our own."

"Oh, Christ. Sorry," I said. "Ian tried to feed me this line. Merlin and Rasputin and shit. Urban legends."

Calvin's brow lifted. "Most legends begin in fact. Anyway, this handful of black sorcerers, along with the actions of my so-called brothers, served to make humans fear magic. The world turned away from it, and it was forgotten. That's why later-generation scions have trouble accessing their power. For you, wielding djinn magic is difficult. Painful. Am I correct?"

"You could say that."

He nodded. "But learn to use earth magic, to tap into the power your brothers have turned from, and you will equal—or even exceed—the power of a djinn in your realm. You in particular, apprentice."

"Yeah, sure. Pull the other one and we can play 'Jingle Bells.'"

"Don't you see? You're Dehbei. Not only are you a late-generation scion, born to this world untethered and pulling from the magic of your own realm, but your djinn strengths are already earth based. Your potential is . . . well, frankly, it's frightening."

"Wait a minute." I shoved my hands in my pockets, afraid they might start shaking. "Are you saying I actually have a chance against these assholes? That I can get Ian and Tory out of there and survive?"

"You might. With the proper training."

"Then train me."

He closed his eyes. "I don't think I should do that."

"Please. Jesus—I mean jeepers. Whatever. Look, what they're doing to him makes the Spanish Inquisition look like a bunch of Boy Scouts. God . . . er, heaven knows what they're doing to Tory. I can't destroy Ian. I don't *want* to destroy him. Yes, he's a bastard, but he has reasons. You know what they are." I stopped for a breath and wondered briefly what Ian would think if he knew I was begging a Morai for help. Probably something like *I will tear your limbs off, blasted thief.* "They murdered his wife. They're cutting him to ribbons. And your sister's planning to make him father a child with her."

"Yes. Which means she'll continue to hunt me. She needs me to perform the *ba'isis.*"

"Then we avoid them for a few days. You train me, I go in and get them. And your sister leaves you alone."

A deep frown etched his lips. "She'll be expecting you to come for him. She probably wants you to, so she can use you to further command his obedience."

"Yeah, she said as much. But she won't be expecting me to know what I'm doing when I get there. She thinks I'm weak. And she doesn't know I can spy on her." A chill jolted my spine. I didn't exactly enjoy the spying method. Maybe Ian wouldn't think about me over the next few days.

And maybe Vaelyn would call off the whole torture thing and sit Ian down for a nice chat over milk and cookies.

Calvin propped his elbows on his knees and stared at me over steepled fingers, like a principal considering the best punishment for a wayward child. Finally, he said, "Very well, apprentice. I'll teach you what I can. But should I believe you intend to destroy me, I reserve the right to defend myself."

"Thank you."

I refused to think further than the next few days. Get Ian and Tory out. I had to concentrate on that. After they were safe, we could worry about the next problem—which was the tiny matter of Vaelyn, who sure as hell wasn't going to say *Oh, well, back to the drawing board* when she lost her favorite torture victim.

And since they shared a tether, we couldn't destroy her without destroying Calvin too.

Chapter 21

I took my jacket off and folded it. "Are you sure I have to do this?"

"Yes. The fastest way for you to learn your power is to discover the source."

"But do I have to take all my clothes off?"

Calvin smirked. "You can leave your underwear."

"Gee. Thanks." If he was messing with me, it didn't show. Much. I rolled my eyes and kicked free of my shoes, yanked my vest and shirt off, and did the rest before I could lose my nerve. At least I'd put on clean underwear before I left the house and got caught in a downpour. I rubbed at the goose pimples on my arms and hopped from foot to foot. "It's kinda cold in here. Is that fireball of yours hot?"

"Not especially. But if you'd like, I can set your pants on fire."

I glared at him. "All right. What am I supposed to do?"

"Lie down."

"On this rock?"

"Unless you'd prefer lying outside in the mud."

Fantastic choices. Groaning, I lowered myself to the ground

and stretched out flat on my back. Cold stone nipped my flesh and sent prickles through my limbs. "Now what?"

"Close your eyes. Feel the earth."

"What, all of it?"

"Concentrate, apprentice."

I closed my eyes and wondered why none of the djinn could bother calling me by name. Except Tory, and he always got it wrong.

I could feel the earth, all right. It was poking me in the spine, digging against my shoulder blades, caressing the back of my head like a brick wall. Unyielding, unwelcoming, practically pushing me away. Why couldn't we have been hiding in a nice, soft meadow? At least it didn't smell too bad in here. It was dank and musty, the way I guessed most caves smelled, but outside of that I caught the scent of fresh rain, moist dirt, the perfume of a thousand pines dashed through a mountain wind.

Below me, the rock warmed—or my skin grew numb with the cold. I couldn't tell which. I tried to concentrate on that, on the feeling of stone against me, the idea that I was touching the world. And I felt . . . something. A deep-seated buzzing, like an itch that I couldn't quite reach. I strained for it, attempting to break it open, but the sensation hovered just beyond my grasp.

Come on, you bastard. Instinct told me the key was right there, directly at my mental fingertips. All I had to do was touch it, take it into me, and I could use it. But the circuit refused to complete. The buzzing intensified, filled every muscle and vein until I was convinced I'd start flopping around on the cave floor with smoke pouring out of me like a downed power line.

The electric flood ceased abruptly. I opened my eyes. "Ow."

"Nothing?"

"Not exactly nothing." I pushed up and drew my knees to my chest. "Something's there. I just can't touch it."

"Hmm."

"Hmm, what?"

Calvin shook his head. He stood, stretched. "We'll have to try again later. For now, there are a few important spells you should learn right away. Shielding, for one. And paralyzing. And suspension."

"If by suspension you mean flying, forget it. These feet were made to stay on the ground."

"You'll learn it anyway." He pointed past me and gestured. My pile of clothes floated off the ground, drifted toward me, and landed in my lap. "Most spells have more than one use. Get dressed. I'm going to reactivate Barzan's wards. We should stay here as long as possible—the more we venture out, the greater the chance Vaelyn will find us."

After I managed to reel my jaw back in, I redressed quickly and watched Calvin work. He used blood to retrace some of the symbols on the walls, and words that made them glow like the identifying marks on a tether. The light eventually faded and vanished. When he'd done half a dozen of them, he returned to his seat. "All right, apprentice," he said. "We'll start with shields."

Hours later, I decided Brother Calvin had missed his calling. He should've been a drill sergeant, or maybe a prison guard. If he'd been Rocky's trainer, Apollo Creed would've been on the mat in round three.

"I'm tapped," I groaned from my latest flight crash position. Since I hadn't figured out how to get to the earth magic—if it even existed, and after the last three tries I'd started to think Calvin was as crazy as his sister—I had to rely on the old painful and draining method to learn this stuff. "I got nothing left."

"Try again."

I didn't even have enough strength to glare at him. Learning shields hadn't been too bad. They were for deflecting minor spells, and they could keep other djinn from detecting power for a short time. The lockdown spell was harder. I'd managed it, eventually, but the effect lasted less than a minute when I cast it. And flying . . . ugh. I'd get airborne, wobble around for a few seconds, and then drop like a lead balloon.

I struggled to my feet and leaned on the wall for a minute. No point in asking for a break. At the rate we were going, I figured he wouldn't let me stop until I passed out. I closed my eyes and tried to convince myself that flying wasn't so bad. Birds did it. Planes did it. Bats—no. Bad example. I decided to think of it as a really high, really slow jump.

When I opened them again, I was ten feet off the floor and rising.

"Shit!" The minute I opened my mouth, I started losing altitude. Fast. In desperation, I ordered myself to stop before I hit the ground and broke something important. Like my spine.

It worked. Sort of. I slowed and floated down to land with an ungraceful stumble. "Enough," I gasped. "I can't do any more. I'm tired, I'm in pain, and I'm extremely cranky."

For an instant Calvin looked like he'd laugh, but he gave an imperious little nod and said, "Very well. You should rest. You are human, after all." He shifted position, stretched his legs out. "And I need some time to think."

"You do that." I limped over to the wall and sat with my back against it. No way I was going to lie down on that damned rock floor again. I figured I'd just relax for a few minutes, close my eyes, and maybe inventory my pockets. Try to come up with some masterful one-man invasion strategy involving shields, weak-ass lockdown spells, and a three-inch switchblade.

I was asleep before I could fully appreciate the fact that I wasn't flying anymore.

———

I smelled smoke.

My body reacted before my brain and jolted me awake. Flames leaped and crackled in the fire confined in a circle of stones ten feet from me. Between the firelight and the weak rays of sun slanting through the roots that covered the cave entrance, I made out the enormous snake heading for me.

I yanked the Sig from my pocket and took aim. "Don't even think about it," I said. "If you think passing out is an indication that I'm going to destroy you, I'll be happy to get the hell out of this cave and away from you."

The snake hissed. It sounded annoyed. It glowed, coiled in on itself, and became Calvin. "Don't be ridiculous, apprentice. And save your strength. You'll need it for today." He turned and walked toward the fire. "I had to heal myself," he said without turning around. "I broke my arm."

"How'd you manage that?"

"Catching breakfast." He sat on his rock and pointed. There was a spit over the fire, with four fist-size black lumps skewered on it.

"Um. What are those?" *Please say hamburger.*

"Bats."

"Of course they are." I swallowed and scooted closer. "I don't suppose you have anything else on you? Loaves and fishes, maybe some stale communion wafers . . ."

"Don't worry. They taste like chicken."

"Yeah. Cannibals say that about humans too." The aroma of roasting bat wafted over to me. My brain said *Oh, hell no,* but my empty stomach overrode it with a snarl of *Meat!* I was about to eat a flying rodent. This'd be the first item on the list of things I wouldn't share with Jazz when I got out of this. If I got out of this.

If she'd even speak to me when I got out.

Damn, it hurt to think about her. How she'd been at the end—not furious, but finished. She'd had enough of me, and I couldn't blame her. Love wasn't enough to put up with the constant threat to her life and Cy's just because they were with me. I should've left them alone.

I would, when this was over. I'd tell her they were better off without me. Take my djinn and go home. The fact that the only home I'd ever known was with her didn't matter. I could go back to living in cars and hotel rooms for the rest of my life, if it meant Jazz and Cy would be safe.

My pocket buzzed. When I figured out it wasn't the power of the earth failing to work through me, I dug my cell out. The screen was still cracked and flashing, but I caught the incoming number. Jazz. Maybe she'd been reading my mind. "'Scuse me a sec," I muttered in Calvin's direction. I wandered off to a corner of the cave and answered with a neutral, "Hello."

"Donatti, what the fuck is going on?"

She sounded so shaken, I immediately envisioned hordes of Morai scions invading Lark's place, and them hiding in his bunker while the bastards trashed the house. "Are you all right?"

"We're fine. Except for Lark—he's a wreck. He can't get hold of Tory. Where are you guys?"

"Um." My gut churned like a tornado. There was no way to break things gently, but I couldn't make myself spit anything out.

"Um is not a good answer. What happened?"

"Jazz . . ." I sucked in a breath that burned my lungs. "They killed Akila."

Her silence was shattering.

"Jazz?"

Her voice trembled when she finally spoke. "Did you see them do it?"

"We didn't have to." My jaw clenched in memory of the devastation on Ian's face. At least I wouldn't have to explain too much. Jazz knew how djinn marriage bonds worked. "Ian's ring broke. Exploded."

There was a long pause. "But there's another way to break them," she said. "Remember? She was going to do it at Trevor's."

The whole scene with Trevor and Lenka flashed through my head. Akila begging the Morai leader to spare Ian's life in exchange for a bond with her. Lenka, sneering and cold: *You would mutilate yourself for him?* No one had to spell out what that meant. The bond could be broken if her finger was cut off.

Still, it wasn't enough. "She was tethered to her ring," I said as evenly as I could. "If it's been destroyed . . . so has she."

Jazz covered the phone, but not in time to completely hide a wrenching sob. I waited. When she came back on, her voice was hoarse but steady. "You still haven't told me where you guys are. Lark's losing it here."

I couldn't help noticing that she didn't express any concern about me. The observation killed any lingering doubt over the decision to get out of her life. She didn't need me fucking things up. "Ian went crazy when they killed her, and took off for their little nest. You know, the one they lined with lethal hardware. Tory followed him. He said—" I swallowed hard. "He said to tell Lark he'd come back if he could."

"Great. That'll cheer him up." Her attempt at sarcasm fell flat. "What about you?"

Christ. Why did she have to pretend she cared? "I'm in a cave, learning ancient wisdom from a monk."

"Not the Morai."

"Yeah. It's a long story." I closed my eyes and leaned back on the cave wall. "Look, I'm working on getting them out of there. I don't know how long it's going to take. A few days, I hope. Tell Lark I'll do everything I can to make sure Tory gets back to him, okay?"

"Gavyn . . ."

My breath caught. "What?"

Seconds ticked by. "Never mind," she whispered. And hung up.

I replaced the phone and made my way back to the fire. Calvin didn't ask about the conversation. I would've been grateful if I could have felt anything at that point. He handed me a flat stone, vaguely plate shaped, with two blackened lumps on it. "Soup's on."

"Yummy." I took it and sat cross-legged on the floor. Despite the loud demands of my stomach, I wasn't quite ravenous enough to dive right into crunchy bat nuggets. Maybe it tasted like chicken, but it sure as hell didn't look appetizing. It might be better if I didn't look at what I was eating.

Or if I used a little magic to boost the appeal.

I closed my eyes and thought hard about chicken. The colonel's best, extra-crispy all-white breast meat. I held a hand out and passed it over the bat carcasses a few times. A slight twinge in my chest said it was working. When I looked down again, I had two golden brown hunks of fried chicken on my plate. Much better. I grabbed one, already drooling.

"What did you do?"

Calvin looked as stunned as he sounded. I shrugged. "Ian told me that magic doesn't change what something is, just your perception of it. Bats are edible—I guess—but I'd rather it looked and smelled like chicken too instead of just tasting like it."

His shock morphed to a smile. "An excellent idea. Maybe there's hope for you." He held his plate toward me. "Would you mind? I'd prefer fish, if possible."

"It's easy. I think you can handle it."

"I will not—"

"Use your powers. Yeah, I know." I had a feeling he was going to end up breaking that particular vow soon, like it or not. Since I only knew one kind of fish, batter dipped and fried, I concentrated on it and made the transformation. "There you go. Consider it payment for services rendered."

"Thank you." Calvin drew his plate back with obvious approval. "I have water for us too. Perhaps you could turn it into wine."

"Make mine a beer, and I'm in."

Grinning, I dug into my Kentucky Fried Bat.

Chapter 22

Another round of lying on rocks brought me no closer to becoming one with the earth.

Calvin made a weary gesture, signaling me to stop, and scrubbed a hand down his face. "Perhaps it's been too long," he said. "For you, or for this realm. I can feel the reluctance of the magic. It doesn't want to be used, possibly because of the black sorcerers, or even the djinn."

"Terrific. So I'm trying to crack the whole damned planet's defense system?" I sat up and brushed rock dust off my back. "I'm a good thief, but not that good."

"Yes. Well." He stood and paced a few steps. "If you're unable to draw on your magic, maybe you should consider calling off your mission. It'll be suicide."

"What's your problem?"

He blinked. "Excuse me?"

"How can you keep telling me to forget about them?" I yanked my clothes back on and held in a scream. "Haven't you ever cared about anyone? I can't walk away from this."

"You should. Vaelyn will destroy all of you."

"Jesus Christ. Yes, I swore. Sue me." I finally understood

why Ian and Tory both hated cowards. "What about Mercy?"

He gave me that castrating look. "What about her?"

"If they had Mercy, would you walk away, let them do whatever they wanted with her?"

"Mercy has nothing to do with this," he said. "She's not involved with the djinn, at all. I've made sure of it."

"Yeah," I said. "Except for you."

"I would never—"

"Come on, Calvin. Stop thinking like a monk for a minute." If he really didn't get it, I'd have to make him understand. "I can't possibly know more about your clan than you do. Get offended if you want to, but you know damned well the Morai aren't above using people you care about to get to you. And you do care about her, don't you?"

He flushed brick red. The color drained fast and left him pale. "More than life itself," he said. "She's so . . . well, you've met her." He smiled a little. "She told me about that, you know. You and your ridiculous campfire story."

"So I'm a terrible liar." I grinned. "Mercy's something else. You're a lucky guy to have her."

"I don't exactly have her." He stared at the ground. "As far as she knows, I'm a monk. And monks don't . . . engage in romantic relationships."

"Then maybe you should tell her the truth."

He snorted. "I can't. She'd never believe me. And . . ." He looked at me with pain in his eyes. "You're right. If Vaelyn knew about her, she'd use her to get to me. I can't let that happen."

Finally. "In that case, you'll help me bring these guys down. Right?"

Calvin's features shuttered instantly. "No. I won't."

"Damn it! You—" I drew in a breath and tried to calm down. If he wouldn't let me play the damsel-in-distress card, maybe some of Ian's pride bashing would help. "Are you that afraid of your sister?"

His mouth opened, closed. He sat down slowly. "I don't fear Vaelyn. I fear . . . myself."

"Oh, yeah. You're terrifying, Calvin."

He narrowed his eyes. "My legacy has not always been one of peace."

"Right." He sounded serious enough, but I couldn't quite picture him as a warrior. "Let me guess. You caused the ten plagues of Egypt."

"I've never harmed this world. But in the djinn realm, I was . . ." He looked away.

"You were what?" I got as comfortable as I could on the stone floor. "It couldn't have been that bad. You seem like a decent guy."

"Really." He stared at me as if he were deciding whether I could be trusted. Finally, he said, "I came to your realm as a scholar, but not by choice. The Council banished us both— Vaelyn confined to her tether, and myself stripped of power for a thousand years. I was to have a hearing before my sentence expired, but by then the clan wars had begun and the Council had forgotten me. Which was just as well, because I'd already decided not to return."

"Whoa. What did you guys do?"

He offered a rueful smile. "We were mages. Powerful even by djinn standards. We worked as mercenaries—the two of us, and our brother, for territorial disputes at first. Then we moved to more political missions." He hung his head. "The particular talents of the Morai lend themselves well to torture and death. As I'm sure you've discovered."

"Yeah. I learned that the hard way."

"I can imagine. And for that, I'm sorry." Calvin let out a sigh.

"Our reputation for violence, bloodshed, and absolute success made us known. Feared. It seemed we could not be touched by djinn law, until we accepted a mission to assassinate certain members of the Council. We failed. Our brother managed to keep his hands clean, but Vaelyn and I . . . well, we're here, and he's not."

"Okay," I said. "So you were a bastard. But you've changed, right? I mean, you're a different guy."

"I've tried. I entered the monkhood to find a place in this realm, but also to convince myself that I'm not the monster I was. To prove that I could dedicate my life to peace and knowledge, instead of hatred and violence. But I am still djinn. Still a Morai." He stared at his hands. "I have spilled blood. Destroyed souls. I've done things so horrendous that I dare not speak of them. And I don't trust myself not to turn back to my old ways."

"I'm pretty sure you have a choice there."

"Do I? To the djinn, and especially my clan, power is everything. We crave it. Hoard it. It's in our nature to seek domination." His eyes met mine, and I caught the weariness in them, the defeat. "Gahiji-an is right. There are no innocent Morai."

Damn. Now I was feeling sorry for a snake. Ian would've kicked my ass if he'd been here. "I think he's wrong," I said. "People can change. Djinn too. I mean, look at me. I used to be a thief. I didn't destroy anybody's soul or anything, but I did a lot of stupid things. I'm not like that anymore."

Calvin made a dismissive noise. "It seems to me you're still doing stupid things."

"Maybe. But I'm choosing the things I do. Before, I was hiding behind the thief role, using it as an excuse to do what I wanted. Now I'm taking responsibility for my decisions." I shrugged and stared at the ground. "I'll never be completely innocent—but I wouldn't want to convince myself that I was. Because if I did, it'd be easy to make the same mistakes all over again. I won't bury what I've done."

"So you believe I'm hiding?"

"Not exactly. I just think you're trying too hard." I smirked at him. "You don't have to be a saint. Nothing wrong with embracing a little of your dark side now and then. Hell—er, heck, if I let go of everything that made me a thief, Ian and I would've died when we went up against Lenka."

"Hmm."

I raised an eyebrow. "You say that a lot."

"Yes. You frequently rob me of words, apprentice."

"What's that supposed to mean?"

"Only that I don't often hear such wisdom from tadpoles."

"Hmm."

"Isn't that my line?"

I grinned. "Guess I should be glad to be a tadpole. It's better than pond scum, right?"

"I suppose you're not as terrible as I thought you were," he said.

"That sounded convincing." I frowned. "So why are you really helping me? I know it's not because I talked you into it."

He stared past me for a minute. "Because you may be able to stop Vaelyn. And I'm not certain I can. She must not be permitted to have a child—especially not with Gahiji-an."

"Why? Will it blow up or something?"

"It's worse than that." A heavy sigh escaped him. "A pure djinn, born of this realm, would not be bound by the limitations of a tether. Under Vaelyn's upbringing, this child could, and likely would, tear your world apart." His eyes grew haunted. "I never should have released her. You must destroy her . . . even if it means destroying me too."

"That isn't going to happen." I couldn't take killing another innocent djinn. "If I'm as strong as you think, I'll find a way to work things out. That's a promise."

"I do hope you're right, apprentice."

"I am." *No pressure, Donatti.* Now three lives were riding on my being able to tap into this alleged earth magic. Four, if you counted mine. "So let's get back to work. Maybe you can show me some of those badass spells you know."

"You may not be so eager to learn after I demonstrate them on you."

"I can take it." I stood and tried to stretch out some of the kinks left over from yesterday's crash landings. "Okay. What are we doing?"

Calvin opened his mouth—and then his relaxed expression hardened. "Vaelyn," he whispered. "And . . . no. It can't be."

"What?"

"Shield yourself. Now. Get as far back as you can." He stood and took a step toward the cave opening.

"Why? I don't—" I felt it then. Bright ribbons of power, seeking, invading everything. The fury behind it chilled my bones.

I decided not to argue. I went invisible, retreated back into the cave, and concentrated everything I had on putting up shields.

Unfortunately, I had the sinking feeling that it wouldn't be enough.

I tried not to breathe too loudly.

Calvin held a hand out and produced another ball of blue flame. Ahead of him, the roots parted to admit two figures in white robes. Vaelyn and the mystery djinn, who had the hood pulled up to conceal his face. At least they hadn't brought any of their thugs along.

"Hiding again, brother? You know you can't hide from us." Vaelyn moved in front. "We grew weary of waiting and decided to come and fetch you."

"It looks like I'm not the only one hiding something." Calvin's voice was tight. "How long has he been here?"

The other djinn spoke. "Fifty years. Give or take."

"You . . ." Calvin backed up a step. "It was you. Not Barzan. You took his form for the *ba'isis*."

Vaelyn let loose a frigid laugh. "Poor Barzan. We may have unhinged him a bit when our brother confronted him, wearing his face. But we wanted strong scions, and we knew you would never perform the *ba'isis* for us. Barzan served his purpose."

"So you did drive him mad." Disgust filled Calvin's voice, and he turned to the hooded figure. "Did you run out of lives to destroy in our realm? Bastard. You should have been sealed away long ago."

The figure stepped forward. "Why, Khalyn. You don't seem at all happy to see me. You're ruining our little family reunion, brother." He held a hand out just as Calvin's came up. "Careful. You may be older, but my scions give me strength. And you know what I'm capable of doing."

It wasn't just the damning revelation of what I was up against now—the other mercenary, the twins' brother, who had a fuck-ton of scions running around powering him up—that made my spine crawl. It was his voice. I'd heard that smug, superior tone before. But I couldn't place it, because all the Morai I'd ever spoken to besides Calvin were dead.

Vaelyn glided past Calvin and kicked at the smoldering remains of the cooking fire. "Where is the mongoose, dear brother? We'd like to take him along."

"He's gone. Probably halfway home by now." He kept his gaze on the other djinn.

"Is he, now?"

I felt something push against my shield. I pushed back, as hard as I dared. Eventually, it moved away.

"Vaelyn," the brother said. "Don't concern yourself with that insignificant Doma spawn right now. He'll come to us eventually. Perhaps he'll find the Bahari brat Taregan and bring him along, and save us the trouble of seeking him out again. But I'm not finished with Gahiji-an yet. And Khalyn will accompany us back now." He gestured, and Calvin's fireball went out. "Won't you, brother?"

"As if I have a choice." Calvin glared at him. "Why did you come here?"

"To take what I should have had centuries ago. And this time, I have the blessings of the Council—or at least one of them. The only one who matters, really."

"You're working for Kemosiri."

"Better the devil you know. I would have destroyed Gahiji-an for nothing, but to be rewarded for it is so much better."

If my blood ran any colder, my teeth would start chattering.

"Our time grows short, brothers," Vaelyn said. "The *ba'isis* must be performed soon. And if we do not have our child, we shall be very disappointed indeed."

"Lead the way, sister. Khalyn will follow you."

They filed out one by one, with Calvin moving like someone had shoved a tree up his ass. The brother stopped at the mouth of the cave. "If you are in here, thief, it's here you'll stay," he said. "Unless you'd like to exchange Gahiji-an's tether for your own miserable life. It's your only chance to survive. We will find you."

Fuck you. It was hard not to say it out loud, but I managed.

He waited a moment, then backed out and spoke a few djinn words. The whole cave rumbled and shook—and the faint light from the entrance vanished behind a curtain of rock.

Chapter 23

I stayed huddled in my corner and made myself wait as long as possible before I lowered the shield. They were gone. They hadn't found me. But I was still completely fucked. I couldn't dig through stone unless I figured out a way to transform something into a couple sticks of working dynamite.

Something told me with absolute certainty that djinn magic wouldn't work like that.

I took slow, deep breaths to calm my racing mind. I had to think, before I went crazy and started beating on the walls or trying to claw through them. I wasn't exactly claustrophobic— just allergic to being trapped. Holing up in a place with only one way out was hard enough, and this cave now had zero ways.

Not thinking about that yet. Instead, I worked back through the overheard djinn conversation and looked for something useful. I got that Kemosiri had enlisted the brother to kill Ian. Not exactly shocking. The old bastard probably hadn't bargained for his daughter being destroyed in the process, but I had a cold suspicion he might not care.

The Bahari brat comment gave me a little hope. It seemed Tory had managed to escape. Wherever he was now, at least he was free of the compound, so I'd only have to worry about getting Ian out. Right after I tunneled through solid rock.

Finally, I lingered on the bit about the scions, and how the brother had fathered them. What did Calvin say? *You took his form.* This guy had made himself look like Barzan to fool Calvin into performing the fertility spell on him. That was a pretty handy fucking trick. And as limited as my knowledge of the clans was, it didn't seem like something a Morai should be able to do. Illusions were Bahari specialties.

Barzan's warnings seemed to leap from the walls around me. *Beware the deceiver. He of two worlds will destroy all.* Two worlds . . . two faces? He had to be talking about the brother. The guy made Lenka look like a slightly perturbed, declawed kitten.

And that voice. Damn it, I knew I'd heard it before. How was that possible?

My muscles twinged in protest of the cramped position I held. Time to wander uselessly around the cave, looking for an exit that didn't exist. The only way I'd get out of here would be to somehow figure out how to access earth magic, and then guess how to use it. And I needed it now, before the Morai decided to come back and make an actual effort to find me.

Need. Djinn magic worked on need. Maybe earth magic worked the same way.

I shifted forward, knelt, and put my hands on the cave floor. *I need out of this cave. I need to get to Ian.*

Twin shocks slammed up my arms. For a minute I thought it was another aborted attempt. Then it hurt like hell—or like a tortured djinn chained to a wall. I was with Ian again, but it was different this time. It took me a few seconds to work out why.

I could still see the cave.

Ian's vision was superimposed on mine, like a double-exposed photo. Blurred snatches of rough block walls, wood stairs, and a hard-packed dirt floor splattered with blood ghosted over the dark contours of the cave. All the pain was his. My own body felt warm, as if I'd been sitting in front of a fireplace for a few hours. Everything inside me tingled with the pins-and-needles sensation of blood flowing to numb flesh. The magic was waking up.

Holy shit. I'd actually done it—I'd broken into the entire fucking planet. For an instant I could feel the enormity of it, the sheer power it contained, and thought I'd pass out. I'd never experienced anything this intense. I could feel the earth's heartbeat, a massive, pulsating thrum that wound through and connected everything in existence.

And I knew how to get to Ian. I could move through the earth, the same way the djinn moved through mirrors. His blood on the floor was a compass guiding me there.

The moment I understood, I sank into the cave floor without thinking.

Mirror transportation was cold, but this was hot. Like climbing into a car that had been sitting under the sun in an open parking lot for hours. The heat lasted a few seconds, and then, like a cork surfacing in water, I popped up through dirt into cool darkness. A surprised gasp whooshed out of me. I shook myself and stood.

Ian spit in my face.

"Thanks," I murmured, wiping away blood and spittle with my jacket sleeve. "Nice to see you too. Hope you haven't contracted any diseases lately."

He shivered hard enough to rattle chains. "Thief?"

"Yeah." Christ. His voice sounded like metal scraping on pavement. A quick glimpse told me enough to keep from really looking at him, unless I wanted to lose my last meager meal. "Time to go. Talk later."

"Destroy me."

"I can't."

"Blast . . . compassion. Do not wish to live."

"Will you shut up? I can't, Ian. I tried. It didn't work." An odd combination of adrenaline and terror pulsed through my veins. I'd made it here in one piece. Now, how the fuck was I going to get both of us out in the same condition? I couldn't go back the way I'd come in. I had nothing to anchor to. This was obviously a basement, but I had no idea where it came out. I'd have to try and get a look around, and then come back for him.

Ian laughed. The haunted sound ripped at my soul and left it bleeding. "No escape," he whispered. "You will die. Both realms burn."

"No I won't. Now be quiet." My own voice broke at the end. Whether it was the bond between us or just being physically close, I felt the aching emptiness in him every time he spoke. He'd already died with Akila, but his body couldn't let him finish the job. Saving him was almost crueler than leaving him here. At least the torture occupied his mind for a while.

I couldn't take the time to explain everything now. Couldn't even heal him yet. If anyone came down here and found him unhurt, they'd know he had help. "I have to check things out," I said. "I'm coming back for you. And this is gonna sound weird, but—try not to think about me, all right?" If he managed to pull me into his anguish while I was skulking around the compound, I wasn't sure I'd be able to maintain a shield.

"No! Please . . . r-release me." He tried to look at me, but his eyes wouldn't focus. Tears shimmered in them. "Begging you."

I had to turn away. "I can't."

A single choked sob followed me when I went invisible and

started up the stairs, inflicting more damage than a bullet in the gut.

Six steps led to a landing, and then a door. Metal, with vents at the top and bottom and long vertical slits in the middle. And a guard on the other side. I could smell him—sharp sweat and stale cigarettes. He didn't move around much, but I knew he wasn't asleep because that would be lucky for me. The slits were too thin to shoot him through. I could open the door, even if it was locked. Then I'd either have to hope he went past me to investigate, or try to engage him and take him out before he sounded an alarm.

Before I could make a choice, Ian decided for me.

"*Coward!*" he screamed. The chains rattled and clanked, like he was trying to wrench them from the wall. "Should have killed you when I met you. Worthless, sniveling thief. Gods take you to hell!"

The guard banged the door open—right into the shoulder I'd turned to retreat. I grunted at the impact and moved out of range. Maybe he hadn't heard me over Ian's raving.

"The fuck's goin' on down there?" The guard came through gun first, then stuck his head cautiously around the edge of the door. I recognized him. Kit, the other brother from the forest. And Jesus, he was young. I didn't realize it while we were fighting for our lives, but the kid couldn't have been more than fifteen or sixteen. His efforts to hide the fear in his face behind a tough mask failed miserably. "Gahiji-an?"

Another violent chain rattle. "I will rip your head from your shoulders!"

"Aw, *shit.*" He withdrew, and I heard the distinct tones of a phone being dialed.

I couldn't let him call for help. I lunged through the gap

in the door and cast a lockdown spell at him, barely noticing that it didn't hurt me like calling on magic usually did. He froze with a finger pressed to one of the numbers. The digital tone stretched out in a continuous whine until I pulled the phone from his hand and thumbed it off. I shoved it in a pocket, and my fingers brushed the barrel of the Sig.

Kill him.

I hoped that cold voice came from the part of me that was connected to Ian and not myself. Either way, there wasn't a chance in hell of me shooting a kid. Especially not one with his eyes bulging from his head in terror, unable to move and trying desperately to see what was attacking him. I shut the door in an attempt to close off Ian's lunatic shouts and searched more pockets. Wire, switchblade, napkins—no idea what I was thinking when I grabbed those—handcuffs. Bandanna. Perfect.

"I'm not gonna hurt you, kid." I stayed invisible while I cuffed his hands behind his back and gagged him with the bandanna. The less he knew about me and my plans, the better for both of us. "I just can't have you calling for the cavalry yet. Don't worry. I'm sure they'll find you soon, if you don't get out of this yourself first."

I sat him down on a stair and frowned. Best thing would be to make sure he couldn't get up, at least not easily. The walls at the sides of the stairs were hard-packed dirt. No protrusions, no railings. Maybe I could make something. I put a hand on the wall and thought about hooks.

Heat flowed into me. A spot near the bottom of the wall bulged out, extruded to a point, and curved up. It looked solid enough. I bent to touch it, and found a smooth, cool surface like stone or marble. That'd work.

The kid groaned against the gag. I didn't have time to

marvel at my new abilities. Had to work fast before he came out of the lockdown. I moved him closer to the hook and slipped the cuff chain over it, then I touched the wall again and made the hook an enclosed loop.

It would've held him, if he was just human. But I still didn't know everything these guys could do—hell, I didn't even know what I could do—and I wasn't going to risk being discovered before I got Ian out.

"Sorry, kid," I said. "You're gonna have to take a little nap." I considered whacking his temple with the gun, but if I hit him too hard it'd be the same as putting a bullet there. So I balled a fist and cracked his chin with a hook. His head snapped aside, held for a second, and rolled forward.

After a quick check to make sure he was breathing all right, I sprinted up the rest of the stairs. Ian's little outburst had cost me a lot of time. I wouldn't be able to make a thorough canvass of the place—I'd be lucky to find a way out and get back here before someone who'd give me a lot harder time than Kit found out what had happened.

At least I had no further qualms about giving back whatever they wanted to dish out. Harder, if I could manage it. Anyone who threw kids out for cannon fodder like this deserved to suffer. And for once, my conscience agreed.

Chapter 24

Halfway up was another landing, with tunneled hallways leading left and right that suggested there was a lot more underground to this place than just the dungeon they kept Ian in. More stairs bent around the other way. I headed up, and a closed wooden door with no windows greeted me at the top. I stood behind it and listened for a minute. Didn't hear anything. I cupped my hands on the door and held an ear against them, waited. Still nothing. Of course, that didn't mean whatever lay outside this door was safe. I pulled the gun out, took a breath, and tried the knob.

It wasn't locked. For some reason, that fact failed to comfort me.

I pushed the door open a few inches. A light brighter than the bare bulbs in the stairway spilled through the crack. No one shot or shouted at me. I kept going until I could see into the room beyond. This was the place Akila had spied on. Same round table with chairs—empty now, two of them pushed back as though they'd been recently occupied. I couldn't see much else.

If I waited any longer, I'd probably lose whatever small

opportunity the deserted room gave me. I slipped through. The instant my feet touched the floor, a familiar and unwelcome sensation slammed through me. A massive shock, as if I'd grabbed the spitting end of a severed power line. I'd walked into a snare spell like the one Lynus had cast at Jazz's place. And I wasn't invisible anymore.

So much for exploring the compound. At least tripping the spell didn't seem to alert anyone. Just like back at the house, it only screwed me if they saw me.

I could see the whole room now. It was unoccupied, and didn't contain much outside the table and chairs. Against the wall to my left was a big free-standing cabinet closed with a padlock. A huge mirror, big enough for two or three to pass through side by side, dominated the right-hand wall. They must've used that to invade the house. The building's entrance was kitty-corner from the basement door. It was ajar. Cigarette smoke and low voices—one male, one female—drifted through from outside. Thanks to Ian's unintended enhancements, I made out what they were saying.

"We're gonna get in trouble, Billy." That was the girl. And I remembered the name Billy from Akila's thought-form—one of the gate guards. The younger one, but now that I thought about it, they'd both been smooth faced and still in their mid or late teens.

"No, we ain't. They're busy. 'Sides, I'm not gonna smoke inside with you." He paused. "Don't wanna hurt the baby," he muttered.

Baby? Damn, how many more kids were these assholes planning to destroy?

"I didn't think you cared."

"Shit, Penny, you know I do."

"Well, ain't you sweet." She let out a breath. "Billy," she whispered. "D'you think we could . . . you know . . . leave?"

"Don't ever say that." There was a flatness to his breathy tone. "If Val or Father heard you . . . just don't."

"He ain't *my* father," Penny murmured.

"Mine neither. But we don't wanna fuck around with him, do we? I already done a week of diggin' just for usin' the damn mirror to get smokes."

"Yeah, but at least you got a way out. Me and the girls ain't got magic like y'all."

Billy gave a bitter laugh. "Kind of a good thing for me. I'm surprised they don't make us fuck our cousins, jes' to see if it'd make the babies stronger."

Silence stretched out. I told myself to move, get back down to Ian before they came in and saw me, try to figure some way out—but I didn't listen to my own advice. I wanted to hear what else they'd say, to understand a little more about what the hell had been going on out here.

"I hate this," Penny said at last. "Why'd we have to guard him?"

"Everybody takes a turn. And it's Kit's ass, anyway. He's closer."

There was a slight thud, as if she'd slapped his arm. "Don't say that. I don't want nothin' to happen to Kit neither. Damn, he'd kill us soon as look at us, wouldn't he?"

"I guess." He paused, probably to drag on his cigarette. "Don't you worry none. He can't. You ain't seen . . . what they done to him." The edge of horror in Billy's voice suggested that he'd seen more than he wanted.

"Yeah," Penny said. "But you know what he did to the elders. Tore 'em up like meat. I heard he ate 'em some too. And he killed Davie, and—"

"Hush up, Penny." He changed his harsh tone, and added,

"Won't be much longer, anyway. Now they got him, Father's gonna go soon. Val said we'd have the world then. We c'n go anywhere we want, long as we keep to the plan."

"Yeah, but . . ." She sighed. "I just don't wanna be around *him*."

"Guard change in an hour. I got the next shift off." A grin practically oozed through his words. "You got a room alone now, right? I ain't tired."

She giggled. "Me neither."

Rough as they were, the love between them shone like a torch. My soul ached—for them, for me and Jazz, Ian and Akila, Tory and Lark. So many torn apart by these stupid-ass clan grudges. I decided I'd do everything I could to make sure their torch kept burning. Even if it meant I'd never be lucky because I wasn't trying to kill them. I'd dealt with bad luck for so long, I almost missed it. At least it'd been reliably bad.

I withdrew to the stairs and closed the door quietly. Still had to get Ian out somehow, and I had the beginnings of an idea. A typical Stupid Donatti plan. So dumb, it just might work.

If I was lucky. Which I wasn't.

Kit was still out cold. I stepped over him and entered the basement with caution, expecting another volley of curses.

Ian slumped in his chains, head hanging slack. He must've exhausted himself screaming. My brilliantly doomed plan included healing him and keeping him calm long enough to explain a few crucial things, like the fact that I was physically unable to destroy him. It was the keeping him calm part I'd have trouble with.

I approached him slowly. He didn't move, didn't twitch. I would've tapped him to get his attention, but I didn't see an inch on him that wasn't bloody or bruised. This close, I couldn't escape seeing the damage they'd done to him. It turned my gut inside out.

His clothing, what was left of it, hung in tatters. All his fingers were broken. He had at least three bullet holes in him, ruptured flesh crusted with black blood. Dribbling puncture wounds that looked like they'd been made with nails—or fangs—dotted his arms and legs. His chest and stomach had been flayed raw. I suspected his back looked the same.

"Ian," I managed through the hitch in my throat. "Are you . . ."

His head winched up a few notches. His eyes opened, and his mouth followed.

I cast a lockdown at him before he could threaten me with gruesome murder at the top of his tortured lungs. This time I paid attention to the magic. It came up through my feet, where I made contact with the ground. I filed that away for future reference. "Sorry to do this, man," I said. "But you have to listen, and we don't have much time." I gave him the CliffsNotes version of all the fun things his little soul bind had done to me, and watched the fury in his eyes change to shock. "Now, if I let you go, are you going to keep screaming at me? Never mind. Just stay quiet, all right?" I undid the lockdown before I even registered that I knew how.

Ian sagged forward. "Paralysis spell," he gasped. "How . . ."

"Old dog, new trick. Long story." I frowned. "You understand why I can't kill you, right?"

He made a choked sound. "Cannot destroy your own tether."

"Ding, ding. You win. So, right now our only option is getting the hell out of here. And we're not going to kill anyone doing it." I felt the rage rolling off him, and added, "We're taking a hostage with us."

"Never work."

"Maybe not. But you're in no shape to plan, and I don't have any other ideas. So that's what we're doing. Now, do you want me to heal you or get you down first?"

He stared at me. Finally, he said, "Heal."

I nodded and held a hand near his throat, looking for the bright red spot. Found nothing. I closed my eyes and made out a weak glow that was probably all the energy he had left.

When I honed in on it, his pain flooded me.

"Ah, shit," I ground out. My legs went limp and tried to buckle. Every bit of me shook like a wet dog. I concentrated on the warmth rising up through me, felt it turn white hot. Sent it all toward the dim light at Ian's throat. *Heal him. For fuck's sake please . . .*

The glow increased, blazed crimson. Through the pain clouding my head, I reminded myself that I had to pull the light through him. Like threading a needle. But there were so many holes to patch, I barely knew where to start. The indecision had me trying to direct it down and up at the same time.

It worked. The light split, branched, seeped into his body like ink spreading through water. Bones straightened and fused back together, muscle and skin rejoined. Three faint metallic clicks reached my ears—bullets being ejected from him and dropping on the ground.

The heat in me started to burn. I pulled out and dropped to one knee, panting, hoping I'd done enough. I didn't feel drained the way I did when I ran out of djinn magic. It was more of a wrung-out, raw sensation, like someone had scrubbed my veins with Comet. Probably could've kept going if I could take the heat. "Get you down in a sec," I said. "Gotta catch my breath."

Chains clanked and popped. Ian dropped in front of me, landing on hands and knees.

"Or you can do it yourself," I said. "You okay?"

"No."

"All right. Stupid question. How about this, can you walk?"

He looked at me. "This is not possible. How could you have done that?"

Calvin taught me. I caught myself before I said it out loud. No way he'd believe that right now, and it'd probably start him screaming and calling me a liar. "Tell you later."

He crooked an eyebrow. "Old dog?"

"New tricks." I stood and held out a hand. "Can we please blow this place?"

He let me help him up. "Your eyes."

"Yeah. Thanks for the makeover. You coming?"

"I suppose I must."

I would've felt better if he sounded pissed at me. Anything but this broken devastation. "There's a mirror up there," I said. "Hopefully, we'll use that to get out. One guard on the stairs—he's our hostage. Two in the building, if they're done smoking. Don't bother with invisibility. They laid a snare spell on the place."

Ian shook his head. "Where have you been to know such things?" he whispered.

"In a cave. Let's go."

Now we'd just have to live long enough for me to explain everything else.

Chapter 25

Ian didn't try to attack Kit when we reached the first landing. He didn't even hurl so much as an insult. I wished I could take that as a good sign.

The kid twitched and groaned. He'd come around soon. Knowing what I had to do, and not liking it one damned bit, I got my gun out and laid my other hand on the wall to rearrange the earth again. Kit slumped sideways against the stairs and flinched into consciousness. His eyes flared wide when they found Ian.

I knelt and pushed the Sig against his throat. "I will if I have to," I said, hoping my voice didn't shake too much. "Understand? Blink if you do."

He blinked. Sullen fury replaced his fear as his attention shifted to me. Like Vaelyn, they all probably thought I was weak. No threat. That was good. A nasty bruise darkened his chin where I'd clocked him. I thought about healing him, but decided to leave it. He might try to defend himself if I threw magic at him. If he had something I couldn't counter, we were fucked.

"You're coming upstairs with us. You'll live if you don't do anything stupid. Got it?"

Another blink. Slow, and somehow sarcastic. He didn't believe me.

That was good too.

I hauled him up by the arm and moved the gun to his back. "Walk."

Kit muttered something. A single word, muffled by the bandanna. It sounded like *asshole*. But he walked.

I stayed one stair behind and kept my grip on him. Ian followed without a word. This new docile attitude of his scared me more than anything else. I kept expecting him to snap, turn into a wolf and go for Kit's throat, try to carry out the threats he'd made to me. But he just plodded along, silent and stiff. A motorized husk.

I stopped the kid on the second landing and took the gag off. "Where do these tunnels go?" I dug in with the gun, just in case he'd forgotten it was there.

Kit coughed and spit on the ground. Bright blood winked an accusation from the glob. He didn't try to run, or scream for help. Smart kid. "Different places," he rasped. "Whole nest of shit under here."

Something Billy had said flashed through my mind, about doing a week of digging as a punishment. Christ, it wasn't bad enough these bastards sent the kids out to fight their battles, to die for them. They used them for slave labor too.

"You ain't gettin' out of here," Kit said, in that same flat tone Billy had used. "Nobody does. Think they won't kill me to stop you?"

"Your friends up there won't," I said with more confidence than I felt. "Now move."

He stood still. A muscle worked along his jaw.

"Jesus!" I whirled him around, forced him to the stairs, and wrenched his mouth open before he could pop the suicide cap. He fought hard, whipping from side to side like a snake. I planted a knee on his chest and shoved two fingers in his mouth.

He bit down. His teeth broke skin.

Somehow I managed not to scream. I snarled a lockdown spell and pried his teeth out of me. "Fine," I said. "We'll do it the hard way." I probed until I found the hollow point in a back tooth, extracted the glass capsule, and threw it back down the stairs. I checked to make sure it was the only one, then released the spell. "That was stupid, kid. Didn't I tell you not to do anything stupid?"

He stared at me, mouth hanging open like a loose tent flap.

"What was that?" Ian half-whispered.

I glanced back. "Poison. He tried to kill himself."

Ian turned an alarming shade of pale and backed away—almost the same reaction as Tory's with the other one. I got the impression that the djinn had a thing about suicide, at least the deliberate kind. But Ian didn't seem to have a problem with one-against-a-hundred kamikaze attacks that basically amounted to suicide. Or asking—make that demanding—a friend to do it for him.

Kit shivered under me. "The fuck you do that for? You ain't supposed to save me. You're the enemy."

"A dead hostage wouldn't do me any good." I got him up and turned around before he could see the bluff written on my face like a banner. "You don't walk, I'll drag your ass."

He hesitated. When he started moving again, it was with a lot more reluctance.

We reached the door at the top without further complications. "Okay," I said. "We're going out there, and Ian and I are using your mirror. Then we'll be out of your hair and you can run off, sound the alarm, marshal the troops and all that shit. I'm sure somebody around here can get the cuffs off you."

Kit laughed. It was a low, desperate sound. "No, you ain't."

"What?"

"You ain't gettin' through that mirror. You think Father's stupid? It's spelled so only we can use it." He jerked a little, but not enough to pull away. "There ain't no leavin' here, 'less you're dead."

"We'll see about that." Shit. There went phase two of the plan. I'd have to improvise. I kept the gun against him, reached around, and pushed the door open. "Showtime. Stage is yours, kid."

Kit moved into the room. The other two must've come in, because the minute he stepped up, Billy said, "Damn, Kit, you're just buckin' for—*what the fuck's goin' on?*"

I pushed in behind him and made room for Ian. Billy already had a hand in his coat. "Uh-uh, Billy," I said. "Hands up, unless you wanna take a shower in your buddy's blood. You too Penny."

They both complied, with identical expressions of shock. Billy kept his eyes on me. Penny, a pretty brunette of sixteen or seventeen with the mound of her belly clearly showing her condition, stared at Ian with quivering lips. "He's gonna kill us," she moaned. "He's gonna *eat* us, Jesus, Billy, do something!"

"Quiet," I said, noting with relief that the outside door was closed. We might have a few minutes. "Whatever they said about Ian, it probably isn't true. Well, most of it. He's not going to eat anybody."

A soft thump behind me drew my attention. I glanced around. Ian leaned against the wall by the basement door, staring back at the girl. "Children," he whispered. "They are all children."

"Not all of them. There's at least two generations here, maybe three."

"Two. Penny's havin' the first number three." Kit let loose another wild laugh. "So how you gettin' out, genius?"

"I know how," Billy said quietly.

"Billy, don't!" Panic shrilled Penny's voice to a high, breathless whisper. "You can't help them. They'll—"

"Hush up, Penny." Billy hadn't looked away from me. "I tell you, and you don't hurt Penny. Neither of you. Deal?"

I nodded. "Deal."

He flipped a hand back, indicating the table. "Trapdoor under there, goes to the crawl space under the building," he said. "The snare don't work there. I got a hollow spot dug out around the back. Lets me sneak a joint now and then."

"Billy, you slime-dog," Kit said. "You ain't never told me that."

"Well, you know now, don'tcha?" A sardonic smile stretched his lips. "Ain't much to do 'round here except smoke, and train, and fuck. You prob'ly noticed we do that lots."

Penny blushed at that and ducked her head.

I bit back a smile of my own. "How do I know you're not sending us into a trap?"

Billy shrugged. "You don't."

I looked at Ian. He nodded once.

"All right. You keep your end, and we'll keep ours. You first, Ian."

"Wait." Billy's mouth thinned. "Before you go . . . mess me up like you done Kit. Maybe they think we tangled with you, they'll let us off easier."

A small sob escaped Penny, but she didn't argue. The fact that she understood so quickly made things even worse.

"Okay." The lump in my throat made it hard to talk. "Ian, can you—"

"I'd rather you done it," Billy said. He tried to laugh, but fear colored his tone. "No offense to you, uh, Prince, but you might break somethin' that can't be fixed."

Damn it. He did have a point. "Yeah, I'll take care of it." It was hard to say. It'd be harder to carry out. "You come here and take this, Ian." I wiggled the gun, still pointed at Kit. As cooperative as they seemed to be, I wasn't going to take any chances.

Kit blanched when Ian approached him. He didn't say a word, but he seemed to almost shrink, like he was a turtle trying to pull into his shell. Ian showed no expression as he took the Sig from me. But I thought I saw something soften in his eyes, just a little.

I walked over to Billy. "Let's do this."

"Yeah." He shivered once. "Don't look, Penny."

She closed her eyes. I wished I could afford the same luxury.

The longer I waited, the worse it'd be for both of us. I drove a fist in his gut, doubled him over so he wouldn't see the other blow coming for his face. My knuckles met the bridge of his nose with a dry snap. I pulled the punch at the last second, but it still dropped him to his knees.

"Mother*fucker*," he gasped, and clapped a hand under his nose. Blood leaked from between his fingers, ran out over his mouth. He shook loose and spat a few times. His shoulders heaved. "Goddamn. Think you cracked a rib too." He raised his head. "Thanks. I guess. Now get the fuck out."

I nodded, backed up, and held out a hand toward Ian. He pushed the gun into it. "Go on," I said to him. "I'm right behind you."

Ian went to the table. He didn't look at anyone, didn't smile or frown or speak. He crawled under, found the trapdoor and opened it, slid through in silence.

Once he was out of sight, Kit turned to face me. "Take me with you," he whispered.

My eyes bugged and tried to pop loose. "What?"

"You could still use a hostage. Take me." His mouth twitched. "I can't stand it here. Tell 'em you killed me."

"Stop it, Kit," Billy said hoarsely. "You know what happened last time you tried runnin'."

Kit shuddered and bowed his head. He didn't ask again.

All the moisture in my mouth and throat evaporated. "I'll come back," I said. "Swear to God I will. I have a score to settle with your leaders, and I'm going to get rid of them. One way or another."

Billy's hollow laugh echoed Kit's earlier sentiments. "You can't. You just a low-gen scrub, same as us. These bastards are gods."

"Maybe. But I'm a thief, and I'm gonna steal their fire."

Three sets of eyes regarded me with doubt. "If you say so." Billy grimaced. "Better shag ass, thief. Somebody'll be comin' along soon, and they won't wanna chat."

I didn't bother repeating the promise. I went for the table and climbed down after Ian, pulling the trapdoor shut after me, expecting to immediately hear shouts and pounding feet above. No one up there moved.

"Ian?" I whispered. My vision adjusted quickly to the dark, but I didn't see him anywhere.

"Over here." His voice came from a dimmer gray patch near the back of the building—the hollow spot Billy had mentioned. "They were not lying about the snare spell, at least."

"Good." I went invisible and made my way over. "We crawl out, you fly us away."

"With all your newfound abilities, you cannot fly?"

"No. And I'm real broken up about it too."

I wanted to imagine him grinning, but the picture wouldn't form. His smiler was permanently out of order.

Small puffs of dust formed in the air as Ian squirmed his way out. I followed fast, forcing my throat closed so I wouldn't cough. Outside, I stood and risked a quick glance around. The rows of buildings seemed quiet. No one occupied the immediate area. I didn't feel any surges of angry power, didn't hear any alarms or shouts. The kids inside were probably giving us a few minutes to get away.

Or it was a trap. I still couldn't rule that out.

I found the slight depressions in the dirt that marked Ian's position. Feeling for him was awkward, but once I made contact I could see him. I threw up a shield around us both. Ian gave me a strange, questioning look, but he didn't say anything. He turned his back and I held on. Christ, this part always made me feel like an idiot.

Ian tensed and took off. In less than a minute, we cleared the compound fence and headed out over the endless forest. No one came out to stop us.

That sealed it for me. I'd come back and free them. Somehow.

Chapter 26

"Can you get to the monastery?" I shouted over the rushing air.

Ian took a long time replying. "That does not seem wise. We should evade them."

"I don't think they're going to look there, and there's something I have to check out." Ian didn't know about the fire. I had to hope they wouldn't expect us to head somewhere so obvious. At least not right away. I suspected they'd try there eventually, though. All of them were smarter than the average Morai.

I caught myself thinking in generalizations and stopped. That was a bad idea. Besides the turning-into-snakes part, I couldn't assume I knew anything about any of them—the full-bloods or the scions. They were individuals, just like people.

Aside from deciding where to land, neither of us tried to chat in-flight. I knew I'd have to talk to him soon, and the conversation wouldn't be easy or pleasant. But that could wait until we weren't rushing along five hundred feet from the ground—which was something I was trying really hard not to look at. I watched the sky for a while. It was gray and overcast, deepening to almost black in a few spots, the thick kind of cloud cover that made it impossible to tell where the sun hid. I'd lost track of time so completely that even if the sun was out, I wouldn't know whether it was late morning, afternoon, or early evening. I was on survival time now. Every minute I didn't die stretched to five or ten on the flip side.

I smelled the monastery before it came into view, an uneasy blend of charred wood, spent magic, and death. Ian stiffened beneath me, giving me momentary flashbacks of our unplanned skydive before I realized he'd caught the scent too. "They burned it down," I said. I didn't bother explaining who "they" were. It'd be hard enough convincing him that it hadn't been Calvin beating the shit out of him for the last two days.

He relaxed a fraction. Soon enough, the remains of the place were visible. Calvin had been right about the fire not burning farther than the building. In fact, it didn't even look like any of the ground outside what used to be walls had been scorched. The pile of blackened rubble remained a perfect square. The stone wall bordering the grounds, and the statue of St. Jude, were untouched. At least the bodies of the three scions I'd shot were gone.

I leaned closer to Ian. "Can you take us down at the back, where that phone booth is?"

He didn't say anything, but we dropped lower and came in where I asked. I slid from him with a familiar swell of gratitude for solid ground under my feet.

Ian staggered a few steps and sat down abruptly, his back to me.

I stood there, torn between investigating my hunch and talking to him. Everything in his body language said *fuck off*—slumped shoulders, bowed head, arms tucked in defensively. But we wouldn't be able to stay in one place for long until this whole mess was settled one way or another. And there were things he had to know, even if he refused to believe them.

I circled him and sat on the ground facing him. "Are you still hurt? Physically, I mean."

"Tired."

"Yeah, me too." I sighed and fidgeted. Where should I start? "Look, Ian. I have to tell you—"

"The children let us go."

He spoke with horrified discovery, like he'd just waded into the ocean for the first time and found it full of blood instead of water. Whatever I felt, it had to be infinitely worse for him. He'd spent a thousand years hating the Morai, killing them, and it wasn't all because of the curse. He wanted them wiped out.

"They fear me." His body curled in tighter. "Children. I would never . . ."

"It's a cult," I said. "They're brainwashed, at least the older ones. But I don't think it's taking so well for these younger guys. Ian, they've grown up hearing stories about you. Lies. Or at least embellishments. They can't help it."

He shuddered. "They are too strong. I have failed . . . everyone."

"We're not done yet."

Ian lifted his head. He didn't speak, but his eyes said everything. He was done, even if I wasn't. He had no fight left in him. If I couldn't get him to care, I'd be on my own.

"Don't you want to know how I learned all this weird shit?"

He blinked. "Yes."

"Calvin taught me."

"You . . ." For an instant life flashed into his features. He went slack again fast. "Why would you say such a thing?"

"Because it's the truth." Once I started, the words wouldn't stop. "He has a twin sister. She looks exactly like him. Sounds just like him too. Her name is Vaelyn, and she's batshit nuts. She's the one who's been working you over. See, she's coming into her cycle, she knows you're already fertile, and she wants a djinn baby. Calvin knows a spell that temporarily restores a djinn's reproduction, for three days. That's how they got these scions."

Ian held up a hand. A cautious interest crept into his expression. "Slow down, thief." He frowned. "This still does not make sense. A female could not have produced these descendants and become fertile again so soon."

"They're not hers," I said. "The twins have a brother. He's the one those kids keep calling Father, even though he's not. Their father, I mean. He's their grandfather, or something. He impregnated a bunch of human women, and had his spawn breed again when they got older. Now they're working on generation three."

"There are three djinn?"

"Yes, but Calvin isn't on their side." *I hope.* "He was with me, trying to teach me how to use my power, and they came for him. He helped me get away."

Ian shook his head. "I am trying, thief. But I cannot believe a Morai would help anyone associated with me. And what could he possibly know of your abilities?"

"Earth magic."

"Excuse me?"

"He's been studying this realm for two thousand years. He said the human sorcerers died out, but the magic is still here. I can use it." I pressed a palm to the ground and felt the warmth bleed through me. "I think I have to be in contact with the earth somehow. But it doesn't hurt to use, like djinn magic does."

"Of course," Ian whispered. "If there is magic native to your realm, you should be able to use it as we can our own in the djinn realm."

"Right. Only problem is, I have no idea what I can do. It's not exactly common for humans to wander around using magic. You guys all grew up with it."

Ian sat up straighter. "How did you get to me?"

"I used the ground, the same way you use mirrors. Only it's backward. There has to be blood on the other end to guide me, instead of me providing it on this end." I glanced away. "Plenty of your blood on the floor back there."

"Hmm." A pained look crossed his face, and he fell silent and retreated into himself again.

"Ian," I said. "There's something else you need to know."

"I suspect I will not wish to hear it."

"Yeah. You won't." I traced a finger idly through dirt. I hated to mention anything associated with Akila, but there was no getting around it. "Your fertility isn't the only reason these assholes wanted you. The brother is working for Kemosiri."

Ian jerked stiff and went deathly pale. His eyes flared wide. For a minute I thought he'd pass out. Finally, he let out a breath and slumped on the spot. "Perhaps I should save him the trouble and present myself to Kemosiri," he said. "I have no reason to fight him any longer."

I wanted to tell him he was wrong. To assure him that he had something to live for, a purpose in being here. But anything I said would've came out awkward and meaningless. I couldn't even point out that nothing would have changed what happened, because I knew he'd find in hindsight a hundred things he failed to do, that he never could've guessed needed to be done. I'd torture myself the same way if anything happened to Jazz. And I'd never stop.

I leaned back and stared at the threatening sky. Above the clearing that held the remains of the monastery, a lone bird flew in looping circles, catching air currents and banking with graceful ease. It completed a circle and wobbled. Then dropped a few feet.

The bird steadied, made a tight loop, and dove straight for us.

My jaw fell in my lap. "Ian," I said. "Did I mention that Tory escaped?"

He favored me with a bleak stare. "No."

"Incoming." I pointed.

The bird—definitely a hawk, a big one—was fifty feet away now, and shuddering like a plane with a blown engine. It gave a few feeble flaps of its wings, failed to straighten out, and hit the ground rolling. It glowed when it stopped, the shape of it swelling and forming arms, legs, torso, head.

Tory flopped on his back with a gasp. "I don't suppose either of you has a frog or a rabbit on you," he said in cracked tones. "Never been very good at that whole dive-and-snatch thing."

A laugh ejected from my throat before I could stop it—and Ian cracked a hint of the first genuine smile I'd seen from him in days. It wouldn't last, but it was nice to pretend for a minute that we would be around long enough to feel normal again.

It took Tory a few minutes to remember he wasn't a bird. He'd been circling the mountain for two days, looking for me. His shock at finding both of us settled in after he stopped compulsively scanning the area for small game and trying to clean his feathers.

I brought him up to speed—the unexpected effects of the soul bind, the twins, the brother, the kids who'd helped us get out. He avoided looking at Ian while I talked. When I finished, he ran his fingers through his hair and grimaced. "They'll come after us," he said. "I'm sure they're already looking. I don't know . . . fuck." He broke off hard, stared at the ground. "I thought you were dead, Ian. I left you there alone. Shit. I would've come for you. I swear I would've."

"You would have been destroyed." Ian roused himself from his stupor and cast him a stricken gaze. "Do not punish yourself for that, Taregan. I am glad you escaped." He clasped his knees to his chest. "Though I do wish you had not followed me there. What they made you do . . ."

Confusion flickered through Tory's mask of misery. "What did they make me do?"

"You do not know?"

"I do," I said. "I saw it." The unwanted memory branded me—being in Ian's head, watching Tory come after him with a knife, the horrified out-of-control expression on his face. "They made you torture him. They were controlling you."

"No. They couldn't have." Tory looked from me to Ian, then back to me. "They swarmed us the second we got there. There were so many. I tried fighting them, but they were human and . . . well, hawks aren't very lethal to humans, so I didn't bother trying that. I knocked some of them out, but I couldn't kill them. Ian must've taken a dozen of them before they brought him down." He swallowed and dropped his gaze. "That's when I took off. I knew you were supposed to destroy him, and I couldn't . . . I just couldn't."

"Impossible." Ian's voice wavered and dipped. "You *were* there. You cut me. You broke my bones. They took control of you, used you."

Tory looked like he'd been gutted with a dull spoon. "I didn't," he whispered. "I swear, Ian, whatever you saw, it wasn't me. I wouldn't have let them take me like that. Not to torture you. Never."

"Shit," I blurted out. "It was the brother."

They both stared at me.

"Calvin and Vaelyn's brother. It was him. He tricked Calvin into casting the fertility spell on him by making himself look like a different djinn, a guy Calvin thought was a scholar like him. He must've taken Tory's form." The only reasoning I could think of for it disgusted me almost as much as the way they used the kids. "He did it because it'd hurt you more."

"Hold on." Tory's hands clenched and turned his knuckles an angry white. "The Morai can't do that. It's powerful illusion magic. Only the older Bahari can pull off shit like that." He pounded the ground with a fist. "This whole thing reeks. Nothing is right."

Something pricked at my subconscious. A whispering, muffled voice. I tried to tune everything out and listen—and at last I realized the voice wasn't in my head, and it didn't come from Ian or Tory. It sounded like it was saying *apprentice*.

Ian's brow furrowed. "Your pocket is speaking," he said.

"Huh?" I reached into the one he was staring at and pulled out my cell phone.

Calvin's face appeared on the cracked screen, faded and opaque, more reflection than image. "There you are," he said. "I don't have much time. They aren't going to let me leave, and they're furious that you rescued your friend." A small smile flickered across his lips. "Well done, apprentice."

"Thanks. Now what the hell's going on? And how are you on my cell phone? The battery's dead."

He smirked. "The surface is reflective. I'm using a mirror spell."

"Oh." Nice trick. I'd have to remember that one. "Okay, so what's with your fucked-up brother?"

"Half-brother," Calvin practically spat. "We share a mother, but his father was Bahari."

All the breath went out of me. I glanced at Ian and Tory, whose expressions said they'd heard him loud and clear. At least that explained a lot.

"Listen to me." Calvin looked away for a second, like he'd heard something he didn't like on his end. His voice dropped to a harsh whisper. "The princess is alive."

My throat collapsed. Before I could react, Ian beat me to it.

"Lying snake!" He launched himself from the ground on a collision course with me. I rolled clear fast, but he was already turning when he hit the ground. He'd destroy the phone before Calvin could finish his message.

"Tory, hold him back!" I scrambled away, tried to get up, and felt Ian's fingers brush my ankles before Tory tackled him. I started running. "Talk fast, Calvin," I said. "Ian doesn't believe you, and I don't blame him. She can't be. We all saw his ring shatter."

"She's here. She's to be part of my brother's reward for destroying Gahiji-an. Her father has promised her to him."

"My God." Everything came together in my head so suddenly that I actually saw a blinding flash of light. I glanced back and saw Ian bucking violently under Tory, screaming obscenities in djinn. Falling apart. Tory wouldn't be able to hold him long. "Your brother is—"

"They're coming. You must save her, apprentice, and stop them. My brother can't be permitted to claim a place on the Council. It would be the end of both our worlds."

He vanished, and my phone was just a useless hunk of shiny plastic again.

I jammed it back in my pocket and walked back toward the warring djinn, every one of my muscles twitching and sizzling like water on a hot griddle. "Stop it," I said.

Ian kept yelling. Tory wrenched his arm back, and Ian promised to rip his intestines out if he didn't let go.

"Goddamn it, Ian, knock it off or I'll break your fucking teeth!"

Something in my voice must've conveyed how much I meant it. They froze.

"She's alive," I said, and held a hand out when Ian's mouth opened in a protest. "Shut up and listen. Vaelyn knows how to transfer tethers. She did it with her own, joined herself to Calvin's so he wouldn't be able to destroy her." My stomach lurched hard at the thought of the rest. "They must have cut her finger off to break the bond. But she's alive."

Tory crawled away from Ian with a thick sound that could've been a sob. He stayed down and curled inward, moaning incoherently.

Ian struggled up to his knees. Moisture streaked through the dirt smudged on his face, and his breath came in hitches and gasps. "Akila," he rasped, the name torn from him like a forbidden word. "She lives?"

"Yes." I knelt in front of him and grabbed his shoulder. "Don't run off this time. We can't afford to fuck this up. It's worse than you think, and it's going to take all of us to get her back."

A violent tremor worked through him. "I cannot leave her there another moment."

"Yes, you can. They aren't going to destroy her. We will go after her, but not yet." I glanced over at Tory, who'd managed to pull himself from the ground. "I know who the brother is, Ian. And so do you." The familiar voice, the spells he used—I hadn't put it together because he was only half Morai, and I'd only seen the Bahari part of him. Not in person, but through a vision from the past. From Akila's memories. Even the reward Kemosiri promised him made sense now.

"I do not understand," Ian said. "Who is he?"

My teeth ground together. "Nurien."

Chapter 27

Ian bolted to his feet, the broken pieces of him cemented back together with rage. "That disgusting, preening, worthless sack of dung! How *dare* he—" He stared at me. "How could you know of Nurien?"

The switch from furious to baffled was so abrupt, I almost choked on a laugh. "Akila told me," I said. "Showed me, actually. I asked her how you two managed to meet, and she made one of those thought-forms. I got to watch the whole story." I grinned at him. "You were a cute kid, Ian. And your temper hasn't improved since then."

His neck flushed. "I have never had cause to control my temper. Particularly now." He paced in a tight circle, stopped, and spat on the ground. "Sniveling bastard. Of course he would have to produce descendants in order to best me. And Kemosiri sent him here?"

"Yeah. Apparently, he's been promised rewards for destroying you."

Ian's jaw clenched. "What rewards?"

I cleared my throat. "A seat on the Council," I said. "And . . . Akila."

A dark expression twisted his features. "I will destroy them both," he said. "Nurien first. And then Kemosiri. Council leader or not, he will die for this."

"Whoa. Take a breath, Ian." Tory lurched closer, rubbing his forehead. "Let's just worry about Nurien right now. Damn." He crossed his arms and looked at me. "Well, at least we know what's wrong with him now. He's part Morai."

"Yeah, but he looks all Bahari. At least, he did when I saw him."

Tory nodded. "It doesn't happen often, but djinn born of two clans always favor the father in appearance. And this explains why he's able to use air magic so well."

"The scions," Ian said roughly. "Their blood is mixed as well. I knew it did not taste right when I . . . killed the boy." His voice broke, and he buried his face in his hands. "Gods, what have I done?" he whispered.

I felt his pain, a hot knife under my ribs. "Ian, don't blame yourself," I managed. "You didn't know."

"Who should I blame, then?" His hands fell away and he raised wet, red-rimmed eyes. "I chose this hatred, this ignorance. These children have only done what they must, as I believed I had been doing. I cannot fault them." He drew in a shuddering breath. "Khalyn protected you. He gave you strength I could never have offered, enabled you to save me. And risked his safety, perhaps his life, to bring news of Akila. How many others like him have I destroyed?"

My chest tightened until I could barely breathe, much less speak. Even if we weren't soul bound, I would've felt the same way. After all, I'd helped him quite a bit in the destruction department.

"You didn't have a choice." Tory sounded as awful as I felt. "You want someone to blame? How about Kemosiri? He's the one who cast the *ham'tari*—"

"Blast the *ham'tari!*" Visible tremors shot through him. "Misfortune be damned. I will no longer kill without discretion. I will not spill innocent blood." Lips pulled back in a snarl, he pounded a fist into the tree beside him, splintering bark. And probably his knuckles. "I will *not* be Kemosiri's butcher."

Some of the tightness eased, and I let out a long breath. "Well, I guess we feel better now," I said.

Ian raised an eyebrow. "We?"

"Yeah. Soul bind, strong emotions—you almost killed me there."

He smiled a little. "I believe some of them belonged to you, thief. This bond does travel in both directions."

"Lucky us." I straightened from an unconscious slump, rubbed my stiff neck. "Okay, guys, we need a plan. Anybody got one?"

Tory glanced at Ian. "What, exactly, are we trying to plan?"

I took a deep breath. "We have to get Akila out, neutralize Vaelyn without destroying her so we don't kill Calvin too, take Nurien down even though we don't have his tether, figure out which scions aren't actually evil brainwashed puppets and save them, and decide what to do with the rest of them."

"Is that everything?" Ian said dryly.

"Damn. I never thought I'd say this, but it's good to have your cranky ass back."

Tory laughed. "I'll second that. So, Donatti, what should we do?"

"Um. Shouldn't you ask Ian? I thought he was in charge."

"My strategy was obviously flawed." Ian caught my gaze, nodded. "I believe we should try things your way."

My first instinct was to say hell no, forget it. I knew how much trust he was putting in me. Akila was more his life than his tether could ever be, and to leave saving her up to me was huge. Especially since I was a complete fuckup. Had been all my life. Ask anybody who knew me, and they'd tell you they wouldn't trust me enough to lend me five bucks, because somehow they'd end up in jail, or in traction, or worse— because of me.

But I couldn't let him down.

"Right," I said. "My way. Er. Well, I do have a hunch about one thing. I think I know where Calvin's tether is." I walked over to the incongruous, phoneless phone booth with its padlocked plastic box. "Bet you a dollar it's in here."

Ian actually smiled. "I believe you are right."

"I hope so." I knew I'd brought a pick set. I shuffled through pockets until I found it and checked the underside of the lock. A wide key slot, nothing apparently jammed inside it. I flicked one of the thicker shims out and jimmied it around until the shackle popped with a dull click.

My hopes sank. It was too easy. I slipped the lock off and opened the box, expecting to find nothing inside. I wasn't disappointed.

"Anything there?" Ian said.

"No." I stared hard at the empty space, as if I wanted something to be there badly enough it'd show up. It did seem a little strange that the plastic box didn't have a back. There was just a stark rectangle of tree bark outlined in gray. I reached in and touched it.

Echoes of magic vibrated through my fingers at the contact.

"I'll be damned." I pressed a palm against the surface of the tree. There was something in there that didn't belong. I could almost feel the shape of it. I tried to let the magic flow through me, into the wood, and pushed gently. My hand slid inside the trunk like a rock sinking in mud. The pliant wood around it hummed and pulsed and sent small, tingling shocks up my arm. At first I thought it was some kind of protection spell.

Then I realized it was because, unlike dirt, the tree was alive.

My fingers brushed something cool and solid and definitely not living. I worked them forward carefully, hoping trees couldn't feel pain, and finally wrapped my hand around whatever it was. I pulled it out slowly, until the tip of it cleared the bark. It was a curved knife, about eighteen inches long including the handle. The blade was wider at the business end. A series of serrated hooks, six in all, ran from the hilt to a third of the way up the blade on one side. The carved bone handle was a coiled snake with blood red gem eyes. It looked like a weapon designed to seriously injure instead of kill. The kind a mercenary-for-hire might carry.

"Holy shit. How'd you do that?"

Tory's voice at my shoulder made me flinch. I turned and lowered the blade before I could manage to cut myself with it. "I have no idea," I said. "Totally winging it here. But I'd say this is the right thing. Wouldn't you?"

"It's definitely Morai," Tory said.

Ian stared at the knife. "Did you not say that Khalyn is also bound to this tether?"

"Yes," I said.

"And you are not going to destroy it."

"Hell no."

"Very well." There was relief in his voice. "But perhaps you will explain why we had to find this, if we do not intend to use it."

"Oh, I intend to use it." I flashed a quick smile. "Just tell me how you seal a djinn back inside one of these things."

His answering grin said he liked that idea.

Ian walked me through the procedure for sucking a djinn back inside a tether—the blood of the caster and the one to be sealed, an incantation, and as much power as I could throw behind it. Tory already knew the drill, so this way, any one of us would be able to take the first opportunity we saw to put Vaelyn away. Now all we had to do was get some of her blood on her tether. And figure out how to accomplish the rest of the impossible items on my to-do list.

The only thing I knew for sure was that we all needed a little time to rest. Ian sat against a tree, looking about as lively as a funeral. Tory wasn't much better. And for all my fancy new mojo, I felt more human than ever—specifically, like a human who'd slept maybe four hours in two days, eaten nothing more than a couple mouthfuls of bat, and would've given a kidney to see the inside of a hot shower.

No one was in any shape to fly far, and even if I could figure out how to get through the ground without blood to guide me, I had no idea whether I'd be able to take passengers. We could probably find a stream or a pond and use reflections to move elsewhere, but we couldn't risk going back to the house, and no way in hell I'd let anyone get near Jazz right now, including us. Especially us. I assumed Tory would feel the same way about Lark.

That left staying on the mountain. So much for a five-star meal and a posh hotel room. We'd be lucky to get a handful of berries and a nice flat rock to sleep on.

"We'd better move," I said. "They'll be looking for us soon, if they aren't already. I know a nice cave where we can hole up and get our shit together. Spacious, cold, plenty of bats. Don't worry. They taste like chicken."

"Really, thief. Bats?" Ian stood and looked at Tory. "We will hunt."

Tory grinned. "Sounds good to me. There's plenty of whitetail around here. It'll be just like the *mau-het* back home." He hauled himself to his feet, brushed a few pine needles from his legs. "Oh, man, I'm drooling already."

"You're serious," I said. "You really want to go deer hunting?"

Ian shrugged. "We must eat."

"Yeah, well, I hope one of you guys is a better shot than I am, or we'll be eating pinecone salad. I've never been hunting in my life." I pulled out the Sig. "Who's doing the shooting?"

They both stared at me like my last marbles had just rolled out of my ears. "The wolf does not require a gun to bring down his prey," Ian said.

"Oh. Right."

Tory gestured farther up the mountain. "There's a good-size stream up that way. Maybe five hundred yards, by . . ." He glanced at the sky. "Damn. I don't know your points here. Let's go with north by northeast for now, and I'll correct you once I'm up."

Ian nodded. "Stay lower than usual. We should not separate for long."

"True." Tory sent me a smirk. "Try and keep pace, Donatti. And don't shoot anything." He glowed, became the hawk, and lifted off.

"Come." Ian started through the trees.

I half-jogged after him. "So I take it you guys have experience at this."

"Of course. Did you think there were grocery stores and refrigerators in the djinn realm?" He slowed for a few paces, studied the ground, and kept going. "The Dehbei have always hunted, though our homeland more resembled your deserts than your mountains. But there were creatures similar to your deer. And after my village . . ." He drew in a sharp breath. I knew what he didn't say—after the Morai army slaughtered every living thing in his village. "I spent some time in the Bahari lands, while I courted Akila," he went on. "I was not welcome, of course, but Taregan was too young to let the court dictate his relations. He would often hunt with me, scouting prey in the wooded depths where my visibility was limited."

"Yeah? I guess this is like old times for you, then."

"Old times, indeed."

A hawk's cry sounded above us. Ian looked up, hesitated, and shifted his course a few degrees. "Your stealth has improved," he said. "You no longer sound like a herd of *jembai* crashing through the underbrush."

"Thanks." I was marginally aware that *jembai* were kind of like elephants. "That's mostly because of you. I picked up a lot of your wolf traits with that soul-bind thing. These eyes do more than look pretty, you know."

"I am sorry for that." He glanced at me, looked away. "I am afraid it will be permanent."

"Hey, don't apologize. If you hadn't done it, you'd be dead right now."

"What?"

"Maybe you didn't hear me when you were all fucked up." The thought of what I'd almost done gave me a serious case of the shudders. "I tried to destroy you, like you told me to. I went through the whole spell. I didn't want to, but after a couple rounds of being there with you, feeling what you felt . . . Christ, I wanted to die myself. But I couldn't do shit about it."

"And if you had succeeded . . ."

"Akila would be on her way back to the djinn realm with Mister Fancy Pants right now."

Ian blinked at me. "Who?"

"Nurien." I made a face. "When Akila showed me the thought thing, he was wearing this gold outfit that would've made Liberace die of embarrassment."

Ian laughed. "Fancy pants. You do have a unique way with words, thief." Another call from Tory had him slowing, and he shifted direction almost imperceptibly. "Though I am glad you were unable to destroy me, I thank you for the attempt," he said in coarse tones. "It means much to me that you would be willing to do what is necessary."

"I've done a lot of things in the past few days that I never thought I'd do." I tried to shrug it off, but levity eluded me. "I guess I'm more like you than I realized."

"You are nothing like me." A deep sadness filtered into his features. "You are not a barbarian, or a monstrous slayer."

"Neither are you, Ian. And if you need proof of that, just ask those kids you didn't kill, even though you're bound by that damned curse." I made a mental note to happily pitch in and kick Kemosiri's ass later. "You've had to make some tough choices, but that doesn't make you a monster. It makes you—well, a prince. And I may be a really small kingdom, but I'll follow you to the end. Wherever that ends up being."

"I do not wish to be followed." Ian smiled faintly. "I would rather have a friend."

"Then you've got one."

The hawk swooped in close with a low whistling sound. Ian glanced up, then peered ahead and grinned. "We are near," he whispered. "Do you hear it?"

I listened. Through the steady rush of wind, I heard a low

and liquid muttering, a silvery splash. Running water. The sound sank fishhooks of thirst in my dry throat, and it was all I could do not to sprint for the stream. "Oh, yeah," I said. "It sounds like dinner."

"Can you track my progress if I go ahead?"

"No problem. I don't know that I want to see you take down a deer, anyway." I swept a hand out. "Go for it. I'll catch up."

Ian transformed. I caught the predatory gleam in the wolf's eyes just before he vanished into the trees without a sound, and decided I was grateful not to be a deer.

Chapter 28

I'd always thought a wolf attack would be loud and messy, punctuated with snarls and growls and the screams of whatever luckless animal happened to be on the wrong end of the teeth. But what I heard was so unremarkable that I half thought Ian hadn't caught anything. There was a bit of running, a few light splashes that I guessed were the extras getting away. A single brief bleat, a thud. Some almost rhythmic rustling. Then only the stream again, a continuous throaty note underscoring the stillness.

I pushed ahead and emerged into a wide clearing along the side of a rocky, rushing, step-down stream. Ian, still a wolf, crouched with his fangs sunk into the throat of a medium-size buck. No puddles of blood or streaks of gore. No torn chunks or flaps of flesh. Ian shook his head, and the buck twitched a little—but the reaction was pure nerves. The deer's eyes were dull with the blankness of death.

For a minute I ignored him, and the hawk circling to land on a boulder overlooking the stream, in favor of my body's demand for cold wet anything. I stretched out bellydown on the bank and caught frigid water in my cupped hands. My throat clenched in anticipation.

The first sip damn near brought me to tears. I'd never tasted anything so sweet, so real. The best steak dinner I'd ever had in my life cost me upward of a hundred bucks, and it might as well have been seasoned cardboard compared to this. I could've started a religion. The Way of the Mountain Stream After Two Days Without Sustenance. Even Jesus would've signed up.

My hands weren't fast enough. I stuck my face in the bubbling water and drank, deep, sucking swallows, like I had an invisible straw. Damn, this was good. I was pretty sure I heard clouds parting and angels singing. I kept going, and wondered if it was possible to drink a stream dry.

Until something small and wiggly slipped between my lips and lodged in my windpipe.

I jerked back with a splash and flopped over. A deep, hacking cough failed to loosen whatever it was—and air suddenly refused to move in or out. I bucked and jittered across the ground, slapping the air, one hand on my throat, trying to squeeze the obstruction out while black flashes dazzled my vision.

Rough hands hauled me upright, pounded on my back. I made a desperate bid for breath. The wiggly thing worked itself down and finally dropped past the sticking point. Everything whooshed from my lungs at once, and I drew a burning gasp of air that forced itself out fast in a series of barking coughs. Tears scalded my eyes and squirted from the corners.

At last I managed to stop coughing. Ian stood beside me, one hand under my arm and the other supporting my back. Tory was a few feet away, losing a fight with a smile. "Did I mention how much I hate nature?" I croaked. "Think I swallowed a fish."

Tory howled with laughter and dropped to the ground,

clutching himself. "A fish!" he gasped between cackles. "Oh, damn. You're killing me! Guess you won't need dinner, then . . ." A fresh laughing fit overcame him.

The gale force of his amusement cracked a smile across Ian's face. "Will you live, thief, or shall we begin the burial preparations now?"

"I think I'll make it. Thanks." I staggered a few steps and sat down. "That was fun. I hope it isn't swimming around in my stomach or something."

"I would conclude it is not." Ian glanced over at Tory. "Taregan, if you would be so kind as to stop rolling about long enough to gather wood for a fire."

Tory sat up, wiping his eyes. "Sure, yeah. Wood." He snorted. "Hey, maybe if we hold Donatti's head in the stream, we'll catch enough minnows for a side dish."

"Taregan."

"I'm going." He stood and wandered off with a grin. The occasional chuckle escaped him and rolled back on the breeze.

Ian shook his head, but a faint smile lingered on his lips. He blinked and looked down at me. "I presume you have a blade somewhere in those pockets of yours?"

I'd almost forgotten about the deer. "I have a few," I said. "The tethers are probably the biggest." My ankle blades were four-inch jobs, not much better than shivs, and the switchblade was even more useless at three.

"I would prefer to use one that is not bound to a djinn," Ian said. "Particularly me."

"Sure." I freed one from an ankle holster and handed it to him. "Here you go. Have fun."

Ian took it. "How quaint." He held it sideways and made a few passes over it. The blade lengthened and thickened, grew teeth on the lower edge and a sliver-sharp sheen along the upper half of the top. "You should consider carrying more efficient weapons, thief."

I shrugged. "I have a gun."

"Yes. And it is far simpler for a djinn to stop a firing gun than a flashing blade." He walked over and bent to the deer carcass. Wet ripping sounds commenced. "Also, knives do not run out of bullets."

I nodded absently and tried not to watch him. "I hope you know how to cook that stuff," I said. "Never had it personally, but I hear venison is awful if it's not made right."

"I have sufficient experience." The blade sawed through flesh with a faint squelching noise that tried to rid my stomach of all the water I'd drunk. And the fish. "Have you never prepared meat?"

"Are you kidding? I can't even boil water." I stretched my legs out. My muscles had finally stopped shaking from lack of oxygen. "I don't cook food. I just eat it."

Ian chuckled. "How have you managed to survive this long?"

"Takeout is a man's best friend." I grinned. "Plus, there's TV dinners. And prepackaged stuff. I'm a big fan of cherry Pop-Tarts." The idea of food had my mouth watering again, despite the awful sounds of the butchering. "The nuns never taught any of us how to cook—especially me. I wasn't allowed in the kitchen. The one time I did go in there, Sister Maggie beat my ass. Said I was stealing bread or something." A startled laugh escaped me. "Figures I'd catch hell for the only time I was actually innocent."

I trailed off, not sure why I was talking about this. I'd never brought it up to anyone before. Not even Jazz.

"It must have been difficult for you." There was a catch in Ian's voice.

"Hey, everybody's got a sob story. It wasn't like they kept me chained in the basement and flogged me every day or anything." I grimaced. Bad choice of words. But Ian didn't seem to notice. "I did steal food, you know. Not there. But when I ran from the orphanage, it only took a couple weeks of rooting through Dumpsters to figure out a better way to survive." I stared at my feet. "Wasn't a huge leap, graduating to stealing money instead. Bought food tasted better. After that, I just kind of didn't stop. I was good at it." I looked away, focused on nothing. "I'd never been good at anything else."

"I am sorry," Ian said softly.

"Don't be. You didn't make me a thief."

"Not for that. For doubting your integrity." He half-turned. Dark blood streaked his arms to the elbows. "You have made hard choices as well. Your world demands it. I cannot fault you for surviving."

"Thanks." I nodded at the carcass, feeling a change of subject was in order. All this bonding was making me itch. "You gonna finish that? I'm starving."

Ian laughed and went back to cutting.

Whether it was Ian's culinary skills or sheer hunger, venison tasted a lot better than chicken-fried bat. By the time we ate and washed as best we could in the stream, the suggestion of sun behind the clouds had disappeared and it was nearly dark. It would've been nice to sit around the fire and dry out, but Ian had doused it the minute he finished cooking, reasoning that a fire was easy to spot from a distance. The reminder that we were being chased didn't do much to lift the mood.

Marginally less grimy, my full stomach broadcasting a false comfort, I craved sleep. I would've crashed right there if we weren't so exposed. Ian and Tory both looked ready to pass out too. I made myself stand and grab a last quick drink—just water this time—then cleared my throat. "I guess we should keep moving," I said. "I can probably still find that cave, so we can get a little rest."

Tory, stretched out on the ground, threw an arm over his eyes. "Sounds cozy," he said. "Can't wait."

"Donatti is right. We must not remain in the open." Ian unfolded himself from his crouch by the stream and glanced at the sky. "Besides, it will rain soon."

I opened my mouth to ask how he knew that, and thunder muttered in the distance.

"Crud." I did a fast check of the area to make sure I hadn't left any useful things lying around and waited for Tory to stand. "Should we do anything with that?" I gestured at the decimated deer carcass.

"There is no time to properly prepare it. We will leave the rest for other animals." Ian stirred the remains of the fire with a foot. "This cave of yours. Do the Morai know of it?"

Shit. "Yeah, they do."

"In that case, we should not stay there. We will be found."

"I hate it when you're right." Lightning flashed across the sky, and thunder chased it almost instantly. "Okay. Any idea where we should go?"

"Perhaps we should—"

"Get the fuck out of here. Right now." Tory pointed downstream, his features somber. "They're coming."

Ian grimaced. "Into the woods." He started back the way we'd come up.

I followed without bothering to ask how he knew. The first whispers and spatters of rain came just before we plunged into the trees. Great. And I'd just gotten comfortably soggy.

"Shouldn't we fly?" I said. "We're not going to get very far this way."

"No. We would be too visible." Ian moved fast. He looked like he knew where he was headed, but I doubted that.

I glanced over my shoulder. Still didn't see anyone chasing us. "Wait. We could use the stream, right? Reflective magic works with water."

"Yes, with reflective water," Ian said. "That stream moves far too quickly for the spell to take hold. We would need a calm surface."

Tory passed me and matched Ian's stride. I hadn't even heard him come up behind me. "There's a lot of them," he said. "At least one full-blood, maybe two."

"All right. Good to know. But do not scry any further." Ian glanced back at me. "That goes for you as well, thief. Use no magic. They will sense it."

"Right," I said. Tory's expression suggested he was just as happy about that as I was. "So what are we supposed to do—climb trees and hope they don't look up?"

"It is dark and raining. If we put some distance between us, and do not use magic, they should not be able to find us. They do not have the senses of the wolf."

He did have a point. Only I didn't like the fact that he'd said *should not* instead of *will not*. "Maybe that'll work, but we can't keep wandering through the woods all night. We've got to rest for a while. I'm beat, and I know you guys are too."

"We may not have a choice."

"Yeah? What are we gonna do when one of us passes out and can't get up? And don't tell me it won't happen. We can't—"

The sharp retort of gunfire cut off my rant.

A rolling echo washed through the trees. The shot wasn't

close—but it wasn't nearly far enough away either. "They're firing blind," I said. "Have to be."

"Or they have night-vision scopes," Tory said.

Damn. I hadn't thought of that.

"Move." Ian picked up the pace. "Do not speak unless you must."

I bit back a retort and tried to go faster. The rain misting down became fat droplets, and then a steady spatter that soaked me through and resurrected the chill in my bones. Lightning strobed the spaces between branches. The whip crack of thunder that followed almost had me diving for the ground.

Another gunshot chased the thunder. I swore I heard the bullet splinter wood somewhere close. And now I caught the sound of feet pounding over ground, snapping branches and crackling through leaves and needles. I had no idea how to judge distances with my amplified senses, but there was no doubt the sounds were closing in. Fast.

"Ian." The urgency in Tory's voice carried over the rain.

He cursed, glanced back at me. Slowed his ground-eating pace. "We change," he said. "Come, thief."

Tory nodded. He was glowing before I caught up with Ian. The hawk looked up at me, blinked, and let out a single low sound, a warning. His senses were probably better in that form. I sighed and half-wished we were flying instead. "If we get out of this, Ian, I'm buying a saddle for you. You're really uncomfortable."

He glared at me while he transformed. I'd probably get an earful for that later.

The wolf snorted and pawed the ground, an impatient stallion. I beat back reluctance and climbed aboard, lying as flat along his back as possible and clutching handfuls of wet fur. "Don't drop me, all right?"

Various muscles bunched and tensed under me, as if he were saying *It will not be my fault if you fall.* The hawk took off first, and Ian bounded after it.

At least I didn't have any broken bones this time. But that didn't stop the impact of his feet with the ground from jarring me with every leap. As a wolf, Ian moved damned fast. The trees blurred by, a mass of mottled shades on either side. I tried to watch where we were going, but with the rain lashing my face and branches whipping at me, I had to assume a more protective position. I'd have to trust Ian not to run headfirst into something that wouldn't get out of his way.

A piercing whistle sounded. Ian slowed a fraction and changed direction abruptly. My back end slid, and I tightened my grip while I righted myself. Ian let out a brief yelp.

"Sorry," I muttered. "Never did take those wolf-back riding lessons."

Another report cracked behind us. Whether it actually was, or I'd just engaged in some serious wishful thinking, it sounded farther away. We were gaining ground.

Ian ran. I concentrated on gritting my teeth so they wouldn't break while my jaw chattered with the cold and the erratic motion. Every few minutes, a call from Tory would change Ian's course. I managed to lean into most of them and only pull out three or four hairs. Eventually the sounds of pursuit disappeared, and I dared to breathe again when Ian slowed to a fast sprint.

Tory glided down and kept pace with Ian. He shrieked, and there was worry in the sound. An instant later I felt the same black ribbon of energy that had invaded the monastery when we first met Calvin. Faint, but definitely there.

"Ela na'ar."

The words whispered and reverberated around us like

the voice of God. A shiver worked through me, completely separate from the damp and the vibrations of Ian's motion. Something massive rippled the air. Lightning and thunder clashed in heightened crescendos, as though the storm was responding to the spell—a spell I'd heard a lot more than I wanted to lately. *Fire.*

Fifty feet ahead, a line of flames zipped across our path, like someone had dropped a match into a stream of gasoline. They rose fast, feeding on magic and wet wood, until we were facing an impenetrable wall of fire.

Chapter 29

Ian skidded to a full stop. Somehow I managed not to fall. But when I tried to dismount, he snapped at me until I held still.

"We have to turn around," I said. "Change back. Maybe we can fly over this."

A low, steady growl issued from his throat. He paced back and forth, raised his muzzle to the wind. Barked once.

Tory dove down and pulled up at the last second before he hit the ground. He banked right and flew alongside the fire wall, a dark-winged silhouette backlit with flames, a phoenix in hawk's clothing. Occasionally he recoiled and flapped furiously, as though he'd caught a draft of heated air.

And it was hot. The flames were immense, pulsating, alive. Angry as their maker. Heat undulated from them in growing waves, parched my skin, singed Ian's fur. But he held his ground and watched the hawk.

"Goddamn it, Ian, what are you doing? This isn't going to stop burning." I tried again to slide down from his back.

He whipped his head around and brought his teeth together a whisper from my arm. I took that to mean they'd sink into flesh the next time.

Tory wheeled away, let out a shrill cry, and rose in the air. He flew at the same spot in the flames a few times, as if he were challenging them. Finally, he turned away and glided over us with a low whistle.

Ian trotted a good distance away from the fire. Just when I started to feel relieved, he paced in a half circle, tensed, and crouched. And bolted directly at the flames.

"Jesus!" My first instinct was to let go—but Ian was already moving so fast that I'd just end up rolling right into the fire. So I threw up a shield, buried my face in wet fur, and prayed the crazy bastard knew what he was doing.

The roar of the flames filled the world. Ian left the ground completely, and searing heat clamped down like a fast-food restaurant grill, transforming me into a sizzling piece of meat. For an instant I felt everything in a progression of colors— yellow, orange, red, white. The blazing intensity negated sweat, crushed even the idea of breathing. My bones were melting.

After an eternity, or maybe a few seconds, we broke through. Ian landed at a sprint, and I did my best to find out whether I'd emerged looking like Freddy Krueger. Everything seemed normal except for a few throbbing patches on my face, and the smoke rolling off me in billowing clouds.

He slowed to a lope and finally stopped, sides heaving against my legs. I tumbled to the ground and laid there in sweet, cool muck, eyes closed, letting the rain soak my stinging skin. Eventually, Ian changed back; I heard him gasp and plop on the ground. I didn't bother looking at him. "Don't ever fucking do that again."

"It was the lesser evil." He almost sounded apologetic. "They are watching the skies. If we had gone over, we would have been seen. They will assume, at least for a time, that we are still on their side of the flames."

Damn. That made sense. But I decided not to swell his head by admitting it. "How did you know we'd get through that without turning into torches?" I said. "I made a shield, but that was real fire."

"Yes, it was. Taregan found the weakest point to pass through. And we were soaked, and traveling at a high speed." Ian shrugged. "Do humans know nothing about fire survival?"

"No. Most of us just avoid jumping through bonfires," I grumbled. "Where's Tory?"

"Coming."

A light tread approached. "You made it," Tory said.

"I'm not so sure about that. I might be dead." I held back a groan, pushed up to sitting, and sneezed hard. "Fuck! Okay, that hurt. Humans can die from pneumonia, you know."

"If you die tonight, thief, I am certain it will not be from this 'pneumonia.'" Ian got to his feet slowly. "We must keep moving."

"This is news?" I muttered, and made myself stand. "Oh, Christ. Look at that."

The fire was spreading. Not California-drought fast, but quickly enough to watch the progression. The sheer heat it threw out dried the next bunch of trees and caught them in the flames. Smoke poured from the blaze, blacker than the cloud-strewn sky. And the rain had already tapered off to a light mist.

My stomach clenched. "They're crazy," I said. "They're going to burn the whole mountain down looking for us."

"Vaelyn cast the spell. She likely does not care how much life she destroys in her pursuit." Ian crossed his arms. "Their compound is no doubt protected."

I turned away and frowned at the woods. "Yeah, but the town there isn't. And . . ." Something in the endless uneven ranks of trees grabbed at my awareness. A clearing just ahead of us—one I'd definitely seen before. "Mercy. Jesus, Ian, she's five minutes from here! She'll never be able to get away from this."

Tory's brow furrowed. "Who?"

"A friend," I said. No time for an explanation. "We have to get her out of there."

Ian nodded. "But I do not know the way."

"I do. I think." *I hope.* At least I'd been conscious on the way. "Come on."

I set out at a fast walk, not bothering to make sure the djinn followed. They could keep up. After a minute, my feet took over and I ran.

I'd never find the place.

The certainty weighed on me like a shroud. I didn't know where the hell I was going. Even with the new and improved vision, every damned tree looked the same. But I ran anyway, dodging a dozen little dips and rises and roots that would've sent me sprawling if I'd tried this before Ian borrowed my soul, or whatever the hell he'd done.

When I hurtled into the clearing where Mercy's place stood, I almost kept running.

Ian and Tory came right behind me. Her porch light was on, and Zephyr stood on the ground next to the steps, sporting half-filled saddlebags. I glanced back and saw the flames licking toward the night sky, probably half a mile away.

Mercy must've seen them too.

The front door banged open and she strode out with two little raccoons in her arms. A cloud of strong and pungent odor rolled out with her, reaching across the yard. I recognized the scent of weed immediately. Good shit.

She staggered down the porch steps, flicked a red-eyed

glance at me, and did a double take. "Who in the—oh, it's you." Her gaze hardened. "If you bastards started that blaze, I'll shoot ya where you stand."

I stopped and shook my head, temporarily too winded to speak. "You're stoned," I finally managed.

She snorted with laughter. "Still the smart one. Ol' Mary Jane takes good to the mountain soil. I'd give y'all a hit, but I'm busy. There's a fire, see?" A giggle escaped her, and she wove on her feet.

"Mercy, you won't get away fast enough on a mule." A pointless argument. She wasn't exactly in a reasoning state of mind.

She set the raccoons on Zephyr's back and unzipped one of the bags, then responded as if she hadn't heard me. "Lightning, then," she said. "Don't know how it got going wet."

"No. This isn't a natural fire."

"Yeah?" She coaxed the little furballs into a bag with a handful of dog food, then zipped it almost closed again. One of them chirred a little, but they didn't try to escape. "If you ain't started it, how do you know what did?"

"Donatti," Tory said softly. "We might have a problem."

Mercy's glazed eyes moved to him. "Who's this one?"

"This is Tory. Tory, Mercy." Shit. We didn't have time for introductions. "Look, we have to—"

"I'm goin' to get Sister." She headed back to the house.

I started after her, but Tory's hand on my arm stopped me. "Let her go a minute," he said. "We're in trouble here."

At last, I noticed the strain in his voice and really looked at him. He was falling down exhausted. Ian too. "Lemme guess," I said. "You're both tapped."

He nodded. "Transformations took the last of it out of us."

"Shit." That left out flying away. I could barely float myself.

No way in hell I'd be able to carry even one more body through the air, let alone three plus a mule and three raccoons. "What about mirrors?" I said. "Even if she doesn't have one, there're windows at least." Tiny windows, I noticed while I said it. The glass between the molded frames was only about four by four inches. None of us could squeeze through that.

Ian frowned. "You would have to cast four successive bridge spells yourself. Impossible, even for one of us. It would exhaust you." He looked from the fire to the house, as if he were judging how long until we all got toasted. "Your new abilities are impressive, but they are earth magic. Not reflective magic."

"Hold on," Tory said. "What new abilities?"

Before I could answer, Mercy emerged with Sister tucked in the crook of one arm and her shotgun in the other. "Y'all better get movin'. Fire's comin' fast." She kept her eyes averted while she walked to Zephyr and settled the big coon on the mule's back. "Ain't gonna make town. Maybe the Holler cave down the ridge."

"You're seriously going to hide out in a cave?"

She whirled on me. "What the fuck else 'm I gonna do? Ain't got a helicopter up my ass. Don't got nobody to come fetch me. Shit." Her eyes glossed with moisture, and she turned away. "This place's all I got. And it's already gone. I jus' hope Calvin makes it out."

I almost blurted out that Calvin was all right—more or less—but that'd be way too much explaining right now. Besides, even that would be small comfort on top of losing her whole world to Vaelyn's insanity. And there was the trifling fact that with Ian and Tory drained, we didn't have a chance in hell of escaping the flames either.

That left two options. Die, or stop the fire. I didn't feel like dying, and I doubted the Ridge Neck Fire Department was equipped to handle this. They probably still used a bucket brigade. So it'd be up to me.

Which meant we were screwed. But I still had to try.

"Do me a favor," I said. "Don't leave yet."

Mercy glared at me. "Why? You gonna ask God to dump a lake on that blaze?"

"Not exactly." I faced the fire, knelt, and put both hands on the ground. Tingling warmth pulsed up my arms, shot with threads of pain. It wasn't hurting me, though. What I felt was the pain of the mountain at the unnatural scourging. Only thing was, I wasn't sure how to put it out. So I'd just have to wing it.

Tory cleared his throat. "Donatti, what are you doing?"

"Stopping the fire," I said. "I think."

"Are you nuts? You can't—"

"Leave him be, Taregan." Ian spoke low, but there was a hesitant note of hope in his voice.

"Y'all are pullin' my leg." Mercy giggled. "He some kind of Injun mojo man, right? Gonna do a little dance, bring the rain back."

Good thing she was stoned, or she'd have blasted me by now. I tried to tune them out and concentrate on whatever the hell I thought I was doing. The border of the fire was a raw, jagged line out there eating through everything. I pushed at it, thinking maybe I could churn things up, throw some dirt on the flames. Dirt was supposed to put out fire.

Nothing happened.

Too bad I didn't have a handy lake to dump on the thing— not that I could've done anything if I did. I had a suspicion that water wasn't my thing. "Come on. It's for your own good," I mumbled at the ground, and shoved harder.

Nothing . . . and then something. The warmth under my

'hands turned hot. A distant tremor, groaning and growing. The ground shook beneath me.

"What the *fuck*?" Mercy yelled over Tory's gasp. "A goddamn earthquake? Shit, all we need's a cloud of locusts now."

I ignored them. The heat filled me, pulsed through my blood. Sweat broke out over every inch of my skin. An awful buzzing sound filled my head. I hoped it wasn't Mercy's locust comment manifesting itself.

A faint glow from the ground caught my attention. I glanced down at my hands just as Mercy let out a startled shout. Red-orange light flickered under my skin, like someone had emptied my veins and filled them with fire. I stared at them, watched the glow spread and seep through my wrists and into my arms.

At once, the sensation ramped up from hot to scorching.

I would've screamed if I had enough breath. They hadn't invented a word for pain that came anywhere close to this. It was a hundred times worse than any flame curse. Fire raced through me, flooded my torso, scalded my throat. Even my toes sizzled. A hot, thick smell choked the air, bitter and sickly sweet—singed hair, charred meat, cooked blood. My stomach tried to turn, but it was burning too.

A hoarse cry rang out. It didn't come from me. Ian dropped to one knee with a gasp. He said something, but I couldn't even make it out, much less answer him. Apparently the soul-bind thing was giving him a taste of my stupidity. I tried to stop thinking about him.

It wasn't hard. I had plenty of pain to occupy my thoughts.

Once the blazing light filled everything under my skin, blisters bubbled into existence on my flesh, like the stuff was a living thing forcing itself out the hard way. A huge one formed on the back of my hand and burst. Tendrils of smoke drifted from the rupture—and the edges blackened, sparked, then formed a ring of glowing red embers that ate through the remaining skin.

I was actually on fire. Not magical fire. Real burning-to-death flames.

Something primal hijacked my senses and flipped the *you are on fire* switch somewhere in my brain. I made a reflexive jerk and panicked when I couldn't move. Finally I realized my hands had fused with the ground. I wrenched free, pulling clods of dirt and leaving behind moist bits of things I didn't want to think about. Then I threw myself flat in the grass and thrashed around like an epileptic eel. Stop drop roll. Put-it-out-put-it-out-put-it-out.

I thought I was screaming, but I couldn't be sure. It was hard to hear over the massive shaking, cracks, and pops that erupted everywhere when I started flopping.

Eventually the immediate burning stopped—either that or I'd flash-fried all my nerve endings. I rolled facedown in the dirt and went still. The only sound in the world was my own ragged breath, the only sensation a bone-deep agony that hollowed me to the core. I had no idea whether I'd succeeded. And I hurt too much to care.

A voice attempted to penetrate my ears. It almost sounded like Mercy, if someone had shoved a sock in her mouth and then kicked her in the stomach. There was a lot of cursing mixed into it. I managed to turn my head and open my mouth, with the vague idea of offering reassurance, but all that came out was a splintered groan.

Someone touched me. I recoiled, tried to say *Don't,* and failed. My vision was a patchwork of dull red and gray. I couldn't blink. A blotchy shape loomed in front of my throbbing eyes and hung there, shimmering like hot blacktop.

"Well done, thief." Ian, shouting through the wrong end of an invisible megaphone. Great—now Mercy knew I was a thief. If she hadn't gone drooling nuts watching whatever had just happened. "Very impressive. But perhaps you should refrain from attempting anything like that again. Particularly if you must drag me into it."

I guessed that meant the fire was out. At least I hadn't torched myself for nothing.

Ponderous scuffing sounds somewhere close. Ian hauling himself to his feet. "By the gods," he said. "If I was not seeing this . . ."

Seeing what?

The instant I thought it, a ghostly image formed over the burned-out haze of my eyes. I could see what Ian saw, just like back in the cave. It still took me a minute to process what it was—the forest, or what was left of it. A wide swath of blackened, smoldering land marked the path of the fire. Torn roots buckled the ground, formed an alien landscape of ridges and craters. Charred and splintered trees stood in a few spots, but most of the area had been reduced to flattened rubble. As if some immense body had rolled around on the flames until they'd gone out.

Damn. Had I really done that?

The strain of looking through Ian's eyes just about split my head open. I pulled back. Blackness drowned everything for a minute, and the rest of the mottled world bled back slowly around the edges. Some of the thick burnt stench dissipated and let in a breath or two of rain-scrubbed air. I still couldn't move, but control of my eyelids mercifully returned and I blinked a few times. Scalding moisture welled in my eyes and blurred some of the patches together.

"Shit. Ian, is he alive? Are *you?*" Tory's voice buzzed like an electric fence. I couldn't tell if it was my hearing, or if he was really that shaken. "How did he do that? That's impossible. We can't even do that."

"He will live. But he is badly injured." Ian almost sounded like he cared. "Perhaps the lady will allow us to take him inside."

The lady in question didn't respond. Maybe she'd fainted. More likely she was deciding who she wanted to shoot first. Before I could glean a clue about what was going on outside my little sensory-overloaded cocoon, a new voice cut through everything like a cold blade.

"How convenient of you all to gather in one place. Please take the human's weapon, before she makes a foolish mistake. We don't wish anyone to die at this moment."

I really wanted to believe that was Calvin—but I knew damned well it wasn't.

Chapter 30

"**D**eceiver," Ian spat. "I knew we should not have believed you."

"I have no more choice than you, *rayan*."

The voice was more reluctant than the one that demanded Mercy's surrender. So Calvin was here too. Terrific. Vaelyn must've found out about him and Mercy, and had probably threatened to take her out if he didn't cooperate. I wondered what else she'd gotten out of her twin. Like maybe that fertility spell she wanted.

"Calvin." Mercy's whisper barely carried. "What the hell . . . ?"

"Keep her silent. She has no place in these negotiations."

"Then let her go inside, Vaelyn. You don't need her."

"No. She stays, to keep you in your place."

Christ. Listening to the two of them talk was beyond weird. If it wasn't for Vaelyn's abrasiveness, I wouldn't be able to tell them apart—she almost sounded more male than Calvin.

Ian snarled something in djinn. It sounded extremely unpleasant.

A beat passed in silence, then Vaelyn laughed. "Really,

Gahiji-an. Even if you had any power left, my children would bring you down before you could cast so much as a shadow. I am afraid you're surrounded. *Rayan.*"

Damn it. Tory had said there were a lot of them. How many did she bring? And how many were kids? I strained to make my eyes work, but they refused to focus. The scions were probably invisible anyway, wherever they were.

"I will destroy you, snake." Despite the fact that Ian didn't have a shot in hell at carrying out his threat, he sounded completely assured. "Do what you wish to me, but I will end you."

"Oh, we don't want you anymore." Vaelyn was practically purring. "We want him."

Him? Why the fuck would she want Tory?

When no one reacted, Vaelyn continued. "That was quite the display, little mongoose."

My gut tightened. And I didn't think anything in me still had the capacity to function. She was talking about me.

"Taregan, no!"

A shotgun blast followed Ian's warning. At the same time, Vaelyn spoke a single word. There was a second muffled explosion, peppered with metallic pops and splintering cracks. Tory cried out. I felt the thud when he hit the ground.

"We trust there will be no more interruptions," Vaelyn said.

I had to see what was going on. And somehow, I had to get myself moving and talking fast. I almost borrowed Ian's eyes—but he'd definitely react to the pain, and Vaelyn might be able to figure out why. It didn't seem like a good idea to let her know about our link. So I concentrated on remembering all the stuff Calvin had told me about healing. I'd have to hope I could scrape together enough energy to even find the damned points.

Ian let out a controlled breath. "He is useless to you. If you must take someone—"

"Things have changed to your advantage, Gahiji-an. In fact, we no longer require your pretty wife—who lives still, as we're certain our dear brother has informed you. You may have her back."

Dirty, lying bitch. I could practically feel the kick in the guts from that one.

"Explain," Ian croaked.

No! The involuntary attempt to shout emerged as a thick grunt. Opening my mouth would hurt too much. Was he really going to listen to her? I closed my eyes and tried to envision the spot at the base of my throat. Somebody had to talk some sense into him before he got me killed.

There. A faint yellow pulse flickered on and off like a heartbeat. I seized it and sent everything I had through the point. *Please work.*

"Perhaps you can be reasoned with." The rough edges vanished from Vaelyn's tone, and she sounded almost feminine. "You've misjudged us, *rayan*. We desire only a place for ourselves in this world. A place to rebuild our scattered clan. Surely you can understand that."

"Lies," Ian said. "You claimed you would rule both realms."

Vaelyn snorted. "Our brother's goals," she said. "Why should we care for a realm that cast us out? We have no designs on the places and politics of the djinn. In fact, we will give Nurien to your young Bahari friend here, to face the wrath of the Council as he should have two thousand years ago."

She sounded as reasonable as the sunrise. But I doubted she meant a damned word of it. I managed to get the healing point to a strong, steady red glow, and my vision started to improve. All the better to see how screwed we were.

Ian hadn't responded in too long. Just when I thought I'd have to smack some sense into him—as soon as I could move one of my arms—he came around by himself. "Do you truly think I am stupid?" Disgust layered his voice, and he spat on the ground at her feet. "You would not betray your own kin."

"Kin! We despise that foppish, idiotic *duohl-et*. He is no more Morai than we are human." Vaelyn practically snarled the words. "Powerful he may be here, but we are a thousand years and more beyond him. He is a parasite, a fool, and a disgrace. Once we have what we want, we will destroy the scions and send Nurien to his end. Here, or in our realm."

Ian forced a strangled cough. No doubt he'd picked up on the same thing I did—she'd just announced her intention of killing the kids. I wondered, if they were really there, how many of them had heard. Or let themselves understand what she meant. "What, exactly, do you want?" he said.

"A child." The words emerged on a longing sigh. "We . . . *I* desire a child of my own, and I have no wish to wait three more centuries. I took you, Gahiji-an, because you are fertile, though I knew you would never willingly breed with me. Now there is no need. Your scion is a better choice—he is powerful, and of this world. The child would belong as I can never hope to."

Oh, *hell* no. Not this scion. Apparently she had forced Calvin to perform the fertility spell, but I wasn't about to touch her long enough to find out.

"Ian, don't . . ." Tory stirred and tried to get off the ground. I could finally see enough to put together what had happened. The shotgun had exploded in his hands and turned him into a shrapnel pincushion. "Don't trust her."

"I do not," Ian snapped. "Not for a moment."

Footsteps approached. Vaelyn stopped right beside me. "Do you have another choice, Gahiji-an? We're offering everything you want. Take it."

A wave of emotion hit me like a hurricane. Anguish and fury and desperation all at once. Ian, longing to believe he could have Akila back, painfully aware he had a better shot at destroying Vaelyn with a blade of grass.

I drew a harsh breath and slammed every bit of my consciousness against the healing point. New heat flared through my body, but this time it was pure magic. Charred skin smoothed and fleshed itself out. Frozen joints relaxed. Screaming pain calmed to mere agony.

Through it, I felt something strange. Small spots of pressure on the ground around me. I could sense where everyone was standing—and I felt the other scions. A dozen of them, positioned in a loose circle around the yard. Shit. She hadn't been lying about that.

My tongue didn't fill my whole mouth anymore. I forced it to move. "No." I sounded like I'd swallowed a cheese grater, but at least it was a discernible word. "Fuck you. Not happening."

"Oh, yes. He'll do very well," Vaelyn said. "Be reasonable now, child. One simple act, and you and your kin will never hear from us again."

"Bullshit." I pushed up a few inches and fell. Swore, tried again. Finally I propped up on one elbow and rested there to heave in a little oxygen. "You . . ."

The thought that arrested me closed my throat and almost gave it away before I could try what might be the dumbest idea ever conceived. I had to get close enough to draw her blood. Sex guaranteed that I'd be really damned close.

"You want a kid," I said slowly. "With me."

"Yes. Nothing more than that."

I hauled in and gained a knee. Every motion sent knives through my blood. I paused again, panting, and stared at the ground. "You'll leave us alone? *All* of you?"

"You have our word."

I managed to lift my head and meet Vaelyn's eyes. "All right," I said. "I'll do it."

If the shock was any thicker, I could've used it to fix the Berlin Wall.

Tory glared, and Ian's jaw hung somewhere around his knees. Even Calvin stared openmouthed at me, as if I'd just spit on a stack of Bibles. Mercy was the only one unaffected. She sat on the ground next to Zephyr, her gaze fixed on a point in the distance. I suspected she'd stopped trying to participate in reality for a while. Couldn't blame her for that.

"Interesting." Vaelyn subjected me to a long stare. "We expected greater resistance."

"It's like you said. What choice do we have?" I kept my features neutral and worked to keep up the healing process. It was going a lot slower than I'd hoped. "I do want something from you first, though."

Her eyes narrowed. "What?"

"A snare spell." I tried to gesture, to indicate the whole area, but my arms were on a union coffee break. "I don't want anyone to be able to surprise anyone else." I would've asked for disarmament too, but she'd probably insist on the same from us. And I couldn't let her see what I had in my pockets.

She nodded. "A reasonable request. We will grant it." She backed away a few steps and raised a hand. "*Sukkayati,*" she said, and waved the extended arm in a slow circle. At the border of the clearing, the scions popped into view one by one as she gestured. I recognized Kit, and Billy.

And Lynus. Who still looked like he'd hit thirty-something overnight, and held a speargun pointed directly at Ian's head.

"Now, then." Vaelyn smiled, but there was no warmth or

welcome in it. "What shall we do to ensure your cooperation?"

I probably should've known she wouldn't make this easy. "You have my word, just like I have yours," I said. "I don't know what else I can give you." The heat from the power I was using to heal kept rising. Sweat drenched me, soaked my clothes and plastered my hair to my skull. But I could almost move. I stayed on my knees and looked as weak as possible.

"Are you crazy, Donatti?" Tory struggled to his feet, but didn't come any closer. "She'll kill you! She's not going to turn anyone over to us. We're outpowered and outnumbered. You're just going to—"

"Hold your tongue, boy. Let the thief make his own decision." There was something lethal in Ian's tone, an edge that demanded obedience. He knew what I was going to try. I'd thank him later for playing along, if there was a later.

Tory shut up. But his expression said he'd slit Ian's throat if he could. And mine.

Vaelyn paced a few steps, stopped, and sent me a speculative look. "There is little you can do," she said. "Still, we can't have you attempting anything . . . noble. A paralysis spell won't do. We will need some parts of you working, won't we?"

"Ergh." A mental shudder worked through me. "Yeah," I said, trying not to sound like I was about to puke. "Guess we will."

"And we can't kill the prince or the Bahari brat—until we find their tethers. However." She looked at Mercy, and a smile oozed across her face. "The woman is another matter."

Calvin beat me to the protest. Only he did it in djinn, explosively, with a lot of nasty words that didn't have English equivalents.

"You have nothing to fear, Khalyn, so long as the mongoose performs as he's told." She made a beckoning gesture, and two of the older scions broke from the circle and headed toward us. "And this will ensure you remain on our side, won't it?"

"Vaelyn, I swear . . ."

The two scions reached Mercy. She blinked up at them and said, "What? Ain't you never seen a beauty mark before?"

"Look here, Luke. It's the coon lady," one of them said. "Even uglier up close, ain't she?"

The other one, Luke, grunted. Each of them grabbed an arm and hauled her to her feet.

Mercy smiled sweetly at the one who'd spoken. "Got somethin' on your face there, sunshine."

His brow furrowed. "What?"

"My fist."

In the space of a breath, she jerked out of Luke's grip and clocked the guy a teeth-rattling blow to the chin. His head snapped to the side, his eyes rolled to white, but he didn't fall. So Mercy kicked him square in the junk. He crumpled like a wet towel.

I couldn't help it. I laughed—deep from the gut, an action that hurt every inch of my battered body. Damn, did she ever remind me of Jazz. I clutched my ribs and bent almost double, gasping, aware that I had to stop before I caused more damage.

Vaelyn launched a spell in a guttural voice. That sobered me. For a few seconds I couldn't breathe, until I saw it was only a lockdown. Luke grabbed the motionless Mercy and hooked his arms through hers to wrench them behind her. "Really, Luke," Vaelyn said with a sneer. "Can you not handle one ordinary female? Shall I have one of the others help?"

"Got her," Luke grunted.

"See that it stays that way." She returned her attention to me. "Now then, thief. The arrangements are quite simple. Once we have finished, we will release all of you. But if you should attempt anything foolish, the woman will be injured. She will not die immediately. It will give you the opportunity to rectify any mistakes, and possibly save her."

"Sounds great," I muttered. At least the laughing fit had accomplished something. With my arms folded, I could get at the inside zipper of my jacket without drawing attention. I hoped. I worked it open slowly, concealing the movement with a couple of weak coughs and twitches. "So, should we get a room, or what?"

"No." She licked her lips. "Remove your clothing."

I froze, stared at her. "Come again?"

"You heard me." She flashed a predatory expression. "We will do this here, with witnesses. You will be far less likely to change your mind this way."

I swallowed hard. This wasn't in the plan. "Um. Can you say performance anxiety? Because I seriously doubt I'm gonna be able to get it up with all these assholes watching."

"We have ways to ensure your . . . preparedness."

"Terrific. You planning to cast a Viagra spell on me?"

"A what?"

"Forget it." I managed to slide a hand in my pocket, and gripped the handle of the twins' tether. "Look, I'm not exactly in the best shape here—"

"Undress. Now."

Her tone said I'd run out of stalling time. I was as healed as I was going to get, and if I didn't try this now, I'd never have the chance. "Okay," I said. "I'm doing it. Give me a second." I reached my free hand back like I was going for a shoe. My throat felt like I'd eaten a sandbox, and my spine crawled with tics and shivers. If I fucked this up, and Mercy died, I didn't think I'd be able to live with myself. Of course, Calvin would probably kill me, so I wouldn't have to.

I drew a deep breath. *Make it fast, Donatti.* The first waves of heat seeped into me as I tapped the earth, sought out Mercy, and undid the lockdown spell on her. She'd have to be able to get away or this wouldn't work. I heard her give a little gasp. And now I really had to move.

I twisted around and threw a lockdown at Luke. He went rigid, and Mercy slipped away from him. One step down. One giant, impossible leap to go.

Vaelyn's mouth opened in silent surprise. The second of hesitation was enough. I lunged at her and brought her down, clamped a hand over her mouth. She glared at me, and I could practically read her mind. *You are a dead man.*

Maybe. But I'd damn well bring as many of these assholes down with me as I could.

I produced the tether and plunged the blade into her throat with a grimace. Might as well make sure she couldn't cast any spells for a few minutes—at least the ones that required words. Blood gurgled and spurted, splashing me and staining her robes. I figured that was plenty of hers. I pulled the dagger out, ready to add my blood to the mix and hopefully seal her inside forever.

Something wasn't right. My gut lurched when I realized what it was. There were no glowing symbols on the knife. Not even a little glint of moonlight. No blood tell.

This wasn't Vaelyn's tether.

Chapter 31

Something told me the only chance we had for surviving the next few minutes was to keep Mercy safe. And I had no time for secret plans. "Tory, get her in the house and protect her," I shouted. "Right fucking now! And don't let her back out, under any circumstances."

I couldn't tell whether he went for it or not, because right after I got the words out, the rest of our little party finally realized what I'd done.

The knife didn't glow, but Vaelyn did. I stabbed at the light a few times, hoping to force her into expending more power. I didn't get too many in before she finished transforming and wiggled free. Before I could give chase, the first gunshots cracked from the perimeter—and something rammed into me hard. It felt like I'd been smacked with an eighteen-wheeler, and then had a tank dropped on me. I landed facedown in the dirt and tried to figure out where I'd gotten hit.

But it wasn't a bullet. It was Ian. He'd knocked me down, covered my body completely with his own. And the scions were still firing.

Shot after shot rang out. Not all of them found a target,

but I felt every bullet that ripped through Ian and sent him into jittering spasms. He didn't even have time to scream. After five or six direct hits, he passed out, effectively jolting me from his head.

They kept shooting. His body jerked again, and again, mashing me farther into the ground. His blood drenched me. I clenched my jaw and resisted the urge to throw him off, to run at the bastards and tear them apart. Ian hadn't saved me just so I could get my stupid ass blown away. I had to think, had to come up with something before Vaelyn managed to get back to her stubbornly not-captured self.

Through the sick pounding in my head, someone shouted a spell. I shuddered. *Too late, damn it, she's back and she hasn't lost an ounce of power . . .*

A series of dry clicks echoed in the air. Some of the scions snarled curses. The gunfire stopped.

"Get up, apprentice." The strained voice belonged to Calvin.

I struggled out from under Ian's inert form, cringing at the wet crunching sounds his body made when it moved. I deliberately avoided looking at him when I got clear. Couldn't bear to see the damage just yet. I scanned everywhere except the place where Ian lay. From what I could tell, Tory and Mercy had gotten inside. Even Zephyr must've taken the hint and run off somewhere.

Calvin had both hands wrapped tight around the neck of a huge black-and-red snake. The rest of the thing coiled around his legs, and it looked like it was squeezing hard. Light pulsed around the snake. Calvin clenched his jaw, and the glow faded. Somehow, he was keeping her from transforming.

"I can't hold her long," he said. "But I'll keep her busy. You take care of them." He jerked his head to indicate the scions.

"Right. No problem." Some of them were still trying to unjam their weapons, but a few had started toward us. They didn't look like they wanted to pat me on the back either. I glanced at the blade still in my hand. "Isn't this your tether?"

"It is." The Vaelyn-snake glowed again, and Calvin let out a grunt of effort. "She must have transferred herself to another tether without telling me. I don't know . . . what, or where." He gasped, swayed a little. "Thank you for saving Mercy."

I nodded. "Let's hope she stays saved."

"Yes. She can be a bit—"

Faint light washed through the snake. This time, it kept getting stronger. Calvin uttered something that sounded an awful lot like *shit*. "Stop them," he said. "Please."

"I will."

He managed to kick free of the glowing coils and started dragging Vaelyn away. I tried to stop paying attention to them, to trust that he'd keep her occupied for a while. I had bigger problems.

Like Lynus. Who'd ditched the useless speargun, and advanced anyway, with an expression that said he'd tear me apart with his bare hands if he got close enough.

I still had the Sig. But I didn't know if it'd work. If the spell Calvin cast was like a snare, covering an area instead of specific objects, it would've shorted out all the weapons. I pulled it out, aimed at the ground in front of Lynus, and jerked the trigger. The answering thunder of the gun let me breathe again, and the clearing fell silent in its aftermath.

Lynus glared at me. "You gonna kill me now too, thief? I ain't armed, you know. Not that it matters to you. Cold-blooded murderin' bastard."

"No, I'm not." I struggled not to show how cutting the remark had been, and raised my voice. "I don't want to kill

anyone," I said. "Look, you guys have been lied to. All of you. I
don't know what they told you, but they're full of shit."

Shouts behind me drew my attention. Calvin and Vaelyn. I
glanced around—just long enough for Lynus to lob a paralysis
spell at me.

It didn't take long to undo it, but Lynus had sprinted a good
ten feet before I shook free. I raised the Sig level with his torso.
"Don't," I said. "I won't kill you, but I'll injure you if I have to."

He froze, and his eyes flared wide. "How the fuck—"

"Never mind that." Beyond him, two figures were
approaching fast. Kit and Billy. The rest of the scions seemed
content to hang back and look either pissed off or terrified.
"If you don't believe they're lying to you, ask Kit," I said. "He
knows they're full of shit."

"Don't you even fuckin' mention my brother! You already
killed one of 'em."

I went cold. It was true enough—I hadn't technically killed
Davie, but I sure as hell didn't try to stop Ian from doing it. And
I probably would've done the same if I'd had the chance.

Before I could formulate a response, twin groans rose
from the ground. Luke and the guy Mercy knocked out were
coming around. In a rare flash of logic, I realized that if my
gun still worked, theirs did too. I knelt and frisked them one-
handed, keeping the Sig trained on Lynus with the other. Luke
had a Desert Eagle .44 Mag. Hell of a piece. The other guy
turned out to have a custom Glock. I tucked them both in my
waistband and stood.

More shouting behind me, farther away. A tremendous
crack, like a tree snapping in half. I didn't look around this
time. Kit came up beside Lynus, looking grim, and Billy hung
back a bit. Neither of them said a word. But at least they didn't
try to attack.

"I'm kind of at an impasse here," I said. "How do we work this so nobody else dies?"

Luke sat up with a gasp and reached for the place his weapon used to be. When he didn't find it, he fixed me with a wild-eyed stare. His jaw worked. A tiny snap of breaking glass sounded.

"No!" Kit dove for him and tried to wrench his mouth open. "Luke, don't . . . Lynus, do somethin'! Please . . ."

"Ah, *shit*." I dropped next to him and sought frantically for a healing point. By the time I found it, Luke was already convulsing. I tried anyway. But whatever poison they used in those things, it worked too damned fast. Foam bubbled from his lips, and his eyes drifted in two different directions and froze there.

Kit held the bigger man's head until his body stopped twitching. When it ended, he sobbed once and raised reddened eyes to meet mine. "He weren't bad," he said hoarsely. "Just not all that smart, is all. He followed orders same as the rest of us, but he never hurt nobody."

"I believe you. And I'm sorry," I said. "It's just too fast. I couldn't stop it."

"Bullshit! You wasn't—Kit, shut your damn mouth." Lynus was practically spitting. "Don't you talk to this piece of shit."

Kit shot him a narrow-eyed glare. "This has to stop, Lynus," he said. "He ain't gonna kill us. Neither is the prince. It's Val and Father who's pickin' us off, and pretty soon they ain't gonna do it one by one no more. They don't care fuck all about us."

"He's right," Billy said quietly. "The thief let us go when he busted the prince out. He coulda killed us then."

Lynus opened his mouth, snapped it shut. He looked from Kit to Billy, then back at me. His face was a blank.

"She said she was going to kill all of you," I told him. Kit and Billy winced at that, but Lynus didn't even twitch. "You're batteries, powering up Nurien—the guy you call Father. She hates him, wants him dead, but she can't destroy him unless you're all gone."

"Ricky," Lynus whispered. "He did somethin' to Val. It was a joke. But she was furious. She made him dig for three days straight, wouldn't let him stop until he . . . just dropped dead." A shudder went through him. "I heard Father screamin' at her. Said she was gonna make him too weak to take the prince out. I didn't get it, but . . ."

I shook my head. Couple of sick bastards, both of them. "They're using you," I said. "For their own reasons, they're playing you all like chess pieces. And only the king's supposed to stay standing."

Lynus shook himself and frowned. He hesitated for a few seconds. "Can I take care of Jackson, there?" he finally said, nodding at the injured man. "That coon woman knocked him a good one. I might be able to heal him some."

"Go for it."

I stepped back to give him some room, and scanned the clearing. Some of the scions had vanished. Since the snare was still in effect, I figured they must've just wandered back into the woods. The ones who stayed were the younger ones, the second generation. They were edging together, moving closer to our little gathering. Probably following Lynus's lead.

A fresh, distant cry erupted just behind the lingering scions. Calvin tumbled out from between two trees, landed hard. He bounded to his feet almost instantly and rushed back into the woods, screaming a spell. There was a terrific crack, and a pine tree toppled over.

Nothing I could do out there. I'd have to hope he could

handle it. When I looked back down at the injured scion, Lynus had a hand down Jackson's boot. Not exactly a healing gesture. He pulled it out—and there was a gun in it.

Damn. I hadn't thought to look for spares.

"You go to hell," Lynus snarled, and swung the weapon up.

I'd dropped my guard enough so I couldn't react in time. My brain couldn't decide whether to cast a spell or shoot him. All I knew for sure was that I was about to take a bullet. I could only hope he didn't hit me anywhere instantly fatal.

A blur of motion caught my eye. With sick clarity, I understood what it was and tried to shout a warning, tell him not to bother, I could handle this. Too late. Kit lunged at me and barreled me aside, just as Lynus fired.

I heard him hit the ground seconds after me. The silence that followed was painful.

Please don't be dead. I could save him. I had to. Gagging on panic-induced bile, I righted myself and staggered toward Kit's fallen form. He'd been gut shot. I had a few minutes at the most before he bled out.

"Kit!" The wild, pitched scream tore through the air. Lynus popped up like a demonic jack-in-the-box, still clutching the gun. "You," he said through his teeth. "Fucking. Die."

And he emptied the rest of the clip into me.

The pain was immediate, blinding. Beyond excruciating. I had time to marvel that anything could hurt worse than being set on fire from the inside. At least it wouldn't last long. I'd be dead in a few seconds—he'd pierced my stomach, both lungs, my breastbone just under the hollow of my throat. I was over and out.

But there was no light at the end of the tunnel. No choirs of angels or lakes of fire. Not even nothingness. There was just the pain, and it kept getting worse.

Why wasn't I dead?

I coughed. Blood and bone splinters bubbled from the wounds in my chest. I could barely see, and couldn't draw in more than a sip of air with my ruined lungs. But I was definitely alive.

I really did have a tether, in every sense. I was just as immortal as Ian.

Kit. Maybe I could still save him. He wasn't too far away. I flung an arm in his direction. A strengthless cry ripped from my throat as the motion spiked new levels of agony. Probably should try to heal myself first, but I didn't know how much time Kit had left. And apparently I had all the time in the world . . . as long as I could stand the pain.

I dug my fingers into the ground and pulled myself toward him, sobbing with every tiny movement. Jesus fucking Christ. No one, human or djinn, should've been able to withstand this much hurt without at least passing out. I was less than thrilled with this ability.

"The *fuck*!" Lynus bellowed. "You dead, you cheap-shit sumbitch. Quit fuckin' movin' and be dead already!"

Shut up, I tried to say, but what came out of my mouth was a thin gurgling whistle and a river of blood. I'd reached the end of my hauling limit. I threw my arm up again, and my hand came to rest on Kit's chest. Had to be close enough. I couldn't move anymore.

Lynus threw the empty gun at me. It struck square in the gut wound. Dazzling white burst across my vision. I didn't have enough breath to scream. "Get your goddamn filthy paw off my brother," he snarled.

I had to get this going before Lynus physically removed me. With an effort that flash-boiled my blood, I pulled at the earth, demanding every drop of power my body could take in.

I closed my eyes and found the flickering red pinpoint that was Kit's dying energy. The second I focused on it, it winked out.

Fuck threading a needle.

I pushed everything I had at the spot. *Come back, goddamn it, don't you dare die on me, kid.* For a few seconds I got nothing—and then the light flared like a close-range camera flash. The backlash shattered my concentration.

But it was enough. Kit's wound closed in on itself, a pond ripple in reverse. The slug oozed from the diminishing hole just before it knit completely shut, and rolled to the ground. Kit snapped back to consciousness with a shocked intake of breath.

And my shattered body still refused to let me pass out. Lucky me.

"Kit?" Lynus croaked. He took a shambling step forward. "Kit . . . *how*? You're healed. I thought you were . . . Jesus, I'm sorry. I didn't mean . . ."

Kit sat up slowly. Looked over at me. "You killed him." His voice was raw, shaking.

"No! I mean, a minute ago he wasn't . . . shit, how'd you *do* that?"

"You asshole. You fucking shot me!" His tone gathered strength. "You know I ain't got healin' power. He did it."

"No," Lynus whispered. "He ain't with us. He killed Davie. They're evil, both of 'em."

"Goddamn it, Lynus, you *seen* what happened!" Kit stood with clenched fists. "Val and Father's the evil ones. We're on the wrong side. And you just killed the right side."

I tried to speak, to tell Kit I wasn't dead. No sound came out. But I managed to lift one arm a few inches and execute a tiny wave. *Hello, still alive. In a fuck ton of pain, but not dead.*

"Christ." Lynus staggered over and dropped next to me. "I'm sorry. I'm so sorry . . ."

He held a hand out. A small, tingling ripple spread through my chest. The congealed mess inside me started to separate and firm. Some of the pain evaporated, revealing new layers I hadn't been able to feel before. I didn't know if that was good or bad.

I was a long way from healed when Lynus sagged back, panting and gray faced. "Can't," he gasped. "Billy. Get Payton over here. He c'n heal some."

"It's okay," I tried to tell him. It sounded more like *iz-ay*, but at least I was making audible sounds. I didn't want them wasting all their mojo. They might need it if Calvin didn't win. I knew better than to hope the twins would take each other out of commission.

Speaking of the dynamic duo, where the hell were they?

Couldn't worry about that just yet. I drew in what I could and worked at putting myself back together. After a few minutes, I managed to pull in a deep breath that didn't feel like I was drinking molten steel. I let it out with a groan, flexed a hand. "Fuck," I whispered. "Don't think I like being shot."

Kit loomed over me, then knelt down to stare. "Sweet Jesus. You healin' yourself? How've you even got any juice left?"

I almost smiled, but it hurt too much. "My power works . . . different. Be okay soon."

"Shit, I hope so." He looked up, and his face fell. "Don't think your friend will be, though. He ain't moved since . . . well, you know."

"Ian can't die." I wasn't ready to confirm that I couldn't either. They'd probably figured that out. Still, I didn't want it getting back to the wrong djinn, if I could help it. They might try to test that theory. "But he needs help," I said. "I have to get to him." I attempted to get up. And failed explosively. Had to heal some more first.

Lynus sent a miserable glance at Kit, then turned it on me. "Thank you," he said. "For saving my brother. I didn't know..."

"I don't blame you," I said. "This is all on your so-called leaders."

"They ain't leadin' shit no more." A fierce light came into Lynus's eyes. "I'll kill 'em both. Swear to God I will."

"You can't. Not alone." The hole under my throat had almost closed. I sat up with a guttural snarl, caught my breath. "But we're after the same thing now. If we work together, I think we can bring them down."

"No, you can't." The flat statement came from Jackson. "You're dead. We're all dead. Dead men walkin'." He laughed, but it was a hollow, hopeless sound. "And I ain't gonna die their way."

I knew what was coming. Knew I couldn't stop it, even if I hadn't been crippled. The muffled crunch of breaking glass might as well have been a gunshot. Twenty seconds, and Jackson's twitching body stilled forever.

Lynus stood slowly and stared at the rest of them, who'd gathered in a tight knot around Billy. "We got any other chicken-shit cowards here?" he said quietly.

No one moved.

"Go on! Poison your fool selves like the elders if you want." He thrust two fingers in his mouth and extracted his capsule. "I'm through servin' this death sentence." He let it fall to the ground.

Billy grinned and fished his out. One by one, the others followed suit.

Lynus nodded. "C'mon, Kit," he said. "Let's help the thief get to his friend."

"My name's Donatti," I said.

"All right. Donatti."

I let them help me up, and tried to steel myself for the sight of what was left of Ian. But I didn't get much of a chance to look—because two figures emerged from the woods and demanded my immediate attention. One of them was dragging the other. And the one still standing had never read the Bible in her life, but I figured she was probably down with the whole eye-for-an-eye thing anyway.

Chapter 32

Lynus and Kit stiffened when they caught sight of Vaelyn. As tough as they tried to sound, they were still just kids. I couldn't let her hurt them.

At least I knew she couldn't kill them. But I doubted they did.

"Just take me to her," I murmured, hoping she didn't have super hearing like Ian. "Act like you're on her side."

"Fuck no." Kit's grip on my arm tightened. "She'll tear you apart."

"No, she won't. I'll handle this." Damn. I'd hoped the twins were a little more of an equal match than this. My only shot now was to hope she still wanted to be impregnated. And if she did, I'd probably have to go through with it.

The thought of having sex with Vaelyn didn't exactly inspire my libido.

"Do what he says," Lynus whispered. "We got no other choice, Kit."

Kit glared at his brother, but he moved.

I half-stumbled along between them and pushed hard in a desperate bid to heal before I had to face the crazy bitch. For a few moments I succeeded. Despite the gallons of sweat pouring off me, I felt torn flesh closing and shattered bones mending. Then the heat fizzled out of me and everything stopped.

Apparently, I didn't have unlimited power.

I wasn't healed all the way. My body felt like a heavy punching bag at a public gym—sweat stained, thoroughly beaten, weighed down and full of sand. I still bled in half a dozen places. I hadn't lost my connection with the earth, but I couldn't draw anything in. The tap was broken.

Vaelyn dumped Calvin alongside Ian with a sneer. At least she looked like she'd taken some damage. Her face was bruised, her robes torn and filthy. Blood soaked one arm and dripped from her sodden sleeve. "Well done, children," she said. Her voice didn't betray the least trace of the pain she must've felt. "You will be rewarded. And as for you, clever little mongoose—you will die."

"Thought you wanted to fuck," I said.

Her gaze went diamond hard. "I would no more trust you to keep your word than . . . wait." She waved a hand. "Drop him."

Lynus and Kit complied, though it took Kit a few seconds longer to let go. I couldn't have stayed on my feet if I tried. I hit the ground on hands and knees, felt the impact like knives through the open wounds. My palms tingled at the contact. And my hands sank a few centimeters into the dirt.

I frowned. Maybe it was all the blood soaking the ground, along with an extreme desire to be anywhere but here, prostrate in front of a crazy Morai who wanted to screw me and kill me, or just kill me. A reflexive and aborted attempt to transport myself. Whatever it was, though, it didn't restore the power tap. No warmth seeped into me. Only chills.

"You seem weak enough." Vaelyn stepped forward. Not close enough for me to grab her, I noticed. "Let us find out if you are. Defend yourself, thief." She pointed.

A flame curse surged through me.

I screamed and writhed on the ground. Even if I had the strength, I couldn't have stopped this. Hadn't figured out a way to deflect a flame curse. At least it wasn't real fire. But it still fucking hurt.

After a moment, Vaelyn cut it off with a gesture. I gasped and went limp. "Interesting reaction," she said. "Perhaps you are spent. And we do want all that power for ourselves. Yes. An earthbound child." She ran a hand absently down her bloodied arm and wrung the sleeve. A thin stream of blood drizzled to the ground. "And then we'll destroy you. You should not have crossed us, Gavyn Donatti."

You would've killed me anyway. I didn't manage to say it because I'd caught sight of something that froze my tongue in shock.

Alongside Vaelyn, where her blood had dripped, a faint red line glowed beneath the grass.

The luminous strip curved behind her, then under Ian and Calvin, tapering off near the forest line. It faded fast. I wouldn't have seen it if I wasn't lying on the ground—but I was willing to bet that if I'd been in the air, the line would've formed part of a djinn symbol. It might've been an impressive sight. The biggest blood tell ever.

She'd tethered herself to the whole goddamn mountain.

"Rise."

By the time I realized she'd spoken in djinn, my body had started obeying the command. I could no more have stopped myself from standing than I could've commanded the sun to come up. My limbs moved in stiff, awkward jerks, hauling me to my feet with unnatural and painful motions. I ended up with legs spread slightly and arms held out from my sides.

Vaelyn looked me up and down. An awful smile curled her mouth. "Children. Strip him."

I struggled, but my efforts went no further than my thoughts. I couldn't even twitch a finger. This wasn't a paralysis spell, though. I could still talk. "You don't have to do this," I said. "I'm a big boy. I can undress myself."

"Undoubtedly. But we won't allow you the opportunity to use your weapons again." Her gaze drifted lower. "Save one."

Ugh.

Lynus moved first, peeling my jacket off with brisk efficiency. He tossed it to Kit, circled me, and plucked the guns from my waistband to shove in his own. The vest followed. My shirt wasn't coming off easily, the way she had my arms arranged, so he tore it apart at the bullet holes. Everything in his stance and motion suggested that he hated me as much as Vaelyn did, and looked forward to my humiliation. Only his eyes said he wasn't enjoying this.

When he went for my pants, I closed my eyes. At least she hadn't taken control of my eyelids. The last thing I wanted to see right now was my own tool spring to attention at Vaelyn's command. It'd be more than enough to feel it.

Once everything was down around my ankles, he couldn't go any further. But Vaelyn had that under control. Invisible strings jerked through my right leg. The knee bent, the foot moved back and lifted a few inches from the ground. If I'd tried this pose on my own, I would've done a face-plant in a half second flat.

Lynus went behind me and yanked off boot, ankle holster, sock, pants, drawers. Right foot down, left foot up. He repeated the process while I tried to banish the idea that Vaelyn was making me do the hokeypokey. The obscene version. I really didn't want to think about what I'd have to stick in next.

Naked, bleeding, and cold in places I didn't know it was possible to feel cold, I waited for her next move. It didn't take long.

"Lie down."

I couldn't help trying to resist. Didn't do a damn bit of good. I went down to my knees, then flat on my back. The night sky filled my vision. The clouds had begun to part, and a single bright star shone directly above me, framed in ragged edges of darker gray.

Star light, star bright . . .

Jazz. Cyrus. I thought I'd managed not to think about them through this nightmare, but they'd always been there. At the back of my mind, on the tip of my tongue. In a safe corner of my heart. With me, and still so far away that I couldn't touch them.

First star I see tonight . . .

The image burned in my head—Jazz holding Cy at the window, the two of them communicating in ways too deep for words. I clung to the mental picture, desperate to claim a different reality from the one I found myself in.

I wish I may, I wish I might . . .

Something stirred deep in my groin. More invisible strings, pulling and tugging me erect against my will. The feeling was indescribably awful. This went far beyond humiliation. It was utterly dehumanizing. I focused on Jazz and Cyrus completely, until it almost felt like it was happening to someone else. She could control my body. Not my mind.

Have the wish I wish tonight.

I wished for this to be over, before the safe place in my head evaporated completely and forced me to experience everything.

The thunder of gunfire threw my thoughts into

pandemonium. Before I could speculate on who, what, and where, Vaelyn collapsed half on top of me—and I realized I could move again. She'd been shot in the back. I had one chance to finish this. Ignoring the pain movement brought, I flipped her to the ground, pinned her beneath me. And caught a glimpse of the shooter.

Lynus, grim and shaking, still held the Glock out in both hands, at once weapon and shield.

Vaelyn clung to consciousness like a yapper dog fastened to an ankle. Her weak struggles gained momentum. I clamped a hand over her mouth, just in case, and fought to remember Ian's brief lesson. Her blood, check. With her back to the ground, it'd be saturated. I could see the faint glow again from the curved line of the tell.

My blood—not enough. Not for a tether the size of a mountain.

I glanced over my shoulder. "Shoot me."

Shocked silence, a shake of the head from Lynus. Vaelyn bucked. She almost threw me off.

"Damn it, shoot me! In the arm or something. Hurry!"

Lynus still didn't move. So Kit yanked the other gun from his waistband and fired.

The bullet tore through my upper arm, shattering a bone or two on the way. Blood and flesh spouted from the exit wound. Some of it splashed Vaelyn, but most of the spray baptized the ground. I hoped it was enough.

And now, the spell. I couldn't access the earth, but I still had some djinn magic left. And that was the kind I needed.

"Ana lo sijin na'ar, nee halam akiir lo'ani."

The fury in her eyes took a rapid 180 dive into horror. Her struggles increased—but she was sinking into the ground. I scrambled off her before I could get sucked in too.

The area around her burst into cold blue swamp fire. Tendrils of luminescent smoke wove themselves from the false flames and wrapped around her, plunging into the earth to burst through on the other side and wrap again. Like phantom spiders, they encased her completely in a quivering cocoon.

Blue fire licked around the edges of the light-mummified body. The quivering intensified, and Vaelyn's bound form convulsed and bucked. Every time part of her rose from the ground, a new tendril spun from the flames and lashed her back down. A thin, plaintive cry escaped the bonds when she started sinking into the dirt.

She went under with a resounding pop. The pool of blue light that remained dwindled to a single pinpoint, flickered, and vanished.

The instant she was gone, Calvin gasped and bolted up to his knees. His head swiveled in my direction, and his eyes looked like they were about to squirt from his skull.

I tried to nod an acknowledgment—game over; good-bye, evil twin—but my body decided I'd had enough of being conscious. I was out before I hit the ground.

The first thing I saw when I opened my eyes was Vaelyn. Hopeless panic ramped my heart up to hummingbird speed before I realized she was wearing black robes, and was not a she. "Calvin," I muttered. "You really need to stop looking like your sister."

"I'm afraid I can't help that, apprentice. Though perhaps I shouldn't call you that anymore." He offered a small smile. "You've . . . progressed."

"To what, flunky?" Christ, everything still hurt. At least it wasn't agonizing anymore. I just felt like I'd been hit by a train.

"I'm not as good as you think," I said. "I lost the earth-magic thing near the end there. Got any theories on that?"

His brow furrowed. "You'd been using it constantly, correct?"

"Yeah."

"Then it's likely you reached your physical capacity to handle the power. The earth's energy is virtually unlimited, but your body's not."

My body. Which was still on display. "Um. Can I have my pants back?"

"Of course."

Someone produced my clothes. I struggled into the pants, stopped to catch my breath, and decided the rest could wait awhile. "So, you ended up doing that fertility thing after all," I said.

"More or less." Calvin smirked. "I had no choice, once Vaelyn learned of Mercy. But I didn't exactly perform the *ba'isis*. I'd hoped to have you destroy both of us before she discovered the deception. However, I must say I like your plan better."

I flashed an exhausted grin. "Me too."

A quick appraisal of things revealed a small, huddled group of scions near the bodies of Luke and Jackson. Neither Lynus nor Kit was among them. They and two others were trying to heal Ian. And not having much luck.

"I have to help them." I tried to get up, and almost made it. Calvin boosted me the rest of the way, and I found I could stand on my own. "Thanks," I said. "You healed me, didn't you? I thought you were spent."

A dark look crossed his features. "I was, until you neutralized Vaelyn."

"Whoa. How did she—"

The slam of a door cut me off. Mercy strode from the cabin

and flew down the steps, with a dented frying pan in one hand and fire in her eyes. Tory staggered out behind her, holding his head like he had the world's worst hangover. Blood trickled between his fingers.

"Oh, shit. You'd better go calm her down," I said. "And tell Tory not to hurt anyone." I suppressed a laugh. Like he could if he wanted to. He didn't look capable of swatting a fly. Obviously, Mercy had something to do with that.

Calvin nodded and practically ran for it. He managed to reach her before she brained anyone else.

I left him to handle things and turned my attention to Ian, expecting to find him in bad shape. Reality exceeded my expectations. He'd been shot so many times he looked like raw hamburger. One of his arms had been just about severed at the shoulder. And he'd taken a bullet to the head.

For the first time, I could truly sympathize with him. I'd been savaged beyond the point of human death twice in an hour. It wasn't fun. He'd been through this countless times in the past few centuries—and this time, he'd done it for me.

Lynus sent me a haggard look when I approached. "You sure he can't die?" he said. "Looks pretty fuckin' dead to me."

"He's not," I whispered. Jesus, what a mess. My eyes burned looking at him. What if I couldn't heal him this time? Would he just stay like that, bloody and broken and gray, forever? "Tell them to stop," I said, indicating the two scions working ineffective spells over him.

Lynus nodded. "Payton, Jimmy. Leave off awhile. Clear out of the way."

They pulled back and strayed over to Kit, who sat cross-legged and glassy eyed on the ground a few feet away. He stirred when they sat next to him, and looked over at me. "Did you kill her? Val, I mean," he said in scratchy tones.

"No. She's alive, but powerless. I sealed her away inside the mountain."

"For how long?"

"Forever." Or until someone broke her out again. I wouldn't voice that possibility, though. They were freaked out enough as it was.

The younger of the other two, who looked right around Kit's age, broke out a grin. "That was some shit," he said. "Yankin' her down in the ground like that. Hey, you gonna do that to Father too?"

"Shut up, Jimmy." The other one, Payton, looked exhausted. "The old man'll probably hear you flappin' all the way out here."

Jimmy's smile vanished.

"Some of the elders left," Lynus said. "They'll report back to Father, tell him where y'all are."

I did a quick mental rewind. They'd left just after I attacked Vaelyn and failed the first time. Hopefully, they didn't know I'd taken her down. If we were lucky, Nurien would assume she could take care of herself.

Of course, neither Ian nor I had much in the luck department now. We were surrounded by Morai we didn't intend to kill.

I knelt next to Ian. The whole contact thing was pointless, but I tried anyway, pressing both palms against the least damaged spots I could find. I expected nothing and got it.

A choked curse in djinn erupted behind me. I glanced back to find Tory standing there pale faced and furious. A huge knotted bruise stood out on his forehead, and blood matted his hair on one side. "What the hell happened?" he demanded.

"Ian saved my ass." I turned away so he wouldn't see me

laughing. "What happened to you?" I asked, knowing damned well who'd knocked him down a few pegs.

There was a pause. "Your crazy friend hit me with a frying pan," he finally said.

Well, nobody could say Mercy wasn't resourceful.

Tory came around and squatted at Ian's opposite side. "How long's he been gone?"

"Not sure. Awhile."

"Damn." He reached out with a trembling hand and brushed some of the hair away from Ian's face. "Can you heal him?"

"Don't know yet." I'd have to hope I could get to the earth magic again. I gave a tentative prod, and felt relief along with the familiar warmth. But when I directed it toward Ian and looked for his points, I found nothing.

I tried again, longer this time. Everything inside him was dark.

"He's so far gone. I can't . . ." I let out a sigh. Cyrus wasn't here, and the thing we'd done before wouldn't work with anyone else. I could think of only one other possibility. "Maybe if we give him some blood," I said.

"That won't be necessary."

I looked back. Calvin was crossing the yard, with a protective arm draped around Mercy. "I can heal him, if you'll help me," he said.

"Heal?" Mercy snorted. "Shit, Calvin, you're full of crazy today. First I find out you ain't blind, then y'all are magic, and now you're sayin' you c'n heal dead people." Her tone stayed light enough, but she'd gone pale and kept her gaze averted from Ian's body, like she'd go insane if she looked for too long.

I noticed Brother Calvin didn't take offense at her language.

"He's not dead. He's djinn." He rubbed her arm gently and disentangled from her. "So, apprentice. Will you help me?"

"Hey, I'm willing to try anything." I stood and moved a few steps back. "But I don't know how much help I'm gonna be. I don't think I can hold anything for long."

"That's all right. I'll provide the power."

I frowned at him. "How'd you get this much mojo all of a sudden?"

"Vaelyn." A fresh jolt of fury infused his features. "She performed the *rohii'et* on me years ago. Unlike your bond, ours was unequal. It strengthened her and crippled me."

"So that's why you didn't heal yourself after the fire, then," I said.

"Yes. I was weakened until you sealed her. Which was, by the way, brilliant on your part. Now it seems I possess her power along with mine, since she's unable to use it."

"Thanks." I barely registered that he'd called me brilliant—a quality no one had ever accused me of having. "All right. How are we going to heal Ian?"

"I'll focus the spell through you." He smiled. "You won't even have to drink any blood, since you're his scion."

"Gee, thanks. So I should . . ."

"Lay your hands on him."

"Right." I went back down and tried to find a few spots on him that weren't covered with blood. There weren't any, so I settled for places without bullet holes.

Calvin gripped my shoulders. I beat back the urge to start confessing my sins.

"Ready?" he said.

I nodded, closed my eyes. "Okay, Ian," I muttered. "Come back, or I'll kick your ass."

Calvin's power was red. Like fire and blood, like the snake he could become. I let it fill me and shut out everything except Ian.

The blackness inside him was frigid. A wasteland. Nothing beat or twitched or flowed. Mercy was right—I was trying to resurrect a corpse.

A tiny flicker caught my eye. Black on black. The faintest glow, like the afterimage of a black light in deep space. I seized it and hammered magic through it. Every last scrap I could summon. Slowly, the flicker solidified and shimmered through a washed-out rainbow of colors, black to dark gray, flat silver, ghost white. Pale yellow. Orange. Crimson.

Blood red. And I was burning.

Something slammed me so hard, I rocked back and fell on my ass. It felt like I'd run full tilt into an electric fence. I gasped out a breath, exhausted at a cellular level, and cracked my eyes open.

Ian glowed. The familiar brightness of his transformation flickered along the lines of his body and grew steadily stronger, until he looked made of light.

"Thank the gods," Tory said. "You all right, Donatti?"

"Fantastic. Let's run a marathon." I scooted closer. Through the light, fur bristled. Bones shifted and raised thick ridges. Usually the change happened too fast for me to see. I hoped this didn't mean he'd stall out in midshift and get stuck as half a wolf.

Eventually the glow fizzled out. A few streams and sparks of light ran down the wolf like water beading on glass. He slept, tongue hanging crookedly from his parted mouth, sides jerking with erratic breath. But he wasn't full of holes anymore.

"He'll come around," Tory said. "Just needs to sleep for a while."

"He's not the only one." My eyes watered with the effort to keep them open. I made a bleary search for Calvin, and found him just behind me. He seemed tired, but not spent.

Mercy, on the other hand, looked like she'd just seen Elvis.

"So I'm dreamin', or my weed's got more kick than I thought." She blinked and shivered. "How many more of y'all are werewolves?"

"Just him." I focused on Calvin until the two of him merged together. "We all need a few hours. How strong are those wards you put on Mercy's house?"

Calvin blinked openmouthed, then laughed. "I suppose they'll have to do."

I tried to smile back, but the situation failed to amuse me. Vaelyn had been hard enough to deal with. Now we had to face Nurien, who had Morai and Bahari magic, a big bunch of scions powering him up, and Akila to use as a shield.

Lucky us.

Chapter 33

Eleven of us, from human to djinn and everything in between, hung around in the bloodied yard. Six Morai scions, three djinn, Mercy, and me. Lynus was the obvious leader among the scions. Calvin, the oldest and most powerful djinn. And we were on Mercy's property.

But for some reason, they all looked to me to decide what we should be doing.

We had to bury the bodies and get everyone inside, including Ian, who couldn't get there on his own. I managed to prod Mercy for shovels and a blanket to carry Ian with. Somebody—might've been Lynus—brought up the possibility that Nurien might send an unfriendly search party out.

I responded to the effect that my give-a-shit was broken. We'd take our chances.

Eventually, everyone straggled into the house. I limped in clutching the rest of my clothes, which I hadn't bothered to put back on. Someone had gotten a fire going in the fireplace, and they'd arranged Ian on a blanket on the hearth. Tory was helping Mercy with pillow-and-blanket detail, bringing armfuls of bedding out from the back rooms and distributing them.

Deciding they could handle things without me, I picked an empty spot and stretched out on the floor. Didn't bother waiting for a pillow.

Sleep swallowed me whole.

Sometime later, I woke with a start, sure I'd heard something. Breathing, soft snoring, and the low crackle of a banked fire filled the room. I lifted my head a bit and scanned the area. The door and windows were still closed, and a red dawn crept through the screens to stain the glass. Sleeping bodies scattered the floor and draped the furniture. Nothing ominous seemed to be lurking anywhere.

The sound came again—a low, mournful whine. Ian, still in wolf form, twitched and shivered on the hearth.

I hauled myself up, shrugged stiffly into my jacket, and headed over to him. Couldn't tell if he was in pain or dreaming. Maybe both. "Ian," I whispered. "You in there?"

His eyes opened, and he whined again. At least he didn't try to bite me.

I knelt and laid a hand on him. A shudder rippled under my palm, and light seeped from the contact point to infuse him with the changing glow—faster than the last time, but still not quite up to speed.

"Thief," Ian slurred when he was himself again. "Please tell me you have defeated Vaelyn."

"She's gone," I said.

His body sagged. "Gone does not precisely mean defeated."

"So you're an English professor now?" I grinned. If he could make smart-ass remarks, he was definitely feeling better. "She's defeated. Sealed back in her tether."

"How?"

"Long story." I glanced around again. No one else was awake, and I wanted them to sleep as long as possible. "Feel like stepping outside with me?"

He groaned. "I feel like excrement. But if we must . . ." He pushed up and took in the room. "Ah. The young ones have stayed."

"Yeah. Their survival instincts are busted." I waited for him to stand and led the way to the door, then outside onto the porch.

Ian shut the door gently, frowned at me. "You look terrible."

"I don't doubt that." I searched my pockets and found a crumpled pack of cigarettes. When I pried the flip top open, tobacco and torn bits of filter paper dribbled out. Crud. I found one that still looked smokable, straightened it out, and lit up. "Don't give me any shit," I said. "It's this, or I'm gonna start smoking Mercy's weed."

Ian declined to comment.

We sat on the steps and I told him what had happened, telegram style. Calvin distracts Vaelyn. Stop. Lynus unloads a clip into me. Stop. I don't die.

Full stop. Ian gaped at me. "You are no longer mortal?"

"Apparently not." I took a deep drag and let it out slowly. "Whatever you did to me, I'm completely attached to your tether now."

He stared across the yard. "I did not expect that."

"Well, it was definitely one of the more welcome surprises today. Dying wasn't on my to-do list."

I explained the rest—how I'd found Vaelyn's tether, Lynus plugging her, the way the ground had swallowed her. When I got to the part about Calvin healing him because I had nothing left, his features contorted. "I would not have blamed Khalyn if he had left me injured," he said. "I have not treated him well."

"I think he understands why," I said. "And I wouldn't worry about him right now. I'd worry about Nurien."

"As would I."

I drew a fast breath at the voice behind us and damn near choked on smoke. "Shit, Calvin," I sputtered. "I thought monks had better manners than to sneak up on people like that."

"I've been considering retirement." He leaned against the porch rail and sighed. "Nurien won't be easy to defeat," he said. "I can't imagine how we'll be able to contain him, or even enter the compound in the first place."

I took a last hit and pitched the cigarette. "Any ideas about his tether?"

"None whatsoever."

"There's a shocker." I looked at Ian. "You think Tory could find it?"

"Perhaps," he said. "It would depend on whether he has wards in place, and how strong they are."

"Nurien is well protected." Calvin grimaced. "I believe Mercy would say he's dug in like an Alabama tick. Whatever that means."

This called for another smoke. I fished out a rumpled one and pinched off the torn end. "It means he's probably smart and paranoid as hell, and he's had years to make the compound a fortress. Kit said there's a huge subsystem of tunnels under that place, so God knows what he's got down there. Sorry, Calvin." I lit up and snorted at Ian's surgeon-general face. "Come on, man. If a half dozen bullets aren't gonna kill me, neither are these."

"They smell terrible."

"Stop breathing, then." I almost blew smoke at him, but decided to be nice. "Anyway. There's at least one permanent snare, on the building with the big mirror. That's probably not the only one."

Silence dropped like lead. I smoked, Ian stared, Calvin frowned.

"Maybe we could . . ." I stopped before the word *fly* left my mouth, and a different idea presented itself. One with a higher stupid factor, but if it worked, we'd be in a better position to survive. "Either of you guys ever seen *Star Wars*?"

"No," they both responded in stereo.

"Man, are you ever culturally deprived," I said. "Okay. I think I know how we can get in the place."

"How?" Calvin said. Ian just raised an eyebrow.

I summoned a grin. "As prisoners."

Tory didn't particularly like the plan. Especially since he had the dangerous part.

"Tell me again why I have to pretend to be Vaelyn," he said after I'd explained what I was thinking. "And try to make sense this time."

I shook my head and glanced around the room. Most of the scions appeared to agree with Tory—at least, the ones who weren't glazed with shock and exhaustion. Ian and Calvin were with me, mostly because the other options would get us killed faster. Mercy had so far kept her thoughts to herself. "Look," I said, "you won't have to keep it up for long. We just need to get inside the gates."

"Yeah, we get in. And what're we s'posed to do then?" Lynus stirred from a semitrance by the banked fire. "Go back to playin' tin soldiers and takin' orders? If y'all go up against Father and lose, he'll know we was helpin' you. He'll kill us. Hell, he won't even have to lift a finger. The elders'll do it for him."

Kit, who'd been listening to his brother with a deepening frown, stood suddenly. "Then we make sure they win," he said. "Damn it, we fight back. This has to end one way or another, Lynus, and you know it."

Lynus clenched his jaw. "We already out. So let's just stay out. We don't go back, they can't kill us."

"What the fuck happened to you?" Kit crossed the room to the fireplace. "Last night you was ready to take 'em out yourself, and now you wanna run?"

"Yeah. I wasn't thinkin' clear last night. Now I am."

"Father'll find us. You know he c'n track us down."

"I don't give a flyin' fuck. We ain't goin' back, Kit."

"We have to go—"

"Goddamn it, I can't lose you!"

Silence ebbed in after the hoarse shout. Lynus turned his back on the room, and his shoulders heaved once. "I already got Davie killed," he said, his voice breaking against the wall. "Don't ask me to let you die too."

Ian sent me a pained look, but he held his tongue. Interrupting would only make things worse. I nodded and hung back.

"Lynus." Kit put a hand on his shoulder. "I don't know about you, but I'd rather die fightin' than live like a damn slave, or keep lookin' over my shoulder forever wonderin' whether he's gonna come after us. I think we can win. And I'm goin' back."

"Me too." Billy moved toward them and hesitated. "They gotta be stopped, Lynus. And Penny's still in there. I'm with Kit."

The other scions murmured reluctant agreement. Lynus turned slowly and fixed Kit with a red-eyed stare. "You really think we got a chance?"

"Yeah, I do," he said. "I mean, with the thief's plan, we're gonna surprise 'em, right? Maybe we can take out the elders before they know what's goin' on."

"And what if we don't?"

"I think Calvin can help you there," I said.

Everyone stared at me. Especially Calvin. "How am I going to do that?" he said.

"Teach them your gun-jamming spell."

"Ah." He nodded, smiled. "Yes, I believe that will help."

One of the scions on the couch—Mack, the one who'd barely spoken to anyone—raised his hand like he was in school and had to use the bathroom. I tried not to laugh. "What's up?" I said.

"I . . . um, I ain't got a gun." He flushed crimson and looked at his feet. "I had one, but when we was chasin' you guys, I got spooked and shot at Jackson. So he took it away."

"Val never give me one," Jimmy piped in. "She said I ain't got the guts to kill nobody."

Lynus bowed his head and pinched the bridge of his nose. "This is gonna be fuckin' suicide," he said. "There's twenty more elders in there, plus Father, and enough firepower to take out the U.S. goddamned Army. We're just flat outgunned."

"I can fix that," Mercy said.

I blinked at her. "Your shotgun's a pile of scraps. Remember?"

"Yeah." She gave me a cool stare. "Come on back here a minute. Got somethin' to show you," she said, and headed for the addition at the back of the house.

I shrugged and followed her. Calvin came right behind me, as if he didn't trust me with her alone. I didn't blame him much. He'd almost lost her last night—and I knew exactly what it felt like to watch someone threaten the woman you love.

There were two doors leading from the short hallway, one straight ahead and another on the right. The door at the end stood open a crack and afforded a view of the corner of a log-frame bed built into the wall. The other door, made of rough wooden planks, was held shut with a padlocked hasp and staple.

Mercy produced a small ring of keys, opened the lock, and rolled the door aside. "Don't get your robes in a twist now, Calvin," she said. "I never had plans to use most of this stuff, 'cept for target practice. I just like bein' prepared." She reached in and pulled a chain switch, and a single lightbulb flickered on to illuminate the room.

Which was full of guns.

Mercy motioned for me to go in, and I stepped through, dragging my jaw along. Three walls held racks and shelves and mounted display cases stocked with more pieces than a state fair gun show. Boxes of neatly stacked ammo lined the fourth wall on either side of the door. She had shotguns and rifles, revolvers, pistols and semiautomatics, everything from the latest Glocks and Magnums to a couple of tarnished six-shooters that looked like they'd last been fired by Wyatt Earp.

The biggest piece in her collection caught my eye. "Is that . . . a machine gun?"

"Yep. It's an M249 SAW, military issue. Light infantry," Mercy said. "Got a pretty hard kick to it, but if you shoulder-mount the bitch, it won't knock you down too fast."

"Holy . . ." I fingered a gleaming Remington sharpshooter with a bayonette blade. "How'd you get all this?"

"From ebay." She winked, brushed past me, and picked up

a Ruger .357 with a scope and laser sight. "I'm bringin' this one. Y'all help yourselves to the rest."

"Bringing?" Calvin shook himself and moved into the doorway. "Mercy, you can't go—"

"Stop right there." Mercy leveled him with a blazing look. "You ain't about to tell me I'm not goin' with you."

He stiffened. "Actually, I am."

"The fuck I ain't. Bastards almost burned my place down." She checked the clip on the gun, rammed it in her waistband. "And another thing. Those boys out there, they're just kids. Seems to me they're pretty unwanted kids too. Christ, their own father wants to kill 'em." Her good eye brimmed, and a tear spilled over. "I know how that feels," she said. "And I'm not gonna stand here wringin' my hands by the window while they . . . while *you* go get yourself shot up, and maybe killed. Am I?"

Calvin managed a smile. "No," he whispered. "I suppose you're not."

"Damn straight." Mercy nodded curtly and turned to me. "You pick out whatever y'all think you need and start gettin' those boys geared up. I'm gonna go make us some tea." She walked out, catching Calvin's hand to squeeze it on the way past.

I shook my head. "You officially have my sympathy, Brother Calvin."

"Really." He frowned. "And why is that?"

"Because I've got one of those at home."

"One of what?"

"A gorgeous crazy woman who doesn't need me to protect her and will kick my ass into next week if I try."

His eyes widened—and then he laughed. "She would, indeed. Man of the cloth not withstanding." He stared at his hands. "I love her," he said. "I've never told her that."

"No time like the present," I said. "You'll regret it if you don't. Trust me on that one."

He let out a long breath. "Perhaps I'll go and help her with the tea."

"Good idea."

I waited until he left, and allowed myself a minute for some regrets of my own. Then I got back to work.

Chapter 34

At least we didn't have to fly.

I'd gotten everyone to agree not to waste power before the attack. It had taken only about an hour to walk. We'd come within sight of the compound, and things were as prepared as they were going to get. Ian and I appeared beaten and bound with the same blue-black pulsating rope stuff they'd used on Akila—illusions, courtesy of Billy and Mack. We were flanked by Calvin and "Vaelyn." It hadn't been easy for Tory to make himself look and sound like her, but he'd had Calvin for a model. He was convincing enough to make my blood run cold every time I caught a glimpse of him.

We knew what waited for us inside. Twenty elder scions, two younger ones—both female—and four human girls that Nurien referred to as breeders, the very pregnant Penny among them. And somewhere, Akila. Nurien hadn't told Calvin or any of the scions where he was keeping the princess. And I wasn't about to dig Vaelyn back up and ask her.

From our position, we could see the outer edge of the compound, but not the gate. Which meant any guards they'd posted couldn't see us yet. Nothing in the range of sight moved. That probably wasn't a good sign. The more of them hiding, the harder it'd be to spring anything on them.

Ian drew himself straight. "Are we ready?"

"Hell no," I said. "Let's do this."

Tory grabbed Ian's arm, and Calvin gripped mine. We started for the path leading to the gate with the scions moving behind us. There were guards—two of them, both elders, stone faced and visibly armed. Beyond them, the compound looked deserted. One of them shifted his attention to us and nudged the other. Both drew weapons, but neither aimed them.

The guard on the left flashed a nasty grin as we neared the gate. "We got comp'ny," he drawled. "Welcome back, Mister High-and-Mighty Prince."

"Maybe we should bow or somethin'," the other one said. His free hand moved to the gate. "You takin' them down below, Val?"

"Of course, child."

Vaelyn's voice coming out of Tory made my skin crawl. But it didn't seem to bother the guard. He unlatched something, rolled the gate back, and stood aside. When we passed through, the left-hand guard leered and snapped off a mock salute. "Enjoy the hospitality, Yer Highness."

Ian growled. Tory gave him a rough shake and shoved him so hard he almost went sprawling. Whether it was for show or to remind him that he was supposed to be helpless, it worked.

"Father's busy," the other one said. "And he don't want to be interrupted. He said to tell you if you come back, wait for him 'fore you off the prince. Guess he's got a surprise for him."

"Oh, we'll certainly respect his wishes." At least Calvin didn't have to hide his disgust. It dripped from his words like venom. "Where is he?"

The leering guard motioned toward the cabin with the big mirror. "Think he's in the tem—"

"Shut *up,* Johnny," the second one snapped. His gaze had fallen on Mercy, who wore a bulky hooded sweatshirt that hid most of her face. "Who the fuck's that? Jackson? Can't be Luke . . . hey, where is the big moose, anyway?"

"Luke popped off, back at the fight." Lynus managed to sound steady enough.

I risked a glance back. The other scions were shifting around Mercy, moving her away from the guards, farther into the compound. Everyone had cleared the gate. Almost time.

"What's the matter with Jackson? He don't look right." A wary edge slipped into Johnny's voice. "Hold up. Why'd Luke pop off if y'all won?"

The second guard raised his gun. "Val, what the hell's goin' on?"

We couldn't wait any longer. I turned to face the guards and flashed a grim smile. "Looks like rain," I said.

At the signal we'd worked out, magic and bullets went flying.

Kit and Jimmy launched jamming spells at the two guards. Lynus and Billy drew on them and fired. The second one went down immediately. Johnny took a slug in the side, staggered back, and vanished—only to reappear when Calvin cast a huge snare spell on the entire compound. Two more shots slammed Johnny against the gate and dropped him.

The snare revealed an elder crouched beside the nearest building, preparing to fire. I moved to dissolve the rope illusion and went for my Sig. Before I got it out of my jacket, Mercy had taken him out with a head shot. And she hadn't even put her hood down.

I gaped at her. She offered a one-shouldered shrug. "Ain't

you better go find whoever you're lookin' for? We got this."

"I guess you do."

Ian shook himself loose and headed for the building with the mirror. I started after him, and stopped when someone touched my arm.

Kit had a gun in each hand. "The temple," he said. "I think that's what Johnny was gonna say. Where Father is. Take the right-hand tunnel all the way down."

"Okay. Thanks, kid."

He shook his head. "No. Thank *you*."

"Tell me that after we live through this." I grinned at him. "Give 'em hell."

"They got it comin'," he said grimly.

The sounds of doors opening echoed across the compound. They must've heard the gunshots. I ran for it, and slipped into the big cabin after Ian. "Know where we're going," I said. "Sort of. Come on."

I pulled the door open on the stairs leading down, and descended gun first.

Ian stopped me at the first landing, where the tunnels ran to the left and right. "What do you mean, you 'sort of' know where we are going?" he said.

"Kit said he thinks Nurien's in the temple. Whatever the hell that is," I told him. "And it's that way." I pointed right.

"A temple." Ian sneered. "No doubt to honor the glory that is himself."

"That sounds about right." I stared down the tunnel, a rounded corridor of hard-packed earth that sloped slightly down, with just enough room for Ian to walk upright. Torches lit with cold blue flame had been mounted about every fifty feet. The glow from them didn't reach quite far enough to cover the entire stretch, and gaps of dark shadows bridged the lit spaces. The other direction looked exactly the same. "Is it me, or does it seem way too quiet down here?" I said.

"It does."

"Yeah. Well, I guess that's not going to stop us. But . . . hang on a second." I knelt under the bulb that illuminated the landing, laid the Sig aside, and got one of my blades out, then sliced a palm and let it bleed on the ground. When the flow stopped, I healed the cut almost without thinking. "Okay. Let's take a walk."

Ian's brow furrowed. "Why did you do that?"

"In case we need to make a quick exit. Remember how I got to you down there?"

"Ah, yes. Very well."

I didn't mention that I hadn't tried to take passengers with me on a through-the-ground trip yet. Hopefully, we wouldn't need to test it.

I started down the tunnel, still holding the gun ready, listening for any hint of life or movement. Only the faint crunch of our feet on the earth and my own shallow breathing reached my ears. The occasional muffled gunshot from the surface sounded like branches breaking. I couldn't help worrying about them, the young scions, and Mercy. With Vaelyn out of the way and Nurien occupied, Tory and Calvin would be all right. The rest of them didn't enjoy virtual immortality. And I couldn't make any more miraculous saves, like I'd done with Kit.

I packed away grisly images of twisted, bullet-riddled bodies and faces too young to die. Time to concentrate on the here and now, on the strange stillness that shouldn't have been. In my experience, this kind of quiet screamed *trap*.

The tunnel continued unchanging. Same packed walls,

same width and height, same torches and pockets of shadow that granted a moment of blindness while we moved through them. The heavy scent of earth permeated the cool air, traced with an ozone whisper of blood. I glanced back at Ian, beyond him. Couldn't see the landing anymore.

But ahead of us, still nothing.

"I don't like this," I murmured. "Any minute now, we're going to fall through a pit onto a bunch of spikes, or a giant boulder's going to roll through and crush us. Or we'll step on a hidden switch and release the poison darts. Or—"

"Where do you get such ideas?" Ian cut in.

"Indiana Jones," I said. "Don't tell me you haven't seen any of those."

"What is an Indiana Jones?"

I stifled a laugh. "Man, you really need to get out more. They're movies. Entertainment. You know, fun?"

"Giant crushing boulders and poison darts do not sound like fun to me."

I stared at him. He returned the look with blank features—and then a corner of his mouth twitched into a smirk.

"Holy shit. You're making a joke?" I grinned. "There's hope for you yet, Ian. Maybe you won't need that operation after all."

He raised an eyebrow. "Operation?"

"To take the stick out of your ass."

Soft laughter escaped him. "Yes. Perhaps."

We passed through the next dark stretch. When we entered the light again, the tunnel ended abruptly in a wall of solid earth, a few feet beyond the torch.

"Great." I walked up to it and stopped. The tunnel branched to the left and right, both directions sloping down, both paths identical in appearance to the one we stood in. "Just go straight down to the temple. Sure. Now what do we do?"

Ian joined me and glanced down both ways. "I do not know. I still sense nothing."

"Oh, this is gonna be fun." I got a blade out and crouched. "Do you care which way we go?"

"I suppose not."

"Okay. We're going left." Might as well mix things up a little. I scratched a thick arrow into the dirt, pointing left. "Let's try it. If we run into a dead end, at least we'll know where we've already been."

We headed down the left-hand tunnel. Eventually, another wall loomed out of the shadows—and this time there were three corridors branching away. Every direction looked the same. "Shit!" I palmed the blade again. "You pick one this time."

Ian pointed down one that slanted away to the right. I marked an arrow, and we kept going. Only to find another wall, and more turns into more identical tunnels.

"This is ridiculous," Ian said. "There is nothing straight here."

I sighed. "Let's give it a few more turns. If we don't find anything, we'll follow the arrows back." And probably get lost in the other direction. I didn't mention that idea—no doubt Ian was thinking the same thing.

Three random passages later, the tunnel no longer sloped down—it was rising again. After we crossed a few stretches of light and dark, I made out a whiter glow beyond the next pool of torchlight. A lightbulb. For some reason, the sight of it didn't inspire the hope that we'd found the temple.

I slowed as we neared it, and stopped at the edge of a landing that looked exactly the same as the one we'd come down. A glance at the ground confirmed what I feared: the dark splash of blood under the lightbulb. My blood.

It had been a trap. Not crippling or deadly, but a trap all the same.

Ian let out a frustrated snarl. "Blasted coward! How like Nurien to conceal himself rather than confront his enemies. He does not have the strength to face a warrior."

"Rather deal with the crushing boulder, huh?" I muttered. "Yeah, me too." It was cowardly, all right—but it was effective. We'd have to search all the tunnels, and continue marking them so we didn't keep going the same wrong way. It'd probably take a while. And I was pretty sure time was the one thing we didn't have.

Before I could suggest getting back on the horse and trying again, a muted whisper sounded close by. I swung the gun up and swiveled toward the closest shadow. "Who's there?" I said.

As if anyone trying to sneak up on us would've answered me. Ian shook his head and pointed. "Your pocket."

"Oh. Right." His hearing was still better than mine. I fished out my cell phone, expecting Calvin. For once I was right about something. "You guys okay up there?" I asked his weak reflection in the faceplate.

"So far. Is the prince still with you?" Concern and faint horror stitched his features, and dark patterns splashed his face. It took me a second to realize what it was—blood.

"Yeah," I said. "What happened?"

"This is not my blood." He closed his eyes, crossed himself. "I have information for you. About Nurien."

Jesus. Somehow I understood what had happened. He'd tortured one of the scions to find out whatever he knew. "Go ahead," I managed.

"The so-called surprise he had planned for Gahiji-an. He is . . ." Calvin stopped and swallowed hard. "He is in the midst of a bonding ceremony. With the princess."

I glanced at Ian. He hadn't made a sound, but his rigid stance and furious expression said he was barely holding himself in check. "Okay," I said to Calvin. "So he hasn't finished it yet, right?"

"Correct."

"And he's definitely in this temple Kit mentioned?"

"Yes. He also knows you're here and seeking him." There was a broken moan in the background, and Calvin blanched. "We've dispatched all but four of the elders, and searched everything on the surface. The rest, we assume, are down below."

"I guess that makes them our problem," I said. "Listen, don't let anyone—including Tory—come down here. You've done enough already, and I'm sure you have some damage control to take care of up there."

He nodded. I didn't press for details.

"Khalyn . . ." Ian's voice wavered between rage and sorrow. "Thank you."

"Yes. Just be certain you put this information to good use, *rayan*." He flashed a quick, sad smile, and the reflection vanished.

Ian glared down the right-hand tunnel, practically burning a path in the air. "Oh, I will," he said in a simmering growl. "I will."

In that moment, I was extremely grateful not to be Nurien.

Chapter 35

This time, we took the tunnel at a run.

"You are certain about this?" Ian said.

"No." I wasn't sure about anything, except that Kit wouldn't have lied to me. He'd said to take the tunnel straight down, and that was what we were going to do. Whether or not there was a wall in the way.

When the first obstruction came into view, I slowed and stopped. The arrow was still scratched into the dirt at my feet. "Okay," I said. "Straight is that way, so we're going through this thing."

Ian frowned. "Did you not say you required blood to pass through the earth?"

"Yeah. I'm not gonna try that here."

"Then what are you doing?"

"Not sure yet." I'd shaped dirt before, so I thought maybe I could move things around and make a hole. Of course, if I was wrong and the temple wasn't this way, I could be digging through for a long time. I flexed a hand and pressed it against the wall.

It went right through like there was nothing there.

Startled by the lack of resistance, I lost my balance, pitched forward, and landed on my hands and knees. Even though my eyes were open, I couldn't see a damned thing. I backed up until the lights came on again and got to my feet. "I don't think we'll need blood for this," I said. "It's an illusion."

Ian scowled and thrust his arm through the wall. "A childish defense," he said. "Nurien mocks us. He does not believe we are important enough to deal with properly."

"Well, it bought him some time. Maybe that's all he's after." I knew better than to get into a discussion about djinn politics with Ian. "There's no more light on the other side. You should probably make one of those flame-ball things." I went through pockets and located the battered flashlight I'd dropped in the mud half a dozen times. The lens and the barrel were scratched to hell, but a steady beam still shone from the end when I switched it on.

Ian extended a hand and produced a globe of white flame. "Ready."

"Let's move." I walked at the wall, through the wall, half expecting a spike pit or poison darts after all. Nothing happened. I played the flashlight beam around the darkness on the other side. Same packed earth, same tunnel dimensions. The light ran ahead a few dozen feet and dissolved in blackness.

We settled at a fast stroll, and I tried to think ahead a little. I almost didn't say anything to Ian, because I knew the subject was a tough one, but there were a few things it'd help to know. "How long does this bonding ceremony take?"

Ian bristled. "Several hours."

"Okay." It would've been nice to think we had time, but we had no idea when he'd started. "How does it work? If it takes a lot of power, maybe he'll be drained by the time we find him." *If* we found him. We didn't know anything about this temple thing.

"It is a sharing of blood, of life." The words dragged out of him like he'd rather eat a handful of thumbtacks than think about it. "The spells involved do not require a great deal of magic. The time, the commitment, is more important." He let out a breath. "There is typically an official present to perform the ceremony. A ranking member of the clan. It is possible to proceed without one, but it takes longer that way."

"That's good, isn't it?" I said. "I mean, there aren't any ranking members of any clan around here. Right?"

"No. There are not."

The pain in his voice stung me. "We'll find them," I said, with a lot more confidence than I felt. "We'll get Akila back. And if he finishes the ceremony before we get there, we'll just destroy the bastard, and the bond will break. If one dies, the rings shatter. Right?"

Ian didn't respond.

I decided to change the subject. Before I could think of anything brilliant to say, my light found another wall of earth straight ahead. I frowned, walked up to it, and stuck a hand out. It passed through without resistance. "How original," I said. "I guess he really does think we're stupid."

"Yes. Nurien's arrogance leaves little room for strategy."

"So we keep going." I moved through the illusion without waiting for Ian's agreement.

By the time I realized there was nothing under my feet on the other side, I was already falling.

My warning shout cut itself short when I hit the ground hard enough to drive the breath from me, then bounced a foot and started rolling. The lightless tunnel dove down at a steep incline. Protrusions that might've been rough steps battered me into an erratic tumble, preventing me from slowing my descent. I tried digging the end of the flashlight into something to stop the momentum—and only managed to vault myself airborne.

I finally crashed to a stop with my face in the dirt and one leg jammed against the tunnel wall. Various bruises and scrapes throbbed in sync with my pounding heart, but nothing seemed broken. Except my pride. I groaned, shuffled into a semiupright position, and spat out a mouthful of sludge. "That sucked," I muttered.

A blurred patch of light approached me, with Ian behind it. His lips twisted into a crooked smile. "Interesting strategy, thief," he said. "Did you perhaps intend to beat the steps into submission?"

"How'd you guess?" I got my feet under me and tried to brush myself off. "At least there weren't a bunch of spikes at the bottom. Christ." I directed the flashlight beam back the way I'd fallen. The incline was so steep, I could make out only about five feet of tunnel before the ceiling got in the way. "When Kit said down, he really meant *down*. How far d'you think that went?"

He shrugged. "Perhaps thirty meters."

"And how far is that in plain, normal distance?"

Ian rolled his eyes. "I believe it would be approximately one hundred feet."

I gave a low whistle, winced, and rubbed the back of my head, where a good-size knot had formed at the base of my skull. "We're pretty far underground," I said. "Have to be getting close to the place."

"Yes," Ian said slowly. "Though I still do not sense anything."

"Well, they did say things were well protected here." I took a minute to heal the worst of the damage. Without knowing my own limits, I wanted to use as little power as possible until we had to confront Nurien, or the other elders. "We should get going. Um . . . but let's slow down a little. I think I've had enough falling for one day."

Ian declined to comment, but his smirk resurfaced.

The tunnel stayed fairly flat and even for a while. We didn't run into any more illusion walls. Eventually, something changed. The tunnel was getting taller and wider. And brighter.

A faint, distant glow loomed ahead. We slowed by unspoken consent, and soon made out two blue-flamelit torches mounted in the floor, at either side of an opening. Beyond the torches, a dingy gray light revealed part of a cavern and some kind of pattern sculpted into the far wall. It almost looked like a couple of columns. Nothing moved where we could see, and there was no sound. Not a scratch or a scuff or a single breath.

But that didn't mean the place was empty. Nurien was expecting us. There had to be guards somewhere. Four elders left. I was sure we'd run into them before Nurien.

I held a finger to my lips. Ian favored me with the I-am-not-stupid glare and gestured his fireball out. I switched off the flashlight. Pre-soul-bind Donatti would've been blind as a corpse in here, but my new sight enhanced the dim glow and cast everything in kind of a blue version of night-vision goggles. I could actually see better without the flashlight.

Which was how I noticed the smaller tunnel ahead, branching off to the right, and the two suspiciously human-shape silhouettes just inside it.

Instinctively, I brought the Sig up into position—just as two lockdown spells were shouted simultaneously. Neither of them had come from Ian. My body froze, and the shapes of the scions withdrew. I heard running feet headed away from us. Ian stayed silent, so I assumed he'd been hit with the other lockdown.

As I worked to undo the spell, panic sizzled through my

gut. Why were they running? They should've tried to shoot us, or cast more damaging spells, or something. Lockdowns only held for a few minutes. These bastards were willing to die for Nurien—so they shouldn't have turned tail now. It didn't make sense.

I broke free and managed a single step toward Ian before a white flash swallowed the mouth of the tunnel. The blast wave slammed my ears like twin hammers, and the tunnel came crashing down.

For a few seconds I couldn't figure out why it was so dark, and why I couldn't move or breathe. It felt like there was a truck parked on my back.

Then I remembered the explosion.

I must've passed out, for God knew how long. No point in shouting for Ian. Even if I could speak, he wouldn't be able to hear me. So the first thing I had to do was get sixteen tons of earth off me so I could breathe. No problem.

I tried moving various body parts, to see if I had any wiggle room. Both legs were pinned solid. Ditto torso and head. I managed to shift the fingers of my right hand, but the movement sent bolts of pain screaming through my arm. Definitely broken. And that probably wasn't the only set of shattered bones I currently possessed.

Crud. How the hell was I going to get out of this? I couldn't use the blood marker I'd left. It'd mean leaving Ian buried here, and we'd definitely run out of time then. If we hadn't already.

I decided it would be easier to think if my head wasn't being crushed. Just as the idea occurred, the warmth of the earth's power flooded me, and the dirt pressed against my face receded. Loose earth rained down around my ears, and a sound like sandpaper whispered from the new space as it deepened. Soon, there was a small hollow carved out around my head.

This earth magic shit really had some kick when I was buried alive.

I concentrated on digging out the rest of me until I lay in a flat pocket of air with a few inches to spare. Once I relieved the pressure, I could really feel how broken and mangled I was. Damn it. I'd have to use a lot of my power to heal myself, and Ian. I'd almost think Nurien knew that, and had the scions take the crippling explosion route just to force us into expending as much magic as possible. But he thought I was weak. Insignificant Doma spawn.

Or did he?

Some of the elders had been with Vaelyn, right up until I took her down the first time. They'd seen what happened with the forest fire and knew I'd done it. Vaelyn had announced it. And they'd wandered off, reported back here—and must've filled good ol' Father in on the new tricks the Doma spawn was learning. So much for the element of surprise.

I healed myself as quickly as I could. My body was prickled with sweat by the time I finished, and I hadn't even found Ian yet. I'd lost the flashlight and the gun too. Jazz was going to be pissed—the Sig was her favorite.

The flashlight was a problem because with absolutely no light to amplify, I couldn't see a damned thing. Blackness pressed against my eyes like a living thing, actively stealing my sight. The sensation of wide-open eyes that saw nothing—not a shape, smudge, or shadow—creeped me out completely. I contorted my way through my pockets until I found my lighter, and gave myself a mental pat on the back for investing in a butane flip top instead of a plastic disposable. I shut my eyes, sparked it up, and opened them again.

Endless, suffocating dirt. Much better.

Ian had been ahead and to the left when I'd faced him just before the explosion. Now, though, he could be anywhere. I didn't think I'd been thrown with the blast, so maybe he hadn't either. I shuffled as far left as possible, picked an angle that seemed like an Ianish direction, and started collapsing dirt out of the way.

The process wasn't exactly efficient. I'd clear a few feet, scrunch forward with an awkward elbow-driven crab crawl, clear a few more, scrabble forth again. Eventually I passed the point where I thought Ian should have been, and had to form a space big enough to turn around. I started a new tunnel back toward my original position, adjacent to the one I'd just dug and a few feet out.

I hadn't gone far when a muffled *whump* sounded behind me, and a brief whisper of moving air flickered the lighter flame. I twisted to look over my shoulder. The turnaround had collapsed and filled itself back in.

Great. If I didn't find Ian soon, I'd lose what little sense of direction I still had.

I pressed on. The enclosed space and constant use of magic conspired to raise the heat level to volcanic proportions. Perspiration ran rivers across my skin, mingled with the dirt, and caked in muddy streaks. My elbows stung with the scraping they endured, and my forearms cramped and throbbed under the strain. But I cleared more space, dragged ahead.

My right arm banged something solid jutting from the dirt, and the lighter fell from my fingers and closed on itself with a tiny metallic snap.

"Damn!" Resisting panic, I patted the ground ahead of me until I felt smooth metal. I snagged the lighter and fired it up. Had to shimmy backward to see what I'd hit—the toe of a scuffed brown leather boot, almost the same color as the dirt packed around it. Presumably attached to the rest of Ian.

I shifted earth around until I had him uncovered and made room to crawl up next to him. He was unconscious, and bleeding from the nose, mouth, and ears. I couldn't tell by looking at him how bad the damage was, but I suspected there were a lot of crushed bits inside.

At least I didn't have trouble finding a healing point. But by the time I finished fixing him, I could've fried an entire truck-stop breakfast on my skin.

Ian came to with a full-body jerk that showered both of us in cascades of dirt. "Take it easy," I said. "This thing's about as stable as a house of cards."

"Donatti." He turned toward me. "The tunnel collapsed."

"Yeah, it had a little help from a big boom. I'm guessing dynamite or C-4."

"How long . . . ?"

"No clue." I'd probably been crawling for at least an hour, but if I told him that, he might give up. I tried to remember the approximate direction of the side tunnel the scions had been in. Pretty sure it was forward and right. "So we'd better get moving."

He glanced around the shallow space and frowned. "I do not see anywhere to move to."

"Got that covered." I focused in front of me and cleared a few feet. "Follow me. And try not to sneeze or anything."

Ian nodded, his mouth stretched in a grim line. "Thank the gods for your new talents."

"I'll have Calvin convey the message," I said.

I decided not to tell Ian that I'd already hit four alarm and was on my way to five. One of us had to believe Nurien wouldn't be able to crush us like flies the second we found him.

Chapter 36

Somehow I managed to pick the right direction, or close to it, anyway. I couldn't see farther than the end of my worm-trail-in-progress, but I could smell the change in the atmosphere—less dirt, more air. I made my way toward the source of the higher air concentration, and after the next few shifts, a small hole formed at the edge of the path.

The feeble light creeping into that hole blazed like a sunbeam bursting through clouds.

One more pass, and I tumbled from the dirt into the wide-open spaces of the tunnel. My body sobbed with relief, and I flopped flat on my back. Didn't want to move another inch. But I managed to slide over and let Ian clamber out. We'd have to get going again soon, but right now if somebody poured gasoline on me and lit a match, I'd just lie here and burn.

Hell, I was practically on fire anyway. I wouldn't even feel actual flames.

I expected Ian to snap at me, tell me to get off my ass and keep moving. But he shuffled aside, sat against the wall, and closed his eyes. He looked awful. Streaked with dirt and drying blood, accidental war paint in brown and red and black where they'd mixed. I probably didn't look much better.

"I believe you were right," he said.

The defeat in his tone overruled my shock. I was never right. Especially according to Ian. "About what?"

"Nurien was simply attempting to gain more time." He let out a sigh. "And he has succeeded."

"Maybe. Remember, we don't know how long we were out. It could've been just a few minutes."

Ian cast me a doubtful glance.

"Look, it doesn't matter," I said. "Whether or not he finished the damned ceremony, we're going to find him and destroy him. Right?"

A fierce light came into his eyes. "Yes."

"Good." I sat up, still hot but not blazing. More like sitting on a Florida beach in August. "I'm sure we're gonna run into at least a couple of scions once we leave this tunnel," I said. "And I lost my gun back there. I'm thinking maybe you should go wolf, so you can take them out."

"How do you plan to defend yourself, then?"

"I've got these." I pulled both blades from the ankle holsters.

Ian raised an eyebrow. "I thought you did not have the stomach for such methods."

"Yeah, well, it's them or me." I wasn't sure I did have the stomach for it. But I knew, without a doubt, these guys wouldn't hesitate. They'd been conditioned. They wouldn't stop until someone died—and I'd prefer that someone wasn't me. "So let's make it them," I said.

He smiled. "A good plan, thief."

"I always do the smart thing."

I stood and waited while he transformed, then started slowly down the tunnel, away from the collapsed part. The passage curved to the left, so I couldn't see where it emptied out—or who might be waiting at the other end.

We rounded the turn. The mouth of the tunnel stood ten feet ahead, with no apparent guards, gates, or other obstacles. That wasn't necessarily a good sign. Like the main tunnel, it opened into the cavern we'd glimpsed before, with the same sculpted pattern on the far wall. I took a breath and headed for the exit.

Ian padded next to me. When we reached the opening, he let out a low, rumbling growl, and as we stepped into the cavern, I caught the scent he must have found first. Death. The place reeked of it. The ripe stench of ruined flesh and spilled blood choked the air, painted everything with a black brush.

I couldn't see the source of the smell. But I did notice the temple.

The sculpted patterns were columns, six of them in two groups, stretching up what would've been three or four stories and blending back into the earth ceiling above. Torches blazed in sconces set into them a few feet above the bases. Behind them, an elaborate replica of a building front had been carved from the wall. Six stairs stretching the width of the temple led to an arched doorway placed between the groups of columns. More torches flanked the entrance.

The thing looked like something straight out of Greek mythology. A place of worship, and sacrifice, and fear. Somehow I got the feeling that was intended.

A light pulsed at the corner of my vision. Ian was changing back. When he finished, he snorted and shook his head as if he had something stuck in his nose. "The wolf cannot tolerate the stench," he said. "And there does not seem to be anyone to kill."

"Yeah, looks that way." I stared at the entrance to the

temple, a gaping maw of hungry shadow, and shivered. "So, we going in there?"

"We are."

"Terrific." I swallowed, gripped the knives harder, and started for the stairs.

The closer we got to the place, the stronger the awful smell grew. I tried not to breathe through my nose, but the stench still reached down my throat and pulled at my gut. Christ, how could anything stink this bad? We passed between the columns—and found the answer lying on the steps behind them.

The bodies of the last four elder scions rested in various heaps. Two on the right, two on the left. Their throats had been slit, their torsos split open at the center and pulled apart like gruesome cabinets. No trace of pain or fear showed in their frozen features. They'd died with the slack expressions of cows chewing grass.

And there was no blood. There should've been gallons of the stuff, splashing the bodies and spilling on the ground, soaking into the packed earth of the temple stairs. But only a faint, dark crust of maroon at the edges of the wounds indicated they'd even had blood to spill.

My stomach jerked and convulsed. I had to bite my tongue to keep from puking. They hadn't been dead long, as far as I could tell. The ravaged flesh inside sundered rib cages still glistened moist and pink. Fresh meat.

Something seemed wrong, outside of the lack of blood. "I'm no doctor," I muttered. "But aren't they missing something?"

"Yes." Ian choked on the word. "Their hearts have been removed."

I blinked slowly and said, "Oh." Nice and calm. Then, with the same calm, I walked back to the other side of the columns and emptied my stomach onto the ground.

For a few seconds I stood there, bent and cradling my gut, the taste of bile scalding my mouth. Nurien had killed them. I knew that as surely as I knew water was wet. Not with his own hands, he couldn't have, so he must've made them kill themselves—or each other. He'd drunk their blood and ripped their hearts out, and left their mangled bodies on the steps of his temple like so much garbage.

Brainwashed killers or not, nobody deserved that.

I spat, wiped my mouth, spat again, and rejoined Ian. We had a djinn to destroy. And I had no remorse left.

It wasn't hard to find Nurien. Ian must've underestimated his arrogance, because the bastard wasn't even trying to hide.

Inside the temple was one long room with cavernous ceilings and more torch-bearing columns marching along both sides. At the far end was a platform with an altar table, complete with candles. Nurien knelt at one side of the table, Akila at the other—though she was restrained with the blue-black rope spell the scions had used to bring her here. No longer clad in the shirt and jeans she'd had on when she was taken, she wore a sleeveless white gown, dirty and torn where she knelt. On her bowed head was a gold tiara streaked with blood.

Without the cult robes, Nurien still looked like an embarrassment to drag queens. His clothing was gold—skintight pants, billowing shirt, vest, sash. He wore white boots and white gloves. He had on a tiara that matched Akila's, except for the blood. His was clean, gleaming. It should've looked ridiculous, but he managed to pull off the overall effect of royalty the way fairy tales made it sound. The real deal. His face looked royal enough—narrow and pinched, with high cheekbones and a thin blade of a nose that he couldn't seem to stop looking down.

Neither of them noticed us right away. I suspected Akila had left her mind for a place where none of this was happening to her. And Nurien seemed to be listening to someone. A deep voice spoke in djinn, but Nurien's mouth didn't move. He and Akila were the only two up there, and it didn't look like there was anyplace in the room to hide.

Without a word, Ian bolted past me and streaked toward the platform. I ran after him, and halfway across the vast space I finally realized where the other voice was coming from. Behind the altar was an ornate frame mounted on the wall. A mirror. But it wasn't reflecting anything. It was an open portal.

Kemosiri's face filled the frame, his features sharp and unforgiving. Akila's father looked just like I remembered him: impossibly old for a djinn, his black hair and beard marbled with white, practically oozing smarminess and power. The bastard was bonding her to Nurien. Or had bonded her already. I had no idea what he was saying, whether it was part of the ceremony.

And I doubted Ian gave a shit.

"Nurien!" Ian's hoarse bellow filled the room. I was surprised he didn't shatter the columns with it. "Preening, prancing *deceiver*. Get away from my wife!"

Akila shivered all over at the sound of Ian's voice. She raised her head like it weighed a thousand pounds and faced him with wide, shocked eyes. "Gahiji-an." His name emerged a dying butterfly of sound, barely lifting from her lips. "You are . . ."

"Alive!" Kemosiri hammered over her. "Blast you, Nurien, you told me you'd destroyed the whelp. My terms are clear."

"I know the terms," Nurien said curtly. He flashed Ian a chilling smile. "Come any closer, *rayan,* and you'll watch her die."

I grabbed Ian's arm before he could do just that. We were still a good twenty or so feet away from the platform. "Wait," I said under my breath. "Look at her crown. I think that's—"

"Yes," Nurien said. "I'd heard you were more clever than we suspected, little scion. It is, indeed, her tether . . . but it is not her blood."

Damn it. I didn't want to be right this time. The spell for destroying a tether only required the blood of the caster. All Nurien had to do was speak the destruction spell, and Akila would die. This close, I could see her hands tied behind her back—and the missing index finger of her left hand. The one he'd cut off to break her bond with Ian.

I hadn't wanted to be right about that either.

Ian blanched and turned his attention to the mirror. "You," he said. "You disgusting coward. You would stand by and let him murder your daughter?"

Kemosiri's eyes narrowed. "I would rather see her dead than bound to a filthy Doma barbarian. Even one who claims to be a prince."

"No!" A wrenching sob escaped Akila. She struggled against the ropes, almost tipped herself off the platform. "I will not be—"

She froze in place as Nurien cast a lockdown spell on her.

Ian glared at him, then looked to Kemosiri again. "So a barbarian prince is unacceptable, but a snake is not?"

"Enough! I am Bahari!" Nurien shot to his feet. "I will fulfill my end of the bargain, Kemosiri. And when I do, you'll hear his death cry all the way to your precious palace." He made a vicious gesture at the mirror. Kemosiri's image vanished, and the surface of the mirror cracked like rotting ice. Pieces of glass sloughed from the frame and landed on the ground in a rapid succession of tinkling crashes.

Ian sneered. "He does not know of your mixed blood."

"I am Bahari," Nurien repeated, calmer this time. "I am a Bahari *noble*. I belong on the Council, and I will take my place. With or without the princess."

"You would not destroy her." Ian managed to sound steady, but I could feel him shaking.

"I would, if I'm forced to choose between her and the Council," Nurien said. "But test me, if you like. Come closer. Cast a spell. Convince yourself that I won't delight in destroying the last ray of light in your pathetic life, before I take that from you as well."

Ian didn't move.

Nurien loosed a wintry laugh. "You have always been weaker than me, Gahiji-an. How it must pain you to realize that now." He circled the altar and wrapped an arm around the motionless Akila. "If you'll excuse me, *rayan,* I have a marriage to consummate."

Before either of us could react, he dragged Akila back and ducked behind the altar. There was a creak, a rustling sound, and a hollow bang. Then silence.

Chapter 37

Ian jerked away from me and ran for the altar.

"Whoa!" I went after him, but his legs were longer than mine. And he was a lot more pissed off. "Ian, this is a bad idea. Didn't you hear what he said?"

"I will *not* allow him to—" He stopped when he got to the back of the platform, and stared down. He didn't say anything more.

I caught up to him. Behind the altar, shards of broken glass littered a hinged wooden square set flush into the ground. A trapdoor, like the one in the mirror building on the surface. I had a sinking feeling we'd find more damned tunnels under there. And this time, we didn't have a single clue as to which way to go.

Ian glanced at me, then knelt and ripped the door open. The hinges that had held it into the frame twisted. Wood cracked and splintered. He tore the whole thing free and flung it across the altar, knocking the candles down.

Faint light flickered in the hole, revealing a drop of at least ten feet—no ladder, no stairs. Not even a knotted rope. "He will not defile my wife," Ian said through clenched teeth. He swung his legs into the opening and whispered, "Gods help me reach her in time." Then he pushed off and dropped straight down.

"Well, this'll be fun," I muttered. Kicking away a few of the larger mirror fragments, I sat on the edge of the hole and threaded my legs through. It seemed like a long way down. Ian moved aside, and I held my breath and launched myself.

The landing impact jarred me, but I managed not to break any bones or fall on my ass. Unfortunately, things didn't look much better from this vantage point. We stood in a small alcove with two guttering torches on the back wall. It was a T junction, with tunnels branching left, right, and ahead. Each tunnel petered out into blackness after a few feet.

Even if we split up and took separate tunnels, the chances were good to excellent that we'd never find Nurien down here.

Ian growled and drove a fist into the nearest wall. He left a crumbling, two-inch dent in the hard earth. "Blasted coward!" he shouted, and turned a stricken gaze to me. "We must find her," he said. "Please. Can you not do something?"

I almost screamed at him. What the hell was I supposed to do? I wasn't Superman. Couldn't see through the damned walls, no matter how much earth magic I used.

But maybe Ian could.

"How much do you know about scrying?" I said.

He frowned. "Why?"

"Because Akila's tether is on her head. If you can find that, we can find her."

Ian's mouth opened and closed. "I had not thought of that."

"So can you do it?"

"I can," he said slowly. "But I cannot make a visual thought-form. It would only appear in my head."

"That'll work. If you can see it, I can see it."

"Yes. We must do something about that," Ian muttered. "And there is another problem. Air magic is not my element. If I perform a sustained scrying spell, it will drain me. I will have nothing left with which to face Nurien."

"Let's worry about that when we find him," I said, despite thinking something along the lines of *We're fucked*. I had no confidence in the idea of me taking Nurien down alone. But I wasn't about to let the bastard rape Akila either, if I could help it. "Besides, magic doesn't solve everything."

"I suppose not."

He sounded about as convinced as I felt. I handed him one of my blades. "Just in case you find a way to use it," I said. "And look at it this way. Do we have another choice?"

"Other than running about aimlessly in the dark while Nurien has his way with my wife? No. We do not." He took the knife and leaned back against the wall. "Have your look, then," he said. "I will begin now."

I closed my eyes. It was easier to look through Ian's vision when my own wasn't in the way. I concentrated on him, and a torrent of fury and frustration signaled the connection. The tunnels came into shivering focus, a few shades paler than reality, like a worn-out movie filmed with a cheap handheld camera.

The image canted to one side and stopped at each direction in turn: left, center, right. Back to center. Far down in the blackness, a pinpoint of blurred light cast a faint corona. The vision plunged into the tunnel and raced ahead. Thick gloom threaded with smudges of light paled slowly, became dark gray, then earth brown as an opening appeared.

It wobbled through the opening, and into a cave. Not a forced-labor dug space, but a natural cave complete with rock formations and dripping water. The place had to be directly under the compound. Most of the light came from an opening that led outside the mountain into full daylight. The rest came from Akila's crown. She lay on the ground near the tunnel exit, still bound and unmoving. Her tiara glowed like a beacon.

Ian's vision wandered drunkenly past her, presumably seeking Nurien. It rounded a boulder, dodged a patch of jagged rock spears, passed over a shallow water-filled depression. Finally, Nurien came into view, inspecting a dark crevice in the wall of the cave.

His crown was glowing too.

The image vanished, and Ian gasped. "Arrogant fool. He wears his tether in plain sight."

"Never thought I'd meet a djinn dumber than me." I hitched a grin and grabbed one of the torches off the wall. "Let's go down there and explode his ass."

By the time I turned around, Ian was already in the tunnel.

Even at a sprint, it took longer than I'd hoped to reach the cave. Apparently, scrying spells traveled faster than the speed of desperation-fueled running. I started to think we'd taken a wrong turn somewhere. But we finally found the end of the tunnel.

Ian blasted out first, and stopped almost immediately. I followed him—torch in one hand, blade in the other—and found Akila lying in almost exactly the same place she'd been in Ian's vision. Half conscious. Alone. There was no sign of Nurien.

"Love," Ian said in a broken whisper. He stretched out a trembling hand, as if she would disappear if he touched her. She stirred, murmured something, and he stumbled the few steps to her and collapsed on his knees. "Oh, my heart. I thought . . . never . . ."

This stunk like a Dumpster at a fish fry. "Ian, something isn't right," I said. "Where's Nurien?"

He ignored me. Slid an arm beneath her and held her to him, murmuring djinn words I couldn't quite hear. Her eyes fluttered, on the verge of opening.

The crown. There's no blood. "Ian! Damn it, listen to me—" An involuntary sharp intake of breath stopped my tongue. I could see her hands now, and her fingers. All ten of them.

That wasn't Akila. It was Nurien.

"Drop her. It's him!" As soon as the words left my mouth, I realized they didn't make any sense. But before I could clarify, "Akila" opened her eyes and cast a lockdown at me.

Ian drew back and stared. His brow furrowed. "Akila, why would you do that?"

She smiled and spoke a short stream of djinn. I couldn't quite understand every word, but I recognized this one. A flame curse.

Ian cried out, fell back. He landed hard and arched up, gasping, then curled on his side clutching his stomach.

I tried to undo the lockdown faster.

The thing that wasn't Akila stood, still smiling. The illusion evaporated—bonds first, then everything else. Nurien pointed at Ian and cast another flame spell, eliciting a hoarse scream from him. And then he turned his attention to me.

I could move again. I stepped back, tossed a lockdown of my own, and lunged at him, grabbing for the crown.

He sidestepped me. The fact that he could still move unbalanced me, and I came down on hands and knees.

"You are no marvel, boy," Nurien spat. "You aren't even shielding. Pathetic." He floated off the floor and hovered a few feet above me. "Be still while I play with the false prince. It will be your turn next." He cast a spell I'd never heard before.

I scrambled upright. Nurien drifted up and back. I stepped forward, intending to levitate after him. And I finally saw the smoke.

Wisps of black smoke formed in the air around me, curling and thickening, gathering substance and form. Ropes. They solidified and took on a blue sheen. I bent at the knees, trying to get under them—but they moved with me.

The ropes drew themselves taut around my torso and pinned my arms at my sides. I lost my grip on the torch, but managed to keep the blade. More of them wrapped around my neck and squeezed, not killing tight, but enough to restrict my breathing to shallow draws. The stuff was cool and dry. Solid. It pulsated like a sluggish heart where it touched flesh.

A final coil looped over my head and wrapped across my mouth, and a greasy slick formed in my gut. But the sensation of a snake against my lips wasn't the only thing making me want to pray to the porcelain god. The rope stuff was draining my energy, feeding on it. The weaker I grew, the faster it pulsed.

"Akila." Ian strained to speak. He pushed himself partway off the ground and flopped back down. "What have you . . . done with her?"

Nurien touched down, slashed a gesture in the air, and Ian went slack. "What if I've destroyed her, Gahiji-an? What would you do?"

"Kill you."

"How original." Nurien shook his head. "Well, come on and try, then. You've got nothing left to lose."

Ian shifted and slowly got to his feet. "You lie."

"Not this time, *rayan*. The truth, you see, is so much sweeter."

"No!" Ian ran at him.

Nurien held a hand out. *"Ela rey'ahn."*

Wind?

Ian flew back in midrush, like a flicked bug. He sailed through the air and slammed against a boulder with a sickening crunch, hanging in place for an instant before toppling face-first to the ground.

A gust of backwash hit me and almost knocked me over. My legs didn't want to hold me up anymore. If I didn't get these things off soon, I wouldn't be able to do a damn thing. Other than wait for Nurien to go through my pockets, find the tether, and kill us both.

Magic wouldn't help me here. I couldn't unmake something I didn't know how to make. But I still had the knife. Had to hope it'd cut through whatever this was. I flipped the handle so the blade pointed up, and bent my wrist until the tendons bulged and strained to lay the edge on the lowest rope.

I could only move the blade a few centimeters up and down. But a rough purring sound suggested it was working.

"No." Ian groaned and hauled himself up. One shoulder hung lower than the other, and, favoring a leg, he lurched toward Nurien. "You did not destroy her. It is another of your tricks."

Nurien frowned, a parody of sympathy. "If it helps, she did beg for your life before she died," he said.

"Lying . . . *snake*."

"I am Bahari." Nurien sketched a pattern in the air, closed his hand, and pulled it back. Ian jerked forward as if he were on the other end of an invisible string. "And you, Doma, are the son of a dead dog."

Ian gritted his teeth. "There is nothing noble about you, Nurien."

"You'll eat those words. *Rayan*." Nurien moved closer to him. *"On your knees, dog."*

The words were djinn, the same echoing tone Vaelyn had used on me. Ian struggled visibly as he sank to his knees.

I strained harder, sawed faster. A faint pop came from the rope, and something cold, thick, and wet oozed over my hand. I didn't look. Just kept cutting.

Nurien took another step. "If you want to save yourself some humiliation, you can hand over your tether now," he said. "Otherwise I'll simply scry it out when I'm ready."

Ian glared at him.

"Have it your way." Nurien shrugged and raised his arms. Ian copied the motion in trembling spurts. Nurien brought his down, and Ian folded forward until he was on all fours. *"Crawl to me,"* Nurien said.

Ian crawled.

Grinning, Nurien crouched in front of him. "I did lie, Gahiji-an," he said. "Akila—my wife, not yours—is alive." He gripped Ian's chin, forced his head up. "Beg for her life, and perhaps she'll stay that way."

Ian drew in a chopped, stuttering breath. "Please," he whispered, his lips barely moving. "Please spare Akila's life. I will gladly trade mine for hers."

"Not bad." Sneering, Nurien released him and stood. "Keep going. Admit that I'm superior to you."

"You . . ." Ian flinched. "You are a powerful mage. A true noble."

I was almost through the rope. I thought the rest of them had slackened a bit, but I couldn't be sure. The only thing I knew was that Nurien wouldn't keep fucking with Ian forever. Sooner or later—and I suspected sooner—he'd come after me.

I couldn't be helpless when that happened.

"Good. And you?" Nurien said.

"I am Doma," Ian rasped. "Insignificant. Weak."

Nurien laughed. "Well done, dog! Pure music. I could spend the next century listening to that." He gestured again, and Ian jerked to his feet. "But I do have a Council to overthrow, and a realm to rule. Busy, busy." He sighed. "I suppose I'll have to comfort myself with the memories."

Ian closed his eyes. "You will spare Akila?"

"I'll consider it. However, your spawn won't be so fortunate."

"Please . . ."

"Don't bother begging for him." Nurien's smile vanished. He made an almost dismissive wave, and Ian flew off the ground, nearly to the ceiling. He floated back and stopped, hovering above a tall spindle of rock with a pointed tip.

Nurien slammed his hands together, and Ian dropped onto the rock. It punched through his back and out his stomach. Blood sprayed up and drizzled down the spindle, black rivulets against dark stone. Ian twitched a few times and stilled, impaled a foot or so from the top of the rock spear.

"Now, then." Nurien faced me with a cold smile. "How would you like to die?"

Chapter 38

A thin membrane held the rope together. One more pass with the blade should do it. But once I got loose, I'd have to move fast. *Think, Donatti. What are you going to do?*

I opened up and let the heat flow into me. Might as well be prepared. And I would've told him exactly how I wanted to die if this damned rope wasn't in my mouth. Of old age, in my bed.

"I could have you slit your own throat. That always amuses me." Nurien folded his arms and gave me a speculative look. "I can't decide whether to handle you as common or rare. It isn't every day I have the pleasure of destroying the last of a clan. Perhaps I should make it special."

Christ, this asshole loved the sound of his own voice. He probably slept with a mirror.

"Fire is both clean and painful. Maybe . . . no, it's not spectacular enough."

What did I have to work with? A single blade. The tether—no way in hell I'd use that. And the earth. The cave floor was stone, not dirt, but it was the same stuff. Only harder. I could probably work with it. I'd just have to make sure I stopped him from talking and moving. He'd already demonstrated that he could cast spells without words.

"I've got it!" Nurien let his arms down. "You'll share your master's fate. It will be poetic. How long do you think it will take you to bleed to death, pup?"

Time to move.

I sliced through the rest of the rope. It uncoiled, and fell away. I dropped the blade, fell to one knee, and smacked both palms on the ground. No time for a smart-ass remark. I shoved magic into the stone and pictured Nurien encased in the stuff, trapped, immobile, gagged.

The cave floor trembled. Rock buckled and cracked under Nurien's feet, and he sank in to the top of his shoulders like the floor was water. Slack-jawed shock prevented him from casting a spell. The ruptured stone around his head sprouted a circle of thick, jagged slabs that extended up, ran together and curved in to form a dome. Not even a whisper escaped.

Damn. I wanted to seal him in just enough to shut his mouth so I could still get to his tether. But this'd have to work for now. I'd have to practice being more precise sometime when I wasn't about to die.

I had no idea if it would hold, and didn't want to wait there to find out. I ran across the cavern toward Ian. He hadn't moved since he'd been impaled, and I doubted it was because he was comfortable right where he was.

He was stuck just above my head. I could probably float up and pull him off, but that'd take too long. I grabbed the spindle, both hands squelching through half-congealed blood, and urged the rock to break.

It snapped apart, and Ian thumped to the ground.

"Sorry about that," I said in case he could hear me. If he did, he offered no acknowledgment.

He'd landed on his side, and the shard still ran all the way through him. I gripped the end protruding from his back and pulled. It didn't move. I considered trying to crumble the thing, but it probably wouldn't be a good idea to leave pieces of stone inside him. So I sat on the ground, braced my feet against him on either side of the shard, and yanked hard.

It broke loose with a wet pop. Ian screamed.

"Don't move, okay?" Before he could argue, I scooted back and pulled the thing out the rest of the way. He grunted through clenched teeth, but he didn't move. "I'll heal you," I said. "Hold on."

Ian coughed out foamy blood and spit. "Nurien."

"He's . . . um, stuck. Just be quiet a minute."

He did. I worked to heal him, and my body temperature spiked through the red zone. The cave might as well've been a sauna. I pushed on, watched the hole through him knit itself closed. I wasn't sure if he'd broken any bones, but that would have to be enough.

Ian jackknifed upright. "Where is he?"

"Over there." I waved a hand in the general direction of the dome. "Trust me, he can't do anything right now. But I don't know how long it's gonna hold."

"Can we get his tether?"

I grimaced. "Not at the moment."

"We must—"

"I know!" Damn, it was hot in here. I swiped a gallon of sweat from the back of my neck. "I can keep him busy for a while. You need to find Akila. He couldn't have taken her far."

"Yes." Ian scanned the cavern. It was a big cavern. "That may take some time."

I nodded and tried not to play the guess-how-long-before-

Nurien-kills-me game. "You'd better start looking, then. Maybe . . . wait a second. The crevice."

He frowned, and then understanding dawned. "From the scrying spell," he said.

"Yeah. It was up toward the outside entrance." I looked that way and spotted the jagged rock garden the vision had passed over. "Should be right around there," I said, and pointed at the wall beyond it. "And listen. You can cut through that rope stuff with a knife. That's how I got out of it."

Ian stood. I followed suit. "Thank you," he said.

"Don't worry about it." I flashed a crooked smile. "You can grovel at my feet later."

"Do not press your luck, thief."

"What luck?"

He laughed a little. "May the gods protect you."

"If they don't, you'll die too," I said. "So get back there and—damn. Is it hot in here?"

Something glowed at the corner of my vision. I glanced over and did a double take. The rock dome I'd trapped Nurien under blazed molten red. Like he was melting the stone.

"Oh shit," I said. "Make it fast, Ian."

He whirled and sprinted for the crevice.

I made an instinctive attempt to disappear. Nothing happened. Calvin must've laid down a damned wide snare. I threw up a shield so at least Nurien wouldn't be able to lock me down, and waited.

The glowing rock oozed in concentric ripples down the sides of the dome. A hole opened in the top and widened. When the hole reached a foot across, a jet of green flame spurted from it and shot to the ceiling, breaking into showers of sparks against the jagged rock formations above.

Inspiration struck. I tamped down my hatred of letting my

feet leave the ground, tapped into my djinn magic, and thought about light, fluffy things. Feathers and clouds and whipped cream. That last one probably didn't help—but I started to rise.

A brief, clumsy flight brought me to a massive cone of rock almost directly over the fiery spout. The dome had melted completely, and the hole was almost three feet wide. It spread a few more inches. The flames died down, and Nurien came up. Aside from a few black streaks and smudges, he looked completely uninjured.

I grabbed the cone and surged magic through it. *Break, baby.*

The rock obliged. I gave it a nudge in Nurien's direction. Unfortunately, it didn't skewer the bastard, but the thick part slammed into him with a satisfying crack and knocked him to the ground.

I hovered over to the next good-size cone. Pain from expending djinn magic already packed my chest and zapped through my limbs. I wouldn't be able to stay up here much longer. But this one was positioned perfectly. If I broke it loose, it'd pin him in place.

I laid my hands on it—or tried to. They stopped just short of touching. And no matter how I strained, my arms wouldn't move.

Below me, Nurien stood and brushed rock dust from his ridiculous outfit. At least I'd hurt him this time. Blood glistened on the front of his shirt where the stone had struck him. He tilted his head back, held a hand out, and crooked a finger.

My body obeyed without my consent. He'd used the puppet spell, right through my shield, as if it weren't even there.

He stopped and held me in midair in front of him. "I know your secrets now, earth mage," he said. "That is what you are, isn't it? Scion of an earth clan, born of the earth. A fascinating creature. Ultimately, though, no more harmful than a bug, as long as you're not in contact with your element."

Damn. I hated smart thugs.

"Let me help you contact the earth again." With a frigid smile, Nurien swept an arm aside.

I flung due left and smashed into the nearest wall, at about a zillion miles an hour. Bones splintered in my arm. Just before I hit the ground, I was jerked up and dragged back to my previous position.

"Did that help?" He leered at me. "What did you do with the dog, little mage? Tell me, or I'll break the other one. And then your legs."

I shuffled through my short list of spoken djinn spells. Paralysis, shield, mirror bridge, tether exploding. None of them would help. So I decided to go with a time-honored spoken human spell—sarcastic insults. "Gee, Nurien," I said. "Why do you need me to find him? I mean, you're supposed to be some all-powerful noble."

True to his word, Nurien repeated the wall-slamming bit on my other side. I screamed this time. He hauled me back, and I gritted my teeth against the pain. Both arms felt like they'd been stuffed with broken glass and set on fire. "Ian's right. You're pathetic," I said. "What, you couldn't get your own wife, so you had to buy somebody else's? That's kinda sad."

"You disgusting little . . . no. I won't destroy you yet." He pointed two fingers down and spread them in an upside-down V.

My busted arms rose. Bone fragments jarred and ground against each other. It hurt too much to scream. I squeezed my eyes shut—and saw Akila.

Ian had freed her. She was streaked with filth, and her eyes were sunken and haunted, but she was alive. The vision moved down. Ian's fingers rubbed the last of the blood from her tether.

Good thinking, Ian. Now get your ass back here and help me.

"Wake up, Doma."

My eyes wrenched open against my will. I was still seeing through Ian, but as a faded image laid across Nurien's smug features. Ian was moving across the cavern, headed this way. I'd have to keep distracting the asshole. "What?" I said. "Are you going to make me do jumping jacks now?"

Nurien's momentary astonishment gave way to a sneer. "You must be too stupid to fear me," he said. "It's almost a shame you won't be able to appreciate what I'm going to do."

I laughed, though it sounded like rusted nails rattling in a tin can. "I bet it's something really clever. Like you're going to keep talking and bore me to death."

"I believe I can do better than that."

"Oh, I'm quivering with anticipation. Seriously."

"You would be, if you had anything resembling a brain."

For an instant, everything blurred and doubled. I saw Nurien's front and back at the same time. Ian was twenty feet away and closing in, utterly silent.

Nurien flexed one hand, then the other. "Good-bye, little mage."

Five feet. Keep him talking. "Are we going to Disney World?"

"You are going—"

Ian clamped a hand on his shoulder. Nurien's mouth opened, but he didn't even get a single syllable out before Ian spun him around and drove a sledgehammer fist into his jaw. The crack of the blow echoed through the cavern. Nurien folded like a used tissue.

And I went tumbling after.

———

The ground felt a lot farther away than it looked. Especially when I landed on my side and transformed my right arm from splintered to pulverized.

"Tether," I gasped after I finished screaming. Like Ian wouldn't think of that himself.

In fact, he'd already grabbed the crown, and Akila was headed toward our little gathering. "You are hurt," Ian said. "Perhaps I should—"

"Finish him. Don't worry about me." I planted my feet on the ground, then pushed and slid on my back to a safe distance away from the imminent explosion, and started healing myself.

Ian took a few steps back. Akila stopped just behind him. Without a word, he handed the crown to her. He was still too drained to perform the spell. I was getting there myself; I managed to fix my shattered bones, but my body protested using the power. A few more spells and I'd be done.

As though he'd heard my thoughts and sensed weakness, Nurien opened his eyes.

Before I could shout a warning, he launched into the air, pointed at Akila and said, *"Ela na'ar."*

Fire immediately engulfed her arms, white-hot flames a foot high, and spread quickly to her dress.

Ian cried her name. He stripped his vest off and beat at the flames, brought her to the ground and tried to roll them out. The fire caught his pants. And the crown tumbled away from them.

I scrambled up and headed for it. Unfortunately, Nurien noticed it too. He threw a lockdown at me, then gestured at the crown. It floated up and across the cave to settle on the now-flattened top of the rock spire he'd impaled Ian on earlier. He cast another fire spell.

Flames circled the base of the spire and swirled up, all the way up, forming a floor-to-ceiling column of fire.

Nurien touched down. Ian and Akila still struggled to put out the flames. I'd almost freed myself from the paralysis spell, but I was out of ideas. This guy was too strong. He was older than Ian, had a bunch of scions running around boosting him, and he'd drained four of them and drunk a few gallons of blood.

Just as I broke free, Nurien threw his head back and lifted his arms like a preacher beseeching the heavens. *"Ela rey'ahn!"*

A wall of wind slammed into me and sent me tumbling through the air. I caught glimpses of Ian and Akila rocketing in the opposite direction. When I collided with something solid, at least it wasn't with enough force to break bones. But the back of my head cracked stone, and I collapsed in a woozy heap.

"I'll take your tether now, Gahiji-an. And my prize."

Nurien sounded a hundred miles away. I squeezed my eyes shut, trying to clear the black spots that wobbled through my vision, and made myself stand. Ian and Akila, considerably scorched but no longer burning, had hit the far wall near the tunnel. And Nurien stood halfway between me and them, silent and motionless. Scrying.

At once, he pivoted to face me. "Little mage," he said. "Give it to me, or I'll tear you to pieces and feed them to your master."

I threw up a shield spell. And ran.

The terrain wasn't exactly suited for speed. Uneven ground and random rock formations conspired against progress. I kept the bigger rocks between me and him as much as possible. Nurien threw a lockdown, then a fire spell, but either my shield held or he missed completely. I dove behind a boulder and tried to catch my breath. The flame column was on the far side of the cavern, and I'd gotten about a third of the way there. If I could reach it, I'd just go into the fire and destroy his tether right there.

I could heal burns. I couldn't heal dead.

Nurien had stopped casting spells. The silence unnerved me. I suspected he was coming my way, ready to launch some horrible magic that would make my teeth explode or boil all my blood, or otherwise plunge me into excruciating pain.

"Ela rey'ahn!"

Panic seized me. I tried to brace myself, anticipating another bone-shattering collision—and then my brain caught up with the sound and I realized the voice had been female. Akila had cast the spell.

I peered around the boulder, just in time to catch Nurien thud to the ground. He sat up almost immediately, his features a mask of fury.

Ian tackled him back down. Fists flew.

Akila approached them, stopped a few feet back, and looked in my direction. She nodded. I took that to mean they'd keep Nurien occupied while I got the tether.

With a backdrop of blows and thumps and flying spells, I moved toward the fiery vortex. Halfway there. Assorted shouts echoed through the cavern, but I didn't look back. Every second counted. Nothing short of destroying Nurien would stop him.

Fifty feet. I splashed through the shallow pool Ian had scried, tripped over a jutting rock below the surface, and went sprawling. Damn. I got myself back up and slowed down a fraction until I cleared the water.

Ian shouted a warning. I looked back—and saw Nurien casting a spell at me.

He managed to finish whatever it was, then took to the

air and flew toward me. Fast. I could still move under my own power, and I wasn't on fire or in pain. What the hell did he do?

I faced forward again, and my gut oozed into my feet. Now there were multiple flame columns, fifteen or twenty of them, all exactly alike. And I had no idea which one concealed the tether.

Nurien had gained a lot of ground, and I was out of hiding places. I searched the immediate area for loose rocks. I'd have to try throwing stones at him, and hope I could knock him out. I'd never be able to find the right tower of fire in time.

A piercing whistle filled the air and a dark shape streaked toward Nurien. A hawk. Akila's bird form was slightly smaller than Tory's, with paler feathers—and twice as pissed off as Ian's wolf. She fluttered around Nurien's head, shrieking and beating powerful wings. Talons clawed at his face. She snapped at him once, twice. The third time, her beak caught his ear. And ripped it off.

Nurien fell screaming to the ground.

While Akila circled and landed, Ian came charging across the cave. The hawk glowed and became Akila, kneeling, gasping, streaked with Nurien's blood.

Ian caught up and grabbed the writhing Nurien. The blade I'd given him was clutched in one hand. He slammed Nurien on his back, straddled him with knees pinning his shoulders, and drove the knife under his chin and straight up through his jaw, tacking his tongue to the roof of his mouth.

A weak gurgling sound bubbled from Nurien's throat. One hand twitched, tried to move. Ian grabbed his wrists and pushed them against the ground. "Find his tether!" he shouted.

"How?" I yelled back.

Akila rose to one knee. "They are illusions," she said in halting tones. "Powerful ones, and they will burn like fire. I can scry the false flames, but . . . it will take time . . ."

"Yeah. We don't have that." Nurien's struggles were already stronger. I felt Ian straining to hold him down. At least Akila had really done a number on his face. It was gouged to hell, and there was blood everywhere . . .

Blood. Ian's blood soaked the spire with Nurien's tether.

I knelt and placed both hands on the ground. The blood was a whisper, a hum, a vibrating wire pulling at me. I let it take the lead and sank into the ground. The brief trip sizzled my veins and steamed my flesh.

But the heat was summer in Antarctica compared to what pounced on me when I emerged.

Inside the flame column, superheated air feasted on my flesh. I couldn't keep my eyes open or they'd melt. I grabbed the stone, and my palms fried instantly. Jaw clenched, I slid my scorched hands up until they found the top and touched white-hot metal. I had the tether.

And I couldn't draw blood. The heat would cauterize the wound before I could squeeze anything out.

Keeping my back to the flames, I pushed the crown toward the edge until I could slip a hand through. I let it slide down my arm, an oversize bracelet, and stumbled backward. Agony flooded me as I passed through the fire. I cleared it, dropped on the ground, and rolled. Most of the flames snuffed out. I thought my hair was still burning, but I couldn't feel anything specific. Everything was a uniform screaming pitch.

I'd lost my knife somewhere between getting smashed into walls. Fortunately, Nurien's crown had plenty of fancy, pointy bits. I let it clatter to the ground, knelt, and drove the tip of it into a patch of raw, blistered flesh on my arm. Blood, and something much nastier that I didn't even want to consider, flowed over hot metal and baked onto the surface.

Good enough. *"Ana lo 'ahmar nar, fik lo imshi, aakhir kalaam."*

My voice creaked like a windmill, but I managed to enunciate. The crown glowed, spit sparks, caught fire.

I heaved it away from me and curled on the ground with my brain rapidly diving toward oblivion. I didn't even hear the explosion.

Chapter 39

Something pulled me back toward consciousness, but I didn't want to go. It hurt too much out there. I finally convinced myself that Nurien was dead, and if I didn't rejoin the land of the living I'd never be able to drink a cold beer again. At the moment I wanted that more than anything else.

I opened my eyes. It must've been worse than I thought, because I couldn't feel a thing except the cool stone under my back.

Which I wouldn't be able to feel if I was still charcoal.

I lifted a hand. Pain failed to spike through me, and my palm wasn't blackened and sloughing off my bones. There was just a hand attached to an arm . . . a bare arm. My jacket was gone. So was everything else I'd worn. Transformation healing restored clothes, but I didn't have that—and I was lying here naked.

"Shit!" I moved to cover myself and hoped Akila wasn't anywhere nearby. "Um, Ian . . . you still alive? I could use a little help."

"Donatti." Ian loomed over me. He looked a lot less beat up than he should've. He must have absorbed the tether's destruction—something I apparently still couldn't do. His lips twitched, and his gaze traveled to my cupped hands, over my groin. "You seem to have lost something."

"Yeah. Fire and cloth don't mix."

"Well then. I believe it is time you had proper clothing." He gestured over me and said a few words. Smoke drifted from the ground and circled me, covering me from the neck down. When it cleared, I had on brown pants, brown boots, and a brown vest. No shirt.

I almost mentioned that I didn't share Ian's distaste for shirts—but then I realized this was what every Dehbei in Akila's thought-form had been wearing. And what Ian wore now. I was part of his clan . . . and damned proud of it. I closed my eyes so I wouldn't make a fool of myself, and said, "Thank you."

Before he could respond, my empty, snarling stomach kicked the moment out.

"Got any food on you?" I said. "I'd prefer a nice thick burger, but I'll take crispy bat in a pinch."

Ian laughed. "Have you lost what is left of your mind?"

"What? I'm hungry."

"You are lucky. A few moments ago, I was not certain that charred lump was you. I cannot begin to guess how you got through that fire."

"Magic." I grinned and sat up. "I take it Akila healed me."

"No. You healed yourself."

"I did?" Damn. Now I was running spells in my sleep. I hoped this ability didn't go beyond basic survival, or I was going to be in serious trouble with Jazz when I started casting lockdowns in bed.

Then I remembered there was a good chance we weren't sharing a bed anymore, and a different kind of pain lashed me.

Ian crouched in front of me. "I feel your sorrow," he said. "What is troubling you?"

"I'm all right." I forced a smile and concentrated on anything but Jazz. Relationship advice from Ian wasn't something I really wanted right now. "Where's Akila?"

"She is retrieving her tether."

I nodded and stood. "Great. When she comes back, let's get the hell out of here."

"Agreed."

Neither of us spoke for the next few minutes. When Akila approached, fully healed and holding the tiara between thumb and forefinger as far from her as she could get it, I couldn't help smirking. "Did Nurien have cooties or something?"

"If these cooties are something unpleasant, then yes. It is likely he did." Akila made a face, and turned it into a smile that lit her angelic features. "It is good to see you, Gavyn Donatti."

"Same here, Princess."

She blushed and lowered her eyes. "It is far more pleasant to hear that word from you than Nurien."

"Stop flirting with my wife, thief," Ian growled—but his eyes betrayed his good mood. He approached Akila and took the crown from her. "I will hold this for you, love. I would not wish you to catch . . . cooties."

"Keep trying, Ian. Someday you'll be able to speak human." I caught sight of Akila's four-fingered hand and shuddered. "So, um, the bond with Nurien broke when he died. Right?"

Thunderclouds filtered through Akila's features. "He lied about our so-called bond," she said. "The ceremony was never completed. My father . . ." She shivered and stared at her feet.

Ian put an arm around her. "My heart," he whispered. "Tell me you will not despise me when I destroy that bastard who calls himself your father."

"I will not, *l'rohi*." Steel flashed in her eyes. "I have no father."

"Whoa." I threw up my hands in mock surrender and backed away. "Ripping off ears, plotting murder—you are a vicious woman, Akila. Maybe I should start calling you Xena."

She frowned. "Who?"

"Warrior princess?" I sighed and shook my head. "Never mind. When we get home, I'm getting you guys cable." A quick stab of pain pierced my gut. Couldn't think about home yet. "Uh, can we go now?"

"Of course," Ian said. "But I am not certain how to return. The tunnel has collapsed."

"Good point." I'd left the blood marker on the landing, but I still wasn't sure about moving more than myself that way, and I suspected I'd hit my earth magic ceiling. An attempt to tap in proved me right. I couldn't draw anything. "Well," I said reluctantly. "There's an exit to outside over there, and I'm pretty sure the compound is right up above us, a few hundred feet. I guess we could . . . fly."

They both agreed way too quickly. I resigned myself to another trip on Air Ian.

No one had wanted to stay in the compound. So when Mercy offered to let the whole group head to her place, everyone jumped at the chance. Especially me. She had beer.

Despite the collective exhaustion, the hour's walk back didn't seem as long as the trip out. All eight of the younger scions and two of the humans—Penny, and an older girl named Lucy who spent a lot of time holding hands with Lynus—accompanied us.

The other two humans at the compound, both male, hadn't survived the fight. They'd died trying to protect the females.

It was twilight when we reached the sprawling cabin. Mercy had shooed the kids inside with motherly commands to rest for a while after the ordeal. All the djinn, and me, claimed spots on the porch and collapsed.

Tory perched on the rail like a bird, weary with relief. "You missed a hell of a fight, Ian," he said. "Those kids are naturals. Didn't miss a trick. If you'd been leading them . . . man, what a unit they would've been."

Ian smiled. "It seems to me that you have done a commendable job leading them yourself, Taregan," he said. "I am . . . proud of you."

"Gee. Thanks, Dad." Tory's exuberant grin said the praise meant a lot more than he'd dare let on. "I guess you guys had a fairly kick-ass fight of your own, though. We felt some of that power flying around down there. Was that all you, Donatti?"

I shrugged. "Wasn't just me," I said. "But I did burn through a lot."

"He's an earth mage." Calvin stirred from his slouch and sat up straighter. "This realm hasn't seen his like in centuries. In fact, it's possible that no mage has ever equaled him, because of his Dehbei blood."

"Yeah, right," I muttered. "Just call me Merlin."

Calvin arched an eyebrow. "Some day, apprentice, you may realize how extraordinary you are."

I didn't feel extraordinary. I felt like a guy who'd killed four times, been burned and shot to death, and wanted to sleep through whatever would pass for the rest of his life.

The front door opened and Mercy emerged with a frosty six-pack of beer. "Oh my God," I blurted out, "I love you. Have I told you that today?"

"Not yet." She smiled and handed me a bottle. "You get the first one."

Calvin cleared his throat. "What about me?"

"You're a monk. You're s'posed to abstain from the evils of booze, remember?"

He got to his feet, crossed the porch to her, and brushed fingers along her cheek. "I've decided to retire," he said hoarsely. "There is someone I love more than God."

Mercy blinked rapidly. "Well, shit," she whispered. "In that case, have a beer. And . . . this too." Smiling, she leaned in and kissed him hard on the mouth.

Tory let out a wolf whistle. I joined him so he wouldn't feel too lonely.

"All right, boys." Mercy flapped a hand at us, and a blush crept over her face. "Y'all save that for your own women. Or your man, in your case," she said to Tory.

His jaw flopped. "How'd you know that?"

"Sweetie, you're too pretty to be straight." She handed him a beer. "Sorry about that knock I gave ya." She passed a bottle to Ian, and looked at Akila. "Are you drinkin', er . . . hell, I don't know your name. But you c'n still have a beer if you want."

"I am Akila." She laughed and took a bottle. "And today, I believe I am drinking."

"I hear that." Mercy opened the last bottle and drank deep. "Damn, that's good."

"I'll drink to that." I cracked mine. The first swallow just about made me weep. I could've died happy right then. "How are they doing in there?" I said to Mercy.

Her expression sobered. "Best as can be expected," she said. "Those kids are tough. But not as tough as they think. They'll need help if they're ever gonna have real lives." She sighed and glanced back at the door. "If they want, I'll let 'em stay here long as they need to. Only . . . I don't really get this whole magic thing."

Calvin wrapped an arm around her. "I'll stay as well," he said. "If you'll have me."

"You better." She grinned at him. "Gotta have a man around the place now. I'm gonna need a lot more rooms."

"I suppose you will," he said. "So, *rayan*." Calvin turned his attention to Ian. "I'm almost afraid to ask, but what will you do now?"

Ian didn't answer him for a long moment. "I do not know," he said at last. "Four hundred years I have spent in this realm, with a single purpose. And now . . . well, I cannot continue to blindly hunt your clan. I *will* not." He looked down and clasped his hands. "Though it will not be easy. The *ham'tari* will see to that."

"That reminds me." Calvin smiled, gave Mercy a brief squeeze, and approached Ian. "I have a gift for you, if you'll accept it."

"You have no need to offer me anything."

"I do, actually," he said. "If it weren't for you—and your talented, noble scion—I'd still be under Vaelyn's thumb. And I would have lost what matters most to me in this world." He glanced at Akila. "I'm sure you understand that."

I forced myself not to comment on the talented noble thing, even though it made me sound like an expensive horse or something.

Calvin looked at me. "The gift is for you as well, apprentice."

"Huh?"

"You didn't believe me before, and I don't blame you," Calvin said. "But I'll tell you again. I have been able to modify the *ham'tari*."

Something that strongly resembled hope flickered in Ian's eyes, and died just as fast. "It will not work," he said.

"In a thousand years and more, no Bahari has been able to

manipulate that curse," Akila said. "I have attempted it many times."

"Same here," Tory put in. "Sorry, Calvin. You just can't do it."

Calvin shook his head. "Have you learned nothing? You shouldn't dismiss anything simply because of clan differences." He faced Ian again. "The *ham'tari* is a Bahari spell. However, it's used to deceive, to bind and manipulate. These are strengths of the Morai."

Ian's breath caught. "Yes," he said slowly. "Perhaps . . ."

"I can't completely break the curse," Calvin said. "But I can change it, so the consequences won't be so dire. I can make the effects practically insignificant."

"Very well," Ian said. "If you are willing to attempt this for me, I shall be honored to accept."

Calvin nodded and knelt in front of him. "Forgive my familiarity, Gahiji-an," he said. "The *ham'tari* is a bond of the heart, and so I must reach you there." He placed a hand flat on Ian's chest and closed his eyes.

Power flowed from Calvin in almost tangible waves. Ian gasped, stiffened, and his gaze fixed on some point beyond Calvin's head. Nearly a minute passed. Ian flinched like he'd been kicked, and a tear tracked down his cheek.

Somewhere deep in my gut, I felt something shatter. But it wasn't a bad feeling. It was a weight lifting from my soul, one that I hadn't even known was crushing it.

Calvin broke contact and slumped over, panting. "It's done," he muttered. "And I think I could use another beer."

Ian shook himself. "It is done." Awe and gratitude painted his voice. "Akila, he has truly changed the curse. I felt it happen."

"Oh, love!" Akila clapped her hands like a delighted child. She reached out, lifted Calvin's head, and kissed his brow. "We are indebted to you, Khalyn of the Morai."

"The name's Calvin, *rayani*. Calvin of . . . earth." He gave her a tired smile. "And I've only repaid the debt I owed to your husband."

For the first time in my life, I almost felt like singing. *Cyrus,* I thought. *Thank God. Cyrus is safe.* I couldn't wait to tell Jazz. At least I could give her that. "So, Calvin," I said. "You mentioned that there's still some effects. How practically insignificant are they?"

He shrugged. "The consequences won't be dire. I don't know exactly what will happen. You may experience dry skin, or mild nightmares on occasion. Or perhaps your toenails will grow at an unusually rapid rate."

I laughed. After a few seconds, everyone else joined in.

"Well," Ian said after the amusement died down. "I believe we should head for home. It seems you all will have some adjusting to do."

Mercy's brow furrowed. "How y'all gonna do that?" she said. "I mean, you're from up north, ain't you?"

"We are. But if you have a mirror, we can—"

She snorted with laughter. "Do I look like I spend much time starin' in a mirror? Sorry, Ian. I'm fresh out."

"That's okay," I said. "You've got something we can use."

Ian looked at me. "What?"

"The shower curtain. You know, the metallic silver one. With duckies."

"If you say so." Mercy offered a crooked smile. "It's been . . . interestin' meeting y'all. You know where we'll be if you wanna swing by sometime."

"Count on it," I said.

The front door slammed open and Billy stepped out, wild eyed and hyperventilating. "Mercy!" he shouted, and did a double take when he realized she was standing right in front of him. "Sorry, Miss Mercy, ma'am. My . . . I mean Penny . . . ah, *shit*." He closed his eyes, drew a deep breath. "The baby's comin'. Like, *now*."

"Good lord, boy." Mercy grinned. "I thought maybe the army was bustin' through my back door. Don't you worry, she'll do just fine. Get her in my bedroom. I'll be right there." She half-shoved Billy back inside. "Duty calls," she said. "Y'all have a safe trip home—however the hell you plannin' to get there."

She entered the house. Calvin watched her for a second, then turned back. "I believe I should help out in there," he said. "I wish you all a far more peaceful life than you've managed to achieve so far. And I thank you again."

"We thank you as well," Ian said.

The instant the door closed, Tory jumped down from the rail to the ground. "Get me to this shower curtain, quick," he said. "I don't think I can handle the whole birth thing."

I laughed and started down the steps. "Right this way."

Chapter 40

Bridging through Mercy's shower curtain wasn't easy. But the four of us passed through, one by one, and entered the apartment over the garage.

Home. I looked around the place, knowing the house I'd called home for a year stood just outside these walls. We'd been gone four days. Nothing had changed here—but everything had. The same place, but I wasn't the same person. It reminded me of stepping out of prison after a six-month stretch and going back to the old haunts. Wondering why everyone I'd known was different, unfamiliar, and finding out it wasn't them. It was me.

Ian headed straight for the couch and plunked down. "I believe I will sleep for a decade," he said. "And then bathe for another."

"You do need it, love." Akila giggled and drifted over to plant herself next to him. "I do as well. I believe I'll join you."

He smiled and drew her close. "As you wish, lady."

Tory folded his arms. "I need to get home soon," he said. "I didn't die, so Lark's gonna kill me. He won't even look at me for a month." He looked at me and frowned. "Donatti, you . . . want to come with me?"

"Yeah, I guess I should." I had to face Jazz sometime, and find out how much she hated me now. I glanced down and grimaced at the filth and grime ground into my skin. "Mind if I jump in the shower first?"

He shrugged. "Sure. Fifteen more minutes won't make me any less dead."

I murmured thanks and headed out. Down the stairs, across the yard, around to the back door. It was locked, but locks had never stopped me before. I was a thief long before I knew about magic. But since I didn't have a pick set on me, I pressed a palm against the handle and thought about how much I needed it to open. A dull click sounded as it disengaged.

I moved through the kitchen. Bloodstains on the floor, dried and black. The living room. A shattered mirror, maroon smudges on the carpet. Debris everywhere. Up the stairs. The main bathroom, another shattered mirror, more blood. Ghosts of fear in the tub, where Jazz had hidden Cyrus from men with guns, men who would've killed them both.

The bedroom. Jazz in green silk. Bloody footprints on white tile in the master bath. I closed the door, stripped, and climbed in the shower. Hot water washed away dirt—but never guilt.

As I scrubbed through the grime, I tried to work out what I'd say to her, if she'd even talk to me. Should I beg for forgiveness? Spout poetic crap about how my life was empty and meaningless without her? Maybe I should just end it myself. Maybe that was the best thing for her, and for Cyrus.

Things had been complicated enough before. Now I was more or less immortal, beyond freakish—and I'd probably ruined whatever chance there might have been at the normal life Jazz wanted.

Eventually the water cooled. I still wasn't clean, but at least

I'd gotten most of it. I dried off and dressed, and left by the back door.

Tory waited in front of the garage. "They both passed out," he said when I approached him. "I didn't want to wake them. You ready?"

"No." I ran a hand through my hair. It probably didn't help my looks much. "I don't know how you planned to get home, but do you mind if we drive? We can take my car. I really don't feel up to flying right now."

"If I couldn't tell you felt like shit, I'd say no," he said. "Flying's faster. But yeah, that'll work."

"Thanks."

I opened the garage door. Both vehicles—my Chevy, Jazz's Hummer—sat untouched, even though we both kept our keys folded in the driver's-side visors. The crime rate around here was practically nonexistent. We were the only criminals for miles. I climbed in, waited for Tory, and then hit the road.

For the first ten minutes of the half-hour drive, neither of us spoke. It was full dark, a warm and quiet night. We hadn't passed a single other car. My brain insisted on counting all the ways Jazz could break my heart. Eventually, panic set in.

"I can't do it, man." I clenched the wheel knuckle white and fought the urge to pull over, get out, and run. "I just can't . . . she hates me. I'll drop you off. I'm not going in."

"Hold on," Tory said. "We're talking about Jazz here, right?"

"No. I meant Hillary Clinton." I rolled my eyes. "Yes. Jazz."

Tory grunted. "You really are an idiot, Donatti."

"Thank you."

"Come on. She's crazy about you. Can't you see that?"

"Not exactly." I told him about the blowout we'd had

before we went after Akila, how I insulted her, told her she was too weak to fight, how she'd said she'd had enough of me.

Tory stayed silent for a minute after I finished. Finally, he said, "Here's the thing about women. When they get mad at a guy they care about who's trying to protect them, it's usually because they know he's right and they don't want to admit it. Think it'll make his head swell or something."

I shot him a glare. "What do you know about women?"

"Quite a bit, actually." He didn't raise his voice, but the strain in it said I'd insulted him. "They talk to me because I'm safe. They know I won't try to get them into bed."

"Shit, I'm sorry," I said. "I'm a little stressed out right now."

"Yeah. The ocean's a little deep too." He smiled. "Honestly, I'll bet now that she's had time to cool off, she'll be happy to see you."

"I hope so," I muttered. "Thanks for the pep talk."

"No problem."

I stared out the windshield. Clouds filled the night sky, but a bright star shone through a gap just ahead. I wondered if Cy had made his wish on that star tonight.

Star light, star bright...

I went through the whole poem, and wished with all my soul that Jazz would take me back.

When we got to Lark's place, the porch light was the only sign of life. All the windows were dark. I parked in the driveway, and we got out of the car to complete silence.

Tory frowned. "It's not that late," he said. "What is it, ten o'clock?"

"Ten thirty," I said.

"Yeah. Not that late. Somebody should be up." Tory headed for the porch steps. I followed him up. He hesitated, then rang the doorbell. "I'd just walk in, but I didn't tell him we were coming. Don't want to give him a heart attack."

We waited. And waited. Two full minutes. Tory reached for the doorbell again, and footsteps approached the door from inside the house. The knob turned. The door opened a sliver. "Who the fuck, and it better be good," Lark said.

Tory glanced at me and mouthed *Here we go.* "It's me."

Lark threw the door open. He was barefoot, which made him almost as short as Jazz, dressed in jeans and a long-sleeved black T-shirt. Dark circles smudged the hollows under his pale hazel eyes, and his usually immaculate sand brown hair was a tousled rat's nest. "Tory?" he whispered.

"Think so. Can I come in?"

"You asshole." Lark whirled and marched back into the house.

"Lark, wait . . . damn it!" His shoulders slumped. "Come on in and close the door," he said. "Things might get loud in here."

I did what he said. Lark hadn't gotten far. He'd stopped down the front hall next to the living room, and stood with his back turned and his arms folded across his stomach.

Tory went to him, put a hand on his shoulder. "I'm sorry, babe."

"Don't 'babe' me." Lark pulled away from him. "You couldn't have called? Jesus Christ, I was terrified. I almost hired a private dick to go after you."

"I was a bird for two days. Couldn't dial with my feet."

"Yeah? What happened the other two days—were you a fish then?"

"*Adjo,* please." Tory's voice broke. "I've missed you so much. I need you."

Silence. Lark turned slowly, reached up, and stroked Tory's hair. "What you need is a shower," he said in shaking tones. "You're filthy."

Tory folded him in a fierce embrace and bent to kiss him. "Can I have some company?"

"Shit," Lark hissed. He leaned aside and peered around Tory at me. "Donatti. Your woman's in the guest room. All the way back on the left." He grabbed Tory's hand and pulled him into the living room, toward the stairs.

Tory shrugged and waved at me. "Good luck," he said.

I waited until I heard a door close upstairs, and started down the hall like a con walking the Last Mile. I'd convinced myself that what Tory had said made sense. Now my convictions unraveled in the face of impending confrontation. Tory might know women, but he didn't know Jazz. Didn't know how tough she was, how independent, how proud.

I reached the end of the hall. To the left, a door stood ajar onto a darkened room. There was a door on the right, closed, with a weak bar of light spilling into the hallway. I went left and pushed the door open just enough to slip through.

Inside, a double bed sat under a picture window, and a small figure slept in tangled covers. Cyrus, sprawled across all the available space, as usual. A fresh swell of gratitude tightened my throat. *Cyrus is safe.* At least one of my wishes had come true. The *ham'tari* curse would never touch my son.

"Guess there really is something to wishing on a star."

I whirled around. Jazz stood in the doorway, a cool, expressionless stare on her face. Her poker face. She could be thinking anything—I missed you, I hate you, I want to rip your eyes out and stuff them in your ears—and I'd never know unless she chose to share.

"Yeah?" My voice sounded strange, like it belonged to someone else. "Why's that?"

She came into the room. "Because I wished that you would

come back tonight," she said. "And every single night you were gone."

"Oh God. Jazz . . . I'm . . ."

"Hush." She closed the distance between us and wrapped her arms around my neck. I held her to me, convinced I'd pass out from relief any second. "I was wrong," she whispered in my ear. "That might be the only time you ever hear me say that, so enjoy it while it lasts. And here's something else I don't say enough, and should've said before you left. I love you. Always have, always will."

I couldn't speak. Every sentence, every word I tried out in my head, seemed either stupid or inadequate. So I held her and breathed in her scent, and felt her heart beating against me, and knew I was home.

She finally drew back and looked up at me. "What happened to your eyes?"

"It's a long story," I said. "Really long. Like Cap Holland drunk in the bar telling war stories long."

"You're babbling, Donatti." She smiled. "All right. You can tell me in the car."

"Car?" I echoed.

"Yeah. You did drive here, didn't you?"

I managed to nod. The giddy feeling made my head light and my tongue sloppy, and I knew the more I talked, the dumber I'd sound.

"Good, because I need to get out of here." She grimaced. "You wouldn't believe what it's been like the past few days. Breakfast, lunch, dinner, bed. Normal stuff in between."

I grinned. "Thought you wanted a normal life."

"Are you kidding? I've been bored out of my fucking mind."

"Then you'll love this. I've got a lot of exciting new ways to screw with reality."

She narrowed her eyes. Just when I thought I'd pissed her off again, she laughed. "Take me home, Houdini," she said.

"Your wish is my command."

Somehow, the ridiculous saying didn't sound as stupid as it should have. Maybe because I meant every word—and I didn't need stars to make wishes come true. I had the whole world for that.

Chapter 41

Morning had officially been canceled. Everyone, even Cyrus, slept until noon.

Jazz temporarily revoked the injunction against using magic to clean, because nobody was interested in scrubbing off bloodstains. Ian and I took care of the house. The mirrors couldn't be repaired, but we got rid of the broken glass. We'd replace them later.

Akila and Jazz had a tearful reunion. I'd almost forgotten that Jazz had thought she was dead. Now, the two of them sat in lawn chairs in front of the garage, drinking coffee and chattering away. Probably about me and Ian. Cyrus tooled around the front yard with a red wagon, a plastic shovel, and a bucket. Every so often he'd stop and pluck something from the grass. Whatever it was went in the bucket, and he'd move on.

"So," I said eventually. "I guess we're retired now."

Ian, on the other end of the porch swing, grunted. "I do not know what we are," he said. "Other than exhausted."

"Yeah. That too." I'd been thinking about something, but I wasn't sure how to bring it up with him. Finally, I decided to just spit it out. "If you don't destroy the rest of the Morai, you won't be able to go back to the djinn realm," I said.

"Yes." He stared out over the porch railing at nothing in particular. "Perhaps I do not wish to return."

"What?"

He looked at me. "There is nothing for me there," he said. "I have never liked the Council, and I have no desire to lead. My clan is dead. Everyone who matters to me is here."

"Akila," I said.

"And you, thief."

I grinned. "Don't start that bonding stuff again. I'll break out in hives."

"Speaking of bonding." Ian passed a hand down his face. "I believe I informed you that the *rohii'et* cannot be undone?"

"Yeah, you mentioned something like that."

He gave a weary nod. "We must attempt to control our shared vision. There are times I would strongly prefer not to have you in my head."

"You mean like when you're getting it on with Akila?"

"Yes," he said through his teeth. "Like that."

I shrugged. "Don't think about me, then."

He let out a laugh. "I assure you that while I am intimate with my wife, I am not thinking of you."

"Same here." I had to admit, this soul-sharing thing was weird. And neither of us seemed to know much about it. Another first-time situation for Donatti the Earth Mage. "I'll work on it," I said.

The women were approaching. Jazz stopped to talk to Cyrus, and Akila came up the porch steps. "I forgot to ask," she said, "but I assume Taregan arrived home safely?"

"As safe as he could be. Lark was pretty pissed at him, but I think he forgave him." I got up and moved aside. "Have a seat, Princess."

"You do not have to move for me."

"Oh, I insist." I flashed a grin. "Besides, I'm sure Ian would rather have the pleasure of your company than mine right now."

"Thank you." Smiling, she settled next to Ian. He wrapped an arm around her, and she laid her head on his shoulder. "It is so good to be home," Akila said.

"That it is, love." Ian glanced at me, and I didn't need the bond to hear his thoughts: bugger off while I have a moment with my wife.

I headed down the steps, thinking I'd sneak off for a smoke—and almost walked straight into Jazz. "Whoops. Didn't see you coming," I said. "What's the little guy up to?"

"Digging for treasure. Too many pirate movies." She grabbed my hand and linked her fingers through mine. "I hear you've been learning some new tricks."

"Something like that." Last night, I'd told her about the soul bond and why my eyes looked like ice cubes, but that was about it. "I can put out forest fires and break rocks in half. Stuff like that."

She raised an eyebrow. "Forgive my skepticism, but . . . bullshit."

"You know, I kinda wish it was." I smirked. "And if you don't believe that, you're really not going to believe this." I tried to give her the condensed version of what Calvin had explained to me, about native earth magic and why I could use it.

When I finished, Jazz said, "Did he sell you the Brooklyn Bridge too?"

"Yep. The deed's in my other pants." I leaned down and kissed her, knowing how hard it'd be for her to accept this.

"It's the truth, and I'm sorry. Look." I let go of her, knelt, and put a hand on the ground. Something simple, I thought. Like a column. A couple of them, connected, with a road between them . . .

Heat washed into me. Grass parted, and slender piles of dirt built themselves up from the ground, tight packed and solid. Soon I had a clumsy but recognizable dirt model—a single span of the Brooklyn Bridge.

Jazz made a soft, strangled sound. She looked from the crude dirt sculpture to me, and said, "I felt that."

"You did?"

She nodded. "I've been getting these weird feelings on and off for a couple of days," she said. "They were like that. Warm fuzzies. I thought maybe it was early menopause or something."

"Erm." That didn't make any sense. "Are you sure?"

"Yeah, I . . . crap! Where's Cy?"

I turned in the direction he'd been. The bucket sat in the abandoned red wagon on the lawn, and there was no sign of Cyrus. Shit. He'd probably decided to make himself shiny. I straightened and looked toward the porch. "Ian. Did you guys see where Cy wandered off to?"

"I did not," he said.

Akila stood and came to the rail. "He was there just a moment ago," she said, her voice laden with worry. "He could not have gone far."

"Wait." Jazz stared at the far corner of the porch. "I think . . ."

I followed her gaze. There was nothing there. "Uh, Jazz—"

"Hush." She moved like a sleepwalker across the yard and stopped at the end of the porch. Then she reached out, bent slightly, and rested a hand in the air, about three feet off the ground.

And vanished.

"What are you looking at, baby?" Jazz's disembodied voice shook a little.

"Frog went under there," Cyrus said—even though he wasn't there.

All the breath went out of me. She'd seen him. He was invisible, and she'd seen him without being anywhere near him. That was impossible.

"Cy?" Her voice steadied. "You're being shiny again."

"Oh. I forgot."

They popped into view. Cyrus was scrunched down, staring through the lattice skirt under the porch. Jazz's hand rested on his shoulder. "He's gone now," he said.

Jazz smiled. "He probably went swimming," she said. "Don't forget to put your wagon back in the garage when you're done playing, okay?"

"I won't, Mommy." Cy straightened with a smile and wandered toward his wagon.

Jazz made her way back, a shade paler than she'd been a minute ago. "He looked like a ghost," she whispered. "I could almost see right through him, but he was there. How could I see him?"

I shook my head, too stunned to think straight. "Not a clue."

"Your eyes," Akila said.

Jazz and I stared at her. She was smiling. "I knew when I first saw you," she said. "Your eyes are different colors. It is a trait of some magi . . . those you call mages. And because the power is in your eyes, you have the gift of vision."

"But . . ." Jazz frowned. "If I have these vision powers or whatever, why couldn't I see Cy before? This isn't the first time he's disappeared on me."

"Because I woke up the earth," I said slowly. "You said those weird feelings started a couple days ago, right?"

"Yeah."

"That's when I was in the cave with Calvin, and he was teaching me how to use earth magic. He said it was sleeping and I'd have to get it moving before I could access it."

"Well, at least Cy won't be able to hide from me now." Jazz grinned and bumped my arm with a fist. "And you're not the only one with magic."

"You mean you're not the only one without it," I said. "So, does this mean I have to stop hanging around invisible in the bathroom while you're in the shower?"

"Gavyn!"

"What?"

She gave an exasperated sigh. "Never mind."

Before I could decide whether she knew I was joking, Cyrus approached us with both arms clasped around his bucket. "Wanna see my treasure, Daddy?" he said.

"Sure," I said. "What do you have in there? Diamonds? Hershey bars?"

He giggled. "No! It's treasure." He thrust the bucket at me.

I looked inside, expecting blades of grass, or maybe pebbles. The bucket was about a quarter full of tiny green leaves. I scooped out a small handful of them for a closer look. They were clovers. I'd never even realized they grew here. I pinched one free of the pile.

It had four leaves.

"Hey, this is cool, Cy." How I'd managed to grab a four-leaf one from the bucket, I didn't know. I dropped it back in and separated another one from my hand, intending to exclaim over it. Wow, a clover. Awesome.

This one had four leaves too.

Huh? I stirred the clovers in my hand, moving them apart. Every single one had four leaves.

I held one up. "Do they all look like this?" I said.

Cyrus nodded and gave me the *Duh, Daddy* look. "Those are the special ones," he said. "Like wishing stars."

"Yes, they are." I brushed my handful back into the bucket. A sense of wonder filled me, stronger and cleaner than the first time I'd realized I had real magic. Cy hadn't just escaped the curse. He'd gone completely in the other direction—and maybe some of it would rub off on me too. "You're a lucky guy, Cyrus," I said. "This treasure is really hard to find."

"No it isn't, Daddy. It's right here." He hugged the bucket back to himself. "I'm gonna go find more treasure."

I watched him head to the wagon. I couldn't find any words, so I put my arms around Jazz and let myself experience it instead.

Cy was right. It wasn't hard to find.

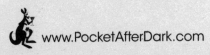